Tony Rycroft was brought up in a military family and spent much of his career working with and around very large engines. From ships to locomotives and power stations. Diesel engines to gas turbines. His work involved extensive worldwide travel. Sometimes to places that are no longer so accessible.

Dedicated to my two grandchildren, Matilda and Oscar.

Tony Rycroft

Present and Clear Danger

Austin Macauley Publishers

LONDON * CAMBRIDGE * NEW YORK * SHARJAH

Copyright © Tony Rycroft 2025

The right of Tony Rycroft to be identified as author of this work has been asserted by the author in accordance with sections 77 and 78 of the Copyright, Designs and Patents Act 1988.

All rights reserved. No part of this publication may be reproduced, stored in a retrieval system, or transmitted in any form or by any means, electronic, mechanical, photocopying, recording, or otherwise, without the prior permission of the publishers.

Any person who commits any unauthorised act in relation to this publication may be liable to criminal prosecution and civil claims for damages.

This is a work of fiction. Names, characters, businesses, places, events, locales, and incidents are either the products of the author's imagination or used in a fictitious manner. Any resemblance to actual persons, living or dead, or actual events is purely coincidental.

A CIP catalogue record for this title is available from the British Library.

ISBN 9781035877317 (Paperback)
ISBN 9781035877324 (ePub e-book)

www.austinmacauley.com

First Published 2025
Austin Macauley Publishers Ltd®
1 Canada Square
Canary Wharf
London
E14 5AA

Many people have read parts of this book during the time I have taken to complete it. Their criticism, encouragement, time and sometimes bluntness was very well received. Thank you all.

Chapter 1
Prologue

During the Second World War, the Allies helped to defeat Germany by relentless bombing from the skies. Just as Germany had done to London and other large UK cities. The bombing on both sides was inaccurate but total, in the hope that the main targets were destroyed. Loss of life was very high on both sides. The rebuilding costs, once the conflict was over, were massive.

During the Gulf War, the Allies brought Iraq down, not, for example, by blowing up a power station but by blowing up the point where the power station connected to the power grid. Providing the very same result, but with less effort and less destruction. Plus, little loss of life.

It was no longer necessary to kill indiscriminately as the technology existed to allow a smart weapon to hit a target with such high accuracy. GPS had provided the means. The weapon could hit a target with an accuracy of inches. Literally, put a bomb down a chimney.

Cannon and tank rounds were capable of being guided by GPS. Program the target, load the round, and fire. Job done.

So, the planning for war became a search for ways to 'disable' a country and not destroy it. After all, when the conflict was over, things needed to be restored.

War had become surgical, and mankind, good and bad, had learnt.

9 November 2015
0625

London Heathrow Airport is the second busiest airport in the world based on international passenger traffic numbers. The only airport that moves more people than Heathrow is Dubai International.

Established in 1930 by Richard Fairey, who paid just £15,000 for the hundred and 50-acre site. He planned to build light aircraft on the site. During the war, it became RAF Heston, when the government swallowed up the village of Heath Row. The first aircraft to operate from RAF Heston was a Lancaster bomber.

Seventy million passengers use the airport every year, more than the total population of the UK. It also employs seventy-six thousand people within its boundaries.

It's a city in its own right, with its own rail network, sub-terrain service tunnels, and dedicated fire service and police force. It even has its own dedicated power station. In less than half a second, Heathrow can go from being connected to the power grid, to being in what is known as 'Island mode' independently powered.

There are actually six terminals at Heathrow. Most people know of the main five, but there is a small sixth terminal that caters for royalty, celebrities, and special guests.

Heathrow lies 14 miles west of Central London and operates two parallel runways stretching east to west. The configuration of the two runways means that depending on the wind direction, aircraft could travel over the city of London on final approach.

This has long since been a matter of concern and controversy due to the risk of an aircraft crashing in the city below. People complain about the aircraft noise above them but then object to plans to create a third runway further out and on a different approach.

Seven hundred and fifty thousand people live under the Heathrow flight path. Historically, 70% of all aircraft approach the airport over the city, the remaining 30% approach over Windsor. However, Heathrow's safety record is second to none.

Today, the wind was in the west, meaning the final approach was from the east directly over the city. The weather for a November day was beautiful. Cold, but very clear.

Above London, moving from the east on its final approach to Heathrow Airport, was the normal queue of early morning inbound flights. If you were to stand near the end of the runway and look downrange directly at the aircraft approaching, you could see the stack of aircraft, one behind the other.

Being one of the world's busiest airports meant that at the time of the day, air traffic control would be stacking the aircraft seconds apart for landing.

Passengers would have a bird's eye view of the capital, much to their delight. This was a sight very much worth seeing. As it was a clear day and little cloud, most of the city would be on show below, lit by the millions of street and property lights.

An Iranair 747-400 was 5 minutes downrange from the runway, it was passing half a mile east and slightly north of St Paul's Cathedral. The pilot was tired, it had been a long day, and he was looking forward to being on the ground and in bed.

The approach was automatic, the aircraft was landing itself. Both pilots were watching over the systems, never having become fully comfortable with letting a computer land the aircraft. However, they embraced the new technologies that continually appeared in aviation.

The flight had originated in Tehran, Imam Khomeini Airport. It was not full but had two hundred and sixty passengers and fifteen crew. This was a daily scheduled flight and was always popular, moving tourists and business people from Iran to the UK. For some, into Europe or beyond.

The flight time of around 5 hours was not too long, but long enough to take you away from the heat of the Persian culture well into Western mayhem.

Exactly 90 seconds behind the Iranian aircraft was another on final approach, and 90 seconds behind this aircraft would be another. And so, it would continue all day, every day, as normal.

Aircraft join the final approach into Heathrow from 7000 feet from two feed in spiral holding patterns. They would normally be between 2500 and 3000 feet as they crossed over the city.

Below and to his left, the Iranian pilot could see the top of St Paul's Cathedral, a beautiful site for anyone to see, regardless of your beliefs or religion. The building was lit and stood out white in all its splendour against the other buildings around it.

A strange parody, as it happens, that one of the Iranian pilot's last sights on earth was a Christian church. On the ground below, he saw a flash not far from St Paul's, an explosion.

The initial shock wave hit them very quickly and knocked the aircraft left. Together with his co-pilot, instinct kicked in, as a result of their extensive training. They took control back from autopilot and slammed all four engines into full emergency power at the same time pulling the aircraft up to climb.

They really needed airspace badly, climbing up from 2500 feet. The passengers were strapped in, and so too were the flight crew having already prepared the cabin for landing. The aircraft, as big as it was, responded instantly and clawed for the height it needed.

The Lufthansa Airbus 380, 90 seconds behind the Iranian aircraft also saw the flash and the 747 being jerked left and start to climb. The German pilot too was awake and very quick to react pushing his own aircraft into full power and climbing to the right, away from the 747 and into non-compromised air space.

He continued his climb, moving up as fast as possible and on a full 180-degree turn, taking the A380 back and high out of what he considered to be harm's way.

Behind him, other aircraft were now taking emergency action, which to anyone on the ground who would have seen, must have looked like some form of an aerobatic display.

As the Iranian 747 was blown to the left, the pilots instinctively used this motion and continued the bank left on emergency power, pulling the giant 747 up and away. Four huge Rolls Royce RB211 engines were providing 240,000 lbs of thrust, pushing the aircraft slowly out of danger's way.

With the big aircraft being only 60% full, it had a better power-to-weight ratio than normal, so responded and moved faster, helping to push them away from whatever had happened below on the streets of London.

Above his head and to the left, a band of orange warning lights suddenly came on, and a loud buzzer sounded intermittently in the flight deck: Fire!

Looking out of the right window, the co-pilot could see that the two engines on the right side of the aircraft had caught fire. He knew that fire control was automatic, they did not have to do anything except keep the aircraft under control.

He had no time to speak the words confirming the fire as both engines exploded, ripping off the wing, igniting the fuel, and taking the two hundred and seventy-five people onboard to meet their Gods.

Chapter 2

SIS London
Friday, 6 November 2015, 0900

The meeting had been called by the head of SIS, controller of the task force tracking the suspected Islamic group that was based around Manchester. They had been given the name, or code name, of Mancunians. SIS had been tracking this group for about 6 months.

It was considered that as a group, they represented a threat to the UK and as such considerable resources were being used to make sure the UK was ahead of them as much as possible.

A full team was permanently based in Manchester and infiltrated many of the areas where the Islamic fundamental type of young people seemed to breed. There were agents working undercover within Manchester University, others were part of the local mosque community, and some worked in supermarkets and local employment areas.

All gathered information on people that could, or just may, become or wish to become involved in the Islamic fight against the West.

What do they look like? What does a terrorist look like? Good questions. Look in the mirror, they look like you and I, no different, ordinary people, going about their business and their lives. The difference is some have been taught that the West deserves to be terrorised and people killed in the name of their God Allah, if not for their God, then for some cause that others believe to be righteous.

Religion is still the root cause of most conflicts around the world since time began. Just how can different understandings of the same theme can cause so much bloodletting and horror?

If you read the Bible and the Qur'an, both are very similar to each other in many ways. Teachings, beliefs, rules, and regulations. It is possible to take words from either book and interpret them as your excuse or reason to kill.

And We ordained for them therein a life for a life, an eye for an eye, a nose for a nose, an ear for an ear, a tooth for a tooth, and for wounds is legal retribution.

From the Qur'an.

But if there is harm, then you shall pay life for life, eye for eye, tooth for tooth, hand for hand, foot for foot, burn for burn, wound for wound, stripe for stripe.

From the Bible.

Mahammad arrived over 600 years after Christ, meaning that in terms of time, Islam is at the stage nowadays that Christianity was in the Middle Ages. The time of the Crusades when we Christians travelled the globe and slaughtered millions in the name of our Christian God. Forced people to kneel to our God, forced our beliefs upon countries thousands of miles away.

Look at any stained-glass window in a church or cathedral. There are always knights in armour, with swords depicted. The Christians believed it was their duty to force any non-believers, or followers of different faiths, to kneel before our God. Do Christians really have any moral ground to stand on?

The difference between then and now is time, civilisation, and the availability of weapons and their ability to kill indiscriminately. You do not have to stand next to the man you are killing now, you can do it from a distance, remotely. Gone is the heat of battle, the actual need to kill up close and personally.

Sitting in the conference room were ten of the most senior officers within the SIS and police, who had gathered to discuss the latest intelligence that the undercover teams had sent through from Manchester.

The word on the street was that something massive was being planned. It involved many people operating in many places throughout the UK. This information was coming not only from the undercover operations in Manchester but from many sources.

Interpol had raised concern and passed on intel from their sources across Europe. Even the USA had passed on other intel pointing to a major attack.

Alarm bells were ringing, and the time had come to consider what course of action was the best.

The man who headed this operation was Commander Si'ad Marachi. A third-generation Muslim who had been brought up in Kuwait graduated from UCH in London with a degree in history and was recruited into SIS directly from campus.

His heritage was Iraqi and lived in Safwan, a town close to the Iraq-Kuwait Border. He had no family however remaining in Iraq. He was fluent in Arabic and Surani a dialect of Kurdish. His family were insistent that he learn the 'Old ways'.

Over the next 15 years, Si'ad had worked in most positions that SIS could offer. His background and obvious acceptance in the various Muslim, or to be fair Islamic communities, allowed him to operate under cover very easily.

Si'ad believed in his adopted country. It had provided security and hospitality to him for many years. To him, the UK was now his home and the home of many similar Iraqi people. Si'ad's family had been killed in some sort of accident back in Iraq.

As such, Si'ad believed the UK was owed his loyalty. He was determined to protect his country, his home, and his new family.

He was devout. He worshipped in the mosque and believed in and followed the Islamic teachings. What he could not understand was why so-called followers of Islam chose to attack people just because they did not believe or were not Islamic. He knew that the Qur'an did not suggest anyone should kill to force people to believe.

The meeting was to update the main ten senior-level officers on the latest information, what his team believed this all meant and to decide if they needed to elevate the situation to a higher security level.

This would mean moving two steps from Substantial, where an attack is likely, to the highest level, Critical, where an attack is highly likely in the very near future. Doing this was out of his control and needed the agreement of all ten together.

What would follow was the UK going onto a semi-war footing with both police and military put on high levels of readiness. The other emergency services would move to pre-planned levels of readiness as would all hospitals.

The prime minister would immediately call a meeting of COBRA and control of the situation would switch to joint civilian/military control.

He had everything he needed, but the one thing that Si'ad did not have was a target. Out of all the intel that he had, from all corners of his control, what was missing was the target. This really worried him and worried him deeply.

In all the operations he has been involved with in his past, successes and failures, they always had an idea or knew the target. A city, a venue, a person, a train. Whatever they were planning to attack, intel had given them potential or possible targets.

Part of the psychological impact of the terrorists' actions was to scare people and frighten them. Where next? Could it be near me? Will I get killed? In doing this, they hope to disrupt what the politicians call 'the British way of life'.

This time, there was nothing, no mention of a target. For some officers, this meant it was all bluff or ballocks, others considered this more of a warning, perhaps multiple targets. But the truth was, no one knew.

There was no traffic on where the target was. GCHQ had found nothing and they were looking very hard, both through traditional means and through hyperspace. The information from the many phone taps and computer taps he had been authorised to use gave nothing.

Perhaps he was wrong, but there was so much mounting intel and evidence pointing to an attack, he needed to act, if only to make sure everyone else was up to speed. He was worried enough to call the meeting and raise the threat level to the maximum. It would be a serious bump in his career if he was wrong, or even failed.

The meeting was set for 0930 hrs. It was now 0900. Si'ad had been ready all night and had been in the building working since 0600 the previous day. 24 hours of continuous nonstop full-on work. The buzz had not gone away. He was wired on coffee and adrenaline. Ready to go, ready to explode; ready for anything they will throw at him to stop him from raising the threat level.

Not out of any issues with respect for Si'ad, he was well respected, and trusted, one of the best and few high-level British security operatives that came from a good solid Muslim background. From the time he joined the SIS, his dedication and effort had been noticed; he was there, in mind and body, always.

It was as always budgets and costs that came into the equation and Si'ad must fight to move past commercial objections, to get everyone to see the facts and threat.

CIS HQ London
Meeting Room 7, 0930

Si'ad rose and welcomed everyone. Each of the main officers had one of their support staff with them. Overall, twenty people were in the room.

Meeting room 7 was four stories underground and access to the room was totally controlled. No one in and no one out until the meeting concluded. Restrooms and other welfare facilities were available without leaving the room.

As he rose, the chatter fell away and the room was silent.

"Good morning, Thank you for coming at such short notice. We do not call such meetings lightly and today, I need to brief you on a growing situation we are seeing that is now, in our opinion, a major threat to the UK."

He paused, a little out of showmanship, but he was actually shaking and needed to get a grip.

"As you all know from circulated reports, my group has been following what we believe to be a fundamentalist threat based in Manchester. This operation has revealed planning and preparations for some form of, shall we say, event. Intel that has been intercepted by our own resources, GCHQ and from Interpol, and beyond all point to an attack on the UK mainland within days. This leads us to believe we should prepare and increase the threat level to maximum."

Whilst Si'ad was saying this, he personally walked around the table and handed out ten file dossiers. These contained the intelligence report and summaries of the findings from surveillance in Manchester and other places.

"Please take some time to read through the data in the files. This is comprehensive and is eyes-only. Once we are finished here this morning, I need to have all ten files back without anything being removed. We have one main concern. From the information you now have, you can see that we are expecting possibly three attacks, maybe more. We have been watching various people and places for some time. What is very disturbing to me, and should be to you, we have no idea of any targets.

"From the surveillance results and intel, we have no real reason to go in and take down the people involved. Nothing of great interest or against the law has been seen or could be proven. Other than intel, we have no legal justification to strike. Please take your time and go through the information. When everyone is done, we can take questions and open this for discussion. Thank you."

Si'ad knew what was in the reports, backwards and sideways. Walking to the coffee table, he poured a large cup of black coffee, three sugars no milk. He had no stomach for food though. Just needed to boost his buzz.

The people that his teams were watching seemed normal everyday folks from mainly Manchester. There were other people that were considered worth watching further afield. Bradford and Leicester. Some work had been done in Birmingham too.

One Manchester pair were a newlywed couple, living with their parents, struggling to raise the money to get a place of their own. In fact, they were a mixed-race couple. Not that this was anything of an issue, but a wonderful sign of the integration between the communities. They seemed to be hardworking. She worked at M&S in Trafford Park, whilst he was an engineer contracted to National Grid.

In total, about another twenty people were being watched. But again, outwardly, they all seemed normal and there was no real reason to suspect that they were involved.

Some of the intel they had was coming back to them from two local mosques where the elders were expressing concern at some of the radical-style discussions they had heard. Other information was from their own SIS officers and local police.

SIS had provided people that could be planted within the mosques. This level of infiltration provided much better information. A better understanding of what was going on. But still no real target information.

Only in the last 14 days had things started to change and only then through secure communications with each other.

GCHQ had pulled the information out of the air and fed SIS in London. These were emails between several of the groups under watch. However, they were encrypted with a pre-shared key required to allow them to be read. Even the SIS did not have the key.

The increase in traffic was causing alarm and the lack of the encryption key was proving a real pain in the arse to Si'ad. Until such time as they can force the company selling the encryption software to give up the key, they are going to be in the dark. This was still ongoing with the company asking for a hearing to decide. Time was not available for this. Time could be running out for everyone. But no one knew.

Si'ad looked around and everyone around the table had eyes on and was now watching him, indicating they were ready.

"Has everyone read the documents I have provided?"

A joint 'Yes' came back.

"As of right now we still do not have the key to read the emails, this is a matter for the courts and will not provide assistance any time soon unless we can bend a few arms and get some cooperation where needed.

"Nothing unusual has been seen except for some meetings between the contacts we are monitoring. Friday last week, contacts 2 and 3 met with contact 4. This has never happened before but confirmed a link between them all. Saturday morning contact 4 met with contacts 6 and 7. Again, nothing major but confirmed a link. They met in a park in the middle of Birmingham; this was odd, or seemed odd as we have been centring the operation around Manchester. Only because a greater majority of the people we are looking at live there.

"It was difficult to get one of our assets close for this meeting but we did try at the second meeting. The conversation that was overheard was only towards the end of their discussions. What was heard made no sense to us, but to them was clearly important judging by the level of excitement and arm waving."

The Met Police Commissioner, Sir Robert, interrupted Si'ad rather abruptly. "Si'ad, please just tell us what did they say."

Si'ad lost his stride for a minute as he did not expect the interruption. He stopped, counted to five in his head, and continued.

"Yes, of course, Sir. What was heard was as follows:

'Are we ready for the Warrington Car boot sale?'

'What about Scunthorpe?'

'What about Duxford?'

'I know they are ready in Norfolk.'

'We have not heard back yet from Kimbolton.'

"Many people had put in many hours of work looking at these towns or locations mentioned in the overhead conversation.

"Warrington: Home to RAF Burtonwood, the biggest USAF base post-war. American link. Nation Nuclear Laboratory is situated in Warrington—a great target. Thelwall viaduct taking the M6 over the Mersey and Manchester ship canal—great target.

"Scunthorpe: Nothing spectacular here. Huge steel plant a lot of heavy industry, nothing that can go bang badly.

"Duxford: Sleepy village near Cambridge; gave its name to RAF Duxford. One of the main Spitfire bases during the Second World War was now a museum.

"Kimbolton: Strangely another sleepy Cambridgeshire village. Home to RAF Kimbolton another USAF bomber base. So again, US links. Closed in 1946 but was on standby until 1960, now an industrial estate. And yes, we have looked at what they make there. Public school, nothing else.

"Norfolk: Too big an area to be able to tie down any possible targets. Several RAF and military bases. USAF bases. For the last week, we have been looking for any link between these three points, but nothing has come up. Military, mainly historical, revenge but against what? Car boot sales target rich environments, normal in a field, away from other influences and pretty uninteresting for security services. Would be an easy target and hard to protect.

"Scunthorpe and Duxford could be other car boot target venues. But I don't have the resources to chase car boot sales, that is just not possible. Norfolk is too wide a description. There could be hundreds of events.

"Initial reaction is that they could be planning something in or around a car boot sale. Possibly Scunthorpe or Duxford. We have checked and Scunthorpe does have several car boot sale events; Duxford has nothing, but there is the war museum there. Aircraft mainly. Local police are checking out the Scunthorpe organisers and we have alerted security at Duxford. Norfolk Police have been advised. Our people are still searching for some form of link between the three locations and car boot sales."

Sir Robert, the police commissioner, stood. "Si'ad, at the risk of teaching you to suck eggs, there has to be a link to these sites, these places, they all seem so uninteresting, but is that a deliberate thing?"

"Believe me, Sir, we have been looking at every possible link, historical, people, military units, everything that could link the places into some reason to want to visit each one. For good or bad reasons."

Si'ad knew that Sir Robert and everyone asking questions were right. His teams had asked the same things, and more, much more, combing anything that could provide a reason to link the places that had been mentioned.

The room went quiet and everyone pondered this information. Car boot sales seemed so harmless, why would you attack such an event? But then where is the difference between a car boot sale or a concert in Manchester? Nothing, just people to slaughter.

Over the next hour, the discussion went around in circles, moving off on different tangents, along a route to finish back where they started. The same questions came back time after time.

- What was on the emails?
- Where were they targeting?
- One target or three as intel suggests?

They just did not know. Over 2600 people employed within SIS were active and looking and thinking continually to protect the UK. They were baffled.

SIS London
12 September 2015, 1145

The Met Police Commissioner stood and coughed.

"I think we have all that we can get from this discussion and we all need to move on for various and plentiful other reasons. We need to bring this discussion today to a conclusion and act accordingly. Si'ad, thank you to you and your teams. What you have presented is thorough and worrying. I personally agree with you that we need to inform the PM and raise the threat level.

"However, there are some anomalies and puzzles yet to be solved or made sense of. Many other people here that have opinions and responsibilities that could be very different to my own. For time's sake, I intend we take a vote. Those who disagree will have an opportunity to discuss their reasons here and now. We simply need a majority but I do believe we should heed the advice and comment from those that do disagree."

There was a rapid chatter back and forth and the room fell silent once again. The commissioner called for a simple show of hands.

"Those who agree with SIS and feel we need to raise the threat level, raise a hand."

One hand remained down. Sir Peter Foster, Home Office. He scanned the room and looked at the rest of the participants all with a hand raised. Some hands were up, just as though you were at school and needed to piss. Others just rose above the table, hardly moving at all.

"I am sorry," Sir Peter said. "I do agree that we need to act, but I would rather like to see these emails broken before we jump to this conclusion and raise the threat level. Si'ad, how long do you think you need to break the emails?"

Although secretly pleased he had a majority and would get his way, he was surprised it was the Home Office saying no, for now anyway.

"Sir, we are in the hands of the courts. They must either hear the case now, or today, or grant us a warrant to seize the data we need. It is in the country's interest; a matter of national security and people may die without it."

This time, Sir Peter remained seated, nodded then spoke, "Very well, I will make sure that we have a hearing immediately, or I will get you the warrant, or whatever is required to seize this data. We must break those emails as soon as we can. In the meantime, I agree, that we move to the highest threat level. I will inform the PM once we finish here.

"One other thing, I think we need to detain the people you have been watching. We have the legal rights and can hold them under anti-terror legislation. Bring them all in and let us see what falls out."

People rose and started to pack away their belongings. Si'ad moved to the door and as everyone left, he took back the files of information he had given to them all. Once complete, he walked across the room to where a shredder stood alongside the coffee and tea. Each and every file was shredded.

Chapter 3

Warrington, Cheshire
Saturday, 7 November 2015, 0900

The transit van was full to overflowing of old household junk. Boxes of books, old toys, a TV set, bikes, and everything you would expect to be able to buy at a car boot sale. It had taken almost half an hour to shoehorn the car boot sale goods into the van.

The weather forecast was good, a dry crisp day, cold, but it was not supposed to rain today. Just in case the last item to go into the van was the gazebo.

November was probably the latest month to hold a car boot sale, but this was the pre-Christmas build-up and gave local people and businesses alike the opportunity to sell not only their junk but festive items to early Christmas buyers.

The Moat Road car boot sale was famous throughout the area and attracted a good group of sellers and massive amounts of buyers. Today was to be no exception and a full turnout was expected by the organisers. So much so that all the available pitches had been pre-booked by number and paid for.

It had taken only 30 minutes to get from their house near Manchester Airport, along the M56 then north over the newly repaired Thelwell viaduct into Warrington.

The car boot sale site was in Moat Lane, just off the A57 Manchester Road out of Warrington, situated on the north side. It lay about 1 mile to the east of the M6. It was well organised, the sales field was separated from the parking areas by fencing, and the whole site was surrounded by tall hedging on all sides except the east side where the entrance was.

The field bordered a National Grid Gas compressor station and the hedging had been planted to shield the various buildings and the two halls that contained the industrial gas turbines. This is one of the many such sites around the UK that push natural gas through the underground pipe network.

Roger and his wife, Amy, were of mixed race, a common thing from their area. As the Muslim and British communities integrated and grew up together, it was wonderful to see how the past discrimination was no longer a problem.

They had been married for only 2 years and shared a house with Amy's parents. Roger, at 24 years old, was an engineer, and a graduate of Manchester University. He was already an important part of the local mosque; helping to teach the younger boys. He had studied both in Manchester and in Syria whilst on years of visit to the area. Amy worked for Marks and Spencer in the Trafford Centre in Manchester.

When they arrived at the car boot sale, the queue to get in to set up the stall stretched from Moat Lane, almost half a mile back towards the M6. They were not bothered too much as each pitch had been allocated and Roger had chosen the pitch on the most north-western corner of the site backing on the corner where the hedge met. Which, after some 20 minutes of waiting, they were directed to and allowed to set up.

This took some time to do, the obligatory wallpaper pasting tables were assembled and covered in their wares. Unstuffing the transit took just as much time as it did to load it.

The bikes were stood up at the front, the TV put on the edge, and the rest of the available area was now being covered with various items no longer needed including decorative gifts for Christmas, made within the Muslim community to sell to the Christians to celebrate the birth of their God. A further sign of the coming together of the various religious communities within this area.

Everything was out of the van except for a large sports bag that was pushed up against the rear of the front seats. Roger made a point of locking the van before he left it. It was only ten feet away from where they were standing but he locked it and checked the doors afterwards.

Within minutes of starting to empty his van, Roger had the locusts appear. Regular car boot sale freaks that like to rummage through your stuff even before you can unpack it.

"How much for this, mate?"

Anyone who has ever attended a boot sale to sell anything will know what they are like. Very aggravating. Their aim is to buy up the better of the jumble or grab a bargain. Then to add these to their own stalls in the hope of a quick profit.

The gates were finally opened to the public at 1030 hrs and soon the whole compound was completely full. Despite the cold, the attendance was huge, much more than could be expected. They were too in search of an early Christmas bargain.

SIS Surveillance Team
Warrington, Cheshire
Saturday, 7 November 2015 0900

It had been quite easy to follow the van from Manchester. Two cars were used and one fell away as they cleared the outskirts of Manchester before the van went onto the M56.

Word from London came in during the night that plans were being made to move in on all the suspects that were being watched. Jump time was going to be sometime on Sunday night. For now, orders were to follow and watch what they do.

'Follow team A' were now behind the van with no idea where they were going at all. Just tailing the van along the M56.

Follow teams are normally planned as a male-female team to give the impression of a couple and to appear less like police or other authorities. Particularly when working in built-up areas where many people could walk past and look into the car.

Beth won the bet as the van turned north onto the M6, Carl was convinced they were going to London. Having been on watch all night, the last thing he needed was to drive to London. Instead, they went north.

Joining the A57, they were forced to drive past the van as it pulled over into a queue of vehicles waiting to go into a large car boot sale field. A mile further, there was a sign for public parking which was almost empty.

Parking at the front of the area gave them a good view down the road to the van, still waiting patiently to get into the boot sale area. Slowly, the van came nearer and took up a place over the far side of the field.

Beth and Carl could see very easily, so sat back to relax a little and watch.

Car Boot Sale
Warrington, Cheshire
Saturday, 7 November 2015, 1040

Roger and Amy quickly became engrossed in what they were selling, and the Christmas gifts were selling well. The true car boot sale junk was not so popular, and Roger was almost giving it away to avoid having to take it home again.

A good rule for car boot sales is to agree that what is not sold is taken to the recycling centre on the way home. This, they intended to follow. Most of the junk they had was donated from within the community.

Over the day, they had many visitors to their plot. The bikes had gone and some of the junk, but they had almost sold out of the Christmas goods. Just a couple of flower decorations were left; dried flowers mounted onto wood slices, arranged and painted with Christmas glitter.

Time was getting later when a couple approached them and spent some time looking at the remaining goods. White, with northern accents, possibly Manchester. They looked through the various old electrical items and poked through some old records, but hung over the Christmas stuff for longer.

"I can give you a special price to clear these last items if you like. We will be packing up very soon and I would rather sell them. How about £10 for the last three pieces?"

"Oh, go on, Carl," Beth said. "Mum would love one of those. They are really nice. Do you make them yourselves? I think they are lovely."

Whilst Roger took the money from a reluctant Carl, they chatted together about Christmas coming and the weather, the cold. All things that normal people would pass the time talking about.

Having paid and said goodbye, Carl and Beth walked away.

Back at the car, the view from where they were parked was now a little blocked by vans pulling back to reload the unsold goods. They could see the van and when it moved, they would follow.

As it was late in the year, the closing time for the day was 1500 hrs and towards the end of the afternoon, as the light was becoming too low, Roger started to clear up the stall and prepare for reloading what was unsold.

He opened the van and removed the sports bag, which appeared from the way he was carrying it to be a little heavy. He stopped briefly to talk to Amy and then with the bag in hand, walked towards the corner of the hedge row. He pushed his way through the foliage stopping at the other side and crouching down onto his knees.

Holding very still for some time, he looked back, just still, not moving a muscle and just watched the people moving around the sale. There were not as many customers anymore but the activity of the sellers packing up their remaining wares more than made up for them. Perfect cover for him as he completed what was the true reason he was there today.

After watching everyone covertly for 10 minutes, he stood slowly and moved back into a small thicket of trees growing in the wasteland that was between the hedge and the wire fencing of the gas compressor station.

The bag was green and as he pushed it into the middle of a dense little thicket, it became almost invisible. Again, he crouched and watched for signs of movement towards him from the crowds. Nothing.

Standing up, he undid his zipper and peed on the tree nearest to him, deliberately he made sure that some of the urine went onto the leg of his jeans, leaving a wet mark.

Moving back to the edge of the hedge, he pushed back through, emerging pulling up his zip, and swearing about his trousers. His neighbour on the stall next to him thought this was hilarious, Roger having missed and pissed on himself.

East Winch, Norfolk
Saturday, 7 November 2015, 1400

The weather in East Anglia was very fine for the time of year. A few clouds and hazy sunshine for most of the day. Even at 1400 hrs, it was starting to dusk, and it was cold. Made worse by the easterly wind blowing in from the coast.

Two ramblers sat in the bar of the Carpenters Arms at a small table near the window. They were dressed in all of the rambler's regalia complete with waterproof trousers and big boots. Their two backpacks were to the side of the table directly under the window, well away from the fire. On the chair next to them were their waterproof tops, Helle Hansen coveralls.

They were halfway through a fine-looking pub meal, vegetarian pasta, brown bread, and orange juice. The pub did a good passing trade from A47, the Kings Lynn to Norwich Road and the walkers who frequented the area. It was one of the main north routes out of Norwich to the East Midlands, or across towards Peterborough and beyond.

Consequently, the pub offered a full range of vegetarian foods and the owner had half expected the Asian couple to ask for a veggie meal. He was happy to cater for all tastes that pass by, from a full-on truck drivers' breakfast to a veggie menu to be proud of.

At 1430 hrs, after coffee and a sweet sticky pudding, they paid their bill, both used the toilets and then spent some time getting dressed to leave. The owner noticed that the backpacks seemed to be a little heavy, wondering what they could need whilst out walking that could weigh so much. But who knows?

Having left the pub, they walked at a slow leisurely pace to the left, south towards Norwich and then turned left again into Walton Road. It was a matter of only 150 yards. At the junction of the A47 and Walton Road, there was a campsite. But the walkers continued, following the road slowly, chatting happily.

About 1 mile further along, there was a farm track to their right. No signs indicating that this was a public right of way or even a bridlepath, they followed this as it crossed a small ditch and headed towards a wooded area known locally as Walton Common.

By now, it was past 1530 hrs and the light was low. It was also getting very cold. As they moved into the wooded area, they turned west and walked towards the western edge of the common.

Less than 300 yards in front of them, across a small field that had been laid fallow this year, was the outer fence of a National Grid Gas compressor station.

From one backpack they pulled out some thermal survival blankets, like the silver sheets you see at the London Marathon. These were far better and more efficient. Along with water and sachets of food; ration packs were given to troops.

Burrowing under a thick and dense brush bush, they cleared an area just enough for two people to lay side by side. On the floor, they spread one of the blankets and some clothes. Then climbed on top together covering themselves with the remaining thermal blanket and clothes they had. Having covered themselves they pulled the food in close, snuggling together to stay warm.

Using the fallen leaves around them, they pushed them out of the entrance they had made, covering tracks and marks as they did it. The light was almost gone.

As they lay together, they expected the silence to be total but that was not the case. There was a distant rumble from the road but there was also a whining noise in the air. This came from the National Grid compound; something was running in there and very fast to make this noise. Both knew what the noise was.

With some cover of background noise, they were able to chat. Cuddled close together, they talked about what was to come and what they had to do. Could they actually go through with it, would they fail? Maybe they would get caught.

"Maybe we would die tonight," she said pulling him closer to him, squeezing him very tightly.

"It will be what it will be, we do what we have to do."

Before he said it, she knew what he would say.

They were cuddled together in the middle of a wood, warm and dry, for now. His hand moved to her breast, she was lying on her right side facing him but did not move away or complain. As he squeezed and played gently, she felt the familiar passion rising within her. Her breath became little erratic, soft pants.

His hands moved up and down the side of her body, squeezing and caressing her, pulling her to him. 6 inches above them was the bush, dense and with some prickles. She could not move too far. But she rolled over to lay flat as his hand found her, pushing under her clothes. Now was their time. Later was time for Allah.

Two Locations: Scunthorpe and Diss
Saturday, 7 November 2015, 2330

Two vehicles, one a small Ford van and the other a Vauxhall Astra van, drove through the countryside. Separated by just over 100 miles as the crow flies, both vehicles had the same purpose.

Driving were two young men and beside each of them was a good-looking young lady, a little worse for wear from drink after their night out. The drivers were sober, completely; considering the promise they were on, the last thing they wanted was to be pulled for drunk driving. Plus, they never drank the demon alcohol. It was forbidden.

The Astra van came through the middle of Scunthorpe, in N Lincolnshire towards the M180. His girl was very drunk and was all over him. She could not wait, wanted to get started right here and right now, pushing herself over the driver and feeling his crotch whilst he tried to drive.

They turned south out of Scunthorpe, along Scotter Road south and headed over the M180 motorway. He turned right into Butterwick Rd and pulled up after a mile, on the left of the road. Cutting the engine, he leaned over, wrapping himself around his new girlfriend.

The second van left St Neots, Cambridgeshire, and travelled west towards Kimbolton. A great time was had by his new girlfriend at his expense. Now it was his turn, payback if you like.

Turning right in Gravely, they headed out into the countryside and on for a few miles. It was completely dark everywhere and he wished his lights were much better than they are. As he passed a go-carting centre, he turned left and left again after another 100 yards. He pulled up on the left side of the road in the darkness. Killing the engine, he too turned his attention to his girlfriend, her also now only too willing and eager to please.

Both vans now sat in the almost complete darkness. In the distance, the orange glow of towns and cities could be seen. On the right side of each van were the security lights of a National Grid Gas compressor station.

After some time cuddling in the front, almost in unison, both drivers received a text message. One word, one word only: 'GO'.

The drivers got out and pulled the girls to the back of the vans. Opening the doors, they each turned and kissed the girls, moving their line of sight away from the rear doors.

From the rear of each van, two figures dropped out and were gone. No sound, no fuss, gone. The clock was now running. 30 minutes to wait but what to do?

In the back of the van, it was warm and there was a mattress on the floor. Bundling in the girls, what better way to pass 30 minutes?

A second message was received by each driver. This time, there was a time difference. Both said the same: 'GO'.

Clothes were put on rapidly and the girls put back in the front of the vans. The black figures returned and the vans left.

***

M11 Duxford
Saturday, 7 November 2015, 2330

The white Renault panel van had made the journey in good time. Lea was on time. As he approached a slip road to leave the M11, Lea reached under the dashboard and flicked a switch. The engine cut out and coughed, plumes of smoke came from the exhaust.

He pulled the van out of gear coasted as far as he could on the inside lane, and then pulled off onto the hard shoulder. The van stopped.

Concerned about passing traffic, he pulled half onto the grass verge and half on the tarmac. Turning his hazard lights on, he got out of the van and moved to the grass area alongside. To the left of him, the verge dropped away downwards into a field. Across the carriageway, it did the opposite and rose up, leading to the runway at what used to be RAF Duxford, now the Imperial War Museum.

Across the far side of the field was the small village of Duxford, whose name the base had adopted many years ago. To the south side of Duxford was another gas compressor station.

At this time of the night, the traffic was very low. Lea had a view along the carriageway for almost 2 miles and a clear view along the slip road joining the M11 from junction 10. It was clear, not a light anywhere.

He moved to the back of the van and opened the door.

"OK, go, go; get on with it."

Two figures dressed in black, black balaclavas, gloves and boots dropped out, pulled a large hold all from the van, and sprinted away over the edge of the verge and down into the field. The edge of the field gave them cover, where it met the built-up bank for the motorway. They squatted motionless, watching, waiting, and moved off. They ran south following the road and then east into a hedged area.

Lea opened the bonnet of the van and using a torch, stared aimlessly into the engine. He did not have a clue about engines but the effect was what he wanted. If anyone did stop, he had just broken down.

***

Diss, Norfolk
Saturday, 7 November 2015, 2330

In the far corner of the car park to the front of the Hartismere Hospital in Castleton Way, the security van started up and the two occupants drove slowly through the exit barrier and left out of the main entrance along Castleton Rd.

The sign written van displayed proudly Property Security Suffolk Ltd. It was bedecked with twin orange flashing lights and two front-mounted moveable spotlights. Aerials bristled on the roof, and the car looked its part.

The two personnel were uniformed, complete with hats, torches, and walkie-talkies, more American than the Americans themselves.

The van progressed along the road and out of the limits of Eye, towards Yaxley. It passed the school and sports centre on the left and then made a right turn into a disused road which led up onto the old airfield.

It was a familiar sight for locals, this company had been patrolling various buildings around the town for the last year. No one really paid it any attention anymore.

It drove slowly along the old concrete road and towards some bright orange lights in the distance. As it got closer, it moved onto the side of the road and pulled up.

Less than 200 yards to the front was a National Grid Compressor station.

One of the guards got out and relieved himself against a nearby tree stump, the second opened the back of the van and another two black figures disappeared into the night.

Chapter 4

SIS Control Room, London
Sunday, 8 November 2015, 2230

The UK threat level was now at maximum. Something was going to happen. That was known. Anytime very soon. Where was the problem?

The PM chaired a meeting of COBRA at 0900 on Saturday, 7 November, less than 24 hours after JTAC's decision had been taken to upgrade the risk criteria. The protocols that were in place for this level of threat were now being actioned.

COBRA—Cabinet Office Briefing Room A—is all that this acronym means. But it has become known as the preface to anything of major consequence to the country. Everyone assumes this is within No. 10 Downing Street, but in fact, it is in Whitehall. It is the Civil Contingencies Committee.

Attendees are drawn from the various parts of government and defence establishments that would be involved in the subject to be discussed. A high-level decision-making committee in the event of a major incident, including terror attacks, natural disasters, etc.

Every police force in the UK was now on high alert. All leaves had been cancelled. They were all preparing for the worst to happen somewhere. Within each police region of the country, their tactical firearms teams were preparing themselves. Vehicles were loaded with the weapons of war.

Under normal operational conditions, there would always be armed response units available. These were kept to a minimum outside of London or the other larger cities. Now, every officer that was firearm certified had been armed and teamed up with trained high-speed drivers in dedicated fast-response units.

They had strict rules of engagement and they needed to follow these very carefully. At this time, they could only return fire if fired upon. If, and when, things changed, they would be advised 'weapons free'. Then they could fire first.

4 hours on, 4 hours off, repeat. For the armed response teams, this is how they would work until stood down. Whenever that was. Each fast-response vehicle would have two crews and a base where they would work from. This could be anywhere and any building. From the police station to a police house on the outskirts of a village.

These officers would race to the scene of any and every event that was considered part of, or the prequel to a major event. First on the scene, first to respond, and first to die if necessary. But they were no longer alone.

Another part of the same response was 22 SAS based at Sterling Lines, Herefordshire. All four squadrons of SAS troops were now also preparing for war. Not in some far of land to protect UK interests or fight for what we all believe, but to fight on UK soil to protect their homeland.

There are four squadrons within the SAS: A, B, D and G. They all have different roles and every trooper trains for all four main roles. Two squadrons of boat troops, one air and one mobility. Out of these main teams are drawn the men, and ladies, required for the Special Projects team. Anti-hijacking and anti-terrorist response.

What is not commonly known is that other squadrons of SAS troops exist, based around the UK. 22 SAS is based in Hereford, 21 SAS has bases in London and Hampshire, whilst 23 SAS has bases in Leeds, Manchester, and Scotland.

SAS specialise in rapid deployment using mainly helicopters. At Sterling Lines, these aircraft were now being prepared to go at short notice, fully loaded with the equipment and weapons the SAS may need to tackle whatever gets in their way.

Leave had been cancelled and people were recalled instantly. Wherever they were, they were summoned back to base.

The NHS operate EPRR—Emergency Preparedness, Resilience and Response. This is a protocol that monitors and reacts to the UK threat level amongst many other such situations, from industrial reactions to terrorist attacks. When the threat level was increased, things started to happen within all the major trauma hospitals across the country.

Beds were being freed up and non-critical patients were moved home or to other more minor hospitals. Operating theatres were being prepared, lists cancelled, staff recalled or put on alert. The mighty NHS machine was being prepared to respond whenever and wherever it was called upon.

Many times this had been rehearsed, making it second nature. This time was no drill, this time everyone knew something was going to happen. They knew it could be something very big.

Si'ad sat in what was a makeshift control room. Everywhere he looked, there were computer screens, keyboards, operators with headsets. Military personnel as well as his own familiar people. The place was buzzing. What was still missing was a target. They had no idea and were nowhere near getting the court warrant to seize the email encryption key.

He too had a headset on and was looking at a bank of three monitors in front of him. Everything that was said, looked at and noted, every single command or decision for the next hours would be recorded. Nothing was left to any chance.

"Heads up, everyone," Si'ad said calmly. "It is now 2230 hours, in 30 minutes we strike. Is everyone ready?"

Slowly, it went around the room, just like in the launch of a space shuttle.

"Comms ready."

"A Team, ready."

"B Team, ready."

And so it went through each of the control points within the room.

The planning was very thorough and complete. As suggested by the home secretary, they were going in to arrest the entire group of people that Si'ad's operation had been monitoring over the last 3 months.

Everyone would be arrested and taken away for not only questioning but also to remove them from any possibility or remote chance of carrying out any form of terrorism.

There were ten strike teams waiting for the command to go. Ten addresses where people were suspected of being involved in the possible terrorist attack. Each team had their own controller and that controller was sat in this room with Si'ad. Everything that was going to happen would be controlled in that room.

There would be no panic, no confusion as the strike teams hit; the controller would see everything from the body cams the teams were wearing.

Each of the ten teams was made up of police tactical firearms officers, SAS and SIS operators. Two cars four up, meaning eight for each target. Parked 100 mtrs further down the road were two ambulances. Better to have them and not need them than to need them and not have them.

Ten targets all within the Greater Manchester area. A grid had been drawn up charting each of the target addresses. A team is allocated to each. At key points within the grid, there were a further four SAS teams. four up in Range Rovers. It was their job to respond to calls for assistance if any of the teams hit problems. If the takedowns were defended by the targets or other problems such as explosives were found, then the extra SAS lads would deploy.

Within the grid were two Royal Ordnance Corp bomb disposal teams. Planning was total. All three of the major trauma hospitals in Manchester were now on full alert—Manchester Royal Infirmary, Manchester General, and the Children's Hospital.

SIS Control Room, London
Sunday, 8 November 2015, 2250

"Strike teams, move to position 2," Si'ad announced. "We have authorisation to go, we have a go."

Each team now moved to a jump of point and a matter of a few hundred yards from the target house. They knew who they were looking for and where they should be. Even down to the room in the house they slept in. Even at this late stage, no one wanted to give them a chance of any warning.

The ambulances stayed where they were, a minute away from the scene if needed.

It was imperative that all teams hit at the same time. Surprise was the key, to stopping warnings from being sent to others.

"Strike teams, deploy now and hold, deploy now, confirm please."

Back came ten responses 'Roger 1, Roger 2...' all the way to ten.

From their vehicles, eight black figures with masks, helmets, Kevlar vests, and H&K MP5 machine guns ran to the front doors of eight houses. Two teams went into blocks of flats and up the stairs to the front doors of two flats.

"Ready 1, Ready 2," and so on until all ten teams had checked in.

"Standby, standby. GO!"

The team was deployed in two lines of four people. Either side of the door but against the side of the building. Safe from attack should anyone try. Adrenaline was pumping and each of the team was ready for anything or anybody. They had no idea of what they would meet, but they were not taking chances.

"Ready? 1...2...3...Go!"

One of the team moved forward up to the door, with a shotgun he blew out the lock and handle securing the door. As it did not move in as expected, stuck at the top, a second shot blew away the bolt. They were in.

"Police, armed police! Come out, come out!"

All that could be heard was a high-level scream and shouting from upstairs. Four pairs peeled off, two up the stairs, working together advancing slowly checking in all directions. When they hit the top, they split. There was no elegance to this, the doors were kicked in and two heavily armed highly trained black figures burst in, ready to kill.

Each room was cleared in turn, leaving the screaming room until last. They knew someone was in this room, just who or what remained to be seen.

Downstairs, a similar pattern was being repeated, each room was cleared and secured by two black figures.

"Clear, clear," as they moved through the small terraced house.

"Control. Downstairs clear, moving outside."

"Roger that, downstairs clear, moving outside."

The garden was tiny, enclosed by a 6 ft brick wall and laid to lawn. In the corner was a large shed.

"Garden clear, there is a shed very large for the size of the house."

"Roger, garden clear, proceed with caution."

The shed was good quality, and well build. It was also wired for electricity. It was around 10 ft wide and 6 ft deep, placed along the rear wall of the garden. To the left side was the door and to the right there was a window.

Out of the team of two, one had his back to the shed and was looking back towards the house. He had to be sure there was no threat from the house at all, protecting his partner, looking down on their six. The upper teams had not yet cleared the house.

"Leave it, wait for the house to clear."

"Control, halting waiting for the house to clear before checking any further."

"Roger that, waiting for the house to clear."

Everyone needed to be sure that what they had said over the tactical radio had been understood. So it was repeated back. If you repeated something wrongly, then the mistake was there and then, obvious, and can be corrected then. Not later with people dead everywhere.

From the upstairs of the house, the screaming got louder and a male voice joined the shouting. The top team had clearly pushed into the room where the people were. Just as abruptly, it stopped.

"Top team clear, two middle-aged people detained."

"Roger that, top clear, two detained."

Outside in the garden, one of the black figures approached the window of the shed and carefully looked through the glass. Inside was not a pile of garden tools, lawnmowers, and years of dumped garden furniture. There was a desk, bookcases and a computer. It was a Home Office setup.

He gave a thumbs-up sign to his partner, who moved to the door and examined the locks, etc. They did not want to risk damaging any potential evidence by blasting the door with a shotgun. The shed was well-built and would have cost some money.

On the door hung a metal crescent. On one side, it was red on the other side it was green. He looked at it for a moment, then let it go, and dismissed it as a religious sign. As it fell back to the door, it assumed its original position with the red side facing out.

"Control, we are now entering the shed."

"Roger that, entering the shed."

The man in black now opening the shed door was 35 years old. He had been in the SAS for 10 years and had seen a lot of action in many places around the world. He knew so much about what the terrorists could do. Not just religious terrorism, but all sorts, homegrown to greedy bastard Russian traffickers.

The door was open, with no lock, just a simple normal door handle. Gun up, he pushed it very very slowly open. An inch at a time. His partner had swapped positions; he was now 6 ft away from him, eyes in the opposite direction covering the six.

He was a Met firearms officer, the UK equivalent of SWAT. Highly trained, very fit, and very awake right now. Looking at every window he could see. No one says that there is a rule you have to be in the target house.

The door was now open about 3 inches. He was not happy; his guts were telling him to stop and he was listening. He stopped.

"Control, we are unhappy with the door on the shed. We need a BD team in here to clear it for any devices."

"Roger that, bomb disposal inbound now. ETA 5 minutes, clear back."

"Roger that, clearing back."

In the silence, as the pair moved back from the door, they heard a metallic ping, like a spring.

The SAS man reacted so quickly, that it was impossible to understand where the reaction had originated from. His head, his training or just the part of your brain that is tuned into protecting you.

"Grenade!" He screamed as he hit his partner from behind, pushing him down on the floor and laying on top of him.

Fusing grenades varies depending on the purpose required. It could be anything from 3 to 10 seconds, or even longer.

5 seconds later, the shed erupted. A ball of flames, burning very brightly and it was very hot. Luckily for the two teammates, this was a phosphorous grenade designed to burn very hot and intensely. If you were there, it would burn you alive. There was no shrapnel with this grenade, no flying debris, other than the tin container.

"Respond, respond, confirm the grenade. Please, what is your status?"

"SAS team, grid 3 deploy, attack team 1 location, backup required, men down."

Cold, calm and on the ball. Not much got the controllers going, even death itself seen online over the internet as the missions unfolded.

One of the SAS standby teams, ready to go, ready to fight, was now screaming through the streets of Manchester. Led by a traffic BMW on blues and twos, someone who knew the way and the local area.

As they raced along the streets only minutes away, four men ran a final check on their main weapons, unloading, checking reloading.

"Control, SAS grid 3, ROE please?"

"SAS grid 3, Control, standby…weapons free, confirm."

"Control confirmed, weapons free, out."

Neither of the two on the floor could hear or see much. The flash had whited out their vision and this would take a few minutes to come back. The bang had deafened them too for a short while. But they were alive.

The others could not yet go to their aid. Nothing was known about the shed, there could be other devices hidden to catch the people that came to help. They had to leave them, just provide cover if needed.

"Team 1, Control, be advised incoming friendly, four up, SAS grid 3, confirm."

"Roger that, Control, four up friendly inbounds."

They could not help the others out in the garden, but from the windows, they provided defensive arcs of fire until they could get their colleagues back into the house out of any further danger. There was a support team coming, they would recover the lads that were down.

"Team 1, grid 3, heads down, flashbangs, with you in 5, 4, 3…"

Three huge bangs erupted, almost simultaneously, and the area was lit with daylight for less than a second. In the three neighbouring gardens, one on each side and one behind, a flashbang had exploded, designed to confuse and disorientate. Should there be anyone nearby looking to get involved, for now, they could see and hear nothing.

A mist of smoke from the flashbangs and the burning shed covered the garden, out of which four masked SAS figures appeared, two covered forwards towards the house, Team 1 resumed cover in the opposite direction. The other two grabbed a man each and hauled them with no ceremony into the house. The rear two followed.

The prone men were lying on the floor of the kitchen, the four SAS lads walked in the back and out of the front door, back into the Range Rover and left.

"Control, Team 1, we need medevac, two down, not critical, phosfo grenade."

"Roger that, ambulance is inbound, ETA seconds, two to be evacuated. Fire service on the way, ETA 10, provide cover please."

Upstairs in the house, in the main bedroom, two people sat on the bed. Their hands were bound using a sort of cable tie designed for rapid use and permanent until cut. Husband and wife, mum and dad, both dazed and confused and shaking still.

"We have some paramedics coming to check you over, and make sure you are ok. They will be here in a few minutes. Please do not worry, no one here is going to harm you in any way."

Their job was finished, the house was clear, both targets were gone. Only mum and dad were home. They appeared to have no idea of why such action had been taken against them. No idea of what the son and daughter-in-law may have done.

The ambulance, they hoped was not needed, drew up and the two paramedics, complete with helmets and Kevlar vests, ran into the house. Within a few minutes, they declared the two stunned men to be OK and not injured. Just the same, they went to be checked over. Their night was over but only for tonight.

Outside, a marked police car drew up and the driver sat and waited. No blue lights, no fuss. Waited.

"Control, transport is in place," the driver called in.

"Roger that, transport in place. Team 1 escort subject to a car outside, one pair to accompany, the rest secure house until relieved. Out."

With that, the attack on the first target was over. Now forensic teams would take over and go through the house to find anything that could help the investigation. Even what is left of the shed can reveal something. Local police would now take over the security of the house, releasing the armed response back to standby. They too would be waiting again.

Team 1 was the only team that encountered anything remotely like resistance. The explosive was not intended to kill anyone, just destroy evidence of what was in the shed. Which it did. Forensics would no doubt turn up some clues, some help for any investigation, but that was going to take time. Time that was now running out.

In the other nine locations, the same thing had happened. There was no resistance, there were only four other people at home. Most of the premises that were attacked by the other teams were empty. It may well be that there was forensics to be found or information that could be of help. Maybe hidden away or on a laptop somewhere.

Unlikely as it would be expected that they would cover their tracks very well. Again, time was needed, which may not be available.

SIS Control Room, London
Monday, 9 November 2015, 0150

The mood in the control room was sombre and confused. It had been expected that the target people would all now be in custody and being prepared for questioning. What they had now was two injured from team 1 and six middle-aged Asian people. Not much for such a massive use of resources.

One thing that had been made clear with the explosion in the shed, was that they were correct. This must be an organised terrorist threat. Why else go to the trouble of booby-trapping the shed? What was it that they wanted to hide?

The effort for now was going to switch to looking for what evidence they could find at each address.

Si'ad sat at his desk looking straight through his monitor to somewhere miles away in his head. The adrenaline rush was coming down, he was calm now. His mind was racing.

Good, he thought.

Turning to the desk on his right, he asked, "Today is Monday. What is the date today?"

"9 November, Sir."

"9 November, 9 November," he mumbled.

"Sorry, Sir, did not catch that, what did you say?"

"9 November...Oh my God, 9/11! Something is going to happen today!"

Si'ad grabbed a phone and stopped. Who should he tell? Who would believe him? His attempts to round up the bad guys just failed.

"Listen up, everyone. Today is 9 November. In the UK, this is 9/11. Spread the word to all points, something is going to happen today and something very bad. We have no idea what, but let everyone know, it is coming."

Chapter 5

Smithfield Market, London
Monday, 9 November 2015, 0200

Smithfield Market, in Charterhouse Street, is possibly the most famous market in the country; it has been held on the same site for over 450 years dating back to the reign of Queen Mary I.

The site is now an integral part of inner London surrounded by the huge buildings of the city. It was once a green field and took its name from 'smooth field' depicting the flat grass area as it was then.

When not in use for the market in the 1500s, it would be used for jousting and other public events. It was not uncommon for an execution to be held in the market area. In fact, Queen Mary earned her nickname of 'Bloody Mary' by having three hundred Protestants burnt at the stake here.

It was here that Sir William Wallace was executed.

The green area developed and hosted other events. The most famous of which was the Bartholomew Fair, which had grown over many decades to become a rough, rowdy, and uncontrollable event. In 1855, the city of London authorities closed down the fair and developed what was now Smithfield Market.

Completed in 1868, it had been restored recently to its original design condition. Parts had to be rebuilt following the bombing in London during the war but were just rebuilt and did not follow the original designs. Part of the market housed the largest single-span roof in the UK.

Charles Dickens made a famous reference to Smithfield Market in *Oliver Twist*: 'It was a market morning and the ground was covered nearly ankle-deep in filth and mire.'

If you came into London in the morning later than 0800 hrs, the market would be gone, packed up, and not a sign of the traders and dealers. Most of the business was completed whilst all sensible people were sound asleep in their beds.

In modern London, the market continued as it has for centuries, still holding its own alongside slick office buildings, cool nightclubs, and coffee bars. It has some advantages of its own too. The market licensing hours still apply in some pubs and you can, to this day, still get a beer with your breakfast.

600 yards to the south sits St Paul's Cathedral; huge, white, and proudly majestic over London. St Paul's withstood the ravages of the Second World War when in spite of their very best attempts, the cathedral strangely managed to avoid any serious damage from the Luftwaffe. Defiance in the face of the enemy.

To the south-east of the market is St Bartholomew's Hospital, affectionately known as 'Bart's'. It has been part of London's history for over 900 years and is one of London's largest hospitals. It was founded in its present form by the amalgamation of two famous hospitals, the St Bartholomew's Hospital Medical College and the London Hospital Medical College.

Due east, the tower blocks of the Barbican stand tall. Opened in 1982, it was now the home of the Royal Shakespeare Company.

The Old Bailey, Lincoln Inns Fields, home to the legal profession in London, and many businesses are all within walking distance of the market, putting it at the very heart of London and its life.

Abdul Qaardir was a butcher's son. They had been buying their meat and produce at Smithfield Market for over 4 years. His father started the family business 6 years ago and it has thrived ever since. They had three shops, all of which were based in Leicester. Serving mainly the local ethnic community but as the Muslim and Western families mixed and integrated, they were happy to provide their services to all in their community.

Their business retailed the meat and vegetables to the public through their own three shops but they were also contracted to deliver the same produce to other shops in the Leicester area. Plus, they held two contracts to deliver meat and vegetables to three schools and two local care homes for the elderly. The business was well-established, well-introduced, and clearly well-supported.

The costs of travelling to London and buying at Smithfield's were therefore shared between his trade customers; the main profit being taken from their own shops. Each day, Abdul and his brother, Mukhtar, would make the journey from Leicester, down the M1 into London to the market.

For 4 years, the routine had never changed. They drove the same route every day from Leicester, leaving home at 2300 at night and travelling the 3 hours to

Smithfield. Their 7.5-ton curtain-sided lorry was ideal. Large enough for the goods they needed but quick and easy to drive.

They travelled down Finchley Rd, left past Regents Park, along Euston Rd, right into Kings Cross Rd, and then into Farrington Rd. As they turned into Charterhouse Street, they pulled up on the left and parked, where they always did, right outside an old Port of London Authority building.

Depending on the time, they may allow themselves a break and a coffee, something to eat, but more importantly, a much-needed visit to the loo.

The old front of the building, against which they had parked, looked worn and tired. All except the modern plate glass front windows and door. A shiny steel box enclosing the intercom system was on the wall to the left of the glass. The front entrance was at least 12 ft across, completely hidden by Abdul's lorry.

The building was originally owned by the Port of London Authority and used as a warehouse for goods, brought ashore in London, intended for sale at the market, or onward shipment out of London. The decline of the London port saw the building's use become unnecessary and it had been closed down in the 1980s. The port authority eventually sold the buildings off to a new company called Capitalgen.

They had put forward a scheme to use the buildings to house a small power station that would generate electricity for the National Grid and supply local buildings with heat and cooling. The scheme was accepted and construction of the station started. It was completed in 1992.

The station generates 31 megawatts of power and another 25 megawatts of steam and cooling. The main power is provided by two huge Volvo marine diesel engines. V18 configuration, each cylinder is more than 18 inches in diameter. Each cylinder has its own individual cylinder head, nine on each side, fed air through a massive inlet manifold and a super huge turbocharger.

When the station was built, these engines were the largest loads ever to be brought into Central London; each one weighing 300 tonnes. They were so heavy that underground tunnels had to be strengthened and underground car parks shored up with huge steel girders.

The engines arrived on low loaders at Farringdon Rd. Most of the traffic lights had been removed; bollards and central reservations also had to be removed to allow the loads to pass. Once the huge transporters had arrived at the entrance to Charterhouse Street, the engines were moved sideways off the trailers and up the street.

Every possible engineering issue or concern had to be dealt with at the planning stages. To prevent the vibration from causing damage to nearby buildings when these massive diesels were running, each was mounted on a 300-tonne concrete float, these in turn were supported by hundred and forty-four airbags. In all, the engines and floats weighed 1200 tonnes.

Unlike most diesel engines, these two had been designed to run on both diesel and natural gas. The gas had to be compressed to 385 bar (385 times atmospheric pressure) mixed with 5% fuel and then injected into the fuel system. Each engine demanded 3000 litres of fuel per hour and the compressors needed to keep up with this were powered themselves by a 1-megawatt electric motor.

The compressed gas was pumped to the top of the building and stored in six huge tanks, together holding enough compressed gas for 2 running hours; 12,000 litres of liquid gas compressed at 385 bars. The equivalent of over 4 million litres of gas.

The heat generated by the engines was used to produce steam and the steam was piped around the local businesses as heating. This is referred to as Combined Heat and Power (CHP).

The idea was to use the waste heat in the engine coolant and oil from the generation process, making the complete cycle of the engines far more efficient. The hot oil and hot water passed through their own heat exchange systems, taking the waste heat to create steam. The steam could then be used for other purposes. In many power stations, the steam was used to turn a steam turbine, generating more electrical power.

For Capitalgen, their steam was to be used for heating local buildings. High-pressure steam could be piped for long distances where it would another heat exchanger would take the heat for use in the building. The steam main went as far afield as the Barbican Centre and into Bart's Hospital.

The supply of gas into the power station was contracted to be interruptible. Allowing an interruptible contract keeps the cost of the gas down. All helping to make their business model viable.

This meant that the gas supplier could ask the station to stop using gas at any time, provided they were given the required period of notice. This was normally up to 3 hours minimum. In the event of a problem with gas supply, maintenance, or peak demand, domestic and other types of high-priority customers were supplied first. Should this happen, then the gas system would be switched off and the engines would run just as well on fuel oil.

Built into the building were two tanks which together held over one million litres of fuel oil. When running on liquid fuel, a full-sized fuel tanker was needed to deliver every 10 hours to keep the fuel topped up; 30,000 litres per 10 hours.

When the weather was hot, the local buildings would not require the heat. This would represent a problem for the operators as they would have no means of dissipating the waste heat. Power stations have large cooling towers for just this reason. They must keep everything cool and running at optimum temperatures.

Many European countries operate local heating schemes, running small gas turbines to generate power and heat for the community. This is a great idea, making the most efficient use of the power the engine creates. They also invest very heavily in the use of wind turbines. So-called clean energy, but once built, there is little in the way of emissions. Until the day when it is very hot, so the local generating or heating schemes cannot run, because they have nowhere to send the waste heat, and then there is no wind.

Bring on the smokers, standby instant access power. Engines restricted to less than 500 hours running per year come online to keep the grid working.

It is vital, therefore, to make sure that there is always a means of removing the waste heat from any CHP or combined cycle generation.

To overcome this issue, Capitalgen used the waste heat to create cooling. Sounds crazy, but it worked. The heat was used to create the pressure and drive the absorption cycle where two fluids were used to absorb heat from the area to be cooled. The fluids were then separated using the waste heat from the engine.

The final part of the design proposal was also to provide cooling for buildings nearby. Using liquid ammonia as the main refrigerant, waste heat was again diverted to produce cooled water for air-conditioning plants. This was also being piped around their private network under London.

30 tonnes of liquid ammonia were stored at road level inside the building, separated from view by a simple breeze and concrete wall.

It had been a fantastic engineering achievement for Capitalgen, squeezing this generation plant into the old building and running it to produce and supply inner London with needed utilities.

Completely safe, computer-controlled, with so many means of shutting the plant down if anything failed or went wrong. For many years, it had been generating power and no one really knew it was there.

From where Abdul and Mukhtar were standing, they could not hear anything from the Port of London building. They were standing to the front of their lorry and only 6 feet from the wall. The way in which the building had been sound-insulated was very effective.

They had arrived 10 minutes ago, parked the lorry, and gone across the road to find the toilets. On the way back, Abdul called in to talk to his meat supplier and making sure the goods were ready for collection. He knew them very well and spent a few minutes passing the time of day. On his return to the lorry, Abdul called Mukhtar over and went to the back releasing the curtain on the side nearest the power station.

Together, they pulled the curtain almost halfway along the length of the rear and then left it to hang. Crossing the road, they disappeared into the butchers. It looked to anyone that could see as if they had opened up, ready to load the truck with goods.

A black figure dropped to the pavement alongside the lorry and looked left, then right, and then up. 10 feet above him on the wall to the right of the main power station entrance was a CCTV camera, it was pointed down and across the glass front of the building. This covered the front door and did not allow too much of a view beyond halfway across the pavement.

The figure removed a small pistol-like device and aimed it at the camera. His first shot missed but the second covered the front of the camera with a white thick liquid. A simple paintball gun. Effective and simple. The camera would be out of action until someone could clean it.

Satisfied, he moved forward again, crossed the pavement, and flattened against the glass front on the far-right-hand side of the door. A second figure had replaced him where he had stood and took up the watch duties.

The plate glass windows were mounted in an aluminium frame about 2 inches wide and sealed in with a plastic strip, just like the replacement windows advertised on the TV.

The whole frame for the front doors and the windows had been refitted when the power station was built, a modern-looking frame. They had left a square hole in the wall and the frame had been fixed at the front of the brick wall. Behind the frame was the remainder of the depth of the wall, about 10 inches in all; with very secure and laminated glass.

Mounted on the inside of the window to the left side of the door, if you were on the inside of the building, was a silver box in the centre of which was a green round mushroom-like button and the words 'door release'. Anyone who was leaving the building could push this button from the inside and the door would release, allowing them access outside.

The green button was mounted on the 10-inch wall behind the metal frame.

From a bag over his shoulder, the first dark figure produced a small cordless drill and started to drill through the aluminium frame. Three times he drilled the hole, each time increasing the size of the drill and the hole got bigger.

The hole was just at the same height as the door release, near where the glass would meet the frame inside. Once the hole he had drilled had gone all the way through the frame, he stopped. The result was a hole 15 mm in diameter right through the frame of the window. He turned and threw the drill to his colleague, who in turn threw it quietly into the back of the lorry.

Using the newly made hole, he inserted a long screwdriver. It was at the exact height of the door release, just 10 mm from the face of the button. Using the screwdriver as a lever, it was a simple operation to just press the green button. The door was open. So much for security.

The control room was on the second floor of the building and was accessible from both sides. As you entered the front door, to the left side was a lift and some narrow stairs. These led up to the control room.

Once in the control room, there was further access out into the plant at the opposite end. Coming in the front door and going to the right side, took you into the lower levels of the plant and by using various steps and stairs, allowed access to the opposite end of the control room.

Two of the operation staff were sitting in the armchairs overlooking a console that controlled the whole generation process in the building. Night shifts were long and very boring. One, George, was asleep, but Steve was awake and noticed the CCTV camera go white.

"Bloody birds, they got us again, George. I will have to go down and clean off the new load of shit from the camera."

He rose and moved towards the rear of the room and the door that led to the stairs and small elevator. It was only the second floor, so Steve walked. The stairs were a spiral, very much like you find in churches to get up in the bell tower.

The door released with a metallic click and both dark figures moved into the foyer. As they did, two more jumped from the back of the lorry and joined them. The second pair moved to the right of the front entrance and in through the door passing into the plant area. The large fire door closed behind them. All four were dressed completely in black and carried a small pack on their backs. Across their chest were slung small automatic machine guns, Uzis, complete with silencers. They all moved as one, like dancers, with grace, as though performing some deadly dance.

Left pair went left and the right pair went right.

Inside the foyer was a metallic ramp built to allow wheelchair access into the building and to the elevator. The left pair moved up and across to the left, one took the small stairs rising up 2 feet, whilst the other ran up the ramp.

Footsteps coming down the stairs could be heard and both men flattened against the walls, out of sight from the stairwell. Steve was coming down the stairs, oblivious as he closed on the entrance, preparing to clean off the bird mess on his camera.

He cleared the corner of the stairwell and both figures moved. One of the men went down on one knee and brought up the Uzi, the second stood behind him to the right and levelled his own gun.

The two dull thuds were almost inaudible. Two kill shots hit home, one from each of the figures. The back of Steve's head exploded onto the wall behind him, he went down without a sound. Job done. They opened the lift door and pulled the body inside, leaned in, and pushed the button to go up.

Racing up the stairs, the dark pair reached the door of the control room and pushed slowly through. They had no idea who may be there but they knew they would not be armed or dangerous.

George was still asleep, snoring like a pig. Figure one spun him around on his chair and figure two shot him twice where he sat, centre of the forehead. He was dead and knew nothing about it. Unlike the others and many to come, he never saw it coming.

Not stopping to look, they both slowly cleared the room, checking each corner, every door, behind desks, the control panels, the kitchen, and the rest of the stairs. It was clear. No one else was upstairs, there was no one else in this part of the building at all now.

The first pair had moved into the plant room and were now searching for the rest of the night shift. They knew there were always four people on duty and it was their job to find and clear any that were working on the machinery. It could only be two people; it could be none. Everywhere had to be checked.

The main access to the road for deliveries was through a garage-like area, fronting the road, and had two rotary doors moving up and over. This area housed the inlet feed pipes for the deliveries of fuel oil and was used as a loading bay for other goods in and out.

As the second pair moved around the edge of the tank containing the ammonia, they could hear the voices of two people talking. Sliding along the wall and up to the edge of the main opening, allowed them sight into the bay. They stood and just watched.

At the far end near the doors, two figures stood, in high-visibility uniforms, hard hats, and smoking. The only place in the building it was allowed but the door was supposed to open. It was too cold tonight, so they were closer to the door frame and almost blowing their smoke through the cracks on either side.

Being so concerned about getting their exhaled smoke out through the edges of the metal door frame, they were totally unaware of death approaching. From 10 yards away, the figures fired two shots each, four dull thuds.

They fell as the others had, dead, doing an honest day's work, slaughtered in the name of some other cause or God too.

The complete shift for the evening was now dead and the station was running on autopilot.

They were sure of the fact that their two targets had now been eliminated. They hid their bodies from sight. Their instructions were then to check the complete plant and look for anyone else. They were not to know that someone could have been working as a maintenance contractor, or other function that does not require a full-time man on site.

Slowly, they worked their way as a pair through the plant room, up the various levels using the stairs provided. The building was indeed clear of anyone else. Happy it was clear, the second pair moved back through the front of the building and up the stairs into the control room. Together with their comrades, they sat in the quiet and waited.

Even though they knew that there should always be four people, and even though they had double-checked, it could be that for some reason, there may have been more this evening. So, they waited some more, silently. If there were more, eventually they would come back to the control room.

The next hour passed very slowly for them, they were high on adrenalin and wanted to move on. They had a job to do; it had to be done that night, and now they had passed the point of no return. Death for them was now inevitable and they all looked forward to meeting their God. To die the death of a martyr was an honour to be rewarded with everlasting life and many virgins to keep them company.

After slightly less than one hour, one of them spoke.

"Go, it is time, and may Allah be with you all."

They separated out into the plant room.

Two moved up through the building onto the highest level. It was a vast room containing six massive pressure tanks holding the compressed gas for the engines. From their packs, they removed two small charges and set them on the sides of the middle two vessels. They set the devices to initiate the explosives. A radio-controlled device, plus fail-safe timers. Doubling back, they checked their own work, then checked each other's work, and left.

Next figure went down to the ground floor and up to the tank that contained the ammonia; from his pack, he removed the charges and set both on the front face of the tank. Setting the radio devices and timers, he too checked, double-checked, and then left.

The final charges were set on the rearward of the fuel oil tanks. Any type of fuel storage was banned in the central city area of London. That was why you could never find a petrol station in the main centre. The border between Central London and Islington passed directly through the main building. These tanks were actually in Islington and allowed.

A door separated them from the rear yard and at the back of the yard, you could see down onto the platforms of the Farrington Underground station. The track ran underneath where he stood. He too checked, double-checked, and left.

Chapter 6

Warrington
Sunday, 8 November 2015, 2330

Roger and Amy lay in the back of their transit van. It was now empty as they had returned home and removed the car boot sale stock, as Roger had wanted everything that was not sold to be taken to the recycling centre.

The best and easiest access for a van was the Lumns Lane Household waste site. Plus they knew one of the people working there and never got questioned about trade waste or how many times they came.

Once empty, they went home, spent some time with their parents, and sat for dinner together. They had no idea if they would be home tomorrow or even alive. The next days would be difficult in many ways for them. Time and Allah would tell.

Now they were back, in Warrington, at the site of the car boot sale, parked up in a layby at the side of the road, only 100 yards from where earlier they had set up their wares to sell them.

Not that it was really worth their while, from a pile of old junk and some rapidly made Christmas decorations, they had gone home with just under £50. Better than nothing Roger had thought.

But the day's outing had nothing to do with the need to earn money.

On the floor of the van was an old mattress and covers. Although he had left the engine running, the heater did not do too well in the back. It was cold; they had sleeping bags each and two old duvets, rescued from the junk before being recycled.

They did not want to go out for at least 2 hours, but the cold may force them to. Amy stood as much as she could inside the van.

"Get out of your bag, zip them together, and make one big bag."

Amy had a glint in her eye and Roger picked it up very quickly. He did not argue. They unzipped the individual bags, then zipped them back up together making one big bag.

"Get naked, get back in and cover us up with the duvets. Let's have some fun whilst we can, eh?"

Roger complied readily; they were down to their underwear quickly. Amy got back in the big bag and quickly threw out her bra and knickers.

"Now you show me, show me you are hard, let me see."

He was and played with himself, making her giggle. Then climbed into the bag, next to her. She was warm and soft and he was hard and he wanted release, so he started to roll on top of her.

"No, not like that, not tonight. This could be our last time together, it must be special. Lay on your back, do it, lay still."

She moved over to his face and kissed him very hard on the lips, almost biting into his lip. Then she moved slowly down his chest, lower. He knew what she wanted to do. They had only ever done this a few times, not sure if it was allowed, or supposed to happen. Tonight, she did not care.

As she reached her goal, she took him in her mouth; he was very hard. There were no complaints from above as she moved, not only giving him pleasure but turning herself on very much.

She knew he was close but did not want to waste any more time. She moved back up along his side, leaned over and kissed him very hard again.

"You taste nice, don't you?" She said, giggling. "Now roll me over and fuck me hard."

He did, they did, she did; they both did. For 2 hours, they did everything they ever dreamed of doing. They had done what any healthy couple would have done to keep warm. Their clothes were piled up around them and they were buried deep under two thick quilts. They were not cold now.

If anyone had come and checked out the van, they would have easily been able to see that two young lovers were passing the time in the back.

Roger knew he had been and was being followed. He knew that tonight he needed to lose the police and get out of Manchester without being stopped. Tonight, was too important; they could not have a tail tonight.

His plan was very simple. He would arrange for other vehicles to delay or block the roads after he had passed along them. His friends would help him; pissing off the police was one of their favourite pass times.

Their parent's house was in the middle of a large estate of terraced houses, part of the post-war rebuilds and removal of the slums, then later came the expansion of Manchester. It was a maze of roads but built on a grid system also.

With some planning, he could break away from the tail. He grew up here and he knew the area like the back of his hand. He did not need a map or sat nav. The driving part would be easy he hoped. But he also needed the police to believe he was still local.

ANPR cameras would locate the van if they managed to get away, so Roger had changed the number plates for some stolen plates from a similar van. This donor van was only 1 mile from his own house, police patrols would see it easily parked up. Swapping the plates over made it look as though his van was parked elsewhere.

He also went one stage further; he had a third set of plates from another identical van. Once out of Manchester on country roads away from ANPR, he would stop and swap again. Better safe than sorry.

Amy left the house first and sat in the front of the van. Roger came afterwards. They drove off moving west along Leslie Street towards Hollywood St. Within seconds, the car appeared behind them. This was odd as the van did not have the correct plates. But it had been outside of his house.

At the junction of Kippax and Leslie Streets, his friend waited. As the van pulled out, his car pushed in behind across the junction blocking the tail car. He got out and ran.

Roger moved off fast, and took the next right and right again. He wanted to make it seem as if he was heading back and away from where he really wanted to go; only to box back in a few minutes.

Looking for the second car, if it came, he would follow the same square and repeat the block. But it did not appear they were looking for the wrong number plate. With a final set of turns and changes, he backtracked the wrong way for their destination but left the area free of his followers.

The journey was normal, he did not speed or attract attention from the police. They just drove normally as if they had no cares in the world. Once on a lonely dark road, he pulled over and switched number plates again, putting the old ones in the van.

Just before 2330 hrs, Roger climbed out of the warmth, got dressed, and then helped Amy dress herself to match his black clothing. At exactly 2345 hrs, Roger sent a text message on his mobile phone; they opened the back doors and slipped out.

The clear day had changed and there was now cloud cover. No light from the moon and very few streetlights to worry them. It did not stop them being very careful. The van was locked and checked. They both stood at the side of the van, not together but one at each end.

Roger moved off and took the lead and Amy followed. They were clearly experienced and had been trained well. Not together, they were 6 ft apart and would always work at this distance, even if compromised. They were trained to keep distance to stop both from being hit by the same gun. They did not expect any armed response tonight, but better safe than sorry. Moving into the nearest part of the hedge row, they both stopped, froze, and waited for movement.

It was almost 5 minutes before Roger was satisfied; they moved on again, behind the hedge row and onwards. Skirting the small fence on the boot sale field, they continued up towards the corner where they had been earlier that day. The closer they got, the more the light from the compound could show them.

Both had spent many nights here at different places around the fence, watching, looking for routine. When did they check, when did they sleep, when did they eat, what happened if there was a problem technically? They knew what to expect.

They needed to move swiftly but surely and pushed through the hedge and reached the small thicket of trees. It was now 10 minutes since leaving the van. Both were now lying flat on the ground; the night was very dark, but the glow from the compressor compound cast a shadow. This was the most dangerous part, the point where they could be seen.

The bag was still where Roger had left it. Picking it up, they moved away again to the far west side of the fencing, directly behind the two large buildings housing the turbines. From here, the two buildings hid them and their activities from the main control room building.

As they reached the fence, they dropped the bag and lay flat, still and quiet. Another 5 minutes to make sure they had not been seen or activated any alarm or detection system. It was a long and cold 5 minutes.

Time was up and Roger opened the black holdall. He pulled out ten sets of wires, each about 2 metres long and had a crocodile clip on both ends. They also pulled out a Uzi machine gun, which Amy picked up.

She unloaded the gun, checked the magazine, checked the breach was empty, and then reloaded. She cocked the weapon and brought it flat against her chest. 15 seconds of almost silent motion, muscle memory completed without even thinking.

Roger worked quickly, the result again of continued practice. He clipped the wires to the mesh in the fence, each clip about 2 feet apart, and he moved down to the bottom of the fence. He then gathered up the excess and taped it above where he had been working.

The fencing had a low current passing through and would detect any breach. The wires continue the circuit whilst they cut a gap big enough to get through. It was a good fence and thick to cut. Part of the weight in the holdall was the cutters. Large and strong, sharp enough to cut with little noise. No 'click' as it cut through.

Within 3 minutes, a hole was available for them to pass through. His forearms burned from the weight of the cutters and the cutting motion continually for the 3 minutes. Roger led and went through, Amy had her back to him and the hole and crouched, swinging the Uzi in an arc from left to right then back again, protecting his six.

"Clear," came from Roger who was now 6 ft into the compound flat on the floor. She moved backwards taking the holdall through and followed.

They both ran up to the back of the first turbine building and flattened against it. Here it was darker, the floodlights position gave this wall a triangular shadow, that they made good use of. With his back to the wall, Roger took the holdall, eased himself to the left, and peered around the corner. Clear, they moved out.

Amy moved to the corner, shrank down, and covered the ground between Roger and the control room. When he was in position and she was ready, she would give a thumbs-up sign. She followed Roger running and shrank into the darkness and waited.

Had they tripped any alarms, any movement would be seen very quickly and they would have to make a run for it.

He ran across the void between the building and the frame structure housing the two huge feed pipes from the National Gas Grid. Two pipes over 1 metre in diameter came out of the ground and arched up, then disappeared back underground. Like the back of the Loch Ness monster on dry land.

These were designed to allow access to the pipeline for maintenance. On each pipe looping out of the ground, there was a small length of pipe on the apex horizontally. This was a 'Pig Trap'. A pig is a wheeled car that fits in the pipe and is used for maintenance.

Just like in the Bond film when 007 travels along the pipe on a cart checking the welding. Totally true, to a point. You cannot ride on these.

Once in the main pipe, it is pushed along by the gas pressure, hundreds of miles, cleaning any unwanted deposits from the walls of the pipe and can check pipe welds as it moves. Throughout the gas grid, many pigs are moving continually.

The two monstrous loops of pipe rising from the ground suited tonight's purpose perfectly. Every gas compressor station in the country had two of the same. Not exact in terms of design as this varies to a point. In principle, they were identical in what they wanted to achieve.

At each side of the loop was a large bolted flange where the loops joined the main pipework.

5 minutes passed and satisfied that there was no threat, Roger moved along and positioned himself at the centre of the arcs to both pipes. He opened the holdall and pulled out what appeared to be a rope. This was a triangular shape in cross-section, and a light copper colour, on two sides. There were four lengths, each around 20 feet long, taped neatly in a coil.

This was a high explosive linear-shaped cutting charge cord. It directs the force of the explosion and propels the cooper 'V' shaped metal lining through anything it is attached to. Used by Special Forces to remove heavy doors, and blow holes in concrete walls, tasks where accuracy is required with maximum force.

Using PETN explosive, it explodes at 6400 metres per second, propelling the copper which weighs a total of 2.5 kg per metre. Force equals mass x speed. But until it is fired, it is harmless.

Roger untapped the first coil and threw the loose end up over the pipe; he taped the end to the huge gas pipe and threw it over again. Then taped both ends tightly together and against the belly of the pipe.

Pulling gently, he moved the det cord along the pipe and up against the two huge flanges. These would hide the cord and make sure that they were not noticed before they were required.

Roger repeated this process three more times, two cords on each pipe, each passing around the circumference of the pipe where it met the flange twice.

Amy did not watch Roger, she crouched continually in the shadows looking towards the main control building, waiting with the Uzi at the ready, the main doors in her sight. The two turbines were running, and a high-pitched whine was in the air, masking any noises they may make.

At this time of the year, demand was at maximum and the pipelines would be carrying over 500 million cubic metres of gas, compressed to over 85 bar, or 1250 psi. The old gasometers that used to be common sites in our towns and cities were now gone. There was no need to store gas above ground when the pipework of the grid was storing it for you.

Supervising and running a gas compressor site at night-time was not the most entertaining work available. The crew would have been relaxing, with only one of them in the control room. Roger and Amy knew this from the months of sitting in the dark watching what went on. Learning the normal regimes that go on at such a place.

Roger pulled two timing devices from the bag and attached each one carefully to the cords on the belly of the pipes. Each timer was set for 0630 hrs. Monday, 9 November. The time now way 1220 hrs on a Sunday morning. Then he ran.

"Let's go, I've done it," Roger whispered to Amy.

Taking the lead, he moved back across the concrete yard to the turbine housings, and Amy guarded his retreat. Clear again, then she followed.

They took the bag through the fence and stopped. Flat on the ground. Waited 5 more minutes, resting, breathing hard but controlled, to see if there was any follow-up.

From the bag, Roger took a pair of industrial cable crimpers. These squash a metal sheath over two ends of the cable to join them electrically. Starting at the top of the hole in the fence, he re-joined each of the cuts with a crimp. Both sides, repairing the break and also reconnecting the electrical circuit. When this was done and he was satisfied, one by one the crocodile clips were removed and the wires returned to the holdall.

If they did not connect well, the alarm would be activated. But all remained silent. There was no point in laying covert charges on the gas pipes, only to be discovered before they went off because of a hole in the fence. It would be very difficult to see these joints from a distance or a vehicle patrolling the perimeter.

Both sat and regained their breath, calming down, watching. One forward, one back. Not talking, not flinching, they each knew what to do. They had been paired up during basic training and continually trained, as were the others until a lot of what they did was automatic. Completely used to working together as a team.

Clear again, no movement, so they moved out together, ran, stopped, looked, checked, and ran again. The van was clear, no one had been near it. Slowly they approached, opened the back, got in, changed, stowed the gun, and were gone.

***

At exactly 0630 on Monday, 9 November 2015, the det cord exploded and literally cut the two main feed pipes at the Warrington Compressor Station in half. The explosion ignited the gas, which was released at huge pressure and formed a plume of flame into the air over 200 feet high.

The gas turbine building nearest to the blast was demolished by the force of the explosion, causing the turbine to move on its foundations and come apart. 2 tons of high-quality aero grade alloys, rotating at 15000 rpm, came apart instantly exploding, sending a hail of shrapnel through the walls of its sister build where the second engine did the same.

Flying engine debris, pipe debris, and shrapnel from the three explosions shredded the control room, the tea room, and the rest of the main building. The night crew of three men had no chance and no idea what hit them.

At exactly the same time, the feed pipes to the compressors at Scunthorpe, Kings Lynn, Diss, Duxford, and Huntingdon, all exploded. Scunthorpe and Diss were unmanned and controlled remotely. No one died that night there. Kings Lynn Duxford and Huntingdon suffered the same fate as Warrington.

In less than one second, during the highest period of demand in the year, the entire ability of National Grid to pump gas throughout the UK was removed, now beyond repair, and was about to get worse.

Gas is brought ashore into the UK at six separate places. It enters the National Gs grid and is pumped around the country. Sometimes in accordance with demand, but there is a normal north-south routing and east-west routing.

If you look at a map of the UK grid, easily found on Google, you can see that there are various points where the grid converges or joins. Like taps or valves, if you turn these off, the gas flow stops.

Tonight, the terrorists attacked the six key compressor stations without which the grid could not function. They had hit not the points where the gas comes from the sea, but they had targeted the main joints of the grid network.

Gas from the north moving south, or from the south moving north has to pass through Warrington or Scunthorpe. Gas from the east moving towards London and the west has to pass through either, Diss, Kings Lynn, Huntingdon or Duxford.

With such a catastrophic attack and loss of pressure, all other compressors would trip and be shut down automatically by their own control systems. The pressure in pipes would continue to force gas out of the holes where it would burn. When this pressure was low enough, the fire would move along the pipe network. Exploding everything as it moved slowly until it ran out of oxygen and died. When this would happen, no one knew, it have never been modelled.

Every gas customer would now be without gas, regardless of your supplier, British Gas or whoever you did your deal with. No gas.

Forty power stations would now no longer have their gas supplies and would change automatically to heavy oil fuel. Fuel stocks would last less than 3 days this time of the year, provided they can be delivered. There were no civil defence plans in place to supply the power stations with liquid fuel. No plans to cover the logistics.

Six bombs, twelve clever terrorists, and the UK PLC was crippled and stopped with the loss of twelve lives.

But this was about to change.

Chapter 7

Capitalgen, London
Monday, 9 November 2010, 0630

For the last 3 hours, the four black figures had been kneeling on the floor of the control room of the Capitalgen power station, all facing to the east, and together they muttered prayers to their God.

Fanatical, radical, religious men; indoctrinated by Islamic preaching from birth. Trained to be the fighters for Allah. Trained to bring the sword of Allah to the non-believers.

It is a strange thing, but nonetheless true, that those who did the training and preaching were never those on the frontline, they were never the ones to give up their own lives for the holy cause.

They considered that they were higher beings, chosen by their God to provide the soldiers of Allah, to find the people who could be used and taught to become weapons. Not to fire a weapon or fight like a man for their family or country, but to die in the name of their God, or a cause.

What were they dying for tonight? None of them had questioned their leaders. None of them even cared. They had been chosen, so they believed.

Go and die, die as we tell you to die; you know you will be killing many people when you die, but this is not important to you. Do not think of the bloodshed you will create or the mothers and children you will kill. You just need to believe that we say it is right to die and your God will welcome you into heaven with the gift of many virgins.

These four men were indeed suicide bombers but with a big difference. They had been highly trained a different level of terrorism. Still blinkered by the indoctrination of their faith but highly skilled soldiers too. They needed to be able to fight, at close quarters, kill without thought, break in, and then die as they had been instructed.

For them, they were on earth to carry out only one cause. Tonight, was their time.

Death was an adventure to be enjoyed. They had no fear just expectation of everlasting glory.

The shift change at the power station was normally carried out at 0730 hrs, and they knew that within the hour, they could expect the first of the changeover crew to arrive. Their instructions were very clear: At 0630 hrs, they must detonate.

This was also the time that London started to wake up. Commuters would then be flooding into the city.

Train after train of people would be arriving from far-off cities and villages. Innocent people come into the city to do an honest day's work for an honest day's pay. Then go back home to their families.

It was a swarm of humanity every day, swarming in and later swarming out. Trains full of people standing, tubes full of people standing. School children on day trips, patients going to hospitals for treatments. Normal daily life continued as every day and it was starting right now.

None had any idea of what was to happen, except the four black figures praying.

At 0625 hrs, a figure, the leader, stood.

"Come, brothers, it is time to go…"

He approached each of the men in turn and hugged them, kissing them on both cheeks.

"Ready?"

"Yes," came as one reply.

From his pocket, he removed a small black device that looked rather like a tiny mobile phone. He pulled out a small aerial from the back and extended this as far as it would go.

He looked hard once more around the room, then pulled out a picture of his wife and children and stood looking for a few seconds.

"They will think I am a hero; they will remember me for all time."

Looking at his watch, it was exactly 0630 on 9 November 2015, he pushed the red button in the middle of the controller and went to claim his virgins.

The two compressed gas storage tanks on the roof blew up in a huge fireball and immediately exploded the other four.

The force of the blast sent the roof debris upwards almost supersonic, a mass of bricks, metal, plastics, and timbers, hurtling skyward with no regard for anything in the way.

It also pushed the floor down into the stored fuel oil and ammonia, which at the same time had just exploded themselves. The compression of the exploding gases multiplied the force and the building just ceased to exist.

Millions of litres of natural gas turned back from liquid to gas instantly, together with a million litres of fuel oil and 30 tonnes of ammonia exploded as one. As much destructive power as the Germans dropped on London in a whole month of the war.

A huge mushroom cloud formed over the hole in the ground where the station used to be. It blossomed upwards into the sky blasting debris in all directions high into the sky.

Heat at the centre of the blast could melt steel, and it did too. The large pieces of shrapnel now moving up and outwards spread with no regard to life.

Above London moving from the east on their final approach to Heathrow Airport was the normal queue of early morning inbound flights. With the wind heading in from the west of London, the approach this morning was directly over the city.

As a strange twist of fate, the Iranair 747 was 3 minutes downrange from the runway, it was passing half a mile east and slightly north of St Paul's Cathedral. It was a beautiful day, very clear and little wind, the descent had been very easy and comfortable. The view for the passengers over London was amazing. Still dark but the lights of the city were so pretty.

90 seconds behind it was another aircraft on final approach, and 90 seconds behind it would be another. Further back, the circular stacks north and south of the Thames were funnelling more and more flights towards Heathrow.

Even the pilots were in awe of the sight out of the cockpit, with the aircraft on autopilot for landing, they could take some seconds to look.

Below and to his right, the Iranian pilot saw the flash as the power station was ripped from the earth. The shockwave from the explosion hit him quickly and knocked the aircraft hard to the left.

It was a big aircraft, but as big as it was, it responded instantly. The two pilots went into autopilot themselves, the result of years of training and practice. They pushed the throttles into full emergency power.

The equivalent of 100 megawatts of sheer power suddenly came online and pushed the aircraft away and out of danger. (Interestingly, three times the power of the station that used to be below them.)

Using the momentum from the shockwave and continuing the turn to the left seemed logical and instinctive, the plane was climbing but not as it should.

Above his head and to the left, a band of orange warning lights came on, a buzzer sounded intermittently in the flight deck and the two engines on the right side of the aircraft caught fire.

"Mayday, mayday, Iranair 237 inbound 3 minutes down range, we declare an emergency; there has been an explosion on the ground and we have been hit."

"Iranair 237, acknowledge, situation report please."

The blasted debris, now supersonic and heading upwards, hit the aircraft on the right wing, smashing through the fuel tanks and erupting them into fireballs. As the aircraft tried in vain to pull left and gain height away from the blast, its engines on the right side caught fire and exploded.

The structure holding them in place failed as did the wings superstructure and the aircraft disintegrated directly over Oxford Street.

The aircraft was only at 2500 feet; it rolled to the right as the right wing came away, held, as if stopped in time for a millionth of a second, and exploded.

Burning fuel, debris, huge aircraft parts, luggage, people, and body parts slammed down into the street below, killing without question. The main fuselage split into two and hit Oxford Circus.

The fire spread in all directions; people ran for their lives only to be cut down a few seconds later.

"Iranair 237, acknowledge, please acknowledge."

Heathrow Tower raised the first alarm of that morning. They reported the loss of contact with Iranair 237 over Central London.

The disaster Heathrow had always claimed would never happen, just had.

Back on the ground, the shockwave moved out from the centre of the explosion. It ripped through the market picking up the steel suspended roof and hurled it headlong towards the Barbican. Then, it continued moving outwards, like a deadly ripple in a pond.

The market roof crashed through the glass sides of the Barbican building at such a force, that it was almost 25 feet into the second and third floors when it stopped. Anything in its path was broken or dead.

The impact of the shockwave and the roof from the market had seriously compromised the structure and it was only hanging on out of pure stubbornness.

Bartholomew's Hospital was in the process of waking up their patients for the day. They were close to the centre of the blast but not so close. Still, the flash and the shockwave were separated by only 1 or 2 seconds.

The blast struck the west side of the building, crashing through the windows, followed by the thin divisional walls. The staff and patients nearest to the windows were shredded by flying glass and small pieces of power station acting like bullets from a machine gun cutting people down where they stood or lay.

As the thin walls gave way and imploded, the concrete pieces squashed anything in their path, blasting through and into the next part of the building. The fire started to rage, fed by broken oxygen lines and spilt medical chemicals; the fire system and sprinklers were not designed to stop this type of horror.

On the far side and to the north of the building, they heard the massive bang of the explosion but were shielded from the flash. They felt the floor shake horribly and then the noise of death approached. The further from the west side they were, the more chance they would have of survival. Impact after impact, the force of the blast pushed internal walls eastwards, but slowly its energy was dying. One-third of the building on the west side was gone.

The steel structure had been critically damaged and was collapsing. Hundreds of people were dead and hundreds more were buried beneath the rubble. To the east side, people ran, anyone who could walk was pulled out of bed and ushered, and more were pushed along out of the way.

The bedbound were left, for them, there was nothing they could do; there were too many walking casualties and no time to push beds. They lay and watched it coming.

The whole structure of the building began to fail beneath them. Their own gas and fuel supply exploded deep in the basement, blowing out luckily westward. This blast was more than the building could stand and slowly it gave up its struggle to stay upright.

After so many years of standing proud to protect and treat the people of London and beyond, it could do no more, its time had come too. The steel was too hot, the strength was going and it could not support the weight. As the top floors gave way, they crushed down on the floors below, like a concertina crashing down and falling over.

Groans of steel on steel filled the air, people rushed out and away; running as they did in Manhattan. As it finally collapsed, it claimed more lives, burying them as they ran.

A staff of over a thousand people and a patient list of over eleven hundred were in the hospital that night; almost eleven hundred died, some instantly. Many more died trying to escape.

To the north, the shockwave hit the Barbican, moving up the streets away from Smithfield, demolishing anything in its path. People, vehicles, buses, and buildings were wiped clean from the ground.

The tall centrepieces of the Barbican Centre were smashed like toys, the glass just disappeared, and both buildings swayed horribly away from the explosion. The steel structures within were not designed to accept this level of pressure and gave way. The tops of both towers broke away and fell down through what remained of themselves below. A strange re-run of the Twin Towers in New York.

The power of the blast was dying in this direction too, the commuters still ran pointlessly they could not escape.

To the south, the top half of St. Paul's Cathedral had been blown almost clean off and the northern wall demolished in many places. It had survived so much over the centuries.

On 12 September 1940, a 4500 lb bomb was dropped close to the West end of the cathedral. It did not explode but buried itself 30 ft underground and right next to the gas main.

Lieutenant Robert Davies led a team of royal engineers over three days who dug to remove the bomb. The team knew that at any time the bomb could detonate, killing them all and destroying much of Saint Pauls.

It took 3 days of hard work in the face of death to remove the explosives, with no regard for their own safety. Churchill had said Saint Paul's Cathedral must be saved at all costs. These soldiers were doing just that. When it was finally lifted out onto a truck, they took it to Hackney Marsh and detonated it there. A crater more than 100 ft across was formed.

Two of the teams that worked so selflessly to save the cathedral were awarded the George Cross. But they were not there today, their war was fought and was won. This war had just started. Traffic was being destroyed, and their own fuel tanks exploded, adding death and fire to the scene around. People ran, they hid, but it was pointless. Against one of the most famous UK backdrops of St Paul's

Cathedral, the people of London were dying. The scene was like a medieval battlefield. Calm to the carnage in a matter of seconds.

Back at what was the power station, the remaining spilt fuel oil from what were the tanks had started to drain rapidly down into the underground train system at Farrington. As it poured over the edge of the flat car park, the suction effect of the underground ventilation and train movement mixed a deadly fuel-air combination. What the military calls a thermobaric bomb.

The mixture ignited and then exploded. The tube tunnels channelled the blast underground in both directions. Two trains packed full of early commuters took full force whilst the road above the tunnels erupted skyward, toppling more buildings as their ancient roots in the ground were destroyed.

As the blast died away in less than 30 seconds, death had come to London, they had their own 9/11. Just as New York rocked and then stood still, so did London rock now.

Smoke, fire, dust rubble, panic, screaming, mayhem, bedlam. People still ran and still hid, looking for shelter from what had happened. Their ears were ringing, they could not see properly, the air was full of acrid smoke, and they were disorientated. But running and hiding was futile.

As a weird and eerie calm began to spread over the scene of so much death and destruction, so too did the 30 tonnes of ammonia now in a gas cloud and spreading to the northeast on a very light breeze.

Anyone who has used a domestic cleaner at home will know that a tiny amount of ammonia can make you gag and burn if you breathe it. Here now, hanging over London was a massive cloud of ammonia gas spreading over a square mile and moving very slowly northwards.

Debris launched upwards by the explosion started to return to the ground, smashing into buildings, adding further devastation surrounding what used to be Smithfield Market. An area spreading outwards for probably half a mile from the centre of the blast had been flattened. People were lying dead on the ground in every direction you could see. Buses turned on their roofs, buildings smashed in some cases to the ground.

Ammonia gas is lighter than air and will normally rise and dissipate, but a release of pressurised ammonia gas can collect at ground level until the aerosol cloud becomes diluted. Plus being mixed with the smoke and gases following such a violent explosion, it was also being held down by the layer of smoke above.

On the ground, people as far away as a mile began to feel the effects of the gas. They ran from the dusty cloud drifting towards them but there was no escape. Within seconds, the victims would feel the burning in the throat, spreading into their chests. Breathing would become hard and rasping. The heads would start to pound with pressure, and within 2-3 minutes, a full pulmonary failure would take place.

As it spread northwards and diluted, the effects were less severe, but this only meant that any victims needed longer to breathe the fumes for the deadly gas to overcome them. Which it did, many many times.

30 tonnes of ammonia would require an evacuation radius of 2-3 miles in case of normal escape. Catastrophic escape was uncontrollable.

London went quiet. Time stood still. Thousands of people had just been slaughtered, but not by a bomb constructed and hidden away by someone with a grudge. They had been killed by turning a deadly device, put in place with the blessing of past and present government, against us.

This had been operated in the heart of our capital city. Completely innocently. No one would ever expect that this could have been used in such a catastrophic way. There was no part of the design or engineering design, or planning procedure that said 'what if?'.

Normally, it would never present a danger, but today, it was a present and clear danger.

As far out of Central London as the M25, the traffic had stopped. People stood at the side of the road and looked at the mushroom cloud that had grown over the city. Every single one of them knew what they were seeing; it had been seen before in New York. No one could believe such a thing could happen again! Not in our country, not in the UK, not the British, not us ! But it just had.

What had happened, no one yet knew. Was it an accident, or was it deliberate? No one yet knew.

The effect of the power station being removed so violently from the grid shut down the rest of the London Electricity Board grid. An area equal to half of greater London was now without power. Including all government offices, inner London hospitals, fire and police.

Many of the grid protection devices would have tripped automatically to stop the damage from a surge or shortage. As the automated circuits started their own checks for errors and breaks or earth leakage, some would reconnect. Others would not if damaged. Partial power might return, but equally, it might not for some time.

Standby power units would now be starting up across the city; individual government buildings and other critical resources would be switching from grid into 'Island mode' where their power supply was isolated from the National Grid; Protected and operational. Diesel-powered generators supply much-needed power.

These too would need fuel, and this may be hard to supply reaching across the damaged areas of the city. They were OK for now and they needed now, badly, someone else would get the job very soon of resupplying fuel for the gen-sets.

Four floors below the MoD building in Whitehall, there used to be a gas turbine, capable of running on gas or liquid fuel. This could supply 3.5 MW of power within minutes of the command to start. Starting was automatic. When the grid connection was lost, the turbine would start.

A huge room full of 24VDC batteries supplied power for what is known as a 'Black Start' when the turbine would need to start without mains or grid power. All systems would be running on 24VDC.

Within a few minutes, the turbine would fire and start to run, hold for 2 minutes at 6000 rpm, then accelerate up to 12000 rpm. The building would switch away from the London grid and move into island mode.

This was removed in favour of cheaper diesel gen-sets which were placed at strategic points around the centre of government. Somebody, somewhere, would now be questioning the decision to take it out.

The BBC had lost their power supply and stopped transmitting from the broadcasting house. This would switch to other facilities, Manchester, or Glasgow. Traffic had stopped, there were no aircraft in the sky, and it was silent, as quiet as the day when the country stopped to watch Dianna's last journey.

The scene of carnage in the middle of London was absolute. Corpses lay everywhere in every direction. The ground was littered with body parts. Vehicles were squashed and thrown. Buildings were gone or just smashed. All that now remained was fire, smoke and dust. And blood.

It was a market morning; the ground was covered nearly ankle-deep in filth and mire.

In the UK, we reverse our dates. Today was 9 November; 9/11.

Chapter 8

Ground Zero, London
9 November 2015, 0930

Not since the war, when Germany tried to bring the British to their knees by the indiscriminate bombing of London, had anyone seen anything like the devastation that stretched before them right now.

Si'ad was standing on what used to be a brick wall. Alongside him were the Met Police Commissioner and the PM himself. Just the three of them, all gazing in horror at what stood before them. Stood, well, used to stand would be a better description.

All three men, including David Cameron, were dressed in a NB suit, complete with breathing apparatus, helmet, and flak jacket. They just stood there, silently; stood and just gazed in disbelief.

This could be a film set. War of the Worlds even. Three alien visitors landed on some desolate landscape of destruction and broken bodies after an intergalactic battle of some sort.

There were tears in Cameron's eyes. This was genuine grief, no one could have surveyed this scene and not be moved to tears. Tears and anger, deep down primitive anger slowly boiling up from the depths of his soul.

"Why? Do we know what type of device this was yet?"

"No, Sir, it is too early to say anything. But we will find out."

60 minutes earlier, terrorists had blown up a power station, deep in the heart of London and deep into what is Great Britain. The attack had hit deep into the heart of the UK financial quarter, deep in the heart of the legal system, destroying or disabling them all.

So too had the terrorist struck and destroyed what was the most famous hospital in the country. Then the biggest symbol of the Christian Church of England; St Paul's Cathedral was gone, blown apart.

A blast area of up to 800 metres in diameter. Total destruction at the centre, reducing only slightly as it moved away. The streets were just rubble covered with scrap vehicles, glass, and water spraying in weird directions. Smoke and fire.

But then there was the dead. Worse of all were the dead. Bodies everywhere, body parts everywhere. Carnage, slaughter. Wherever you looked, people lay dead. It was going to be hard to find a body that was still whole. Blown to the four winds, unrecognisable, untraceable by looks alone.

It would take years to identify everyone and advise the relatives that their loved ones were finally dead. By then, there would be nothing to bury, but it would give closure for them on this horrible day.

Those who were not dead slowly started to scream; the eerie calm that hung over this scene was being replaced with the sounds from hell.

Less than 1 mile to the west, Oxford Circus was burning. The wreckage of the Iranian aircraft fell from the sky in a massive deadly fireball. The streets around 0630 in the morning were quiet and loss of life on the ground was minimal, so they hoped. But scattered everywhere were the bodies and parts of the passengers and crew on the aircraft.

Huge lumps of airframe had smashed down through buildings, one engine had gone right through the road into one of the walkways under Oxford Circus. Burning fuel had fallen onto buildings, setting them ablaze instantly, and falling on people, soaking their clothes in AV gas, kerosene basically. Consuming them whilst they had thrashed to hang on to life.

The devastation here was nothing compared to the scene at Ground A. But it was still massive. Buildings here still stood but were burnt. Fierce fires had been started, and parts of the airframe embedded hideously in buildings and the road. People were still strapped into their seats in the sections of the fuselage, dead luckily for them. The fire was now burning them too. The smell of burning meat filled the air.

Time seemed as though it was standing still, but it was not. Emergency crews had started to arrive on this scene. Fire everywhere, dead everywhere. Where do you start? What do you do first?

London had its very own 9/11; Armageddon; Carnage.

At the same time as the bomb had gone off in London, the terrorists had struck to take down and disable the supply of energy to the UK. Very successfully. The gas grid was down; it had been possibly damaged so badly that it would take years to rebuild.

An existing power plant had been used as a weapon against us to create a deadly bomb. It was there already, harmless, providing services to London. Someone had identified the plant, engineered how to turn this against us, and carried out the deadliest attack London had seen in one night.

These were surgical strikes against the UK, designed to cripple the country quickly. The aircraft was an unhappy coincidence, and bonus, unexpected. Clearly, someone had studied the UK and how best to attack the country to provide the most impact. It had worked.

UK PLC had been brought to its knees; the population was stunned into silence, totally speechless. Initial estimates were putting the death toll at over six thousand in London alone. The toll of injured would be in the twenty thousand. This was literally an hour after the attack. These numbers would rise rapidly.

In two strokes of the terrorist sword, the UK had lost their gas grid and power was out in most of London. Power cuts were coming. UK finance industry had been dealt a massive blow; the UK legal industry a massive blow; even our Christian faith had not been left untouched. St Paul's was nearly gone.

Cameron could not find any words and stood with his head bowed, nothing would come to mind that he could say. Words alone cannot express the horror he had been forced to witness this morning. His country, and the people he led, had been slaughtered like animals. He felt only anger, terrible anger and hatred for these people that had done this. But what people? Who were they?

Foreign or homegrown terrorists. Had they come to our country with the sole intent of attacking us, or did they already live here, benefited from the British way of life and now turned to attack us?

Soon Cameron would have to find the words, the country needed to know what had happened. But it was also going to want to know what he, the PM, was going to do about it.

Buildings were still burning; the fire service would struggle to get to them to put them out because of rubble and no access. The same for the ambulance service. People could be alive, but it was seriously doubted if anyone would have survived the blast near where they stood. Sending in people to check puts them at high risk, but it was what they did. Every one of them knew the risks involved and you try stopping them from going.

The three men in their NB suits got down from what was left of their wall and made their way back to the vehicle that had brought them here. After the blast, they were some of the first people to get to the scene. All of them wanted to come to see, to understand.

No one was speaking, just looking, their minds were racing through, processing the scene and what this means to the country and in terms of rescuing anyone left alive. London did not have the number of resources it needed to deal with this.

Something stupid was troubling the police commissioner. In the back of his mind, he kept asking an insane question. It kept coming back, he would dismiss it but then it came back. In amongst the questions of who did this, and how, he kept asking himself why he was wearing this NB suit. It puzzled him but the thought was pushed away by the huge disaster that was now London.

He had just been given it and told to put it on. In a crisis, you don't ask you just do. But why, why for?

Cameron suddenly turned to the Met commissioner and spoke.

"We will recover, and God give us all the strength to show restraint. But we will find them or die trying. Gentlemen, we need to go to work. COBRA 0900, be there and ready to brief both COBRA and the full cabinet. In the meantime, start sorting this fucking shit out."

But it had already started.

The UK war machine and fighting spirit was waking up. Not since the Falkland conflict had this part of the United Kingdom been released or seen. Nothing brings the UK together quicker than someone trying to attack or kill us, particularly in our own country. Now forgetting all the silly disputes and arguments, it was going to happen again.

Not just the military was mobilising, but everyone. Business, the people themselves. Outraged at the attack in London, they were now going to rise to the challenge. We wanted blood. Only one hour after the bombing, the Met were being inundated with offers to help.

The emergency plans had already been actioned and actioned very fast. It was less than 48 hours since the threat level had been moved to the most critical. But 48 hours to the British Armed Forces was long enough.

The full three battalions of the Paras had already been mobilised to protect key installations. Main grid power stations, nuclear power stations, water treatment, and rail stations. Anywhere that was a valid target.

Every main power station would have armed protection and ground-to-air missile protection. The RAF regiment had deployed to all the main airports.

The Royal Logistic Corps were already on the road, with just about every type of logistic support the country and London could need: Tankers of fuel taken from the UK emergency stocks were heading towards the power stations; food supplies for the troops that had been deployed to help; mobile field hospitals heading into the relief effort; mobile bridges and road repair, JCBs, everything.

They had been automatically put on full standby when the threat level went to maximum. As of 45 minutes ago, they were heading to London.

Royal engineers were preparing to be flown into Central London. As were dozens of the best structural engineering consultants the UK had. Separate planning had already been put in place to make London safe, wherever needed, to begin to recover the dead and injured.

The M25 had been closed. All non-emergency vehicles outside of the M25 were now banned from coming into London. The M25 was being turned into a marshalling area for emergency traffic heading to the relief effort for the London bombings.

Military precision was taking over. Entry and exit slip roads were shut. Not by bollards and signs, but by a Land Rover and two heavily armed soldiers. People were just been told in no uncertain terms to stay away.

London was at war. Londoners too had been told very clearly to stay at home, stay indoors, and let the emergency services do their job. London was under martial law.

Major hospitals in the south of the UK were now on full alert, waiting for their first casualties. Non-essential patients were being sent home or moved; they were going to need the beds. Medical staff had been called back into work, everyone. Most had heard about the bomb and were already on their way back in any way when they got the call.

Every air ambulance in the UK was being drafted down into London for service. For once, the government was paying their costs. An irony. London City Airport had been designated a heliport accepting only civil and military helicopter medical crews. They would ferry the injured to each hospital within flying distance. Approach roads from the bomb sites to the airport were closed off and would soon be guarded. One route into the airport another route out, clearways for the ambulance crews to speed along.

Fire and ambulance crews were called back in. Throughout the south of England, the emergency services were heading to London. They would rally on the M25 and be directed to where they were needed most by the military.

This left the surrounding counties London short on the ground of emergency cover, so planning was now drafting down crews and vehicles from most other counties in the UK.

Comms had been set up to cover the bands of the radios used by all services.

Even two cruise ships had been commandeered. They were being readied for sea, preparing to embark passengers to leave on their next journey. Pre-existing emergency planning was in action. In the port of Southampton, naval and army medical teams had just arrived and started to prepare the ships to become hospitals. Expecting casualties within minutes flown in from London.

Routes in and out of the blast zones, Ground A and B, had been laid out. No traffic hold-ups were being planned. London was shut to everyone.

3 hours from the blast, B+3h, Britain was coming together, working to a common need. There were people alive in there somewhere, they needed help and it was coming.

Four zones had now been designated: Ground A, the blast zone, approx. 600 metres in diameter. Ground B, the crash site in Oxford Circus. Outer zone 1 for inner marshalling, walking wounded medical triage and emergency crew welfare. Outer zone 2 was a cordon to stop all the rubber-necking parasites, press, and anyone that was not directly involved and contributing to the rescue effort.

This zone had already been christened the JFO area: Just Fuck Off.

Overall command and control was established at Scotland Yard. Rooms were being made over for the various services and coordination. Fire and ambulance control continued from their own HQs; live feeds were being established within Scotland Yard.

This all was a well-rehearsed and practiced routine, swinging very rapidly into place with no panic, people doing what they had trained to do. But they knew this time it was for real.

The ambulance crews were now being shepherded into both ground A and B, following the designated routes in and out. Their job was only triage. Find the people that are alive and stand a chance of making it. Forget the rest. Move out only those who could be saved. Hard choices had to be made, but whilst they may fight to save someone who is almost dead and most certainly dies, another person able to be saved might die.

Fire crews had different approach corridors, and all this was set up within minutes. The fire commanders had called on the London 'knowledge'. They got some cabbies and asked to draw the best routes in and out of the scenes, ignoring all one-way streets or diversions; direct routes, one in and one out.

Cabbies knew their stuff and these were the best people to show the emergency services how to get in and out quickly. 15 minutes later, the routes were agreed and set in stone.

Ground A, London
Monday, 9 November 2015, 1030

Medics now swarmed over the rubble, following the screams of those left alive. With them went the fire crews, looking and searching. Already search and rescue dogs were on the scene and many more were coming. This was going to take a long time and resources would soon run dry. People would need rest, food, and shelter, and then back to work.

All food shops, restaurants, fast food chains, and supermarkets within zone 2 have been contacted. Their staff were all now rushing to get to their jobs. They had to feed and water a lot of people constantly over the next critical days and beyond.

Even as far away as France, their government had quickly acted to join the relief mission in London. Our oldest enemy and oldest ally. In Calais, they were now loading car ferries with ambulances and fire equipment, medical supplies, sniffer dogs, search and rescue experts; sending their own emergency services to London. Within 3 hours, these crews will start to bolster the people on the ground.

From Dover, they will travel up onto the M25 for marshalling and then be directed to the areas most in need of support. Kent police were waiting for the vessels to dock and would escort the much-needed convoy into London.

Police vehicles waited on the M25 too, as the ambulances started to come out of London carrying the injured away, they would provide an escort, pushing through towns and roads to clear the way for the ambulance.

B+4h and all of this was happening.

The French President had also put the main hospitals in the northern areas of France on full alert. They were preparing to accept British casualties. French military personnel had also been together with helicopters for evacuation. The

French will evacuate the injured back to France for care. These were already airborne and heading for London City Airport.

Heathrow was now only accepting military or medical aircraft. The USAF and RAF had despatched various types of cargo-shifting aircraft, being configured to move injured people in flight. Once in place within 90 minutes, they would provide air bridges from London to further away points of the UK and France to feed other hospitals.

Flying into Wales, The Midlands, North-East and West. Ambulances would be waiting to receive the grim cargo from the airports nearby, John Lennon Airport in Liverpool. Manchester Airport, Newcastle, Edinburgh. Simple planning but effective.

Treating possibly twenty to thirty thousand casualties was an unimaginable task. If there were thirty hospitals, they would each get a thousand patients. Sixty hospitals, it is still five hundred people each.

Ground A, London
9 November 2015, 1115

Fire crews were laying down water feed pipes all the way from the Thames to supply the crews at Ground A with water. With so much damage done that some fire hydrants would not be available, or accessible. Trucks towing pumps had deployed along the embankment and had linked up many pipes back to around Ground A, all over a mile long. Now pushing Old Mother Thames into the fight to save her city.

The medics and fire crews had whistles. If a live body was found that was recoverable, a whistle would sound. Attention moved to this point and every effort was diverted to get them out. Rubble was being manhandled by frantic medics to get at the injured. A&E consultants were on the ground, making rapid triage decisions that would haunt them for life—leave them and move on or get them out.

Patients were having limbs that were crushed under concrete amputated there and then. A large dose of morphine was all they were given, then in quick, cut and tie it off, the hospitals were to sort the rest out. If they die, then they die, for them death was already close.

Many were lucky, being pulled out from under concrete, or gathered up from hiding in a doorway. People cowering, hiding away, not trusting, horrified, pulled to safety and rushed away. Now ambulance after ambulance was being loaded two up or three up and sent screaming away. As one moved away, the next one was waiting.

There was not going to be enough, it was taking too long to get crews from other parts of the South into support Ground A. Within 30 minutes, they were going to be waiting on returning crews. That was too long. On the fly, rethinking was happening, the command oversight.

Military ambulances were already being used but the decision was made instantly to use trucks, even Land Rovers. Within no time, these were arriving. Ambulance teams were splitting up, soldiers now driving the ambulances whilst they cared for the injured. Loading five or six broken people onto the back of a 7.5-ton truck. Did it matter, they were going, being moved out of hell. One paramedic with his pack was looking after 5 or 6 people. This was war. Do what you can to save who you can.

Even the London cabbies convinced the police to let them help, only taking walking wounded out of the way to treatment facilities being set up away from the rescue effort, relieving ambulances and allowing them to be used for the critical.

Doctors were coming in, unasked, from many GP practices, cars stuffed full of every type of help they could possibly need. Marshalled from the M25, through to zone 3. Even vets were willing to get into the rescue effort and they were there treating the walking wounded.

In the streets behind the carnage, just outside of Ground A, the shopkeepers and food outlet staff now came bringing water, tea, coffee, food, Big Macs, Kentucky, sandwiches, anything to give these heroes something to burn whilst they worked. Crews were being called off as they cleared one casualty and ordered to go and eat, drink, and get back. 15-minute breaks were being enforced. But they were back in 10.

Order was being established within chaos, it needed to be. Working together in a controlled way was the only thing that would make sure as many people were saved as possible. This was going to continue for days. Evacuating the injured would be over hopefully tomorrow. After this, the pace would slow, there was no rush to recover the dead and body parts.

High-level decisions would have to be made on how to deal with the dead and the huge amount of body parts that would need to be recovered. This was already being discussed and plans were made to deal with recovery in a way that would give the victims the respect they all so deserve.

- Bodies with ID
- Bodies with no ID but identifiable
- Body parts.

Field mortuaries were going to be needed to control the process of tagging and storing the bodies and parts. Forensic teams would be called in to take DNA samples, bag and tag, then at a later date, try to identify who it had been.

Where do you store over six thousand dead bodies? How do you move them out away from Ground A with some dignity and respect? They all deserve to be treated well, regardless of colour, race or creed. London is a true multicultural city and very proud of it. There would be many religions represented in the death toll.

Behind the emergency crews on the ground, their controllers and everyone working on the rescue effort, a well-trained military and civil defence planning organisation was growing rapidly as people were seconded or ordered in to bring the massive task of dealing with what had happened under full control.

It was their job to answer and solve all the questions and problems being raised. To deal with problems, needs, requirements, and things unthought of or missed. Plug the holes. They would start to organise the recovery of the dead, where they would go, how they were stored, how they were identified and who moved them and how.

Facilities would be made available very quickly, by fair means or foul, to give the rescue effort what was required to clean up and bring London back to its full glory.

***

A small child, about 4 years old, covered in dust soot and obviously blood, came up to a policeman who was taking time out to drink some water. Her clothes were ripped, and she was crying, sobbing uncontrollably. This took him by complete surprise, his head was blank; he had turned off for a short time.

"Mummy stuck," and pulled on the policeman's jacket. "Help mummy."

Following the little child around the corner and 15 feet into an alley, he saw on the floor an arm and a leg sticking out from underneath what used to be an air-conditioning unit, one of the large roof-mounted units no one ever really sees as they are hidden away behind screens on a roof area.

Whoever was under this was mummy, and mummy was clearly dead. He handed the bottle of water to the child, bent down, and picked them up.

"Let's go and get you warm. We will come back and get mummy later. She is fine now."

Inside, his heart broke and all he could think was, *Fucking bastards*.

Chapter 9

M1 Bedfordshire
10 November 2015, 0220

No one enjoyed working the night shifts, it was just a necessary part of doing the job, a shift system that covered the full 24-hour day.

Seven days of mornings, working 7 am until 3 pm, then two days off. Seven days of late turn, or afternoon, working 3 pm until 11 pm and then another two days off. Then nights, 11 pm until 7 am, after which there were 3 days off.

With only 7 days off in the month, one rest day was paid as overtime. Paid, well that is what they call it, pittance was more accurate. Considering the risk and constant threat under which the police force operates, their pay should be doubled.

All government promised reviews and ended up offering below 3%. Then a week later, the same people sat in parliament and voted themselves a 10% pay increase, relying on the police to protect them. To get in the way of a bullet meant for them. Shield them from terrorism. Ironic to say the least. You had to wonder what the reaction would be if the police just hid.

"Sorry, Sir, You don't pay me enough to die for you!"

That would never happen. Same with nurses and most other people working in the public sector. It was a calling; you would do it regardless of the pay. Government knows it and certainly exploits it.

There were some perks, however, to being a traffic cop and tonight they were enjoying one of them, on patrol in a brand-new E350 Mercedes estate car. Produced by Mercedes as a police demonstrator and loaned to Bedfordshire Police in the hope that they could perhaps influence the police authority into buying a fleet of them.

Well, if the frontline drivers had any say in the matter, then they would want some of these on the fleet. No argument.

The police Subarus and Evos were amazing, but these were racing cars and not overly comfortable for an 8-hour shift patrolling a motorway. The Merc was a luxury in every way. Electric just about everything, loads of room, comfortable heated seats. Above all, quiet.

But the main fascination was the engine. It had a 3.0-litre diesel engine. A motorway patrol car with a diesel engine! Not so many years ago, this would have been funny and the chances of getting a traffic cop in it were nil. The introduction of Common rail diesel not only changed this impression but gave the diesel engine a new lease of life and a new attraction for enthusiasts. A modern, simple, high-performance injection system that turned around everyone's thinking of the old oil burners.

This 3-litre lump was set up so that maximum performance was given by the engine. 'Chipped' as the boy racers called it. This gave the big V6 diesel just over 300 bhp, capable of pushing the car to a very unhealthy speed when required and very quickly. 100 mph and the engine is only doing 2000 rpm. The low-down torque was just amazing.

It comes from Mercedes almost fully equipped with all the necessary lights, horns, sirens, and state-of-the-art communications. Each force will add its own systems, but Merc planned for this and provided the mounting points and wiring. They cannot have Bobbies drilling holes in their precious new Mercs after all.

It was now 2.20 in the morning and things were very quiet. The last two days had been total mayhem. Many of the Beds Police had been drafted into Central London to help with the massive attack that had occurred. This meant the force was shorthanded, to say the least. All leave had been cancelled when the threat level had been elevated on Saturday, but no one expected to witness what had happened. Not just in London but throughout the country, with the loss of gas transmission systems.

Every force in the country was now stretched to the limit. Constant 12 hours on and 12 hours off was the present requirement. Many of the crews were not going home, just resting in the station, eager to get back out there and make a difference.

The army had been mobilised to protect key targets and provide logistics support for all manner of different reasons. Convoys of liquid fuel for power stations and heavy earth-moving equipment were being taken into London. It was a disaster scene from Armageddon.

Dave and Brian were in their treasured Mercedes and were between junction 13 and junction 12 on the M1, just north of the Toddington rest area and services, travelling south. There was a police post in this service area, and it was necessary to travel down to junction 11 and flip back onto the northbound side to get access to the west side of the north carriageway.

A small access road did exist between the north and southbound side of the motorway services, allowing authorised vehicles out of the service area, onto an unclassified road that crossed the motorway and gave access back onto the services. It was illegal to use this road if unauthorised and there was a barrier that prevented the public from gaining access. This often did not work and in times of hold-up on the motorway, it was a rat run for people trying to go around. A good source of business on some days for the lads.

Tonight, it was not necessary to use this road, there was no hurry. Plus, it allowed more time to possibly spot something that could be of interest. At this time of the night, boredom was a big problem. Well, it was a problem.

In their rear-view mirrors, a car was approaching in the outside lane, clearly moving very fast.

"We have a mover coming in behind, very fast," Dave said to Brian.

He was very calm, as though this was something that was just normal. As he said it, the Merc accelerated fast, bringing their speed up from the patrol speed of 60 mph. Within seconds, they went through 100 mph, but the car approaching from behind kept catching them.

"This one is really moving, mate."

As the Merc went through 120 mph, the car in the outside lane flashed past them. What speed they were doing was not clear until it pinged up on the forward speed radar: 160 mph.

"Here we go, call it in. See who is up front of us to help, get the Luton car."

Pulling out behind the car, Dave hit the blue lights and accelerated more; pushing up to 160 mph, the two cars flashed down the M1 towards Luton.

"The ANPR has pinged it, Security services."

"Yeah, yeah, that's ballocks, check with VA."

VA was the Bedfordshire Police Control Room call sign. Dave kept on the tail of the car whilst the ANPR data was confirmed.

"Echo 1, VA, stand down, Security services."

The Merc coasted down in speed back to 60 mph and continued down towards Luton, adrenaline melted away, and they both again started to think about eating and going back to the services at Toddington; a little deflated that their 60 seconds of excitement was over.

Going past junction 11 and on to 10, he would flip around using the Luton Airport exit. There was no rush and he needed to get his nerves back in check.

Dave had already done 20 years in the force and had seen most things. He was not easily surprised, yet did find it very strange that they appeared to have someone following them. He had noticed the car shortly after the security services vehicle had sped passed them about 10 minutes ago.

A Volvo estate car, a V70. It was not doing anything wrong, not speeding, there did not appear to be anything wrong with the car. Nevertheless, it still appeared to be following the police car.

"I think we may have someone following us, mate," Dave said to his colleague sitting next to him.

"Yeah right, I mean everyone follows a police car, don't they?" Brian replied.

"Take a look, he has been there for about 10 miles now, doesn't overtake, doesn't slow down, just there keeping his distance. He is even using the inside lane too!"

"Shame all of the other prats on the road don't take a leaf out of his book then, make our lives easier. I fucking hate people that drive in the middle or outside lane all of the time."

Brian was somewhat intolerant of lane-hogging drivers and loved nothing more than to pull them over and tell them. He had a wicked sense of humour and began to think this was funny, so started to take the piss out of his partner.

"I bet you have been shagging around again and got caught. We have probably got some lunatic husband after us. He is going to beat you black and blue."

"Fuck off, that was years ago, and I learnt the hard way. He is following us, let us see what he does. I am going to play with him a bit."

Indicating right, they took the exit slip road to junction 12 on the motorway. As they drove off of the motorway, the Volvo behind them continued along the carriageway, down towards the service area.

"You wanker! Maybe you need to drink less coffee, you're going mad, mate; following us my arse, he has driven straight on."

Dave drove to the top of the exit ramp, straight over and back down onto the motorway again. Feeling rather stupid, he decided to continue on the planned route to get them into the police post and something to eat.

They passed the services and continued south to junction 11. Again, exiting the motorway on the slip road and moving down, then under the flyover on Dunstable Road, turning sharp right, and back onto the motorway moving north again.

Traffic police are highly trained, not just for their driving skills, but in dealing with almost any type of situation they could come across whilst out on the road. From fatal accidents to stray animals, and crazy driving to crazy drivers. They never stop learning. Within a short time of achieving traffic status, they will have seen and dealt with most types of incidents and most types of drivers.

The level of driver training they achieve is second to none in the whole world. The holder of a police first-class driving ticket is a very good driver indeed. They are not lucky to have it, they have earned it. 10 weeks of intensive driving and theory. More if the driver has pursuit training. These people can really handle a car in all types of stressful conditions.

Moving off onto the main carriageway, Dave accelerated away enjoying the car. He noticed there was another car just joining the motorway behind them but did not take too much notice of it at first until it closed on them.

"He is back, the same car is behind us again. What the fuck is he doing? How did he know I was going to flip-flop there?"

"You sure it is the same car?"

"RT06BHF, it is the same car, run a check on it."

"This is very weird. Let's pull him and see what he is doing."

"No, not yet, see how far he is willing to follow. Go back up to 13 and flip again. I'll get him checked."

Dave increased his speed to just above 70 mph to see if the car followed. It did, he increased it more to 80 mph, and the car followed. Dropping back to 70 mph, he knocked the car into cruise and just drove towards junction 13.

"Has to be a coincidence. Maybe he is lost, turned around also but took a piss first."

"No, fuck off, he is either a fruit or up to something. He is seriously spooking me."

"VA, 475, moving vehicle check please."

Brian was asking control for a check on the car behind them. At the same time, he had activated the rearward-facing ANPR camera and was waiting for any response. The same system also recorded images as the car was moving. The number plate recognition system was already checking the plate for tax and insurance, plus any flags associated with the car or owner.

"475 from VA, go ahead with a check."

Brian read out the index number of the car over the radio. Within seconds, the operator had checked the vehicle on their computer and returned a no trace response. The ANPR system on board also returned no trace.

The video camera was showing the driver and using the zoom facility, Brian could take a good look at who it was. The driver was male about 25 to 30 years old, foreign-looking with a Middle-eastern appearance, normally dressed in a shirt and tie and a body warmer type coat. He seemed relaxed and under normal circumstances, a perfect motorist. Nothing about him would normally give cause for concern.

"Let's wait and see what he does at 13."

The police car continued north on the M1, passing the service area and junction 12, then on towards junction 13. This junction was not a simple junction as it had a roundabout and traffic lights controlling the flow of traffic. During the day, it could be a real problem and there was often a large queue of traffic in all directions.

Dave deliberately slowed down early for the junction, dropping his speed to 60 about a mile short of the slip road. The Volvo followed suit. He dropped speed again to 50 and the Volvo again copied him.

"If he follows us back southbound, I am going to stop him and see what he thinks he is doing. Get on to control and advise them of the situation, just so they are aware. Something is not right and we need to at least cover our backs."

The police car moved off the M1 onto the slip road, up the hill to the roundabout at the top.

The Volvo followed. Brian was in contact with the control room advising them of the situation. It was very bizarre and clearly the radio operators thought it was entertaining.

Indicating the right turn, he moved around the island and back across the motorway bridge to the traffic lights. Here, he took the right-hand lane, indicating right again, and waited to turn back onto the southbound carriageway.

The Volvo had gone. It was not behind them anymore.

"Prat, he was lost, looking for Milton Keynes probably. Can I get something to eat now, Sherlock?"

"Ballocks," was the only response.

Having delayed their meal break to play with a lost motorist, Dave decided to put his foot down. They moved down the slip road and back onto the motorway. As the big Mercedes left the end of the slip road, it was in fourth gear and already over 110 mph.

"Wow, I need one of these cars." Dave laughed.

In the distance behind them, the Volvo too pulled out onto the motorway and followed the police car once again, speeding up to catch them.

"Dave, there is something fast coming up behind us. Slow down, mate, could be the boss."

Dave slowed the car to a normal 70 mph and the lights in the mirror grew larger, but slowed too. Slowly but very surely, the Volvo caught them and fell in behind at a safe distance.

"Your mate's back flower, it's the Volvo again."

"Let's pull this arsehole over, he is beginning to annoy me."

Dave slowed the car again and put the flashing blue lights on, plus the electronic banner in the rear that says stop. Indicating left, he began to move over to the hard shoulder.

"Is he coming with us?"

"Yeah, looks like it."

"Ok, let's have a word with him."

The police car stopped on the hard shoulder, still with the lights flashing blue in the darkness of the night. The Volvo pulled very carefully up behind the Mercedes and stopped when less than 2 feet from the rear bumper. Both Dave and Brian got out of the car and walked back towards the Volvo. Dave approached the driver's window, whilst Brian instinctively took a look around the car, peering in through the windows.

The driver slowly lowered the window to allow Dave to speak to him. By this time, Brian was looking through the passenger window at the front. Both saw the same thing at the same time—what the driver was wearing.

They both knew instantly what it was and what it was not. It was not a body warmer, it was a vest loaded with explosives. In the driver's right hand was a book, the Koran. In his left hand was a trigger mechanism.

"Ru…" was all Dave could actually get out.

The blast blew the Volvo apart taking Dave and Brian with it. Its fuel tank erupted, and so too did the tank in the police Mercedes parked feet in front. The Mercedes exploded and the blast lifted the whole car up into the air, to the right and down the embankment on the left side, rolling and burning as it fell.

The Volvo had more or less ceased to exist. A small tangle of wreckage remained but this was 100 yards from where it had stopped. The surface of the road had caught fire from the fuel and heat igniting the bitumen.

The blast was heard up to 10 miles away. Luckily, the only cars on the motorway at this time were the Volvo and the police car. But other traffic was approaching some distance away. They had seen the flash and heard the bang. All had stopped. The motorway was on fire, there was nowhere to go.

The first call routed to the Bedfordshire Police was from Vodafone.

Brian and Dave's shift mates responded to the emergency calls that went out from the control room in Kempston. They knew that there had been a massive explosion on the motorway and had been advised to approach with extreme caution.

At the same time, two-armed response units were scrambled from Luton Police HQ and were now northbound on the M1, moving at over 150 mph towards the scene. They all had the same thought in their mind. Could they get there quickly enough to help their colleagues? Little did they know, Brian and Dave no longer existed, no trace would be found of them as they were blown to the four winds.

The first unit to arrive was the shift inspector; they were further north of the scene between the junction and Milton Keynes, a matter of a few minutes away at speed. They arrived to see the road on fire, the wreckage of the Mercedes and a fuck off hole in the ground that used to be a Volvo. People had got out of their cars and were filming the scene on their phones.

Within a few minutes, there were more cars, armed officers, an ambulance, and a fire engine on the scene. There was nothing for the ambulance crews to do, except help the other police officers as they threw up.

M1 Leicester
Junction 22 Southbound, 0345 Hours

The police Volvo was now doing over 130 mph southbound on the M1 between junction 22 and 21. In front of them was a BMW 535 saloon that had refused to stop. At this time of the night, with little or no traffic, it was safe to continue the pursuit and try to stop the vehicle.

If nothing else, it was providing some sport during a long night shift. Weather was good for the time of year, cold but dry and fine. Visibility was good and there was no reason to back off and stop this chase.

Leicester police control had taken over command of the incident and were now vectoring other high-speed police vehicles towards the scene, aiming for a TPAC stop, quietly and without risk to the public.

As the BMW hurtled south towards junction 21, the slip road had already been blocked. A large police transit van was parked across the road, lights flashing, obvious to everyone. They were not getting off here. The best place for this pursuit was on the motorway and the control room was making sure of that.

In the rear-view mirror of the Volvo, a set of blue lights appeared and were gaining on the first car very quickly. They were doing 130 mph behind the BMW, meaning that whoever was driving the police car behind them was moving very very quickly.

Speeding through junction 21, the BMW moved out to the outside lane as he saw another police Volvo storming up the slip road joining the motorway. This gave the three police cars the opportunity they needed to attempt a TPAC.

All three cars were Volvos and had a driver and mate. Highly trained pursuit drivers with nerves of steel and very cool customers. The high-speed approach from behind the first police car came through the middle lane and passed the slip road Volvo moving ahead and in front of the BMW. Slip road Volvo moved into the middle lane alongside and the original police car dropped in behind.

"Ready, ready, execute!"

The lead police car hit its brakes, the middle lane car closed in, and the rear car closed up. The BMW had nowhere to go, boxed on three sides by police vehicles and on the fourth side by the central barrier.

"TPAC team, be aware there has been an attack on the police in Bedfordshire tonight, proceed with caution."

"Go, go."

The passengers from each police car opened their doors and ran to the driver's side of the BMW. The window was down and the driver shouted, "There is only one God… Allah God is good! Allahu Akbar, Allahu Akbar!"

The explosion took all four cars, all seven men, in a massive explosion. The blast pushed debris high into the air and blew cars and body parts over both carriageways. No one had the slightest chance of survival just as the planners expected.

The full attention of the police and security services was now focussed on two attacks in the early morning of 11 November. But now people all over the country were being woken up to be told of two further dreadful bombings that had killed eight policemen.

The impact on the ordinary police, men and women would be massive. They were no longer safe and would question any requirement to engage with what was until tonight, routine, normal policing.

The Metropolitan police anti-terrorism teams, plus other internal and external security organisations, were mobilising to deal with this new threat to the UK.

Terror had now come to those that we rely on to protect us. The country was at war.

Chapter 10

Scotland Yard
11 November 2015, 0900

Sir Robert Mark, who was appointed police commissioner in 1972, was the very first incumbent to have come up through the ranks to achieve his position. Prior to this, many were retired military officers or civil servants.

The rules were changed and now the police commissioner must have been a serving chief constable and be British. The post was not open to anyone who was not a British citizen.

Until now, in 2010, there had not been a female police commissioner appointed, but there are many female chief constables.

Modern policing needed a command structure of totally experienced officers. There was a fast-track system for graduates but this still required hands-on experience 'pounding the beat'. There was no quick route to the top of the British police forces. Money, influence, breeding, or education did not gain you the respect and knowledge you needed.

So it was with Sir William Shore. He had joined the force at 19 years old and for the last 32 years, had worked in several different forces across the UK. His experience was vast having worked in anti-terror, murder, fraud, traffic, and major crime.

He had been in place for only 18 months. The position of commissioner was appointed by Her Majesty the Queen and was at her pleasure. Meaning, he would not be removed without royal assent.

32 years of police experience did not prepare you to understand or deal with the attacks that had taken place over the last few days. Yes, he had seen horror before, fatal car accidents, murder victims, fire deaths and gangland slaughter. Nothing on this scale before. There were no manuals he could use.

These were not random opportunistic events. This had been planned.

Sir Robert had not been home since Sunday, sleeping when possible for a few minutes in the office. He badly needed a shower and food. But time was not available. He ate whilst he was working, stale old sandwiches delivered hours ago. Hours that had vanished in seconds. A shower was a luxury he could look forward to when they got the situation under control.

Sir William was a leader. He led from the front and expected nothing of his officers that he would not consider doing himself. He had to be prepared to do what he asked of his men and women on the frontline.

There was one difference, as of Monday morning, Sir William now had an armed guard. Two of the Mets firearms officers were always with him. Right now, they were outside the door to his secretary's office. The only way into him was through this door. Unless they had an appointment, they were not getting in, regardless of rank or standing in government. Not even the PM was going through unless expected.

The whole of Scotland Yard was chaos, very organised, but chaos. Police officers were dealing with everything from ongoing crimes to identifying the bomb dead. Rushing around the building, a constant tide of people was focussed on one goal.

One of the things the British were very good at was managing a crisis of this scale and all the 'powers that be' were now one machine wiring towards a common goal. Revenge. We were good at revenge too. Sooner or later, we would extract revenge for Monday.

Sir William now sat in a large meeting room adjacent to his office. The table was oval and about 12 feet long. Around the table sat eight of his most senior officers and advisors, plus two military advisors. Early morning briefing was held at 0900.

Around the room were whiteboards, flip charts, and huge monitors displaying various diagrams, maps, plans, and charts. Each person sat at the table had an assistant who sat behind them and to their right side. Two rings of people, twenty-one in all. Each of the main ten would present an updated report on the situation.

By design, the relevance of the information spiralled from the outside in. Meaning, that the matters involving the two sites in the city would be last and security measures and ongoing actions in the rest of the country would come first.

The two military men spoke first reporting on the various actions taken to secure what they thought were at-risk targets—the power stations, airports, and other key installations.

But how far should they go, what is sensible and what is panic? The military does not panic, they plan.

- Power stations now all had an armed guard patrolling all entrances and access.
- Remaining gas installation had armed security.
- Fuel refineries and LNG facilities were being guarded, supply logistics of liquid fuel were being controlled and guarded by the Army Logistics Corps. Civilian hauliers were now under military command.
- All operational airports were now guarded by the RAF Regiment, others had been closed and all commercial flights banned.
- UK airspace was closed to all but relief flights. RAF jets were on standby to be scrambled to intercept even the smallest light aircraft breaking the rules.
- The Royal Navy was patrolling close to all major and some minor ports. Only essential ports were now allowed to operate with military control.
- The country was locked down and on a war footing, readying and preparing to fight back.

Next to rise was a deputy chief constable who had been given the NHS liaison role. She was to coordinate and report on the medical relief and recovery effort and the ongoing situation. A grim and harrowing job, one that was not the envy of anyone around the table.

"Over the first 36 hours, there had been 6,122 live casualties from both sites. These ranged from walking wounded to others critical in hospital. Eighty-five UK hospitals had taken casualties and eighteen French hospitals.

1923	Walking wounded were treated and released.
2347	Critical with life-threatening wounds.
986	Life-changing injuries.
866	Seriously injured but will recover.

"Based on computer modelling of previous bomb attacks and events studied at various institutions throughout the world, modelling has put the estimated dead in London as five thousand five hundred people. We expect less than 25% of the dead will be whole. The rest will be dismembered with their body parts possibly scattered up to 10 metres around them. This is going to prove to be the hardest part of the recovery.

"This also represented a large public health risk which must be addressed quickly. Otherwise, there is a risk of disease including cholera. Very difficult decisions have had to be made that will not be popular with the public at large but need to be made nonetheless. A type of triage system had been imposed due to the health risks and the sheer scale of what had to be done.

1. Whole bodies will be kept and stored for identification.
2. Part bodies that are identifiable will be kept. Such as a limbless torso where the head is still identifiable.
3. Large part bodies with identification on them will be kept. Where a part corps is found that has identification in a pocket, wallet, phone, or bag.
4. All other body parts recovered will have DNA taken, logged, and then sent for cremation. A central database will be established to collate matching body parts and arrange identification through hospital records.

"A high-temperature incineration plant had been commandeered to deal with the cremation of the recovered body parts once DNA samples had been taken. South of the river, close enough to avoid delays, sitting between the Millwall football stadium and a school named after Sir Francis Drake. Ironic. One of England's greatest sea captains who pioneered trade over long distances with far-off countries. Now it seems those countries wish to bring us to our knees.

"Here, once documented, body parts will be cremated. There is no other option. The volume of refrigeration required for the timescale of identification was just mind-blowing. Public health is a priority to recovery and normality. Sadly, for some, this will mean there is nothing to bury of their loved ones. For others, it may mean there is never any true identification of a lost family member.

"As much as we would like to be able to provide such a facility, there is no possibility of meeting all the various religious wishes of the families with confirmed dead. We must be allowed due to the forensic process. We expect some issues along the religious routes.

"Work continues at both sites to recover anyone trapped but as time goes on, there is less chance of finding further live casualties. At some time in the next 24-36 hours, we must declare the site dead and allow heavy lifting and mechanical diggers onto the site. Any bodies found will stop the work and they will be recovered with all due respect.

"The workload on the medical emergency services has lessened and is well within the capacity of the NHS service. Some non-urgent or planned procedures and admissions are being delayed. I am informed that the London Fire Brigade is being supported by surrounding counties and is well within operation limits, although most of the crews refuse to go off shift to rest, taking only hours at a time to eat and recover."

Another chief constable, Roger Morris, rose to his feet to address the gathering. He was possibly early 50s but looked very drawn and far away. He was clearly shocked at the report from the NHS and casualty count. His report was more personal.

"Ladies and gentlemen, you will understand that I am reporting on operational matters covering the response and efforts to track down and stop whichever group of people are responsible for this attack on the United Kingdom. Make no mistake, this is how the government, Sir William, and everyone I speak to considers the attack. We are at war in our own country. My brief covers all levels of security clearance and I am not at liberty to report this morning on some of the responses that are occurring. Enough to say that all the UK's considerable security machine is now totally committed to this attack.

"What I can tell you this morning is that there was no bomb near Smithfield Market. There was no trace of any explosive residue. Conventional or otherwise. Police, fire and military forensic testing did not find any trace of an explosive substance. What did, in fact, cause the devastation was the Capitalgen power plant exploding. The power station was attacked and used against us. To cause this explosion took extensive engineering knowledge, plus very good local knowledge. Most people would walk past the building and not be aware there was a power station there.

"The explosion was caused by the ignition of a large volume of compressed natural gas that was stored to run the engines. In addition to the gas, there was 1 million litres of liquid fuel stored for use if required. Not all of the fuel burnt in the blast, this drained naturally into the underground systems where it mixed with the airflow, creating a fuel-air mixture, which then ignited blasting along the underground network. A Thermobaric reaction.

"We also now know that there were 30 tons of liquid ammonia used as a refrigerant. Many of the dead that were found some distance away from the blast zone died from inhaling ammonia. It seems that we built the bomb for them and whoever this was, they just set it off. A good job, Sir, you wore the NBC suit when you went to the site on Monday.

"An Iranian aircraft on final approach to Heathrow was overhead Smithfield when the explosion happened. Debris from the explosion brought it down over Oxford Circus. No one survived. The falling debris and fuel were what caused the added devastation. This was an unintentional act and not a deliberately planned attack. It does have a certain amount of irony attached but none of these people deserved the fate they were given.

"Non-classified activities are continuing with teams tracking down and interviewing all known sympathisers and verifying their locations over Saturday, Sunday and Monday morning. Anyone on the watch lists or related to anyone on the watch lists is being interviewed.

"Finally, as you know, we have lost eight police officers to a new method of attack using motor vehicles. These were two horrifying attacks that leave us all wondering just how they may be countered. The impact on morale and the willingness of our officers to engage is huge. This is now a matter for separate debate and consideration. What I can say is that we are considering providing every patrol car with a trained and armed soldier. The UK police forces only have limited trained armed officers, we need many more, and the armed services are the natural place to obtain these resources.

"As of today, all officers trained and authorised to carry weapons will be armed. I have to say, a sad day in the history of British Policing."

He sat and the room went very quiet. A hush. What could you say, over the last 35 minutes, the information given to the meeting was a little short of a briefing Churchill may have expected during the London Blitz. At least then, we knew who we were fighting.

Sir William rose.

"I suggest we take 10 minutes to get a hot drink, compose ourselves, and then get back to business and progress this together."

At the back of the room, there was a table with coffee, tea, cold drinks, and light food. Sandwiches and small cakes. No one ate a thing, and no stomach to eat, but the coffee went very quickly, many people had been awake for hours and needed the caffeine rush.

Sir Willian was not a man of ceremony and queued up with the rest to get a coffee, standing next to Morris, who had just reported to the meeting.

"Sir," Morris said, "out of interest, how did you know to wear the NBC suit?"

This question had already been in Sir William's thoughts for over a day. Morris served to bring it back to the forefront.

"Not sure, Roger, I was just given it and told to put it on. A precaution I assumed. The PM and that Si'ad from MI6 both wore them too."

The meeting continued and finished at 1230 hrs. Everyone went back to the common cause, finding out what had happened and who had done it.

Sir William was distracted through the rest of the meeting, not noticeably but his mind was wandering back to the same question of the NBC suit—Nuclear, Biological and Chemical protection.

Chemical protection…Chemical protection.

His thought process was simple. Whoever asked for the NBC suits to be provided must have known there was a gas risk. Inconceivable? Not possible? How? Why? It did not make sense.

No one knew the attack was going to happen, or where, or what, or how, except those that were involved.

He sat and puzzled over this conundrum for the best part of an hour, then picked up the phone to speak to his secretary.

"Helen, get me the TFC as soon as possible. Whatever he is doing, get him here now please."

The TFC was the Tactical Firearms Commander. All and every operation involving Met police firearms officers goes across his desk. From normal armed response patrols to specialised operations. Inside and outside of the Met's operational area.

"Sir, TFC is about 30 minutes away but will be with you as soon as possible. Is this an urgent matter, Sir?"

"Possibly, Helen, tell him to blue light it. I need him here now."

Just under 20 minutes later, Chief Superintendent Nottingham was shown into the commissioner's office. A large man around 6 ft 3 inches tall and built like a rugby second-row forward. He wore black police fatigues, boots, webbing, and a side arm.

"Carl, grab a seat, relax, please. I need to discuss something with you, and I need you to arrange something for me."

Carl has only been in this office once before and that was for a ballocking. He crossed the line and went outside of the standard operating procedures. For good reason—to save the life of one of his officers, who would certainly have been shot. He knew what he had done had broken the rules. He was in a concealed position, unseen by an armed and dangerous man who had just bungled an attempt to rob a local Barclays Bank.

The second guy, the robber's less than effective side man, was stood back behind him, about 15 ft to the rear. Carl's position was high and provided a view of the yard below him. It was full of old containers, boxes, and an old car that had long passed its sell-by date.

A second armed officer was moving along the side of the container, towards the position of the bungling pair of robbers, right to where they stood, one with a raised handgun. He was walking right into it.

Carl used the radio to warn the officer but the static crackle told everyone where he was and the gunman moved out to get a firing angle on the officer. Carl did not hesitate; he fired and dropped the gunman with a double tap. Two shots.

The not-so-clever accomplice complained there was no warning. There was no time. An enquiry by the Independent Police Complaints Authority ruled the shot was justified to save the life of his colleague but warned about giving due warning that armed police were present.

This landed Carl a 'Carpeting' with the commissioner. No further action was taken.

"Carl, were you involved with our lads in Manchester and elsewhere last Sunday when we tried to grab the suspected people for the group?"

"Yes, Sir, I was. I coordinated the teams working with our friends from Sterling Lines."

Sterling Lines is the SAS base in Credenhill, Herefordshire.

"Fine, that's good, it is what I had hoped. I need you to arrange a meeting for me. As soon as possible and I mean today as soon as possible. I want you back here this evening with both the leaders of the police team and the SAS team. I want your opposite number from Sterling Lines here with you too. This is not a request, it is an order. I expect everyone here latest 1830 this evening. Any difficulties?"

"No, Sir, I do not see any issues. I have about 5 hours to get everyone here. Works for me, Sir."

"Good, make it work for me. And, Carl, outside of yourself and the other three people, no one needs to know anything, and I mean no one. I have your back; if you have to lie to senior officers, I will cover you off. Please pass the same warning to the others."

"As you wish, I will be back at 1830, Sir."

Carl left the office, worried. Had he messed up? He could not think as to why. Why the secrecy? He could see the rush, everything was a rush right now. His was not to reason why. He came to work on Sunday morning and had not been home since. A few more hours or days would not matter.

Scotland Yard
11 November 2015, 1830

At 1800, Nottingham was back together with a police sergeant, a SAS sergeant, plus an army major. All wore fatigues of some description and all wore side arms. They sat outside of the commissioner's office near where the two police armed guards stood protecting the commissioner. This was a holding area where people gathered ahead of any meetings with the head of Met police.

The commissioner himself came out of the office to greet the waiting four men. Turning to the two police guards, he asked them to reposition themselves, one at each access door to the anti-room.

"I want no one in and no one goes out until I tell you differently. Do you understand? I don't care who it is, what they want or how badly they scream and shout. No one in or out. Get it?"

"Yes, Sir," came the response.

"Gentlemen, please come through."

Sir William led the men through his secretary's office into the meeting room where he gestured for them all to sit. On the table was coffee and tea, provided by his secretary before she was sent home.

He sat at the head of the table with a pale grey folder in front of him. Nothing else. No IT paraphernalia, just a good old-fashioned folder.

When everyone was settled and had a drink, he started.

"Thank you all for coming at such short notice. What we will discuss this evening, as of this point in time, only one person on earth knows about. Me!

What I am about to discuss with you is so secret that no one in HMG has any idea, nor will they until I deem the time is right."

Out of the folder, he took four one-page documents, stood and made a point of placing one document in front of each person. Then sat down again.

"Each of you has already signed and works within the Official Secrets Act. You all know the consequences and penalties of breaching this agreement. In front of you now is a further document I would like you all to sign before I talk with you. This is nothing more than a document which reminds you of the Official Secrets Act and that you have signed it and are aware of the penalties, etc., etc. I want to be sure you know and understand. Do we have any problems with signing this paper? Speak now."

Silence, not a sound. Two of the meetings read the paper, the others did not look at it. Nottingham was first, pulling a pen out of his vest, and he signed the paper. The others followed.

"Thank you. I will have my secretary provide you with copies tomorrow for your own records. Now, gentlemen, please listen very carefully. I want your honest opinions, thoughts, and benefits of your experience. Nothing more. No guessing or maybe. Tell me honestly what you think.

"On Sunday, you carried out several coordinated attacks on suspected members of a group we were tracking together thought to be hostile to the UK. Out of all the planned attacks, none succeeded. Why?"

There was again silence for a good few minutes. It was the SAS Sergeant who spoke first.

"Sir, honestly, they knew we were coming. No other explanation in my mind. Someone had told them we were coming. We looked like a bunch of prats. We got nothing and no one."

Carl seemed a little flustered over this comment.

"That's just impossible. The control we had over target ID and location was total. No way anyone could have leaked it. Until 15 minutes before we engaged, I had not shared the final location."

"Gentlemen, this is not a witch hunt. I want your opinions, that is all, then I will share my thinking. Please what else? How secure were our comms?"

This time, the SAS Major got involved.

"Standard Ops procedure. All were Special Forces secure and encrypted. The police tactical teams use the same gear as us. No way anyone was able to eavesdrop. Anyway, comms were silent until we went live."

"So, if the targets knew you were coming, who else knew before you went in, how many people were in the loop?"

"The four of us, plus MI6 command, Si'ad Marachi, the teams were not briefed until they were in position and ready to deploy. 10 minutes before deployment, we each briefed the team leaders."

Sir William went very quiet again, pensive and worried. He racked his brains, wondering if he should move on. He did.

"So outside of this room, the only possible source of a tipoff is MI6, correct?"

"Yes, has to be, unless we are under suspicion ourselves, Sir."

"If you were, then you would not be here with me now. Please relax. Something happened to me on Monday which I have been puzzled about since. In our briefing this morning, someone made a comment to reinforce my unease. Could the operation on Sunday evening have been a clever way of diverting all our attention away from the threat level and finding the threat, paving the way through for the attacks to go in with reduced risk of compromise?"

"OMG, you could be right; it would be a genius move. We are all focussed on what we thought was bringing down a terror gang, whilst they were én-route to attack the city and the gas lines."

"Exactly, but I have more. On Monday morning, I went with the PM and this Si'ad Marachi to view the site at Smithfield. I was given an NBC suit and told to wear it. Why, what for?"

"That's clear now, Sir, the ammonia gas."

"Exactly again, that is clear now. It was not known on Monday morning hours after the blast. Clearly, the PM would not have known anything; it was all we could do to stop him vomiting in his suit. The only person out of the three, who stood there that morning, that could have known was Marachi. How did he know there was ammonia gas about? It must be him. He could have tipped off the group that we were coming, he could have designed the timing to allow them to cover for their own attacks. He and only he would know about the gas. So, he protected himself. Someone is playing both sides of a chessboard!"

"Then we need to bring this fucker in for a chat, don't we, SAS style? See what else he can tell us."

Sir William stood and started to pace about the room. This made the others have to follow him with their heads like they were all wired together.

"We could but he will not talk. We need to use him I think, and therefore why you four are here this evening. You and only you know what we suspect.

This is how it will stay. From now on, you work for me, report to me only on all matters relating to this issue. No one else. You can use your skills to bullshit and cover your arses with anyone else. At the end of the day, I will have your backs if any trouble is encountered.

"I want you to put together two teams of totally trusted people. We are going to follow this man every second of the day from now on. You will not be seen, compromised or in any other way risk this operation. So, whatever you do, you do not get caught. Absolutely no comms with me. You do not phone me, text me or anything. I will be here each night at 1830. You come to me and me only. I want a report every day. The five of us meet here every day from now on.

"If anything comes up that you need to know, then I will make contact with you. This will come through our own channels over to Sterling Lines. I want the best out of everyone. Use the best, no holds barred. Do as you must but do not lose this man and do not get caught, and don't fucking kill him, yet!

"You have 24 hours to put the teams together and prepare. I will see you all back here tomorrow evening. Thank you, gentlemen."

Chapter 11

JARIC, RAF Brampton
Wednesday, 11 November 2015, 1830

RAF Brampton was a small non-flying RAF station close to the town of Huntingdon alongside the A1, Great North Road.

The history of its establishment boasts many changes that followed the use of the camp during the First World War as a German prisoner of war camp. During the Second World War, it became a site to house babies and children evacuated from London during the Blitz.

The USAF used part of the base as a headquarters until September 1945 when they moved out to occupy what is now RAF Alconbury. From this time until 1957, various parts of the RAF Training and Support command were in residence.

In 1953, JARIC (Joint Air Reconnaissance Intelligence Centre) was formed and they moved into RAF Brampton in 1957.

RAF Brampton was, in fact, part of an unusual three-station combined command, shared with RAF Wyton, the other side of Huntingdon and RAF Henlow near Hitchin. Only RAF Wyton had a runway and flight operations. Henlow had a grass runway and did fly gliders.

The gate guardian at RAF Brampton was an MD F4 Phantom XT914 borrowed from RAF Wattisham in Norfolk.

Huntingdon became an Air Force town. With Brampton and Wyton to the east and west of the town, RAF Alconbury is close by and RAF Molesworth is less than 10 miles further away. A lot of businesses and jobs were provided by the bases in the local area.

There was a time when you could not go far in the town without seeing someone in uniform. With the advent of increased terrorism in the UK, not many would now venture off camp in uniform. Too much of a target.

You used to see squaddies hitchhiking at the side of the road in their uniforms with a big kit bag. They would not be there long before a truck or ex-service person would pick them up. Now though, they are not allowed to do this. Too much of a risk with the terror threat.

JARIC had been established at the end of the Second World War to study and evaluate the huge amounts of aerial reconnaissance captured by the Germans. This information provided unique intelligence on the Soviet Union and Eastern Europe during the early Cold War years, long before any satellite imagery became available. Much of the post-war Cold War planning was based on the information that had been taken from Germany and examined in minute detail. The Allies knew where most of the Soviet threats were based.

The operational capability of JARIC grew and was expanded as rapidly as technology advanced. With the availability of satellite imagery and high-quality photographic images from aircraft, the role they provided was to give target assessment information before and after any strike. Weapon development too kept pace with technology using GPS guidance systems to make the munitions very accurate.

The methods of war changed over a matter of a few years, allowing military strikes to become almost surgical, reducing casualties and the risk to civilians. The Western Allies developed the means of using one small weapon to destroy a strategic target with little collateral damage.

It was no longer a case of dropping thousands of tons of bombs on a target to destroy it. Just as both sides had done during the Second World War. Now one or two smart bombs could be used to disable a target.

Bombs that can steer themselves, guided by GPS, or bombs that follow infrared light to a target. Ground troops shine an IR light onto a target to guide the bomb home.

Instead of flattening a power station completely, a smart bomb can seek and destroy the transformers and connections to the electrical grid, rendering the power station useless until the transformers are replaced and rebuilt. Less reinstatement cost, more accuracy, and little loss of life but it has the same effect.

The same for a bridge. One smart bomb can take out a small section of the structure, rendering it useless, but leaving enough that it can be repaired once all hostilities end.

The RAF use the Panavia Tornado GR4 as their air reconnaissance platform.

Powered by two Rolls Royce afterburning RB199-103 engines, the Panavia Tornado GR4A is an impressive aircraft. It has a wingspan of over 45 ft with the wings fully spread, 28 ft swept to 68° and is over 54 ft long. A top speed of over 1,452 mph and carries a pilot plus navigator in tandem.

A small window below the main cockpit houses the Vicon camera pod. The GR4A has no cannons mounted in the forward fuselage. Replacing these are a Sideways Looking Infrared system and a Linescan infrared surveillance system. It can still carry and deliver over 18,000 lbs of ordnance.

The aircraft can collect photographic data at very high speed, whilst flying over a target faster than sound. The data is streamed directly to frontline troops or battle control.

This meant that over the last years, the function JARIC was set up to perform changed. Expanded may be a more accurate description. Not only had they the responsibility to interpret and identify ground-based threats, or potential target change over time, they were now tasked with examining the infrastructure of a country and designing a way to cripple it, with as little damage as possible, surgically removing parts to disable it.

Before the second Gulf War, during the massive planning that took place, JARIC was involved in target identification and selection for exactly these reasons. Many of the targets attacked in the first wave were designated by JARIC.

Group Captain Will Rivers was JARIC's Commanding Officer. He had been in the post for 8 months now. Prior to this, Will had been OC 2 Squadron at RAF Marham in Norfolk, flying Tornado aircraft.

His life was flying, and he was a veteran of both the Gulf Wars and a few other support and confrontation missions around the world.

Just over 5 years ago, Will took part in an operation in the UK to help recover a stolen weapons-grade virus, using his aircraft on low-level reconnaissance runs.

Having stolen some of the virus, the terrorists had been chased down by the security services and were holed up in a pub in a tiny village in Cambridgeshire. The threat of the virus being released was so severe that plans were made to bomb the pub and incinerate the virus.

Many thousands of people would have been killed within days if the virus got out and went airborne. Many more over the next 12 months would die too. The twenty or so people in the pub, being held by the terrorists, had to be considered expendable compared to the risks to the greater population if the virus escaped.

What was to be a simple high-speed pass designed to get overhead data for the police and security services on the ground turned bad when the terrorist engaged the aircraft with a stinger missile.

Not one of his better days out flying and he ended up safe but in the middle of a huge foam blanket and a wrecked aircraft on the runway at RAF Wittering.

As the commanding officer of JARIC, Will's brief was very wide. There were the standard procedures and daily workload for the unit, which took all the hours his people had. Data to be examined could come in at any time and from anywhere that the UK had an 'interest'. Plus, data from NATO or other Allies.

Will was a workaholic and single. When work was done, Will had some pet projects of his own using the JARIC systems. These were more hobbies, but he quickly learnt how to operate and do exactly what his highly trained team of people did every day.

One of which was an ongoing project to evaluate and map the targets he would choose if he had to attack the UK. He would spend hours poring over maps and satellite imagery. Much of it was high definition and very classified. Will's security clearance was as high as it could be. He had access to almost everything.

A crazy project you may think and one that could land him in a lot of trouble if misinterpreted by his senior officers. Will had this covered off and his project was known to both his boss and his two second in command. He had permission to continue. But the findings and plans he was creating went nowhere outside of JARIC and RAF Brampton that was the agreement. It was top secret, eyes-only, and only a restricted few people. Outside of this, it could be interpreted as treason or at a minimum breaking the Official Secrets Act.

Will was troubled. For the first time in his career, there was 'shit' going on and he was not at the sharp end. He felt frustrated and angry wanting to get in and help. But there was little he could do.

Most of the work at JARIC was done on the day shift; there was a night crew but this was reduced in numbers and dealt with incoming requests as they appeared. The night was when Will liked to get back into his project and attack the UK. He already had a lot of data and a lot of plans.

An attack on any country would go in in three waves.

- Firstly, shock and awe, demonstrate the power and ability to strike.
- Secondly, take out important and smaller targets.
- Thirdly, move in for the kill when ground forces would be deployed.

His own plans against the UK had just moved from shock and awe to considering the second level of attacks. Where would he go? What would he hit to disable his adversary? The list was growing as the targets reduced in size and importance. There was a list of 'clean kill' targets. It was very true that the shock and awe attacks would claim many lives. But after this, it would be minimal.

Working in his own office using the JARIC computer system, he was able to identify a possible target, flag it, and then research the reduced function and impact of removing it. A painstaking process that had to be done very carefully and was time-consuming.

As always, he had the TV on, stuck permanently to BBC News. The main theme was the London blasts and attacks. With one eye on the news and the other planning to destroy another bit of the UK, he was busy but stopped dead.

"Fuck me," Will said.

With a few clicks of the mouse, the display changed and up came a list. His stage 1 target list. This showed five shock and awe targets, Central London blast using existing infrastructure, Overhead London commercial aircraft, and hit command-and-control assets. The other two did not register.

"The bastards have targeted the UK; they have done what I am doing. They must reach the same conclusions. Which means we can maybe figure out where they will be going next."

Will now had a serious dilemma. What he had been doing was above board, he had authorisation. Otherwise, it would look very suspicious. His orders were that his data could not leave the base or be shared with anyone. But surely this was different. He may have something, something that could help to save lives and stop these terrorists.

He had to, or must, share this information. But with whom and how does he cover off the security considerations and limitations?

"Go in at the top, talk to the top," Will mumbled.

All military bases have secure comms. Brampton was no different. Will picked up the phone and called the guard room.

"Group Captain Rivers, who is OC tonight please?"

"Flight Luis Johnson, Sir. He is out on a walkabout at present. Do you need him, Sir?"

Flight Luis, short for Flight Lieutenant.

"Yes, as soon as possible, it is important. Get him to my office just as quickly as you can, thanks."

Clearly, they had called him on the radio and panicked him big time. Less than 10 minutes later, Johnson was banging on the CO's door.

"Johnson, come in, thanks. I need you to set up a secure comms call for me. This is to the Metropolitan Police Commissioner. I need this urgently, as soon as possible. I know we have secure comms but linking to outside systems is not something I am familiar with. So, set it up quickly, get me on the phone to the Met."

"Sir, I will call you once it is ready to go."

"Johnson, only the Met Police Commissioner, nobody else, no assistants, secretaries, etc. One to one call and the line must be secure. Otherwise, just abort, pretend it never happened and you were never asked. Got it?"

"Sir!" And he was gone.

Johnson had no real bloody idea either. Secure comms, he was not an IT geek.

Just how the fuck do I get a call through to the Met? he thought.

15 minutes later, the call was arranged. Johnson had called Scotland Yard and explained the need for a secure priority call coming from the RAF. He made it clear the call was only for the commissioner due to the level of security clearance that is required.

The connection protocols were shared and within a few minutes, the police IT folks were helping to sort out the link and get the call arranged.

Will sat in his office, hovering over his own desk phone. The other magic was happening elsewhere. The call was being encrypted and transmitted, the unencrypted at the other end.

He was concerned that he would sound like a prat, but so what, would not be the first time. Better to have said and messed up than just ignored, it was Will's theory. The phone rang.

"Sir William, thank you for taking the call. Can we be sure that this call is totally secure between you and me?"

"It is, go ahead, Group Captain."

"What I am going to discuss is classified, I am risking my job by talking to you. I need to be able to trust that what I say is confidential if you choose not to act upon it."

"That is fine with me, no one will ever know. Right, what is on your mind?"

"Sir, my command looks at countries and selects targets to allow the UK to attack and disable the country with the smallest damage impact. We do not hit a power station, we hit the transformers outside. Technology now allows this.

"I have an authorised personal project that I have worked on for the last 6 months since assuming command at JARIC. This is mainly designed to familiarise me with the way things work. Simply put, I am plotting and targeting the UK, looking for where to attack and how. The first targets I selected have almost been copied by the attacks on London. There is no way my data has been used outside of the UK military system. It is eyes-only secure to myself, my commanding officer and my two deputies. They have never seen the full project data I have.

"This means that someone like me has sat down and completed an attack evaluation on the UK arriving at similar or the same results. Or, the data has been hacked, which means this can only be from a very high-security clearance level of origin."

Will paused to allow this to sink in and for the commissioner to respond. It was quiet a very long time.

"Let us put aside how why and where this data the terrorist may have used has come from. What you are saying, exactly, is that you identified the same targets in London that have been hit, is that correct?"

"Yes, Sir, exactly right."

"Are we not a little late, it has happened?"

"Sorry, Sir, you do not understand what I am saying. Normally, we identify three stages of attack. First shock and awe, this is where the London attacks match almost. Second, are smaller targets; the second targets are still to come if they are following the same reasoning or have my project."

"So you mean you can provide possible intelligence on where they may go next?"

"That's what I hope, Sir, yes. I may be wrong about exact targets but the methodology is correct. If they have completed their own evaluation, then we will be close. If they have access to my project, it will be exact."

"You're based in Huntingdon, aren't you? I am going to send a car to collect you. Bring your data with you and we can go through this together with the security services when you arrive at Scotland Yard."

"Sir, this data cannot leave RAF Brampton, I cannot bring it to you. You will need to come here."

"Oh, you can now, Group Captain. I will make the necessary calls. Don't worry about that. Bring what you need. A car will be with you in 10 minutes. Oh, Group Captain, wear a sidearm when you come into London. We are on full military alert."

And he was gone. Will stood there holding the phone.

"Shit me and my big gob! What have I just done?"

Back on the phone with Johnson, he informed him that he had been summoned to Scotland Yard for a briefing and needed a sidearm.

"Draw the weapon from security and I will collect this at the gate in 10 minutes."

Will's computer was a desktop model and not a laptop. He did have one but it was his own and not something he could connect to the secure network. There was no way it would allow him access to an uncontrolled machine. He could, however, use a USB drive as this had been vetted and was coded to allow access for internal data sharing. It too was not allowed off camp. Too late now.

Having transferred the data, he put the drive into his briefcase with a laptop. It was only the report he had compiled to date. None of the imagery or satellite data he had access to. This limited any exposure. If they wanted this, then it can be accessed from London.

The walk to the gate was only a few minutes, but a few minutes of fresh air, cold air in fact; a frosty November evening. Signing the weapon out involved more paperwork than when he bought his first house. Sign here, sign there, then again for the ammunition in the magazines.

Sure enough, there was a police car at the gate waiting, a BMW traffic car. It was two up, driver and front seat passenger. Johnson escorted Will from the base. He too was armed.

Will was asked to get in the left side back. Before he got in, the passenger got out and asked to see his weapon.

"I need to be sure it is safe, Sir; no offence, better safe than dead."

With the ease of a time-served soldier, he checked the handgun, checked the chamber, then the magazines, declared it safe, and handed it back.

"Sorry, Sir."

Will got into the car and strapped up, putting the briefcase on the seat to his right. The car started up and pulled out of the gate, turning right onto Buckden Road, then just took off.

Blue lights came on and the car accelerated out of Brampton towards the A1 only a couple of miles away. Will loved his cars and loved to drive, but he had not been driven at these speeds before.

Hitting the A1, the car filtered onto the southbound carriageway. Filtered was perhaps the wrong word, rocketed is perhaps more accurate. The A1 had many obstacles along its route into London, roundabouts and crossover junctions. Once they had cleared Buckden roundabout, the road was clear until the Black Cat and they clearly meant to make use of it.

Sitting where he was, Will could see the speedo. It rarely came below 120 mph and roundabouts were being taken at speeds he thought impossible. What a driver, this was going to be some journey. This coming from the backseat of a Tornado capable of over 1000 miles an hour.

Huntingdon to Central London during the day was 90 minutes by car if you were lucky; bad day 2 hours.

Less than 35 minutes later, they cleared the roundabout at the bottom of the A1 in Boreham Wood. 52 miles in 35 minutes average speed of almost 90 mph. Even now going in towards Apex corner, their speed did not slow much.

Turning left at the roundabout, the car picked up two Met police motorcycle units that sped ahead clearing the way for the traffic car.

This was the second time Will had been given a high-speed ride by the police. Previously it was when he was in Ipswich and had to get back to RAF Marham to fly the recon mission over the pub when the virus had been stolen.

Less than 15 minutes later, Will was outside Scotland Yard. Thanking his two new friends, who now had an open invitation anytime to visit RAF Brampton and JARIC, he headed out of the car and up towards the main entrance.

Security was massive. Three layers of checks as he went through the door. From checking his name, rank and purpose, to the x-ray of his briefcase, side arm check, and body search.

Clearly, no one was taking any chances. It took a full 10 minutes to get through 10 metres of entrance hall into Scotland Yard.

In those 10 minutes, his new friends would be more than 15 miles away heading back to Huntingdon.

Chapter 12

RAF Brize Norton
13 March 2003, 0800

RAF Brize Norton was the RAF's largest station. Over seven thousand people worked on site. It was home to the RAF Strategic and Tactical Air Transport (AT) and the air-to-air refuelling (AAR) squadrons, which made it the hub for all rapid global mobility for UK forces.

It was built between 1935 and 1937 and started life as a flying school. During the war, on the approach to D-Day, it was home to the heavy glider conversion unit. In 1951, it was handed over to the USAF, until in 1965, the RAF took back control.

In 1984, following the conflict in the Falklands, the RAF found it was lacking in strategic transport capabilities. Brize Norton was expanded and 216 Squadron was reformed flying Lockheed Tristar aircraft. In 2001, the first Globemaster III arrived.

For the past 2 months, Brize Norton had been on full alert and was busy supporting the UK forces build-up to the second Gulf War. The West was going back to finish the job after failing to topple Sadham last time.

The West was convinced that Iraq possessed WMDs and Saddam was happy to allow this myth to continue. Poor intelligence, misleading rhetoric from Iraq, plus the lack of hard facts lead the West to agree to go back and make sure. History will judge any decisions the politicians make, but right now, it is happening.

In the most southerly corner of the airfield, adjacent to the village of Alvescot, a single C-130J sat on a small apron across the taxiway from a cluster of three small buildings. These were sitting in a compound that was fenced off. Depending on the direction of the wind, the aircraft was only a matter of a few hundred metres away from the end of the runway. Out of sight and out of mind perhaps? If the wind was in the other direction, it would need to taxi for about a good mile to reach the runway.

Access to the fenced compound could only be made from the airfield itself and that was through two gates in the fence offering an in and an out route. There was no way through from the roads outside the perimeter fence. To the south of the building was an array of antennae. To anyone looking over the airfield perimeter fence, it would look like a communications facility.

In the larger of the three, main centre buildings, six men slept in cots on the floor. They had arrived at 0300 and were already knackered after preparations that had been going on for 24 hours. Their kit had to be drawn from stores and then the final briefing with their commanding officer before the journey from Sterling Lines.

They were a squadron of SAS men ready and waiting to deploy into Iraq. Their mission was top secret and they would be the very first UK or Western forces to deploy into theatre, ahead of the air and ground assault that was being planned. They would go in first. Their presence was known only to a few, a very few.

The mission was critical but almost suicidal. They would be in the area where some of the first waves of bombing would take place. A two-target mission. Succeeding was going to be difficult and the campaign planners wanted it done by the SAS.

Wheels up was at 1000 hrs UK time. They would fly to RAF Akrotiri in Cyprus, refuel, and then head over to Saudi Arabia towards Iraq. Their kit was packed and ready in their bergens. Their weapons and ammunition were ready and would be checked finally before the drop.

To get to where they needed to be without compromising the aircraft too much or the mission, they would be inserted by HALO drop from the C130, High-Altitude Low Opening parachute drop.

Not for the faint-hearted. Jumping out of an aircraft at 30,000 feet free-falling down and opening your chute at 2500 ft above the ground, loaded with a bergen that weighs around 55 lbs plus personal weapons and tactical weapons. In all, each man will be carrying approximately 75 lbs of extra weight.

That's 5 stone; imagine jumping out of an aircraft at 30,000 ft with a 12-year-old kid strapped to your back. At least the pack will not scream.

Their kit was already checked, packed, and ready to go. But the last job before departure would be a final weapons check. Every weapon was checked and rechecked, by different people each time to be sure there were no mistakes. The soldiers, six of them, would sleep on until 45 minutes before wheels up. Another hour of rest.

In the same building, a breakfast was being prepared to feed the lads before they went. Full stomach for the trip. Inflight service on an RAF C130 may not be that good and certainly not frequent. Breakfast was one of the biggest and best fry-ups the lads had ever had. It was a good pre-mission feeding.

"The condemned men ate a hearty breakfast," mocked the squad leader, John.

John was the troop leader, not an officer. All the men except one were sergeants, he was a corporal. In an SAS squad, or troop, they had a leader but most decisions were taken by everyone. If everyone had a say and input, the resulting decision would be well-informed.

Loads of carbs and fat and it was all over by 0900. The lads cleaned up, made a visit to the toilets, and got ready to go. RAF loaders (loadies) came over to their building and tried to take their kit bags.

"We'll get that, thanks, mate. No offence but they do not leave our sight. Same goes for the weapons in that crate. We will bring them aboard with us, then you can stow them. Ok?"

"Sure thing, see you onboard in ten."

There was no way any of their kit would leave their sight from now on. They had to be sure that no one had a chance to do anything, regardless of how small it may be. Just dropping a pack too hard can damage the equipment they would need and would compromise the job.

The loadies had gone, leaving them all alone. Breakfast had been cleaned up and away, not that they could eat anything more. It was just the six of them together alone. John broke the ice.

"Let's go start a war then, shall we?"

Ten minutes later, they were onboard seated towards the aft of the aircraft behind rows of other crates destined to be offloaded in Cyprus. Although the lads would be forced to disembark to allow access to the crates, they would not leave the aircraft's sides. They would just wait whilst it was emptied. Their identities were to be protected, as with all Special Forces (SF) operations.

When they landed and were forced to disembark for a short time, they would protect themselves from being seen or even recognised. They all had shemaghs, a typical Arab scarf that was wrapped around the face to protect it against sand.

During SF ops in the desert, nothing had ever beaten a shemagh for sheer usefulness. Not issued, they bought their own.

1000 hrs on the dot, the C130 went wheels up racing down the runway to the southwest. Meaning that their aircraft had to take a long taxi to the runway to start the take-off. Once airborne, they would turn onto a course taking them across central France, southern Germany, Switzerland, and then across Italy towards Cyprus.

They were expected at Akrotiri at 1800 hrs local time. Unloading and refuelling would take an hour and they were scheduled to depart at 1930 local time. With an onward flight time of just under 4 hours, they should be over the drop zone at 0030 hrs local time.

Iraq had some extensive air defence systems. Mainly supplied by the Western Allies—UK, USA and France during the Iraq-Iran war which ended in 1988. This was back when the Iraqi regime was friendly to the West, or perhaps more 'useful'. By supporting Iraq and supplying them with weapons for both defence and attack, the West hoped to degrade the abilities of Iran's military and delay their efforts to achieve a nuclear weapon.

This had backfired to some extent, just as it had in Afghanistan where we supported the people in their fight against Russia.

Because of their modern and effective anti-aircraft defences, there was a need for a high-altitude drop. The aircraft would cross into Iraqi airspace for a 15-minute incursion over the northern border of Kuwait, flying a semi-circle over the border and back. In and out in 15 minutes.

As there was no declaration of war or any hostilities, it was not expected that Iraq would respond and escalate the whole situation. However, for these 15 minutes, they would be exposed inside what was soon-to-be enemy airspace.

They would be overhead what is just desert. Sand and not much more. Nothing military or strategic, but they would be seen, and with the escalation and tension in the area, the Iraqis could respond in some form. Only time was going to tell.

1930 hrs and the C130 departed Akrotiri, turning east towards Saudi Arabia, the international airspace.

10 minutes later, they got their escort. Two Tornado GR4 aircraft fell in just to the rear one on each side in formation. As the C130 crossed over Saudi Arabia, they expected two more friendlies to join them, two US F16 fighters. No chances were being taken; if Iraq did respond, they were authorised to return fire.

The lads spent some time eating again, stuffing as much food as they could. No one knew when they would next be able to eat safely. A box full of shop sandwiches, crisps, chocolate, and soft drinks was handed around. Once they were all finished, they got their heads down and they actually slept. Even with the noise of the C130 and thinking about what they would be doing next.

30 minutes out of Akrotiri, the C130 came up behind a giant RAF Tristar refuelling tanker. These had been converted from civil aircraft for the RAF by Marshalls in Cambridge, designed to carry 300,000 lbs of aviation fuel, almost 45,000 gallons.

It too had an air-to-air refuelling probe. Sounds crazy with all that fuel on board. With so much fuel loaded, it would not be able to take off. So, it took off with the maximum fuel it could carry and they just topped it up once airborne from another aircraft.

Air-to-air refuelling was one of the most amazing spectacles of aviation. Amazingly, this was done for the very first time in June 1923. But to this day is one of the most difficult and dangerous operations a pilot can perform.

The buffeting caused by the mother aircraft jet stream just adds to the difficulty of the refuelling operation. Plus, there is a lot of highly explosive fuel, several aircraft and people all in one place. There is no room for any error.

With the C130 in the centre position, the two Tornado escorts came alongside right and left to tank up. It would take a matter of minutes to top up the Tornados. The C130 would require longer. 15 minutes later, with their tanks on full, they were good to go.

Although well within their flight range, the fast jets carried ordinance that added weight. Topping up increased their range. If there was any trouble and the aircraft had to fight, this would burn fuel very quickly. Having a full tank was just good planning.

The tanker would be here on the way home too, just in case. Better to have it and not need it.

There rest of the flight was uneventful. Two US F16 fighters joined them as planned 45 minutes out of the drop zone. Just adding extra protection from the Iraqi fighter threat. If Iraq responded with fighters, then the Tornado and F16 escort would see them off.

Should they respond with missile threats, the GR4s would attack the radar sites using HARM missiles. They seek out and destroy the source of radar emissions associated with a missile system.

At this stage in the hostilities, the command felt that Iraq would not wish to be seen to start the conflict. Becoming the aggressor against such overwhelming force would do very little on the world political stage. They may gesture at the aircraft, but this was a chance that had to be taken.

As the big C130 flew on, the lads slept soundly and the crew went about their business and resting themselves.

At 1130, 1 hour before drop time, the loadies woke up the lads with a final brew and even more food, high-calorie cakes and sweets. An hour to go and they knew that these guys needed time to go back over checking their kit and then their weapons, for the nth time.

They had already done it three times before boarding. But who knows? SOP (standard operating procedures) called for them to check again before the jump. Once down, they would not move off anywhere until they had again checked and then loaded their personal weapons.

30 minutes to go and the loadies now helped the lads fight their way into the parachute harnesses. Two chutes, main and spare. The spare was slung low at the front of their body, covering their tummy. The main chute was on their back with their bergen slung below it. Down one side was their HK MP5 machine pistol.

Once this lot was on, they had no choice but to waddle to move. Moving around, overloaded like this, made it impossible to walk anything like normal. The loadies had long since learnt not to take the piss as a head butt hurts.

15 minutes to go and the lads now helmeted up and fitted their oxygen masks. Then, turned to face each other, checking and double-checking each other's kit, everything. Webbing, pull cords, weapon security, stowage. Anything that could come loose or not be tight correctly.

Good to go, six thumbs-up.

10 minutes out, 30,000 ft and the aircraft went red inside. The two Tornados and F16 fighters peeled off and began to fly pre-agreed holding patterns 10 miles north and 10 miles to the south, still over Kuwaiti airspace. They were fully armed and ready to fire if required to intervene.

The C130 went black, turning off all exterior lighting and crossing the border into Iraq. The first coalition aircraft of the war went hostile. It would complete a slow curve with the top of the curve some 5 miles from the east of Safwan, out into the desert.

The curve covered just under 150 miles of Iraq, 25 minutes at 380 mph. From safety back to safety. Dropping off some folks along the way.

"Gentlemen, we have just crossed into enemy airspace. The first hostile incursion of this war. Drop in 6 minutes. Prepare for drop please."

The loadies went into action. They were all wearing thermal suits and completed their own harnesses, which were attached to long webbing lanyards. This would stop them from falling out of the aircraft if they slipped, or anything went wrong. Oxygen masks and helmets too.

The large tailgate whined and started to lower. The rush of air and noise was massive, and it was freezing cold. They were at 30,000 feet. Air temperature was -40° C. They were dressed and prepared for it.

Lessons had been learnt from the first conflict in Iraq when the men from Bravo 20 were caught out by the cold in the desert. All the lads were wearing cold weather gear, which for the next few minutes they were going to need.

To the side of the rear gate, there were the expected lights. The red light was on. This meant wait not ready. Below the red light were two green ones. Red and green, ready, two green no red, go.

The loadies gave a thumbs-up and saluted, the lights went green, and they jumped.

As the tailgate began to close, suddenly the C130 banked hard to the left catching the two loadies off guard. Thankfully, they were attached by lanyards.

In the cockpit, the pilots were reacting to warnings from their own radar and defence systems and from AWACS that they were tracking three inbound Iraqi fighters.

Moving away from the planned semi-circle route, they had decided to run for it, directly back to the border and into Kuwait. Just under 15 minutes of flight time. But the Iraqi aircraft were now supersonic and would be in the area very quickly.

They pushed the Allison T56 turboprop engines into full military power, squeezing out some extra airspeed. All they could do was run until they were within striking distance of the border. Then countermeasures could be used. If they deployed these now, it was obvious they were over the border and operating within Iraqi airspace.

The four escort aircrafts went live and their weapons radar had started to track the bogies. They were at 10,000 ft before they split. The F16s went vertical going for height and a better attack position on the Iraqis. The two Tornados were 70 miles out and went supersonic too, directly towards the three incoming Iraqi F16s.

A crazy situation. Aircrafts supplied by the USA to Iraq were now being used against them.

The C130 was now 30 miles from the border. Warning buzzers sounded in the cockpit as one of the Iraqi fighters achieved a radar lock.

"Firing countermeasures," the co-pilot announced in a tone that he would possibly use when talking to his children. These guys were so very cool.

The aircraft lit up the sky with phosphorescent balls of white-hot fire pouring from both sides and at the same time, packets of chap were released, bags of tin foil pieces that floated in the air and created alternative targets for attack radar.

The Iraqis would have seen the four Allied aircraft long ago, but also noted they were not hostile as no weapons radar was working. But now it was working and all four were coming straight at them.

The first 1000 ft took 10 seconds, then accelerating to 1000 ft every 5 seconds. By turning their bodies belly down and with splayed arms and legs, they could limit their velocity to around 120 mph. Just over 2.5 minutes later, at an altitude of 2500 ft, they pulled the ripcords and fell silently to the ground. All six landed within 20 metres of each other. A bump was all the sound there was as they hit the ground and rolled sideways.

Within the first minute, their chutes and harnesses were off, bundled into a small heap near each of them. Where they landed was where they stayed. SOP, weapons check. Side arms and main weapons were checked, loaded and locked. Safety on.

Some laid flat, some were on one knee, looking outwards from a circle of six, a 360-degree sight line. Weapons were locked and ready. For the next 20-30 minutes, they would be still, watching and listening. They had to be sure their dropping in had not been seen and no response or follow-up was coming across the desert.

It was a clear night, less than 6 minutes since they left the aircraft. To their south, they saw the sky illuminated with the countermeasures the C130 was popping to protect itself. Further south were two red trails going vertical, the F16s going high.

Still, in Kuwaiti airspace, the Tornado escorts were 1 minute out from crossing the border.

"UK escort, confirm we are clear to cross the border? Speed M1.1 inbound head-on three Iraqi bogies, Friendly is 4 minutes out and closing. Two friendlies high on our NNW."

"Affirmative, repeat affirmative, clear to engage if bogies threaten. US escorts acknowledge."

Both US pilots acknowledged and four more Allied aircraft blasted across the border into Iraq to defend their big brother, which having dropped its secret cargo was now running from trouble.

The GR4 weapons radar was now tracking the three Iraqi F16s. Flying side by side, the GR4s were about 1 mile apart and moving very fast. The lead aircraft had tactical command.

"Going low, make them think we are attacking a ground position, it may draw their attention from the C130 to us."

Both aircraft went for the deck, down to 600 ft and at Mach 1.1, this was really something. Ground terrain following radar kicked in and the aircraft followed what the ground did. It almost worked, and two of the three Iraqis changed course and vectored onto the RAF Tornados. The third wanted the C130.

"Good call, UK, you have two bogies. Third is still chasing big brother. C130 is almost clear and he will not cross into Kuwait airspace. We are heading down on you due east from Angels 30,000. I think they will run."

The US F16s locked on to their targets from 5 miles out, alerting the Iraqi pilots to the threat coming in from the east.

At the same time, the two Tornados split up and they too went vertical directly towards the two Iraqi fighters. They turned north, out of harm's way and back to safety.

"Escort, big brother, we still have company and are now in Kuwait airspace, could do with some help. Confirm?"

The Iraqi fighter had continued after its prey and had not known or ignored the fact it had crossed out of Iraqi airspace. Its speed had come down and was closing on the big C130 from behind. A second burst of countermeasures spewed from the aircraft as it tried in vain to get away. It was too big to throw around like a fighter but they had to do something.

Banking hard to the right and it dived to avoid any threats.

"US escort, we will be in range in 5, looking for missile lock now."

The two F16s raced across the sky to defend the C130, from above the two Tornados were closing as well. None of them were inside missile range but maybe achieving a missile lock would spook the pilot. It did not.

From 40 miles out, the two US pilots saw the Iraqi jet explode, break apart, and go down.

"Escort, big brother, strike one for the Kuwait military, they got him with something. We are homebound, thanks for the help."

"Safe journey. Revenge is a bitch, eh?"

10 minutes later, the two Tornados reformed with the C130, coming alongside the cockpit, and dipping their wings in salute. Dropping back, they headed once again to the tanker.

Chapter 13

Iraqi Desert, 5 Miles East of Safwan
14 March 2003, 0100 local time

The drop had put them on the ground about 6 kms (clicks) to the east of Safwan. The terrain where they had landed was desert, sandy and very flat. This provided little natural cover. To the west of their position, the land was cultivated and the local farmers grew a variety of crops when they were able. These did provide cover if, or more likely when they would need it.

It was early March and the daytime temperature around Safwan was normally 26-28° C. At night, it would drop to between 10 and 13° C. Sounds warm compared to the UK in March, but it was the night-time temperatures that could be an issue, dropping very low if there was no cloud cover. There could even be a frost.

The plan was to move at night under the cover of the darkness. This would also help with the cold and keep them warm. During the day, they would lay up, hidden as best the ground cover would provide. If no cover was available, they would have to dig in to hide themselves.

Jock, the squad leader, was the only person until now that had any knowledge of the targets. They had two, primary and secondary. Obviously, the primary was the most important and they had to achieve this. Once done, the secondary target was more diversion than anything else. It was still important and was necessary.

The main problem they had was that as soon as they attacked the primary target, the Iraqis would follow up. So, the attack had to go in allowing them maximum time to get out of the area.

Before this could happen, they expected that they needed some wheels. They needed to acquire a vehicle that could be fast and could carry six heavily armed SAS men.

The drop zone had been chosen as the area was clear of any military or civil interference. They were midway between highways 1 and 26, 2 clicks south-east of the Um Qasr Bulk storage site. This was not a target for them, it was a marker only. Normally lit up like a fun fair, but with the threat of hostilities, it was blacked out. They should be able to see it 2 clicks away, but there was nothing.

Everywhere was pitch black. This was good and would help them when moving across the open country towards the primary target.

Jock was 5 ft 10 inches tall. Not over tall but built like a Scottish prop forward at Murrayfield, all muscle and very fit. A veteran of many conflicts, or operations. He took no shit from anyone and gave none back. This was how he was and he expected people to treat him in the same way.

It would be coldest just before dawn; by then, they needed to be hidden away. Jock was talking about digging in, there was no cover and he did not have the time to waste looking.

"We are going to stay here for the rest of tonight; dig in, get comfy, and wait out the day for tomorrow evening. But before we do this, we need to go through the two targets, sort out who is going to do what.

"Mike and Ian, you're on stag. 150 metres out east and west. No comms. Any fuss, click the mike buttons twice. Otherwise, see you back here in 2 hours. When you get back, I will brief you too."

The two lads picked up their gear, bergens and everything, and walked out to start their stag, sentry duty. They were the squad's eyes and ears for the next 2 hours.

"Listen up, we have a primary and secondary target we must hit. The main air assault will start on 20 March. We have 5 days to get both targets sorted. Primary is a must. Secondary is nice to have, if possible.

"Ok, the primary target. During the first Gulf War, the UK and US Navies destroyed most of the Iraqi fleet. Only a couple of mine layers remained. Or so they thought. In fact, they apparently missed two Lupo class frigates, Russian built and sold to Iraq secretly.

"These are both moored in Um Qasr port, about 12 clicks to our SSE right now. They are hidden from view between large freighters and have camo netting on them. Impossible to see if you do not know they are there from the ground. But the satellite caught a glimpse and the techs confirmed they are naval vessels. Command wants them sorted. They do not want these babies getting out of port. No threats to our own shipping.

"Powers that be want them disabled and not brought into the limelight by the press or anyone else. We are going to put a hole, and a big hole, in each of these ships. As close to the waterline as possible. Big enough to stop them from wanting to go and play. We move tomorrow when it is dark, approx. 1800. We have 12 clicks to cover into the port, gain entry without going noisy, pop the ships, and then get the fuck out. The plan clearly means at some stage it will go noisy. We will use timed charges to give us 30 to get out of the area.

"Any response and follow-up will assume we are heading for the border back into Kuwait. We are going to do the opposite. Head due north deeper into Iraq and then lay up until the heat drops off a bit. This will keep them off our backs, I hope. We need to grab a vehicle sometime if possible but can't risk discovery or trouble. If necessary, we will tab away and hide up.

"So, get to the port, go through the outer and inner fences at 10 o'clock position on the plan. We split into three pairs. One pair attacks the first ship, the other pair attacks the second ship. Pair three move to the fences at 2 o'clock position on the plan, cut through, this is our Exfil, then get back and cover our six. If you can reccy a vehicle, all the better. Once we are inside, we will agree on the timings based on what we see. I want 30 minutes to get the charges in position on the hulls. 10 minutes to get to Exfil and get the fuck away. Timers set for 30 minutes. Meaning, we will be 20 minutes minimum down range when they blow.

"Rally point, if we are compromised and we split up, the rally point will be at these coordinates: 30.08378, 47.76006. This is an irrigation hollow next to the border fences. It is deep and can hide us. Only expect to get in at night between 1200 and 0200. Anything else should and will be considered hostile. Any questions, or suggestions, now is the time."

There followed several questions, answers, and discussions, but this settled quickly. Each man was equipped with a GPS locator. This was not like a sat nav but a small receiver that would give just the numerical coordinates. A lot of training is given to understanding and using this device against a map of the area.

"OK, dig in, check your gear, stow it, and get some sleep. Hard routine."

"What is the secondary?"

"Not now. We take the primary, if we get out and are in one piece, then when we stop, I will go through the secondary. If you don't know, you can't tell. We all knew this was a risky op. Everyone good? Joe, Fraser, you're second stag. Bob and I will do the third. Get moving."

Hard routine means no fires, no lights, no smoking, so sound, shit in a bag take it with you, cold field rations. Cover everything when you leave, no trace.

Through the night, the men changed stag, slept, ate, and prepared. Jock filled the first two stags in on the plan. All was still good.

At 1630, the light began to fade and the desert took on a very eerie appearance. The time between the light and dark was a difficult time for soldiers. It could play games with your sight. Not until it was dark would they move out. For now, they loaded up, checked their weapons, and then filled in the holes they had dug. Nothing was left. A piece of dried-up bracken was used to brush over the hides.

"Mike, take point, heading 130, we have about 12 clicks. Let's go."

A line of six men fell in, each was about 4 metres behind the one in front. Mike led off at a jog. Even with all the weight in the bergens and now the ordnance they needed for the ships, they jogged off towards the port. The charges they would need were dropped in the weapons crate with them out of the C130. It had been recovered.

A gap was left between the men; SOP. With the space between them, one gunner could not hit two men with the same burst of fire. If they were compromised, they needed space.

There was cloud cover tonight, meaning the darkness was more total. It was also warmer. They all had night-vision goggles and could see well. What they did not need was to silhouette themselves against moonlight. Tonight was good.

The area of desert they were crossing turned into more tended land. Further on and less than an hour into the tab, the ground changed again. A pattern of low walls had been constructed rather like hedgerows, but just earth, well sand. They knew these were here and expected this possible cover, it was a welcome sight. It also meant they were progressing well.

30 minutes later, Mike stopped, hand up, and dropped onto one knee. Everyone copied, keeping their distance. But now, six of them were scanning the horizon in all directions. Weapons up, safety off. For 10 minutes, they just waited and watched. Jock jogged up the side and squatted next to Mike.

"What's up?"

"Tank Berm ahead, 1 o'clock."

Ahead and slightly right was a man-made mound. On one side, which faced Kuwait, it was high. The other side, there was nothing. It was a hollow dug out into the desert where a tank could drive in. The front of the berm would offer maybe 60% protection from an incoming round fired low. The tank could sit, hidden from view almost, then engage its enemy's tank from relative safety.

"Good call, we will box it to the northern side. Half a click."

"Roger that."

Mike led off again at a slower speed for fear of noise. He turned left and walked almost half a kilometre, then turned right, half a click, then right again, another half a click, then left again, back onto the original course. In doing this, they skirted around the tank.

As they passed the rear of the berm, a quick look with the binoculars showed them it was empty. But they did not know that they had to assume the worst. Clear, they sped up again.

Jogging onwards, they cleared two more of these fields, separated by mounds of dirt. The third, Mike stopped again, another tank berm and the same box manoeuvrer was repeated. Better safe than sorry.

Just under 3 hours later, they were stopped again behind the side of a low wadi. From here, they could see the road. Highway 26. Alongside the road was a railway yard with sidings. Four long rows of freight cars stood stationary. There was only one loco which was clearly operational as the cab was dimly lit.

"OK, let's sit here for a while and see what is going on. How much traffic? I want to know how often those freight trains move in and out. That could be our way north once we hit the ships. It would be very good to be on one of them and move when it goes noisy. Joe, Fraser, get closer to the main drag over there, we need a way across the road without being seen. See how many people are in the petrol station and possible threats first, then reccy the road and get us across. 2215 now, back here at midnight. Radio silence unless you are compromised. Approach us only from our six."

Over the next hour, the rest lay in the sand, two looking over the berm towards the road and petrol station. The other two were prone on the floor facing the opposite direction covering their rear, or six.

They counted only one train arriving and departing. The new freight cars were left, the two locos, uncoupled and then shunted back and forth to move tracks, coupled up and pulled away for just 100 metres, checking all was connected and all cars good to go. From what they could see, this operation was completed by the loco driver and mate only, no one else was about, certainly none in military uniform.

There were a variety of freight cars in the full train. Some were for carrying containers, others flat for bulk goods. They could not see any that would give them cover for a journey north, but they were a way off. Closer look may show something possible. Nothing like you imagine from the cowboy and war movies, where you slide a door open and jump in.

Hard routine prevented them from brewing up and getting some hot food. But the wait until midnight did give them a chance to eat some cold field rations and get some water. This was still no time to rest and take their eyes off the ball.

Midnight passed and there was no sign of Joe and Fraser. But this was no flap, radio silence. 30 minutes past their due time, their tactical radios, strapped to their ears and throat, clicked twice. Alerting them all to the approach. The pair watching the rear were using night-vision goggles and picked up the two lads coming in as instructed.

"Two in the garage, but no sign of any military, men or vehicles. We clocked only one car in the hour we were laid up. Not a great source of wheels to go north. 200 metres south of the junction is a drainage pipe under the full road. It is clear and we can crawl through. May need to rope the kit though, which could be noisy. Problem is, this will bring us out right behind the buildings next to the shunting yard.

"300 metres north of the junction the light from the garage is no issue, we can tab over the road quickly. Plenty of cover, skirt the rail yard to the north and get down on the port. From where we went south along the road, we could see the rail track going into the port. There is a tunnel. Plus, a hole in the fence. Could be guarded but I doubt it. That must be our way in. There must be a marshalling yard inside too."

For the next hour, they talked it through. All possibilities, all problems, all routes out, and agreed on the plan. They would move over the highway to the north, box around the outer train yard and enter the port through the train access and tunnel.

Still the same plan of attack, two pairs one for each boat, the third pair were now permanently covering their backs and keeping the escape route clear. If they had a flap on, they would go back to escape through the fence on the northeast perimeter.

What was on their side was the lack of lighting. The port was blacked out. They knew an attack was coming and feared they would be hit.

"We go in 30, you two get some food and water in you. Direct line to cross over point head 45."

They crossed the road easily in the darkness and the rail tracks, continued half a click further into the desert, then turned right and tabbed down towards the port.

0230 and they were concealed in a small but deep wadi. They had climbed up and were lying on a sand dune 200 metres north of the hole in the fence that the trains use. They could clearly see the tunnel access to the port. Behind them due north, about 2 clicks, was a large house or residence. Some high-ranking Iraqi official, possibly to do with the port, would be living it up inside.

"Dig in, sort your shit, Joe, Fraser stag. For the next 24 hours, we watch and learn. Two on stag, two watching, two resting. Someone get a fucking brew on."

Being in a deep wadi gave them cover from any line of sight. It was safe to get a brew and some hot food inside them. For now, they would rest, watch and learn. See who moved where, guards, patrols, trains, visitors, trucks, and anything that would get in the way or compromise their reason for being there.

Um Qasr Port, Iraq
15 March 2003, 0200

Having laid up for the last 24 hours and spent the time watching and learning, they knew most of the comings and goings of the port and traffic. It was very little in the way of movement.

Only four trains had moved in and out of the port through the tunnel. Traffic on the road approaching the port from the north was minimal, with only a handful of vehicles. The whole time they watched, only one security patrol was seen, a 4x4 approached the rail tracks near the perimeter fence. But the two guards only got out for a quick fag and one had a piss.

No real threat was seen and now no real threat was expected. The guessing was any military had been deployed to the frontline to face the Allies, leaving the protection and security of internal infrastructure wanting.

At 0245, they moved out; you would not have known anyone had been in the wadi. By 0300, they were through the tunnel.

As they emerged, to their left, they could see there were storage containers, which offered great cover. No hesitation, they all saw the same thing at the same time and went for it. Squatting down in their defensive circle, they caught their breath.

"This is the rally point, come back here when you're done and we move off together. If it turns to shit, get back here and we will fight our way out from here if we can. Otherwise, see you on the border. Let's go."

There was total cloud cover, no moon or stars. It was almost total darkness. It would be crazy to assume that no one else here had night vision, so caution was still required. Moving from cover to cover, they approached the dockside, working in pairs. Move and cover, move and cover. Now 50 metres apart. They crossed what was the base of an old rail track which had been pulled up. Following this made it easier a direct route to the dockside.

Two tower cranes were in front of them, relatively new compared to the rest of this shit hole. In the water alongside the cranes, two merchantmen were berthed. In between them were the two Navy ships, their targets.

No guards, no security, and no lights on the ships. Not even red lights which made it more difficult to see from a distance. It seemed no one was home. The boarding gangways were in place, and it was simple for each pair to go over and hide on the decks, then wait for any follow-up.

Jock's briefing was to place the charges on the hull as close to the waterline as possible. This was easier said than done without a boat or getting wet. They had devised a plan to drop the charge over the side on a rope and allow a magnet to fix it to the side. Each charge pack weighed 10 kg and they had two each. They would all be very happy to leave this weight behind.

The charges were dropped with them in the arms crate from the aircraft and had fallen approx. 500 m from where they all landed. A locator beacon allowed them to find it.

10 kg of Semtex could do a lot of damage alone, but these charges were different. It was a coil of Semtex explosive strip that had a 5-millimetre thick V-shaped copped bottom. The explosive filling the top of the V. This was rolled into a coil. When it exploded, the copper would be propelled by the force and cut right through almost anything in its way. This just makes sure they had a nice hole.

The packs were roped up and the timers were pre-set for 30 minutes. They had agreed to extend this to 40 minutes to give them extra time to get out and hopefully catch a train north.

The first two charges clamped on magnetically easily to the side of the ship. Swinging the bomb about in mid-air may seem a little crazy, but Semtex is like

Play-Doh until you fire it. The third charge fell, dropped into the water, and was lost. One ship only had one charge.

The pair from boat 1 were first back to the exit rally point. 'Click, click' announced their approach. 10 minutes later, they were all back.

"Any flaps? No? Let's go catch a train."

The locos were not moving and were now attached to the long row of freight cars. This was now a good bet. It was possible it would be moving off very soon. Many of the cars were flatbedded and loaded with odd shapes of cargo. It had been pre-agreed this was the best cover if it was available. From a distance, it was not possible to be sure but close up it was good.

They would jump the train and take their chances that it would get them away from the blasts. Now the job was done, it was, and there were only 22 minutes left before the charges were initiated. Then it would go noisy.

On the western side of the tracks, in between two of the buildings, was a Toyota Pickup and one guard. As they came up the tracks from the fence, they clocked the truck.

Moving along the eastern side of the tracks away from the buildings on the western side, as close to the front of the train as they could, they climbed up and pushed in between the freight on two different but adjacent cars.

14 minutes to go. They waited. A good sign as the train jerked when the two locos bumped into the coupling. They expected to move within minutes.

10 minutes to go. Nothing, no movement. If they did move off and the drivers heard the thump and flash of the charges, they may stop. Suddenly, this was not a good idea.

8 minutes to go.

"Fuck this, we can't sit here. Let's go for the truck over there. We need to drop the guard."

On the far side of the compound, the Toyota flatbed was still there. A technical without the gun on the back. They had no choice and could not risk hanging around for the train to move. Dropping down from the train, they crossed over, using other trains as cover to as near the Toyota as possible.

"I got this," Jock said. "Fraser, with me, the rest cover your arcs. We don't need this to go noisy now, don't fire unless it is absolutely needed."

Jock moved in the darkness. He knew his night vision cast a green glow on his face which would be seen as he got close. The guard was about 45 years old. Scruffy, poorly dressed. He wore the traditional Arab Shemag. His weapon was leaning on the front of the vehicle whilst he was near the driver's side door. The door was open and the radio was on. Not loud but he had some music playing. Western music, not Arabic.

If there was a guard looking after the truck, then where were the people that were using it? As soon as they took it, the follow-up would be instant. But what else can they do?

Jock went to the opposite side of the truck and moved along its length, round the back and came up behind the guard. One swift and silent movement with a combat knife and he lay dead, never knowing who had sent him to his God. He did not fall to the ground, Jock held him, and together with Fraser, they moved him back onto the departing train, whenever it was actually going to depart that is.

"Let's go, four in the back two in the front."

"No! push it, push it as far as we can from the building. Then they won't hear it start."

"Good call, let's go."

The radio had been on and the keys were in the ignition. One climbed in to steer whilst the others pushed.

5 minutes to go and 200 metres of pushing, they loaded up, started up and were gone, heading north on Highway 26. At this time of the night, there would be little traffic and they were driving on night vision, so no lights.

They were 6 miles away when the charges blew. They heard nothing and saw nothing, but they knew the damage was done. They knew there would now be a follow-up. The body, the missing truck. They knew they would now be hunted.

What they did not know was that the man they had killed was not a guard; the buildings were empty and he was there to look for things to take from the trains. He was nicking stuff. His body was now moving slowly north on the train and would not be found until it was unloaded in Baghdad. His car would never be noticed. The dead man should not have been there. No one would miss him, except his family of course.

Using a stolen truck on the open road, with full camo clothing and kit was not the best of plans to stay alive. The truck needed to be ditched and they had to get back on foot to move now towards the secondary targets. Dawn was less than 2 hours away and they needed to hide up somewhere for the day.

Turning off the 26 at a place signposted Al Jabid, they made a right towards the Um Qasr site, drove for 500 metres and dumped the car. Puncturing all 4 tyres, they made sure it would not be coming back to haunt them further along the road.

Back out into the desert, they now had to find a layup point. There were many small holdings or farms in this area and this could provide cover. A lot of the people had moved away from the border with Kuwait. They knew the war was coming and wanted to get as far away from where clearly a lot of the ground action would take place.

During the first conflict Iraq had invaded Kuwait, the Allies pushed them out but then had to stop. This time, there was no one in Kuwait. But Sadham was no fool; whilst the attack on his country was taking place, he could try once again to annex Kuwait, the lost state of Iraq. This was going to be denied. The main crossing point into Kuwait from Iraq was Safwan.

The secondary target was to shut down the crossing point.

Jock spent an hour going over the plan to attack the second target. This time, they would not be alone when the attack went in. It would be attacked from the air. They had to guide the ordnance onto the target and light it up with infrared (IR). The lads would shine a laser onto the target. This reflects and forms like a cone of IR light. The aircraft and bomb could see this and the bomb guided itself into the cone. Very accurate.

All they had to do was to get into a position to light up the target for the aircraft. Into position on, or close to a border post, heavily guarded, full of people, trucks, goods, kids and families, all crossing one way or the other.

The attack was timed for 0030 hours on 20 March, the first hours of the air war. Iraq was going to be denied the use of this road and crossing. At this time, there will be few people and hopefully no civilians.

"We have two laser designators, so two teams of three. Joe and Fraser on me. The targets are the roadways Iraq side of the crossing. We will light up the road within 10 metres of the border and our friends will plant a 500 pounder. Create a huge crater. We will also light the area between the two customs sheds. Same again, 500 pounder will destroy these and access around them.

"Once this has gone, our crazy fucking Tornado friends in the RAF will come over low-level and use the JP233 systems to deny the road from here approx. 1 click north. We need to be as far away as possible when they get here. Minimum 1 click and flat somewhere, obviously not to the north."

Again, a lot of discussion, ideas, routes, and exits were gone through. The aircraft crews knew they were in theatre and, to a point, vulnerable.

"In my view, the main issue we have is height. We need to get some elevation to use the designators more effectively. What, do we have any ideas?"

"Nothing and you're right. We need to get in the day before and reccy where to go and where to run. The pre-agreed coordinates are the Exfil 0600 on 20 March. If we miss this, they will come back on 21 at the same time. No comms with base. If we are there and hear the chopper, we will flare IR. Once the bombs hit, we need to be moving towards our Exfil, and quickly. We need to be on target the night of 19, choose our points, and reccy a route back to Exfil."

Safwan, Iraq
18 March, 0100

As agreed, they split into two teams of three. One team had moved slightly north and towards the Iraqi border post. The other team was skirting the border fence towards the actual point where the road out of Kuwait crossed into Iraq.

One bomb would crater the road at the crossing. A second would demolish the Iraqi Army border post and the infrastructure there.

Once these two targets were clear, the RAF would then deny the use of the approach road from inner Iraq to the border post. The aim was to prevent and deny any Iraqi forces trying to cross into Kuwait.

The north team had spent most of the previous three nights looking for an advantage point with some height. They needed to be a good click from the impact site and they also needed to be able to target the correct buildings, so line of sight was important. The terrain was flat, in all directions, flat as flat could be, apart from buildings. The main town lay to the east and north of the Iraqi border facility. To the west, it was desert and flat desert.

Locating on a building would risk being compromised. Plus, they had to be in place a minimum of 12 hours ahead of the strike. This presented even more opportunities to be discovered.

The first night dismissed any use of the town's buildings and highlighted the possibilities of civilian casualties in the event of a firefight. Night two was spent to the west of the border looking for cover with some height. The issue here was that the Exfil point agreed with the command was the other side of the main highway and the other side of the bomb strikes. This meant once they hit, they needed to cross over the area of damage. Possible but not ideal.

Early in the morning, just before dawn, the north team had located a large tank berm about 1 click from the border crossing. This was designed for two large or three small tanks. The berms to the sides and front were larger than they had come across before on the march to the port.

This gave enough elevation to target and designate the buildings in the Iraqi facility. It also gave enough elevation to see and designate the border crossing itself. Meaning that both the north team and the fence team could use the same position.

The following day, it was agreed all six men would move to the berm and the attack would be initiated from there. At the same time, a second berm, a further 10 clicks west, was found and this was to be the new Exfil location.

Details were transmitted to the command and the new pickup point was set.

All six of them in the same location would mean if they were challenged, they could fight their way out more easily, but they risked losing the whole squad if the attacking forces were large.

It was now 2300 on 19 March. All six men were in place. Their kits were packed on their backs and they were ready to move and move fast to get away.

The planned time of the attack was 0030 hrs on 20 March. 200 mtrs out from the berm on the west, north and east points, an infrared flare had been left. This was flaring and could be recognised by friendly aircraft. It marked the position of the covert troops on the ground.

Each man had IR flares on their own belt kits. These too would be lit once the attack had gone in and they were moving north to the Exfil point. These were to allow any aircrew coming in to see their position if there was a firefight or other contact on the ground.

0015 hrs and the two laser designators were turned on, targeted on the points of attack. Each had an eerie electronic wine as the invisible ray was sent to the target, bounced off and formed a cone of IR light for the smart bomb to follow.

The two operators lay still, motionless and waited. The other four covered their arcs of fire, safety off, and waited.

At 0025, the radio crackled, and two call signs, "Inbound 5 minutes, acquired." Then dead. 2 minutes later, two more call signs. "Released, good luck." The distant roar of jet engines on full military power could be heard, turning the aircraft away as quickly as possible.

Time stopped. Everything went totally silent. Somewhere in the blackness two loads of 500 lbs of high explosive fell to earth. Looking and guiding themselves into an IR cone of light. Only during the last seconds would you hear a whine or whistle. It was too late.

Night turned to day with a flash, then seconds later, the sound hit the berm, then the shockwave. In the last 10 seconds before impact, all six had dropped down to the bottom of the inner berm wall. Curled up in a ball, covered their ears and prayed.

The shockwave blows outwards from the blast and hot air rushes with it. As it dissipates and the air cools, it rushes back the opposite way. Then airborne debris will return to earth.

For now, they were going to stay where they were, huddled up, not safe but as safe as it gets this close to the blast.

2 minutes later, they moved out. No looking back, their job was done; they did not give a shit, they needed to move. IR flares on, and they moved out on the heading for the second berm 10 clicks away. Standard operating procedures clicked in on auto and they fell into a single line, walking as fast as they could. The ground was too rough and unpredictable to jog, otherwise they would have moved quicker. They did not need any broken bones.

Every 5 minutes to start, the line stopped. Each man covered his arc of fire. Night-vision goggles allowed them to see anything or any movement. Nothing, move on.

As they put distance between themselves and the attack, the time between stops increased. The risk of follow-up was reduced.

10 minutes into the Exfil, the radios came to life once again. Four call signs, "Incoming south to north 150 ft, 700 knots, out." These were the Tornados. A minute later, four aircraft streaked overhead, silently. The sound followed seconds later.

They crossed the town and hit the road on the approach to the border crossing. In V-pattern formation right down the road and 40 ft on each side of it, small bomblets were released, exploding craters into the surface, destroying the road and any chance of using it. To each side of the road, it was destroyed in the same way.

They were up and moving, not looking back except for looking for any follow-up from Iraqi forces. None came.

The Exfil location was roughly 10 clicks and it would take 2 hours minimum in full kit over this terrain. They would arrive knackered, scared and relieved.

Chapter 14

Scotland Yard, London
2330

Having cleared the extensive security to get into Scotland Yard, Will had just been given his sidearm back and was checking it one more time to be safe. He was in uniform and had refused to release control of his briefcase at the x-ray machine.

A policeman had offered to visually inspect the laptops it contained. He was taken into a side room, away from the main entrance concourse. Two armed police officers were with him.

"Sorry, Sir, please take a seat. We understand the issues and you need to work with us to make sure everyone here is safe, as well as yourself."

"It is fine, Officer. What the laptops contain is, shall we say, sensitive. You must understand that I cannot and will not allow you to see anything that is secure."

"That's fine, Sir, if you could please just turn on the computer. We need to see the boot sequence and witness the log into Windows."

Will hit the button and the laptop keyboard lit up and the power and HDD lights came on as normal. The screen came up and showed the BIOS commands loading, and eventually, the Windows login screen was shown.

He then took the card from the lanyard around his neck and pushed this into the right side of the laptop. This automatically entered the username in the space provided on the screen. The password was still blank.

Typing slowly, Will entered a 20-symbol password and hit enter. The screen changed and waited, then a welcome screen stated BIO. To the right side of the keyboard was a fingerprint reader. Will then had to slowly drag his right index finger over the reader.

The screen changed again and the word 'next' appeared.

Again, he dragged a different finger over the scanner. No one would know the password. Even if the card was stolen, the password was required. If they had both password and card, the fingerprints were required. Not one but two. The only person who knew which fingers was Will himself.

This was about as secure as any login for Windows could be. It satisfied the two police officers that it was a working laptop and that the login was secure and MoD.

He was approached by a different police officer who led the way back to the lift and to the higher levels of the building. As they exited the lift, the commissioner was there to greet Will.

"Group Captain, follow me please, welcome to Scotland Yard."

The commissioner led Will into his office. It was late at night and his secretary was not there. The two armed officers still protected the access to his office suite.

"Help yourself to a hot drink and any of the sandwiches, Group Captain, they are fresh."

Will was hungry, he had not realised the ways things moved so quickly. To be honest, he did not expect to be in London right now, or with the Met Police Commissioner. It was a long time since he had eaten, so he grabbed a sandwich and a coffee and then joined the commissioner at the conference table.

Sir Robert knew that the RAF Group Captain was going to be very tight-lipped over the report he was referring to and his concerns. Although he was here, he was governed by a different level of authority and unless this barrier was opened, it would not be possible for an open discussion.

"Group Captain, everything we discuss here tonight, between you and I, is privileged. When we conclude our meeting, we will jointly decide together if anything we have talked about can be used to help with stopping this carnage, or prevent any more loss of life, however small. Only if we both agree, will we move forwards. If we do not agree, there will be no questions or recriminations. I will arrange to get you back to your own office and this meeting will never have happened. I am fully aware that you are risking the remainder of your career by being here with me tonight."

"Thank you, Sir, But I have to be sure the room is secure, I have to ask. I have a duty to protect this information, I mean no disrespect."

"The room is secure; I will take full responsibility for the security whilst you are here with us. Please do not worry."

Will took out his laptop and his working notes. The laptop did not need to be connected to any network as the files he needed were on the drive itself. He picked up the power supply, plugged it into the laptop, then stopped and looked at Sir Robert.

"May I?"

"Yes, of course, go ahead."

As the laptop came to life, Will considered an opening question for Sir Robert that would confirm that he was on safe ground.

"Sir, what we are doing right now could be considered an act of treason. It contravenes the Official Secrets Act and in short, could land both of us in a whole lot of deep trouble."

"Thank you, Group Captain, I was expecting a comment like this from you, and I am glad to see you had the balls to ask. This meeting is not happening, simple as that. Now, what have you got?"

"Sir, as I have already briefed you from Brampton, part of the work we do at JARIC is to look at countries and decide just how to disable it with as little loss of life and damage as possible. The use of smart weapons and other modern methods of war now allows this to happen. This starts with the team at JARIC looking at both the military and civil infrastructure. The military targets are somewhat easier. If we destroy a runway, then the enemy cannot take off, that removes the air threat instantly. We do not need to destroy the aircraft.

"Remove the command-and-control centres and degrade their ability to act and deploy military assets against us. Likewise with communications. Stop the head talking to the tail. Both military and civilians alike depend on normal resources. Water, gas, and power. Remove these and it will severely disrupt what they consider normal life. When people are cold and hungry, they will look for other means to feed and keep their families warm. Civil disobedience. So, push this along by making it difficult for the authorities within the country to work. If the people don't back the action taken by their governments anymore, change will come about.

"I was working alone on a study of the UK to highlight exactly this, to research and identify exactly these points for the UK. How would I bring the UK to its knees? Looking at what to hit and how to stop it being repaired quickly. What is happening is too close to my report for it to be a coincidence."

Over the next 3 hours, he took the commissioner through the results of the work he had done.

Starting with major targets and working down to minor opportunities and then looking at the ways he had considered disrupting social life and the way society functions.

There were too many similarities to the attacks that had already happened. The shock and awe part of the scenario.

Will had identified the gas pipelines as a valid target, plus the need to hit the capital city of London in some way. Surprisingly, his examination looked for an inner London power facility that could be disabled, only to shut down power to the government. The identification of the city Gen plant, by whoever had found it, was in his view a master stroke. Not only had it damaged London's power grid but it also disabled the underground and put London into meltdown.

Will continued to explain his reasoning through lower grade targets and then moved through the need to disrupt the normal function of society, our way of life.

At no time did the commissioner comment. Will finished, and as a habit, just said, "Questions?"

"Well, Group Captain, impressive. Very impressive. Also accurate beyond what you already know. There is one set of attacks which are not yet public knowledge and we have kept all the data as far as possible secret, away from the press and any form of reporting. Your own plan looks to disrupt the normal way of life. Would you consider that attacking the police and stopping them from functioning, or even wanting to function would fit your scenario?"

There was no hesitation. "Of course, it would bring about a breakdown in law and order and plunge the country deeper into chaos. I have even considered how to do this myself."

The commissioner continued. "Over the last few days, we have seen two attacks on the police themselves, very clever attacks, and we have lost many police officers. In one incident, a motorway patrol stopped a motorist who had been following them for some time up and down the M1. When they got out of the car to talk to the driver, he detonated a bomb killing himself and two officers.

"A second incident involving three police vehicles carrying out a TPAC stop was blown apart in the same way by the driver detonating a bomb of some sort. He waited until all three patrol cars had stopped, then set it off. All six officers died. Net result is that the frontline police are now hesitant to get involved as they fear walking into a trap of some form. Who can blame them?"

"No way, fuck! Sorry, Sir."

"Don't worry, that is far less than I was heard to say when I was told."

Will was shocked further. His own report contained a detailed analysis of just such methods of disrupting law and order. The fact that this was now being used started to worry him greatly.

"Sir Robert, my report suggests exactly such action, hi-visibility strikes on the police, put the fear of God into them and they will not function as they should. This is far too close to my report. In everything that has happened, I have predicted or suggested similar targets. There is no doubt in my mind someone has a copy of this report and has used it to attack us in the UK.

"The only way this could have happened is for someone with security clearance equal to, or above mine, to have found the required document control and then found a way to get to the document itself. The document was on MoD servers only. Even this had been encrypted above and beyond the MILSPEC requirements. Only five RAF personnel knew the document existed. If this has been shared or leaked, then it must be one of these five. Of which I am one."

The commissioner hesitated for a moment before talking. His head was off in a different place but came back quickly.

"Do you agree, Group Captain, that there are too many pointers to the fact that this document has been used against us?"

"Yes, Sir, of course I do. It is clear, obvious."

"Then you must agree, just as we laid out at the start of this discussion, we must act upon what you have brought here today. We need to look at not only how this report has been leaked, or stolen, but how to use this information to our advantage. Do you agree?"

"Yes, Sir, yes, I do."

The commissioner rose and walked round the room, three circuits of the long table, hands in his pockets and his head again somewhere else. It was a hugely long 10 minutes before he stopped and sat down again. His face had changed. No longer pensive but not positive.

"Group Captain, I am going to request that you be assigned to my command until we have dealt with and eliminated the threat we now face to the UK. I will go to the highest levels of government and have this agreed upon within the next 20 minutes. It is possible you may have to brief COBRA but I do not believe this will be necessary. Yet!

"I will prepare a document for you to read and sign. This is just a reminder of the terms and conditions of the Official Secrets Act, which you have already signed. This is voluntary but if you choose not to sign, you will be removed back to Brampton. Sorry. It is paramount that you are fully aware of the severity and penalties of any breach of this agreement. We need to know you are 100% aware and working with us to keep the secure surroundings we need to function."

Will nodded. "Yes, Sir."

What the hell have I done? Will was so unsure, worried if he had acted correctly. He went directly to the commissioner and bypassed his own chain of command. That could be seen as very bad. But there was a clear security breach and he had to do what was best to protect the UK.

Hang me if you must, what I did was correct, Will thought.

The commissioner had been gone less than 5 minutes when Will's MoD email pinged on the laptop. There was a new message in his inbox from his boss, higher up the chain of command.

Here we go, thought Will.

"Group Captain Rivers, you have been temporarily reassigned to work with the Met police. Sir Robert Mark has requested your services as liaison and explained everything fully. The issues with the report and what has happened in London are considered paramount and you have acted totally correctly. JARIC resources are still at your full disposal. Good luck."

"Fuck me, what a relief. Sir Robert has some serious strings to pull on. He has just removed my ass out of the firing line. I need to make this work."

10 minutes later, Sir Robert had returned and Will had signed the document prepared by the commissioner.

There were two copies, one for the commissioner himself or for the record and one for Will. Once signed, he placed the official copy in his desk drawer and gave the other to Will.

"We need to find you some space to operate. Let me know if you're going to bring any of your people in to assist, and get your RAF people to contact this man and set up the data links; whatever they need, we can arrange it. But quickly, time to take the fight out there. Do you RAF Officers still have a Batman chap looking after you on base?"

"Yes, Sir, I have an orderly that works with me."

"Good, write down his details for me. My staff will make contact and ask he packs for you for a long stay in London. All you need in the way of clothes and uniform, personal things. I think a few hours is enough time for him to accomplish this. Then, it will be collected and brought here to Scotland Yard.

On the top floor, we have some small rooms that can be used for overnight stays when major incidents happen. I will get you a room. You live and breathe here now.

"As of now, Group Captain, you're a copper. You work for me. I will explain more very soon. Go to your room, and get your head down for a few hours. I will let you know when your gear arrives."

He called someone and 5 minutes later, Will was on his way to the top floor and given a room. The room was just that a room. A bed, a table, a sink, a window. Further down the corridor was a bathroom and showers. These rooms were designed to be functional, not luxurious. You want luxury, help yourself to a London hotel.

Will looked at the bed, fell on it, and was gone. He was exhausted but jerked awake 15 minutes later, he had to go to work.

It was now 0715 in the morning. The commissioner had not slept now for 32 hours. He needed to let go. Opening his door, he called one of the guards.

"In one hour, bang on the door and keep banging until I answer. I need to rest a bit, not for long."

"Sir."

He laid his head on his arms for 30 seconds, or what seemed 30 seconds before the door was being banged into life in his head.

When he awoke, there was fresh coffee and fresh food, and his secretary was now in place and working.

Instantly, he was back online and working. Focussed. It was said that during the war, Churchill never slept properly. He would sit in his chair and put a bunch of keys in his hand then sleep. As he entered deep sleep, the keys would fall off and wake him. That was enough to refresh him and keep him going. Sir Robert never considered himself a Churchill but he was able to deal with stress and work with small cat naps, just the same.

Phone in hand, he made a call to the police sergeant who was with him the previous day.

"Sergeant, I want all three of you back here for 1000. Drop everything and get here. Just you three, no one else. The teams can wait until later."

He also needed a room to use as a base for the RAF liaison, Will and his soon-to-be team. His issue was that because of the reasoning around Will being here, he could not risk anything, therefore it had to be set up within his own office suite.

There was his own office, plus his conference room. At one end of the conference room was a sectioned-off area where his secretary worked. That was it. She had a large desk with a computer and printer, a separate table, and a coffee machine.

"It would have to do. We may need to move the screens away and open it up to the main room. Jean won't mind."

What was going to be done together with Will had to remain top secret.

"Jean, do you have a minute please?"

He waited and Jean came into the office, pad and pencil in hand, sat down opposite.

"Sorry, Jean, I need to use your office for an RAF Officer who has arrived as a liaison link to the MoD. He needs to be in the conference room but we need this too for our planning. I want him to use your desk. I will get you moved to the space at the end of the corridor where the two guards are now. It will put you in a position to make sure no one gets in here that you don't want. I am sorry. Please don't worry, as soon as this is over, I want you back in here where you belong."

Jean was no fool, this was her third commissioner and Sir Robert was the best. A totally honest and decent man. She was in awe of him and what he had done for the Met. She did not mind one little bit.

15 minutes later, Jean and the coffee machine, most importantly, had been moved and the screens had gone too. The empty desk looked much larger now.

Will came back down from his room and walked past Jean, sitting at a new desk outside of the commissioner's office. She gestured with a smile and he continued into the conference room. No chance to open his mouth to say anything as Sir Robert was in there.

"Ah, Group Captain, we have moved Jean out to bolster the guards and to create some space for you and your men when they arrive. Have you considered anyone that should join you yet?"

"The only people that are cleared are my 2ICs (second in command), so it must be them. I have not done anything about it yet."

"Make the calls, Group Captain, I will have a car at the base in one hour to collect them. Also, get your Batman chap to sort your kit in the same car. One hour, the car will be there."

Will grabbed a phone and got through to RAF Brampton. He knew one of the two men would be working, and the other would be off duty.

"Greg, get your kit together for an unexpected trip, you need enough for at least 2 weeks to be sure. Raise Henry too, kick him out of bed and have him ready with you in one hour at the gate guardroom. My orderly will give you my kit bag. No questions and neither of you is to discuss this with anyone. Am I clear? We will brief you on arrival. Both of you draw side arms from the armoury."

"Arrival where, boss? Side arms?"

"As I said, briefing on arrival, all will become clear. Not a word. A police car will collect you in one hour, no questions. Enjoy the ride."

"Enjoy the ride? What the fuck is going on now?"

Within the hour, both wing commanders were stood at the gatehouse, together with a kit bag packed for Will. Both were in uniform and both had a side arm strapped to their side.

Bang on time, one of the Cambridgeshire police E350 Mercs pulled up. It stopped and two officers got out, one opened the boot. "Your bags please, sirs, in the boot."

Once they were packed, they then asked to check the weapons. Only when they were sure the guns were safe, did they continue.

"Sorry about the checks but we need to be sure always."

Both responded at the same time, "No worries."

They got in the back and the blues came on; the Merc took off south, following the same route that Will had earlier.

Greg looked at Henry, raised his eyebrows, and got a 'who knows' gesture back. They tried to relax back into their seats but it was going to be difficult. Maybe better not to watch.

Chapter 15

Gas National Control Centre (GNCC)
Warwick
12 November, 1000

The conference room was full, eighteen people, from the head of National Grid to the pipeline engineers that run the systems. They were all still in shock at seeing the system removed so instantly and the loss of life, of people they knew.

They were further shocked to get the call from Scotland Yard to prepare for this discussion. Everyone had been working constantly, no one had gone home, sleeping at their desks or wherever they could lay down. But sleep would not come; no one slept, just lay staring into space.

At 1000 hrs exactly, the screens in the large conference system came to life. Facing the eighteen people were just two men in uniform, the Metropolitan Police Commissioner and an RAF Officer.

With no hesitation, Sir Robert started the call.

"Good morning, I am Sir Robert Mark, Met Police Commissioner, and this is Group Captain William Rivers. You will understand that we do not have the time for any pleasantries. I need an update on your status, as of now, plus what is happening. This is not a witch hunt, no one is being checked upon; we just need the hard facts of life as it is now. Is that clear?"

The head of the table rose, then sat down again.

"Yes, Sir, it is clear. John Yates, head of overall engineering. I am leading the operation to restore gas supplies. The situation is as follows.

1. Whoever did this had done their homework and taken out the main junctions of the gas grid, together with a lot of compressor assets. This has shut the grid down dramatically as we all know. Sure, these details are on the internet, but the in-depth knowledge needed to understand where to hit has been assembled with a lot of hard-to-get information.

2. Reinstatement or repair time is 2-3 years. Damage will have spread far away from the sites along the pipe. It all needs to come out and start over.
3. Plans are progressing to bypass these sites with smaller bore systems in place. Although no one ever expected to have this level of destruction, plans were put in place to bypass a failed site. This means within 2 weeks, we could have 50-60% capacity backup on the gas grid.
4. That is as good as we can expect at this time, Sir, everyone here is flat out to get the bypass in place and operational.

"Do you have any questions, Sir?"

Sir Robert responded very quickly, "Please bear with me, I am not being rude but we need to discuss something, and I will cut the connection in the meantime."

The meeting room screens went black and sound was cut. Everyone looked very surprised. Now they are here, now they are gone.

Sir Robert turned to Will, a very concerned look on his face.

"You predicted that the grid could recover from a strike by bypassing the stricken compressors. I don't care how you knew but what have you planned to stop this happening?"

Will was ahead of the commissioner.

"Yes, Sir, that is correct. Hitting other compressors would not have the same impact. Ok, it will hurt, but it is the pipes now. The pipe infrastructure would need to be hit. For us, that is an easy task, plot where the pipes are and then break them with a bomb."

"Oh, that's OK then. How the fuck do we defend it? These bloody pipes are buried in the ground, how can we even follow them?"

The response was a little irritated but Will didn't care. He can see the frustration of the situation. But again, he was there and ahead of the commissioner.

"Simple, Sir. Have you ever driven down the road and seen a white and orange pole, that says 'Gas High-Pressure Main', there to stop some idiot in a JCB digging it up? Every place a pipe crosses a road, it is marked. Even unmade roads. If whoever this is has read my report, they will now be looking at doing just that, finding the pipes and cutting them. We would use ground-penetrating ordinance. Quick and simple. Unless they have an aircraft, they need to dig. Dig down to the pipe and plant a charge. We can stop the bastards they need time to dig."

A conversation took place before they went back to the GNCC meeting.

Again, Sir Robert was straight in, no time to waste.

"I am sorry about that but we operate at high-security levels and some of the conversation was classified. Please forgive us. You mentioned the plans for the bypass to become active. Firstly, 2 weeks is unacceptable, we need this in days, 1 week is maximum. If you need resources to help you, whatever this is, you come to me and ask. Understood.

"Secondly, we expect whoever this is to try to disrupt the bypass and continue the shutdown of the gas system. To do this, they will now target the pipeline itself. We know it is underground, but they will dig to get to it. Access will be from a road where the pipe crosses, or nearby. We, therefore, need a map of all the pipes you intend to use to complete and operate this bypass. It must show us every single place one of the pipes crosses a road. No mistakes, each and every crossing needs to be plotted. I know this may be many thousand but we need to know.

"Every crossing is a potential point that these people may choose to attack again and disrupt the bypass. Have I made myself clear? When can you assemble this data and have it available for our analysis? Plus, we need a list of any such site or position where genuine NG contractors are operating. If you have ongoing works anywhere on the pipeline, I need to know."

John Yates spoke again, rising once again to his feet to walk to a huge map on the wall. He stood studying it for a few long seconds.

"I can see what you are saying but this is a massive task."

Sir Robert cut in very quickly. "The blast in London was massive, 7000 people died."

"Yes, Sir, apologies. We will get on them immediately. You will have this in a couple of days."

Again, Sir Robert was all over John.

"I need data today, as fast as you assemble some of it, I want it. It may be better to suspend all work on the pipes you have in progress. This way, we can assume that anyone with a digger digging a hole near a pipe crossing on the road is hostile. Do you see what I mean?"

John was back and a little pissed off.

"How are you going to monitor so many options continually? There are thousands."

"My problem, Mr Yates, but I have the resources I need, well so I am told. We will expect to see something from you within hours and this will then continue until we get the job done. Stop all NG repair activities on any pipe road crossing until further notice. That order starts now, please clear any site of digging machinery and plant. Thank you for your time. Please do not take this personally, we are all tired and worried. Let us stop these bastards together."

The screens went blank once again and they were gone.

The only person in the whole room that had spoken was John Yates, all the others sat there with their mouths open.

"Let's go to it, people, we all heard the man, we are defending the country. I need that data as quickly as possible, use anyone and everyone who is capable of helping. No point in compiling a list, print maps of the pipelines, just highlight every crossing on the map. As soon as a map section is complete, it goes to Scotland Yard. Keep a copy for us too. Stop all work and recall all our. If it is too far away, move it at least 1 mile away from the crossing and cover it with a tarpaulin or something. It is a way of marking it as one of ours, I guess."

Will and the commissioner sat for about 15 seconds staring into space. Both heads away in different directions absorbing what they had just heard and discussed.

"Group Captain, this is all very well but as the man said, there are thousands of places they could attack the pipe. We cannot stop them."

Will was already there in his head.

"We can I think, Sir, use the RAF. Plot the routes of the pipes and fly down them. Each crossing can be plotted into the aircraft target systems and if we use the camera systems on the Tornados, we can monitor these roads quickly and continually. The crews will soon get used to the pipe runs and see anything they don't like.

"As GNCC pass the locations, we start flying continually and watching. The camera data can be analysed by JARIC; we can have almost instant confirmation of possible threats. We know there is no work allowed by anyone at these points from now. Anything we see will be hostile. If we spot a bad guy, we kill them. No questions, kill them."

Sir Robert came to life.

"How can we hit them quickly? Sending troops or police takes time and will be noticed. We must hit them from the air."

"All very possible, Sir. We will need ground attack aircraft available in the air, just waiting, whilst the Tornados patrol the potential targets. If the cameras and JARIC see activity, it is passed to the AWACS and they coordinate the strike. We don't need massive bombs, just enough to top them, even cannon fire, then we follow up with feet on the ground. This means if we follow the routes of the pipes, we do not need to wait for GNCC to send data, we just need the pipe runs. If we locate some activity, we will know it has to be bad.

"With your permission, we need to escalate this to the MoD and get the balls rolling, then I can liaise with the RAF and yourself."

Sir Robert seemed to relax; his shoulders dropped very slightly.

"Set it up, Group Captain. I will initiate the liaison with the MoD for you, then you take over. I have seen your record; you are more than able to handle this task. Work from this room, let me know what you need. I am going to double the guard on access to my suite. This does not fail."

Sir Robert sat and picked up the phone.

"Get me Downing Street, I need to speak with the PM and his team."

Less than a minute later, the phone rang.

"Good morning, Sir, Sir Robert here, and I have Wing Commander Will Rivers sitting with me; he is cleared to the highest level.

"Over the past few hours, we have discovered some disturbing news and perhaps some better news. We need to brief COBRA and we need to do it now; I need permission to fly attack missions from aircraft within the UK."

The phone was on speaker and so was the system at No. 10. On the other end, Will heard mutters which ranged from 'Fuck me' to 'Jesus'. These folks were tired, haggard, devasted, all in one emotion.

Cameron spoke. "How soon can you be ready, Sir Robert?"

"We are on the way, Sir. I need this approved, and I need this approved now. We will explain as I am sure you all expect."

That was it, the phone went dead, no goodbye, how's your dog or anything, just cut off. Why waste the time and energy? Shit was happening, and Will had stuck his head upright in the middle of everything.

"Let's go, Group Captain, bring your gear with you. You're about to brief the government."

No waiting. Sir Robert picked up the phone and called someone who was now jumping about doing what he had been told. "I need to get to COBRA fast. I need a car and armed escort."

By the time they arrived at the front door of Scotland Yard, there were two BMW X5 4X4s waiting, plus four heavily armed crews, doors open waiting for the passengers.

This could have been walked very easily a matter of a few hundred yards but it was too dangerous. Both are prime targets for terrorists.

As Sir Robert got to the front door, he stopped dead.

"Fuck, come with me, Group Captain, we need to go back upstairs. There is something else you need to understand."

Back they went upstairs, passing the now four armed police officers tasked to protect the commissioners.

Once in his office, he sat at his desk and looked very disturbed.

"What I am going to tell you, only four other people know. This is the highest level of security and you will not discuss this with anyone anywhere except with me directly. Unless I am with you at the time, you do not discuss this. After the carnage in Spittlefields, I went to the scene together with Cameron and Si'ad Marachi. This was less than an hour after the blast, we were some of the first people on the scene. No one yet knew what had happened and what sort of device had been used to create the blast.

"When I arrived, I was given an NBC suit and told to put it on. A precaution I assumed, possibly a very good one too. I took no notice of this and it was somewhat fulfilling seeing Cameron puking up inside his when he saw the scene. I never said that, ok?

"About an hour later, once we had left, I was informed about what had happened and that part of the explosion involved liquid ammonia used as a refrigerant. At the time we visited the site, no one knew this information, but I was given protection. Why? This bothered me and set off alarm bells amongst my staff. Cameron and I had no idea that there was possible gas contamination at the scene. So only Si'ad could have known there was a risk. Hence, the suits.

"I have briefed some very close trustworthy people to start to watch Si'ad. But this has not started. I must initiate this later today. Your theory that someone has your report showing how to disable the UK may be more correct than you originally thought."

Will was now confused.

"Sorry, you lost me, Sir. Who is this Marachi person? Why was he there anyway? Why look at him?"

"He is the head of the SIS, direct control over the operation following the terrorist cells, the attempt to arrest them and bring them down. He would also have free access to your documentation. On or off the base where you work. He can see whatever he needs to see."

Will was stunned.

"Fuck!"

"Fuck exactly, Group Captain."

"Why is he not dead or at least in custody?"

"Cut off the head, another one will grow; we need to take the whole snake with it."

Sir Robert now sat at his desk, picked up the phone, asked for the PM again, replaced the handset and turned to Will once more.

"The problem I have, Group Captain, is that the head of the SIS sits on COBRA. If our fears are correct, then we are about to inform the enemy of our plans to stop him. We cannot address the full COBRA assembly and I need to discuss this with Cameron."

The phone rang and made both of them jump; any free time and both heads go into overdrive within themselves looking at the data.

"Sir, sorry to disturb you further. There is a possibility that internal security is compromised and we consider at this time, rightly or wrongly, that Marachi is involved in what has happened. What we need to discuss can therefore not be heard at a full COBRA meeting. We need to brief only the few people required to decide. I cannot risk the full attendance at COBRA."

"So be it, Sir Robert, who do you need?"

"Yourself, Sir, Home Office and MoD. That is all, no one else."

"Come to number 10, see you there."

Gone, again, no pleasantries.

The four armed police were still in position, had not moved from the vehicles, and were still covering their arcs. Well-trained, totally professional. Both passengers were loaded and they sped off towards No. 10.

No. 10, Downing Street
12 November, 1105

The whole day so far to Will was a dream. He was knackered, hungry, and wondering where all this had come from. It was less than a day ago, he was happily in Brampton. But he was alive, many were dead. It was his job to protect the British people.

Once through the gate into Downing Street, they were soon out of the car and ushered into No. 10. With little pause, they were led into the cabinet room where Cameron was waiting. Michael Fallen and Theresa May sat to each side of the prime minister.

No one rose, no ceremony,

"Gentlemen, please sit. Let us get on with why you are here and what it is you wish to discuss."

No messing about then here, thought Will.

Sir Robert led the discussion.

"Sir, this is Group Captain Will Rivers, Head of JARIC. He contacted me yesterday with some information relating to a project he has been commissioned to complete that looked at how to attack the UK if it was a war scenario. The group captain's report on his findings and research is held within the most secure conditions with only two people officially authorised to see it. Even I had no idea this project was active.

"Group Captain Rivers was concerned that the attacks we have suffered were too close for comfort to the findings within his report. He contacted me to make this known, even though by doing so he risked his own position.

"Further to this, Sir, you will remember having to wear the NBC suit when you visited the site where the explosion was. At the time we went to the scene, it was not known there had been an escape of ammonia gas. The only people who would have known that this was the case were those who had been involved in the planning. Only three people went to the site, and I am sure that neither you nor I had any involvement in the attacks.

"I am dealing with the possible fact that we have a traitor amongst the security service command. Leave this with me, things are happening. But I want him in place for now, so we can use him if necessary. Group Captain, if you please."

Will went to stand but Cameron waved him down to sit.

"Prime Minister, to be brief, my report on an attack on the UK highlights the need to deny the gas supply system to the nation. This has been copied. It also points out that there is a way to bypass the initial damage. National Grid Gas is already working to initiate the bypass. Within 1 week, we expect 50-60% supply.

This is a target for whoever and they will want to break the pipe network used for the bypass.

"We must assume that these pipes will now be attacked. To do this, they will have to dig and dig quite deep to be able to get a charge close enough to do any damage. To get access to the dig, they will need to use the roads to get close to the pipes. All pipes are marked at the side of the road for safety reasons. We have stopped all planned maintenance along these pipe routes. Now, anyone seen digging is hostile. But we need to see them first.

"I need to use RAF Tornado reconnaissance aircraft. They will fly the pipe routes continually feeding JARIC with photo data of every place that they can dig. If we see them, we can act."

Cameron cut in, abruptly.

"Act, how? What does that mean? How can we react quickly?"

"Sir, we need to move the RAF onto a war footing, full alert, highest levels. We must defend ourselves internally.

1. The Tornados will feed JARIC with data and good eye contact of what is happening. They can fly in any condition and fast.
2. JARIC identifies a threat, which will be digging activity, they advise an AWACS which will be airborne. The AWACS will direct in, ground attack aircraft. These will need to be airborne also, which means tankers as well.
3. The attack aircraft will need rules of engagement and the final kill command. I will be controlling the whole operation. You need to agree to my rules of engagement and delegate the kill permission to me too.

"If they damage another pipe, it could be 3 years before the UK has gas again. Simple as that, Sir."

Sir Robert's eyebrows rose as he thought to himself, *Well, that has fucking told Cameron no mistake.*

There was an open discussion between the five people assembled for about 15 minutes. Other options, using the army, the fact we are attacking targets in the UK. But at the end of this time, there was total agreement.

Cameron spoke.

"Sir Robert, we agree, this must happen. They do not get a chance of any further damage to the gas network. Make it so, Group Captain Rivers. If both you and Sir Robert consider what you see is a threat, you have HM Government's permission to act as you feel fit to defend the country."

They rose in unison and left the room. Will's head was spinning. He got what they needed, but what did Cameron just say?

"Make it so, Group Captain Rivers. Is he having a laugh, fucking Star Trek?"

"I heard that, Group Captain," whispered Sir Robert.

40 minutes after leaving Scotland Yard, they were back. Will wanted to go to JARIC to start the balls rolling but he was not allowed. He had to stay in London. Everything was to be done by conference calls.

Will had insisted that the MoD IT people deal with the links to where the operations would be commanded from. Newly agreed encryption protocols to keep out anyone, even those that had legal access from what was happening.

The RAF war machine was waking up very quickly.

4 hours later, Will had the first data coming from GNCC; they had thought about it and provided maps with positions marked. These clearly showed the pipe routes the Tornados would follow. Most of these centred around the same rectangle of the damaged compressor stations, from Warrington in the north to Bedford in the south.

By this time, Will had an AWAC airborne flying a figure of eight over Nottingham. At RAF Scampton and RAF Honington were eight Tornados, loaded up and ready to go, waiting for the map data to arrive. It had, so JARIC were crunching the data to provide the routing and crossing data to the aircraft. Within minutes, the data would be pinged to the aircraft and they would be tasked.

At any time, they expected four to be up and active, four ready to swap out to give the pilots rest. At RAF Marham, two more were being readied to allow for any maintenance issues.

4½ hours after the meeting with the PM, the first four Tornados rose into the air. For the first time in British history, they had permission to kill British targets. At the same time, two RAF air-to-air refuelling tankers took off from RAF Waddington near Lincoln. When they reached the correct height, the second tanker would top up the first tanker to full load, then drop away to land.

The ground attack aircraft were not airborne. Will was using the QRA system (Quick Reaction Aircraft) two pairs of two Typhoons were fully armed and waiting. Within 3 minutes of being scrambled, they could be moving ready to take off. Already cleared to go supersonic over the UK, they could be on target, directed in by the AWACS, within minutes.

Will's plan was now in action. More map data was arriving from GNCC and this was being fed to the search aircraft. It was happening.

The Tornados were following the routes of the pipes, cameras actively looking for unwelcome activity.

Will was knackered still; he had forgotten he was hungry until Sir Robert's secretary put a plate of ham sandwiches and coffee in front of him.

"Thanks."

Chapter 16

Scotland Yard
Commissioner's Office
12 November, 1830

The four men, two SAS and two police tactical officers were shown into the commissioner's meeting room. All four stopped and looked puzzled.

Half of the meeting room table was taken up with three computer screens, a shit load of maps, and a half-dressed RAF Officer.

Sir Robert walked in and began,

"Gentlemen, please sit. Do not be alarmed at what Group Captain Rivers is doing. I will explain his presence first. This is Group Captain Will Rivers, Will for easiness. He is the current head of JARIC, based at RAF Brampton. I will assume you all will know what JARIC does. Part of the brief the group captain had was to look at the UK and identify the best way to cripple the country. His report was not far from being complete.

"He contacted me last night and pointed out that what was happening to the UK was directly what he had suggested. This was too much of a coincidence, so I have Will brought it here. To get access to the report requires authority at the highest levels of security clearance. Only five people, not including Will himself, have this level of clearance. The fact that this eyes-only confidential report may have been used as a plan of attack in the UK means that someone may have copied it. There are too many similarities to think perhaps they did their own research.

"Will is fully aware of my concerns about Marachi and why you are here. Marachi is one of the people with a level of security that could access Will's report, adding more weight to my concerns. As of a few hours ago, the PM authorised the use of force in the UK against UK targets if required. The damage to the gas supply system is massive and will take 2-3 years to repair. There is, however, a way to bypass the damaged parts and restore up to 60% supply.

"This information was also highlighted in the attack report. We must assume that these terrorists are going to follow the report and now try to attack and interrupt the bypass pipework. To do this, they will need to dig down to the pipe and plant charges. No other work is ongoing, any digging is now hostile. Problem is, that there could be over a thousand places they can attack.

"Will is co-ordinating the RAF operation, flying and continually monitoring the pipe routes, any digging or strange activity seen will be analysed by JARIC. If they are digging, we will destroy them. QRA fighters are on standby to react. He is a resident here and has full clearance to overhear anything we may discuss. So down to business. Where are we?"

It was Nottingham who spoke, not out of any seniority, the others would add in as they felt necessary.

"We have the teams of men we need. At this point in time, they know nothing about the task. All four of us have seen and gone over their service records and looked for any issues that could compromise what we need to do. All the men are solid, flawless, and highly qualified. Any along the way that raised any concerns were not included. We are confident."

Sir Robert continued, "Ok, that's good. We now have more reason to believe that Marachi is bad. But we need him in place to use and to allow us time to locate and grab the rest of the people he is involved with. Then we need to know why.

"He is continually monitored for security reasons. His phone is encrypted, and his home and car are swept daily for listening devices. Any possibilities of us using a bug or similar are out of the question. We could involve GCHQ, but again, Marachi has access and they may report back the request. Notwithstanding all of that, I need him followed. We need to be aware of his movements 24 hours a day. Do not assume he is asleep, 24 hours a day, full monitoring. Use your teams to complete this—who he meets, who he calls if we can, where he shops, what he buys, where he prays, who he is shagging."

Will interrupted.

"Sir, sorry to interrupt. What sort of car does he have? If it is a newer car, BMW, Merc or Audi, they have a sim card fitted that reports position, engine data, and all sorts of info we don't know about. It can be used in emergencies to contact the manufacturer. If you talk to them and we know the car, they can let you listen and provide position data. It will require a court order."

Sir Robert continued, "Good point, follow that up, but with the teams; nothing is delegated outside of the teams without my say-so, nothing. It must be kept secure and tight.

"I have commandeered a meeting room on lower level two. You can operate from there with your team. Civilian dress always but you may be armed. You are labelled as tactical advisors. My secretary has your new clearance and access badges. No hard copy records are to be left in that room. Spotless and clean always. We meet every day as and when possible, all information will be kept and collated up here with me."

"Bingo," muttered Will.

"Sir, we have a possible target, one of the Tornados has pinged something 200 mtrs to the side of a crossover somewhere near Nether Kellet."

One of the three screens was showing a live feed from the Tornado, the other showed a slightly older feed after JARIC had tweaked it. It was dark but the thermal imaging showed what appeared to be a digger moving along the path of the pipe.

"The aircraft is going around, it will be back in a few and lower."

Sure enough, the display went sideways as the aircraft banked around and came back lining up with the digger, 10 miles out, and then the screen went back horizontal and normal. Less than a minute later, the digger could be seen pulling a trailer.

"Standby," Will said, he had his hands over a headset to his ears. JARIC were analysing the pictures. Then the second JARIC screen zoomed in on the target.

"It's a tractor with a shovel on the front up in the air, it is pulling a load of hay. 500 metres away, you can see the heat signature of cattle. Off to feed the herd, I guess. No threat."

"Sorry, false alarm, but you can see how quickly we can identify a threat."

"Indeed," said Sir Robert. "I think I need coffee."

"Sir, do we just accept that or follow up? It appears to be innocent. Are we just going to ignore it?" This was the SAS Major talking; it was a good call too.

Will broke in.

"Good call, Sir. It does look OK but who do we send? Whoever goes needs to be armed and able to respond. We need a means of double-checking anything we decide not to hit."

This time, the SAS Sergeant spoke.

"Chopper, teamed up with four of the lads. Base it somewhere in the middle of the theatre, check what bases are available. Make sure it has a couple of 134s bolted on. It could be over the target with 15 minutes of a stand-down call to the aircraft."

What he was saying was that they needed ground suppression fire available if they got to the site and they were mistaken.

The M134 minigun was deployed in the doors of helicopters by the British forces. 7.62 calibre rounds and were usually pintle-mounted to helicopter doorways or firing ports. The high rate of fire made the minigun an ideal weapon for close fire support and landing zone suppression.

Sir Robert stood and walked up and down twice.

"Ok, make it so, Group Captain," taking the piss out of Cameron. "Can you set this up with your end please, Major? Will, you need to add this into your planning and make sure everyone is aware. Group Captain, what do you need?"

Will's mind flashed through the planning and control of this new asset.

"We will authorise the deployment as it is required to check anything we dismiss. Once authorised, I must let AWACS take control, there are too many aircraft about at one time."

That was it, it would happen; other people now would be running around preparing this new weapon that hopefully will not be needed.

"Gentlemen, back to our business.

1. Check how possible it is for the sim card in the car to be used to provide data on his movement and any conversation in the car.
2. Can we get sound from the house at a distance using some of the new tech gear our lads have? Check this out and let me know.
3. Start to follow 24 hours a day. If he so much as farts, I want to know.
4. Any shops he uses more than once, I want to know the background of anyone connected to the shop, owners, staff, etc.
5. Any deliveries to his house, I want to be traced back to where they came from.
6. I will arrange for his banking to be checked.

"We will reconvene tomorrow at 1830. Thank you, gentlemen."

With that, they stood and left the room, leaving Will and Sir Robert alone.

"I am going to get my head down for an hour, Group Captain, which makes me realise you need a second in command to assist you and allow you rest. Think of who that could be and we can discuss this later."

He was right. Will was dead on his feet now, the pace of everything was so rapid and so intense, he was running on adrenalin. He had the biggest war game on three screens in front of him, and it was real and live.

Eight Tornado crew were airborne along with twenty-two in the AWACS and 4 in the tanker. Thirty-four lives were directly responsible to Will, more sat waiting to respond.

"Fuck, I could murder a beer."

SIS Headquarters
Vauxhall, London
12 November, 1900

Si'ad was at his desk, along with many of his colleagues. They had not stopped since the attacks hit London. He was half asleep with his head in his hands and elbows on the desk, dropping in and out of consciousness. On his desk were the details of the people that his planning had tried to detain and failed.

On his wall was a display of their pictures and locations, where they lived. All the details of a well-planned and thought-through operation.

Huge use of the SIS and police had gone to waste, people were now questioning his intel and planning, but he did not care. He knew he was right; he knew it was those people.

He drifted off to sleep but was very disturbed. His nightmare appeared, every night the same nightmare, it would not go away. He was back as a child in his hometown in the south of Iraq. Happy times, warm with his family together, playing with his friends.

The invasion of Kuwait for them, as kids, was something they were proud of, but they did not understand. They thought it was all good, like the history lessons they were taught. They knew that Kuwait should be part of Iraq and Sadham was right to take back what was theirs. It belonged to the people.

When you are taught from a young age about the history of your country and that some injustices have taken place, you do not have the experience or even the means to question this knowledge. You just absorb it.

So, when the war took place to push Iraq out of Kuwait, the population were confused. They lived a simple life, simple things, whilst the government and their leaders lived the lives of kings.

The conflict did not enter Iraq, it was not allowed. The aim was to recover Kuwait and stop. But many people Si'ad knew were forced to go and fight for the Iraqi Army. They did not ask to go, just told to report and train for what the government knew would be a war.

He was too young at 15; 18 and over you had to go when asked.

Si'ad was from Safwan, a small border town with Kuwait. Here, the main road crossed out of Iraq, through a huge border crossing and checkpoint, into the state of Kuwait. When the invasion took place, he could remember sitting on the roof of his house cheering the Iraqi forces crossing the border.

It was a major sight for him to see, so much military might, so much of Iraq going to reclaim their rights. But the horror of what happened to those people and the might that crossed over that day would never be fully known by the Iraqi people.

He was lucky, he was too young so he did not need to go. He had no brothers, just two sisters. Mum and dad worked where they could find work, on the land, loading or unloading cargo at the border. They did all they could to make sure there was food and some future for the family. But it was hard.

Their house was big compared to some families. They were lucky. It was directly opposite the two border crossing buildings on the opposite side of the road. He would often look out of the window and wonder where all the trucks went. It also meant mum and dad could be there quickly to unload and earn money.

The memory of the war faded, and life continued but the pressures of the sanctions that had been imposed on Iraq hit the normal people more than the 'kings' lying around in Baghdad. Food was harder to find, work was harder to find. People travelled further to find work and money.

Rumours of a new war soon began to scare the people. The papers told of rhetoric from Sadham in defiance of the West, and the build-up once again of the Iraqi Army. This time everyone knew they were coming to Iraq; they would not stop at the border with Kuwait. He knew it could be very bad.

Most people just wanted a quiet life and to be allowed to go about their business as their families had for many decades before. But it was not for them to decide. The Iraqi people are not aggressive, they live a simple life. But their leaders have different ideals, driven by greed and power.

Si'ad's father had a beaten-up old pickup truck; he had no idea where this had come from and chose not to ask. He loved to get in the back and go out with his father to get food or carry goods for someone who paid for them. The miles they travelled together in that pickup, these were happy days.

His father was also a scavenger. Going to places that perhaps he should not go to see what he could find. Old railway yards, old factories, abandoned military facilities. Anywhere.

This was good for them; some of the scrap he found, or old radios and electrical goods fetched good money in the town. He did very well, justifying the cost of the truck.

As the deadlines approached that had been set by the West, no one believed it would happen, so life continued as normal, everyone just did what they normally did. Si'ad went to school, and so did his sisters.

No preparation was seen and there was no build of any military around the border town. This gave the people confidence that there would be no war, there would be no invasion. If they were to come, they would need to cross into Iraq through their town.

It was 19 March 2003 and his father went off in the truck very early that day to Um Qasar, a small beaten-up old port to the south. There were some good places to scavenge and he loved it there. He always came back with something very interesting. It did not seem different that he was late back, sometimes he would have to hide to avoid the police or army.

But after 2330 at night, Si'ad began to be concerned and decided to start to walk down the road in the direction his father would return from. The main road, numbered 1, was about 1 mile out of town. It was a cool evening and he enjoyed the cool air as he walked. Everywhere was black. Even the distant factory had no lights on.

"Fucking useless power people. Another power cut!"

The flash lit up the night sky and was gone before the bang and shockwave knocked him off his feet. He was stunned but uninjured. He lay on the floor with a mouth full of dry mud and sand, his ears were ringing, and his eyes showed white spots when he looked. Slowly, he sorted himself out and realised what had happened.

He was a mile away from where something had exploded; exploded in the town near the border crossing. He ran as he had never run before in his life, back towards what was now a hole in the ground and burning.

What he saw was beyond his belief. The two big sheds were gone, rubble, a tangle of iron and bricks. Where the actual crossing was, the road was missing and there was a huge hole there too.

He turned and slowly looked at the scene, realising that his house was gone too. There was nothing left, the whole block of houses was flat, burning and flat. His family, two sisters and his mother, could not have survived. There was no way. Why had that happened?

He ran over to the mound of rubble and started to claw at the blocks, they were hot, and parts of the building were still burning.

"Mamma, Mamma!" He dug and pulled with fury until two older men dragged him away, pulling him off the rubble from other falling blocks.

"Come, come, they are gone. Allah has taken them for himself."

As he stood looking at what used to be his life, once again the sky lit up over to the west of where he was standing. The road out of the town started to explode, a lot of small explosions ripping up the road and the ground on either side. Then the sound of aircraft followed and were gone.

Quiet returned and the people of the town started to scream.

Two days later, the body of his father was returned to the town. It was discovered on the back of a train that had left the Um Qasar port. His truck had been found by people from the village and all the tyres had been slashed.

He was 15 years old, and he had no idea of what to do or where to go; he had nothing. No money, no family, no home. For many days, he wandered the town, people fed him and comforted him, but his heart was broken and so was his mind.

"Whoever did this to my family will pay. One day, they will pay."

With that thought in his mind, he waited until it was dark, the middle of the night. Then found his way through and around the wreckage of the border crossing, walking brazenly right into Kuwait and across the fields away from what was his life.

For two days he walked, without food and without water. Finally crossing a road, he fell, smashed his head on a stone, and woke up.

Always at the same point he wakes up, the same dream, the same nightmare, the same tears and hurt.

Si'ad had been asleep for only 20 minutes but that was enough, he was recharged.

His office was a little secluded from the main room; up to twenty officers worked at the same time, each one following something or someone to track down the terrorists that had wreaked so much carnage on the capital.

Walking to the front of the room, Si'ad stood and addressed everyone.

"Right, update please."

For the next 30 minutes, each and every one gave a summary of where they were and what was next. Si'ad made no notes, he just listened and learnt.

What was clear was that they had nothing much at all.

Nothing at all.

"I am going home to shower and change, and I will be back within one hour. If anyone needs me, you call; I don't care when just call."

He left, locking his office after securing his laptop and other equipment.

His car was in the garage under the building, a Mercedes C250, and was only 1 year old. He did get paid well for doing what he did. This was one of his little perks.

Every car in and out of the garage was swept by the guards. They were looking for any type of tracker or radio device. On the way in, they were looking for explosives as well. With the type of work this organisation did, no one was safe. Safety comes from vigilance.

The follow team was in place. A variety of vehicles. These would swap about very frequently but follow the Merc as a team, reducing the possibility of being spotted.

As he pulled out of the garage, Si'ad nearly knocked a pizza guy off his moped. They gestured at each other as drivers always do and the Merc moved off, with an angry pizza man following him. As the pizza got delivered, another car, bike, and even a paramedic dropped in behind or in front. A second vehicle further back in the traffic was waiting to take over.

So it was that everywhere Si'ad was to go, someone would follow. If he walked or even biked, someone would follow.

With the benefit of a court order obtained very quickly, Mercedes was now cooperating with the police to provide data and a link to the car. 'Mercedes Me' was part of the vehicle COMAND system which provided sat nav, music, vehicle settings, and the displays in the car. It also controlled the emergency links back to Mercedes for breakdown and assistance. You could even message the car from your smartphone and set it to warm up in the morning.

Through this link, the police now had real-time position tracking on the car. It was being followed, but if they were to lose the car, a location would be available at any time.

More importantly, the two-way voice link could be activated to listen. This would show on the display at the top right of the COMAND screen, but unless you knew what to look for, you would not be aware. This was the only risk.

The police tech guys together with the new tactical advisors had put together a laser microphone. This was a laser beam that was directed at a flat surface in a room through the window. Something like a picture or mirror. The surface of a picture would resonate in time with any sounds in the room, very slightly. The resonance would change the frequency of the laser beam a fraction. This can be processed to provide the sound from the room.

Everything was set; Si'ad was being followed and listened to.

Chapter 17

Peterborough, Wellington Street
12 November, 1630

Maghrib, or evening prayers, normally lasts 45 minutes at the Salah ad-Din Mosque situated on Russell Street, a short walk north of the town centre. It starts at around 0430 hrs but this will vary as the time of the sunset is important. Maghrib must begin just after sunset. As prayer finishes and must finish before dark, when Isha prayer will begin.

Islamic prayers consist of different numbers of parts called Ra'kat. Each part itself has a different name. Maghrib prayer has three obligatory Ra'kat called Fard, two recommended Ra'kat called sunnah, and two optional Ra'kat called nafts.

The first two Fard are recited aloud by the Imam, and the third is silent and prayed within yourself. Each part of the prayer must be performed within a prescribed time to be considered valid.

They arrived on time at the mosque, in fact, a little early so had some time to chat with their friends before going inside to pray. The service was expected to last only 45 minutes, but once prayers were over, the Imam rose to address the people in front of him.

As he rose, there was silence. Everyone was kneeling and had been bent over in prayer. They must pray as though they were in the presence of God, head down and prostrate. When they moved back to the upright position, they must chant, 'God listens to the one who praises him'. Then standing up, they must chant, 'To God belongs all praise'.

The Imam was a gentleman of about 68 years old. He had served his people for over 35 years in some form or another. He was trusted and was known for his wisdom.

"Sit up," he said, and as they rose, the familiar chant was recited.

"Before you leave this evening, I wish to talk to you about what is happening. We have all seen the dreadful attacks that have taken place in the last few days, many people, including many of our own beliefs, have been killed, violently and indiscriminately. The Quran does not justify any use of force in the name of Allah. Islam is peaceful and it is only the radical misteaching of some that allows the name of Islam to be seen as an aggressor.

"None of us know who the people are that planned and made the attacks in *our* country." He made a point of emphasising *our*. "We all live in this great nation as have our fathers and mothers for many generations. Together, we have helped to integrate and build communities of trust, living together with all races and beliefs. It is a sad fact that everywhere, the word 'Terrorist' is linked to Islam. So the blame for the last few days will sit with our faith and our beliefs until it is proven otherwise.

"This mosque will never condone, or accept, or preach, or encourage the use of violence in the name of Islam. I warn you all now that I would not hesitate to protect the people I serve and other people in *my* and *our* country. I will cooperate with the authorities to help bring to justice anyone who thinks they have the right to kill and maim indiscriminately. Whatever thoughts you may have need to be good and follow the teachings of the Quran. You must obey Allah and Allah shows you the way of goodness and peace. Now go and heed my words. We live here together, we have no right to hurt anyone in the name of Islam."

The Imam bowed his head turned and left. As the prayers broke up and people started to leave, there was much discussion as to what had prompted this lecture from the Imam. Did he think they were involved?

"He has no faith; how can he have true faith and talk like a woman? You can't kill, you can't hurt, but look at what the West does, and has done. We know our path is righteous and that we are chosen to take the will of Allah to these money-loving womanising filth. How many of our people have the West killed in just the two wars in Iraq? Or Afghanistan, how many, but for them it is acceptable."

"We are just to do a job, a small job for the greater good. We are not going to war to fight the great Satan. Stop being dramatic, you are such a fool sometimes and this could be bad for you one day."

The three of them chatted and argued the reasons for the Imam's comments as they walked. Two were brothers, 26 and 28 years old, the third was a friend and he was 26 also. All three had been friends growing up in Peterborough, same schools and many of the same interests. All three were employed by National Grid Gas, working on maintenance and repairs to the gas pipe system.

About 1 mile away from the mosque in Wellington Street was an old British gas depot and a huge gasometer. A relic from the days of town gas and early natural gas storage. This was now a National Grid depot but little used. A valuable piece of land if you ignore the costs of removing the gasometer and returning the land to greenfield status.

The depot sat next door to Wellington Street carpark, a shopper's parking area, further out of town but cheaper for all day. It also hosted Peterborough car boot sale.

Parked in the bottom corner of the carpark nearest to the entrance was a National Grid truck, a small one, open-backed, full of the necessary kit that the maintenance guys would need daily. On the trailer behind was a JCB excavator.

The trailer was large and had three wheels on each side, high sides, and a tailgate ramp for loading and offloading. The two vehicles together looked quite impressive.

Parked up next to the NG dept, the truck and trailer did not look out of place; hiding in plain sight. No one would question why it was there, it possibly came back late and the depot was closed.

The three agreed to meet at 0600 hrs in the Stanley Recreation Ground, a short walk from the truck, then they would go to get the truck sorted and ready.

By 0615 hrs, the truck was running and their belongings for the trip were in the cab. Three holdalls, food and coffee. They headed out of the car park, right into St Johns Street, then right again off the roundabout into Boongate.

The truck cleared Peterborough heading north on the A16 towards Crowland. The home of the famous Crowland Abbey and the Guthlac Roll, an 800-year-old record of medieval Britain.

There was no rush, the journey would take less than one hour, and they would not be starting work for some time. The new A16 bypass had been completed a few years ago and just before the road cleared Crowland, there was a layby with a very good burger van. Why not get some coffee and a good solid dose of fat whilst they can?

They pulled in and ordered coffee with three of the largest options for a burger imaginable, double burgers, onions, cheese, pickles and tomato sauce. 30 minutes later, they were gone, except for the mess on the front of their overalls.

All wore full orange hi-visibility clothing, jackets, and boots. It was not cold but it was not hot either. They needed to appear genuine and wearing the gear provided that impression.

400 metres further along the A16, they turned off right crossing over Hull's Drove into Falls Drove. Then followed the road back south again. The road was narrow. There was room for two cars to pass easily but their truck and a car would struggle, two trucks may be impossible. Time would tell.

Three-quarters of the way along Falls Drove, there was a double bend. 500 metres out of the bends, they found what they were looking for. On the west side of the road verge were the two gas pipe warning signs. Under the road where they were right now was a 1-metre diameter high-pressure gas pipe.

To the east, 700 metres across a field were two wind turbines, happily turning away creating 'free' energy.

Turning left into French Drove, the truck pulled up and stopped in the gateway to the access road for the wind turbines. Adjacent to French farm. The access road was unmade and secured with two metal gates, one large and one small. Then the fence continued on either side of the gates. It would be very easy to walk around the gates but vehicular access had to be gained by unlocking the padlock.

There was no real need for high security on such sites, anything worth stealing was 100 ft in the air, but tonight they did not want to steal anything. The padlock was cut with some heavy-duty bolt cutters and the truck drove through. They shut the gate behind them. The two wind turbines were no more than 400 metres ahead of them.

Somewhere in the ground in between the two turbines was the gas pipe, buried to a depth of 1.1 metres, slightly less than 3 feet 7 inches. They just had to find it.

From the back of the truck, they pulled out what could only be described as a lawn mower. A wheel on each corner and a handle to push. The difference was that there was no motor or blade, just a pack of electronics to find pipes.

GPR, ground-penetrating radar, uses a form of radar to look at what is under the surface. If a pipe is there, the reflection back from the radar emission is different and will show on the screen. Walk the mower up and down and it will locate the gas pipe they are seeking.

It did and using a can of spray yellow paint, a rectangle was marked on the soft soil to the west of the access road. This was where they needed to dig and remove the soil to a depth of 1.1 metres, and it should expose the pipe. If it did not, then it would not be too far away. Close enough to damage with an explosive charge.

Whilst the mower was looking for the pipe, the others unloaded the digger from the trailer and brought this around ready to go to work. It was as the digger was backing off the trailer that the jet went over. It was dark and they had no idea what sort of aircraft it was. It was quite low and fast; it was gone before they knew it was there.

It did not bother them, they were busy working for the National Grid and had all the clothes and a National Grid vehicle. Why would they not be working? Plus, it was dark and they were going very fast, nothing to worry them at all.

Scotland Yard, London
12 November, 2000

Will was by himself, sat as he was when the SAS and commissioner had left, staring at the screens. His coffee was cold, as was his second cup just to his right.

He needed the loo badly but was reluctant to leave, as Murphy's law states if he isn't there, that's when it will happen. Will was in charge of the operation to stop anyone digging to get access to the gas pipeline bypass that National Grid was arranging, 'Operation Digger'.

His headset came to life.

"Digger control, JARIC, possible target, sending feed now."

Will's JARIC feed came to life showing images of a field with two wind turbines. Right in the middle was a digger being offloaded from a National Grid truck and trailer.

"Confirm all NG operations frozen please?"

Will responded.

"All operations have been stopped. Affirmative."

"Standby, sending index plate from truck, get police to run a check. If this is NG owned, then could be an oversight, if not, it is hostile."

"Send the aircraft around again, give me 5."

Will grabbed the phone and got hold of the desk sergeant in the lobby downstairs.

"Wake the commissioner. I do not know how, get him back into his meeting room now. Instantly, I do not care if he is naked."

The JARIC display changed again and the blown-up fuzzy picture of the truck's number plate could be seen. It was fuzzy but it was readable.

Will was now running on auto, he had gone into some place in his head and was computing all the moves that would be required or possible and all the different issues he may have to deal with.

Through his secure comms, Will made contact with flight control at RAF Coningsby.

"Coningsby, this is Digger control. We have a possible target for you, bring two Typhoon aircraft to full readiness, fully armed. Do not scramble until my word. Acknowledge?"

"Confirm Digger, two aircraft full readiness, standing by, out."

With a huge bang, as the door opened hard and swung back to hit the coffee station, Sir Robert arrived. He was not naked but just in his uniform trousers and his shirt, open at the collar.

"Sit rep, Group Captain, better be good I have not slept for 48 hours."

"Possible target, National Grid truck and trailer offloading a digger. In the field directly overhead one of the bypass pipelines is between Peterborough and Wisbech. Located by the last pass of the Tornado, it is coming back as we speak. JARIC have flashed over the index plate of the vehicle for ownership details. If it is NG at all. I need your help."

"Give it to me."

Will had scribbled it on a piece of paper and handed this to Sir Robert, who already had the phone in his hand.

"Control room, get me a vehicle check on this number, and now."

He read the number out and wrote down something, then put the phone down very quickly.

"The truck is stolen along with the digger. It was taken from a builder's yard in Bradford 3 weeks ago and has not been seen since. It is not National Grid. You have a target, Group Captain. Now, kill it."

The JARIC screen was back and the right screen showed the IR feed from a second Tornado as it went airborne. The original aircraft that had spotted the digging had been vectored back around by AWACS as was now approaching again from the east.

The team at JARIC was now looking at the target from the first pass and the surrounding possible damage area. They did not want to hit and damage the wind turbines, but they were very close. The pipe was only 4 ft under the ground, so any ordinance must be very light. What about the farmhouse? How many people in there? Nearest electricity pylons. Everything and anything that could go wrong.

"Sir Robert, we need an armed response to the farm; if these idiots run, they will go for the farm. We do not want them exiting through the gate either."

Again, Sir Robert picked up the phone and quietly passed orders to his control room. They, in turn, linked to the Cambridgeshire police and called for backup.

Within seconds of the request, two Cambridgeshire armed response vehicles were mobile.

One came from the main Peterborough police station where the crew were on a break in the canteen.

"AV5, urgent response, go, go, possible terror threat, head out A16 towards Crowland and standby for update."

Rob and Brian stood, turned, and ran out of the canteen along the main corridor to the back of the station. In the car park was their BMW X5, now the favoured response vehicle for many forces.

They were both wearing their side arms but the rest of their kit would be in the boot. Brian jumped into the driver's seat and fired up the engine, Rob was in the back and he pulled out two Sig Sauer SG516 semi-automatic rifles, plus four magazines. They were not stored loaded.

As Rob was about to get in the front passenger seat, the rear door of the station burst open and two more armed officers ran out.

"What the fuck are you doing?"

"We are coming with you, no fucking way are we not going to get involved, we are coming."

"You can't."

"Fuck off, drive, we will call it in on the way, they won't call you back. Drive man, just drive, go."

Both climbed into the back, pushing their Sigs between their legs. Weapons checking began immediately, most of the time they were not looking at what they were doing. None of the weapons were loaded.

The magazines were in their tactical vests, but the action and function of the weapons were being checked. Even though they knew them to be unloaded, they swapped weapons and checked each other's handguns and rifles. Three highly trained officers doing what they do.

They went out of the station at Thorpe Wood, under the A47 junction at Bretton, then back up onto the A47 heading east. Dual carriageway, good road and hit the gas.

The second response car was on the A47 to the east of Wisbech. They got the same call.

"AV9, urgent response, terror threat, proceed A47 towards Peterborough turn north on B1040 at Thorney, confirm?"

Now two police armed response teams were blasting their way towards the farm and the two wind turbines; completely unknown to the three terrorists, they were about to dig their own graves.

Both cars were less than 10 minutes out, AV9 was up to 120 mph on the A47 and had pinged two Gatso cameras already. To their right, a low-level jet flashed past, making it appear they were going backwards.

"Fuck, he was low, what's going on? There is shit somewhere, that's the second one in less than 20 minutes."

The comms came to life again.

"AV 5 and 9, control, we are handing over control of your vehicles to the military via a link from Scotland Yard, please use channel 17. From now on, you will be talking directly to the military, confirm?"

"AV9, confirmed."

"AV 5, confirmed."

"Good luck, guys, control out."

"Fucking told you, something bad is happening. Who they gonna call…"

"Shut up and drive, will you? It will all be over by the time we get there at this speed."

The radio was switched to channel 17, a channel reserved for just such times as this. As soon as they had changed the channel, it was live with traffic.

"Police AV 5, online, sit rep please."

"Standby AV 5."

"Police AV 9, online."

"Standby AV 9."

"AV 9, AV 5, you are now working with Operation Digger in place to stop any terrorist attempts to further damage the gas pipe system. We have a target actively digging that the military is about to engage. To the southwest of target is a farmhouse with unknown occupants. They are outside of any damage radius we hope, but if the tangos run, they will go to the farmhouse in our view. That you will not allow to happen.

"They have access to the dig area through a gated road. If they manage to run with the truck, they will exit through this gate; you will not allow that to happen. Understood?"

Both police units confirmed.

"See, Rob, you're glad we came along now. We can point out the bad guys for you."

"Fuck all the way off," was the only response. Adrenaline was pumping now; these lads were super cool under stressful conditions but the build-up was a mixture of fear and humour to mask it.

"AV 9, turn off A47 onto B1040 north, head 2 clicks to the north and turn right into French Drove. Silent approach, no blues, no noise, kill vehicle lights on a right turn. Head slowly along French Drove and drive into the gateway entrance of the access road."

"AV 5, Turn right from the A16 onto the B1040, go south 1.5 clicks turn left onto French Drove. Silent approach, no blues, no noise, kill vehicle lights on left turn. Head slowly along French Drove, drive into French farm, secure buildings, and occupants. We have been advised you are unexpectedly four up, happy days; nice one, lads. Confirm on turns into French Drove. Digger out."

Whilst the deployment of the police was going on, Will and Sir Robert watched the Tornado go overhead for the second time. The JCB digger was in place and the truck was to the east of the dig. This was not a deliberate act on their part but it did mean an attack needed to come from the west. For some reason, Will was thinking of a run from the east.

"Sir Robert, I am going to scramble the SAS Chopper and get them on the way, we can always send them home. Better to have them available."

Will spoke to the AWACS and gave the order to scramble the SAS to have them airborne and quickly available if needed. Within a few minutes, the chopper would be lifting off from RAF Waddington and heading south. Flight time was 15 minutes. 15 minutes that they could be digging.

The JARIC screen came to life and it showed various plans of hitting the target with different weapons looking at the blast radius and depth of penetration. There was no point in stopping these guys but then doing the job for them. JARIC were looking at all options.

Will and Sir Robert looked and both had the same look on their faces.

"We are either going to do their job for them or knock down the wind turbines. Anything we fire must not be able to penetrate the ground too deeply."

"The Typhoons have been loaded with Brimstone missiles. This is an anti-vehicle missile that was developed to hit smaller vehicles. It carries less explosive and a lot of damage is pure impact. It can hit a digger easily or the truck."

"But we don't know how deep a crater it will blast. Do we?"

"Exactly no, we do not. If it hits the truck, then it will lift it off the ground, most of the force being absorbed in the initial explosion. That explosion should take down the diggers. But nobody has ever really worried about how deep the crater in the ground goes down after the strike."

"Then we could end up breaking the pipes ourselves."

"We need to use guns. Attack very low, run in from the SW; meaning any rounds that miss will impact to the northeast of the pipe out of harm's way. It will disable the digger. Then we let our SAS friends clean up."

"Agreed, Group Captain, make it so."

This had now become the new norm and they both chuckled every time Sir Robert used it.

"Police are moving up French Drove now, they will be in position in 5 and we need 5 more for them to make contact at the farm."

"Coningsby, this is Digger control. Scramble Scramble Scramble. Hold for our command. Attack will vector them on to target from the southwest, very low very fast. Use cannon only. No missile strike, considered too much of a risk. Confirm."

It would take less than 3 minutes to get the Typhoons in the air from full readiness; Will and the commissioner had to wait. But within this time, they started to get the feeds from the aircraft.

"Confirmed DC, from SW exit to NW and up. Low-level attack guns only."

Will continued his instructions.

"Bring the helo to a safe distance and hold for instructions. We will need them on the ground or to engage quickly."

French Drove
12 November, 2025

AV 9 rolled very slowly along French Drove past the farmhouse and pulled quietly into the entrance of the access road. The gate was open. The police car now completely blocked any access. But it would not stop a 7.5-ton truck at speed. If that was to happen, they would need to stop the truck by other means.

It was dark and they could not see very well. No cover for them was obvious. To the left of the access road, about 20 metres in, was a mound of dirt or something. That would work, but they would need to be together; not ideal, but that was all they had to work with.

They had been deployed whilst on the move so had no chance to get their main weapons. These were in the boot and secure. But not for long. They too had Sigs, SG516 and were now checking and loading them. Checking again, swapping and checking. They were good to go, and their handguns too.

It was going to be a cold wait, but at last, they were getting a chance to hit back.

AV 5 rolled along a minute later and turned into the driveway of the house. They soon realised that having four up was going to be a bonus. What they had to defend was bigger than they had been told.

The BMW stopped close to the front door but out of sight of anyone in the fields to the north.

Rob walked up to the house, was fully dressed, with helmet, mask, and sidearm, and had his Sig across his chest with his right hand on the stock to stop it banging around. He knew that whoever opened the door could freak out and panic. He had to allow for that.

He banged on the door very hard and shouted, "Police, open the door."

Then he banged again and again.

A light came on in the hallway and he could hear the lock being turned.

"Armed police, do not be alarmed, nothing is wrong."

Rob hoped that this would take away some of the surprises of seeing him rock up on your doorstep like the pizza man. It did and it didn't.

"Oh my god, what's happened? Is it Paul, my son? What's wrong?"

"Please be calm, nothing is wrong. We have some trouble nearby and we do not want you to be worried or involved. I need you to go back inside, turn off all the lights, and go upstairs out of the way. Can you do that?"

"Yes, but what is going on?"

"I need you to go back inside and do as I ask, can you do that?"

"Yes, of course."

"Someone will come and talk to you once we have resolved the situation. Until then, stay upstairs and keep the lights off."

Rob left and joined the others.

"DC AV 5, farmhouse is secure. Two occupants, lights off. They are upstairs and will stay there until someone tells them different."

"Received AV 5, move to your 2 o'clock through small industrial units and deploy to make sure that no one uses the route through the farm as an escape. Targets have orange hi-vis clothing."

"AV 9, site rep."

"DC AV 9 in position, the gate is blocked. We are to the east behind a dumped load of roadstone."

The control then issued the rules of engagement.

"AV 5 and 9. Anyone leaving the site wearing orange hi-vis or not is to be considered hostile and you are free to fire as you feel necessary. Do not take chances, each of the targets could be wearing a suicide vest. Shoot to kill, headshots. No chances."

"Fuck, you two still want to be here?"

"Yes, we do want to be here. So, where are we going? There is a fuck off Calor gas tank over there, not the best place to stand. Two behind that bush at the end of the road and two in the farm crap over there. We can cover your six at the bush."

They moved out, took up positions, and rechecked their weapons.

"Mission is live, comms are open, keep traffic to a minimum."

The first voice they heard was the aircrew in the helicopter now in a hover over Market Deeping about 6 miles away.

The second was the inbound Typhoons. They had left RAF Coningsby and headed southwest towards Huntingdon, then out over the old USAF base at Molesworth before turning north. Once they were overhead Oundle, they would descend and turn on a heading to intercept the diggers. All air movements had been stopped in this part of the country. There were very few anyway following the attacks.

Two aircraft 2 miles apart, one as a backup in case of any maintenance issues.

The lead Typhoon dropped to 600 ft, lined up on the target now showing as a blip on the HUD.

"RAF 1, confirm engage, weapons free."

"DC Control, engage."

The aircraft went black, turning off all normal navigation lighting. Ground following radar was keeping the aircraft at the right height.

The attack would have happened before the aircraft sound arrived, which meant total surprise. They had heard aircraft noise a lot recently around Peterborough. It was on and off all day and night. But none of them really gave this any thought.

There was a faint noise in the distance, the police were in position and waiting. They had no idea what was intended other than these arseholes digging in the field would be meeting the RAF any second now.

Will and Sir Robert watched the feed from the Typhoon, live video feed.

"AWACS, confirm fire?"

"Shoot."

"Be advised Typhoon, 25 seconds out and Tornado inbound east to west 35 seconds for BDA."

They heard the cannon before they heard the Typhoon. From about half a mile out, the sky lit with flashes of tracer rounds, streaking death towards the place where they were digging. It was then overhead and gone.

In its wake, the 7.5-ton truck exploded into fire, riddled, which lit up the area surrounding the dig site, showing the JCB intact.

"AV 5, truck gone, digger still operational, but they are running."

Then came the wup wup in the distance as the SAS were inbound in the helicopter; as the Typhoons commenced their run, so too did the SAS, they were on site and swooping down.

As it came down from the north side of the wind turbines, it flew across the dig site and opened up with the rotary gun destroying the JCB and one orange figure trying to run away. The other two were heading along the track right into the hands of the police.

"H1, cease-fire, friendlies on the ground waiting, land and follow up, repeat friendlies at farm."

The chopper went nose up, sided in towards the running men and dropped, four figures jumped out, spread out and followed.

"Unit 1 down following up, we will hold back and move to the west side."

"AV 5, we have them two running, both are armed, we will engage."

"Rob, take the big guy on the left, I have you covered."

From a prone position on the floor, Rob took aim and fired. The larger of the two orange men dropped, falling on what was left of his face because of his own momentum. He did not go bang.

The second turned to his left and ran across a patch of grass that separated the farm track from the wind turbine access road. He hit the access road, turned right, and ran down the road towards the blocked gate and the police car.

As he saw the police car, he knew he was trapped, so stopped and just sank to his knees. He threw his weapon to one side as far as he could, then put his hands up in the air as far as he could reach.

Just waited, kneeling on the road surface, waiting, like 'Oops sorry, chaps'.

The two police behind the mound rose, weapons raised and slowly approached.

"AV 9, we have one orange man surrender."

"No! Stop, stand down."

A shot rang out 20 metres from the left of the two police officers and the orange man went down face first, motionless.

"Do not approach the bodies, say again, do not approach the bodies."

As they turned to where the shot came from, they saw a heavily camouflaged soldier.

"Easy, lads, easy, weapons down. We are all on the same side, here."

A broad Welsh accent, out of breath, said.

"Sorry about that, boyo, but he was luring you in. I bet he has a vest on. Can't have these cunts messing up our police now, can we? Leave him now for the bomb folks to deal with. You see, the first one we hit from the helicopter went bang, but you would not have known that now, would you?"

"How the fuck did you get so close to us without us knowing?"

"That's what we do. You drive fast, that scares the fuck out of me, but I'm a sneaky fucker."

Chapter 18

Sawtry, Cambridgeshire
B1090, Just Off the A1
12 November, 2230

The journey down from Bradford had been uneventful. Traffic was very light, which was clearly the result of the attacks that had taken place over the last few days. Most people were taking the advice from the government and staying home as much as possible.

The lack of gas and reduced power availability were causing problems for everyone. It was November and it was cold. Everyone was now struggling to keep warm.

There were two of them in the van and they were warm, the heater was working well. The van was not too old. Most of the National Grid vehicles were less than 3 years old. From Bradford along the M62 and down south from there on the A1; 2 hours and they were only 30 minutes away from their destination, near Sawtry in Cambridgeshire.

Sawtry was an A1 town, cut in half by the Great North Road. And together with Stilton a few miles to the north became popular staging towns in the days of stagecoaches. The A1 was later built to the east of the town and then upgraded to the A1(M).

As the new road was completed, planning was allowed to provide infill housing between the new road and the town. Some local farmers got rich and new, badly needed housing was built. Sawtry blossomed into a town that provided easy access to Peterborough and Huntingdon where there was plenty of work.

To the east of the A1, there were some factory units but then open fenland. The builders did not get that far.

Beneath the fields of the UK is a little-known network of supply pipes that pumps aviation fuel directly from the refineries around the country to every RAF base and UK airport. Most people have never even heard about it. At points along this network, there are also fuel dumps or holding areas; huge tanks are buried in the ground holding millions of gallons of aviation fuel. More commonly known as AV gas, or Jet A1. This is kerosene.

The network was established just before the Second World War. A secret pipeline was built between Liverpool and Avonmouth docks, where the fuel went by road and rail to the destinations. With the onset of the war and the vulnerability of any fuel movements to German bombers and fighters, this network was expanded to allow fuel supplies from Western ports to be sent to the airfields in the east.

This was known as the Government Pipelines and Storage System (GPSS) and it supplied all the British and American aircraft during the war. To this day, it is still classified as a national secret, even though there are plans to sell it to a Spanish company.

Once the war was over, the pipeline remained and was expanded to supply fuel to all civilian as well as military airports, stretching some 1500 miles around the UK. Thousands of aircraft every year were refuelled using this system.

Have you ever driven down a road and seen a small white gate in a field in the middle of nowhere? This is a pipe marker for the GPSS. They are more obvious when travelling by train and you can follow them as you go along.

Not so secret after all, plus there was information on the internet allowing anyone to see the approximate routes of the pipelines. The pipes were deep and not large. Unlike the gas grid, it would be very difficult to locate and attack the pipes. But just like the gas grid, the storage areas would be easy to attack. They were old and had little security.

On the B1090, less than a mile from Sawtry, about 300 metres from the road along a driveway or access road, was one of the fuel storage stations connected to GPSS with five underground storage tanks, each capable of holding 250,000 litres of fuel. A total of 1,250,000 litres of highly flammable liquid.

From here, the fuel was pumped east to RAF Alconbury and RAF Wyton, and beyond to all other RAF and civilian stations. It was also pumped south to Sandy, where right next to the RSBP Bird Reserve, there was another storage facility. Another million litres of aviation fuel, just sitting there in the ground.

To the northwest of the storage site was the edge of Sawtry. Two large housing estates grew out of the village as they built on the land islands created by the new A1(M). 99% of Sawtry residents had no idea that less than 1 mile away sat over 1 million litres of highly flammable aviation fuel buried in the ground.

Over a hundred private houses sat within the blast radius of the fuel exploding. If this was to happen, the shockwave alone would demolish most of them. Hundred houses with an average of three people per house, three hundred casualties instantly; plus, anyone on the A1(M). Debris and flying lumps of buildings and the tank would claim many more people.

How the local planning authority would consider such a fact was something that none of us would ever really know. They must be aware that the facility was there and must be aware of the potential damage an accident could cause. The danger was present and very clear.

But this was peace time and why would anyone want to blow up the fuel dump? But then, why would anyone need to blow up the gas grid?

The National Grid van had turned off the A1 slightly north of Sawtry and joined the side road which allowed access to the town and further along to get onto the B1090. The time was 2230 and they wanted to wait until at least 2300 before arriving on site. This gave them time to take a break, sort out their gear and prepare.

The weather was cold, with full cloud cover and no moon. No rain but windy. All the way down the A1 the wind, coming from the east, had buffeted the van. Good cover for the pair tonight.

At 2250, the van moved off and followed the road alongside the motorway, past one of the large factories and to the south of Sawtry. This road was, in fact, part of the old A1 that had remained to be used as a service road for non-motorway traffic.

As the road rose slightly up to a roundabout, the van turned off left towards Wood Walton.

The entrance to the compound was only 400 metres along on the left. They pulled into the compound's driveway and stopped the van. Getting out, they opened the back and removed some of the red and white plastic barriers you see in the road when works are going on, blocking the entrance to the driveway.

Then they each took a black holdall and their weapons and moved off into the blackness. Before closing the door, one of the figures reached inside, pulled out a metal wire and attached it to a small hook that had been fitted to the door. Then went to the driver's door which was still open and flicked a switch under the dashboard.

Without bothering to close the door, the two black figures walked away from the van very slowly, looking around all the time, watching all directions for movement or light. They did not have any form of night vision; they were relying on what light was available and stealth.

The gate was little problem, the chain securing it was old and not suitable for the job intended. A cheap fix from whoever had to maintain the facility. They were prepared and cut the chain easily, leaving the cutters on the floor.

They knew from what they had been told and from studying aerial pictures, they had to walk about 300 metres to the first tank of fuel. This would take them past some old buildings, long abandoned and somewhat derelict. Once past these, the first tanks were very close. They were the ones they needed.

They knew that they would not be walking back to the van, their instructions were very clear. Take the holdalls, position them at the centre of the top of the tank, lay down and initiate the explosives themselves. This was a suicide mission.

The resulting blast would bring the carnage of London to a sleepy town on the A1.

"AV mother. AV 7. We have company. Advise?"

"AV 7. Mother, repeat please, you have company."

"Roger that, two up armed and carrying holdalls moving on the compound. Advise?"

"AV 7, confirm armed?"

"Roger that, look like AKs. Two targets, all black out, no NV. Advise?"

"Standby, AV 7."

"AV 7, where have they come from, any ideas?"

"We clocked them arriving in a National Grid transit van, parked up at the entrance and they have blocked access. Intention is hostile clearly. Advise?"

"AV 7. Mother. Clear to engage, take them down, do not start a firefight, we do not need any more holes in the ground."

"Mother, confirm, clear to engage."

"AV 7, that is affirmative, engage."

In the darkness within the compound, twenty Paras came to life; they were hidden away around the small buildings and in the undergrowth and had been since it turned dark. They did not expect an attack during daylight, although it was possible. But during darkness, there was a high risk. They were right and they were very ready for all comers.

The driveway led about 100 metres to a gate, then a further 100 to the first of the buildings on site. Laying prone on the roof of the first building were two snipers. The other eighteen were at various points, including one man in a ghillie suit lying on top of each tank in the ground.

The terrorists would need to clear the buildings and a further 150 metres to get to the first tanks. Right now, they had stopped at the gate and were about to cut the chains locking it.

Comms came to life.

"They do not get past the buildings. If they get that far, drop them, clear?"

The two snipers responded, "Clear."

"I want these motherfuckers alive; problem is they may be booby'd as a last resort if compromised. If they are going to go bang, they need to do it away from the silos. They need to do it near the buildings."

This was a good call; it may well be that the terrorists themselves were the weapons. They had no way of knowing. Just lay on the tank, pull the trigger, and go to meet whatever God they represent.

"Ok, Jock, change of plan. When they get halfway along the buildings, drop one with a headshot. George immediately put a round in his chest where a vest would be. If he doesn't go bang, we are good to take the second one down by hand. Phil, John, sort yourselves out to take the other cunt down. Try not to kill him. Only kill if he has a device, it could be in the holdall. Any uncertainty, double tap the head; if either of you have a worry, then drop him.

"No mistakes, be very sure, we do not need a stray 7.62 round flying about around this lot. On my call."

The two figures could not be seen normally, it was too dark and they walked very slowly stepping out each foot carefully. They had no rush to be honest, other than dawn and that was hours away. It was a cloudy night with little moonlight. There was some ambient light from the nearby A1(M) but not much.

What they did not know was that twenty pairs of eyes using night-vision kit were watching them, allowing them to get to a point where for the first time since London exploded, the Paras were about to join the party and going to hit back very hard.

Slowly, they advanced along the roadway, step by step, totally exposed, showing a complete lack of training or preparation. It would have been better to hug the buildings and that would have stopped the snipers getting a shot off.

These people were not trained, they were fanatics, willing to do and to follow in the name of whatever God or because they had been indoctrinated with.

"Halfway, almost there, it's now or never, boss."

"Take him."

Two shots echoed out, the first removed most of one man's head, the second hit square on the chest a little to the left, right where any explosive may have been. He dropped like a sack of potatoes and did not go bang.

"Safe, go."

Out of the darkness, two figures rushed and grabbed the second man. Each took an arm and extended it high over the terrorist's head, looking for wires and a trigger device.

"Clear, pat this cunt down."

"No vest, no wires, put him down."

One very violent thump to the head with the butt of his handgun put the man on the floor. He was instantly surrounded. They ripped open his outer jacket and were feeling all over his body for any form of hidden device, nothing.

"Clear. What's in the bags?"

"Who gives a fuck? Get them over the fence and as far into that fucking field as you can, then get back here. They are not our issue right now. Rest of you, back out to the permitter. That was too easy, diversion, tab around the fence. There could be more; heads up, everyone, do not get taken for fools, there may be more of these bastards."

The guys with the ghillie suits were the final defence for the tanks, they were now loaded and safeties were off. Any bad guys would be dropped as soon as seen. The others took a part of the fence and were tabbing up and down in pairs looking for other contacts.

The adrenaline faded away and calm returned. After 30 minutes, they were stood down, leaving only single guards patrolling more of the fence the others returned.

"AV mother, AV 7,"

"Go ahead, AV 7."

"Mother, we have one target down and one alive with a bad headache. I need the bomb guys here as soon as possible and extract for this arsehole and his dead mate, confirm."

"AV 7, confirm helo inbound 15 minutes; will confirm bomb disposal."

"Boss, boss, you need to see this."

Laying on the ground, totally out cold, the second terrorist was being searched more thoroughly, now they were certain there was no risk or hidden explosive devices. Their black combat-style jacket had been removed leaving just a t-shirt.

"What's the fucking panic?"

"It's a fucking girl, she's a girl."

"AV mother, AV 7, be advised prisoner is female and needs attention to a head wound."

"Acknowledged, AV 7, prisoner is female."

They could hear the helicopter inbound a long way off. They had scrambled an AS365 Dauphin aircraft that was on standby sitting at RAF Waddington, 40 miles in a straight line. A SAS unit, aircrew plus four regiment lads.

"AV 7 Helo, inbound estimate less than 5, flare landing, acknowledge."

This meant the helicopter pilot wanted the guys on the ground to choose a place to set down that was safe.

"Roger that, will flare IR. Be advised two unknown explosive packages have been isolated in the field to the east of the site. Approx. 100 metres out from perimeter fence."

All combat troops carried IR beacons, these emitted infrared light, invisible to the naked eye but very visible to aircraft. It would mark the spot where they thought would be best to land.

"Two of you get out to the space behind the main building, lay IR flares, and guide the chopper in. Make sure you have yours lit too, I don't want anyone getting jumpy and mistaking you for bad guys."

The chopper came in slowly, hovered overhead and set down in the middle of the flares the lads had left. Immediately, four guys dropped down crouched and covered their arcs. The threat was gone but they did not know, they needed to be sure, and it was second nature.

"You guys ok?" The question came.

"We're good, we dropped one and have the other secure. You need to know the prisoner is female."

"Jesus, fuck, really? Where?"

"This way."

Only two of the four that arrived with the helicopter left the aircraft, the other two remained, weapons ready as no one was taking any chances.

They followed the Paras around the building to where the unconscious girl lay. They had put back her clothing and she was now lying in the recovery position with a field dressing on her head.

"Where is the other fucking one?"

The body had been moved to the side. It was face down and had been covered with its own jacket. The SAS man lifted the cover and looked at the body.

"What the fuck did you hit him with, a tank round?"

"Sniper 7.62, makes a mess."

"One to the head, one to the vest, that was a great call; nice work. Let's get them gone. Put that one in this."

He handed over a body bag and two of the Paras started the grim task of loading the body into the bag, not as easy as it may seem. As the flap was over, the snipers had come down from the roof and stood watching.

"Boss, this one was fucking female too!"

Both snipers in unison turned away and threw up.

"Guys, who cares? Half of the people they killed in London were females. She is still a cunt. They started this not us, but we will fucking finish it, be sure of that."

A police firearms unit had arrived and was with the van; they had orders to stay away from the Paras. As they approached the van, the chopper lifted off to about 100 ft, dipped its nose, and headed south.

The police would take care of the van and a forensic team was already on the way. The B1090 had been closed to all traffic.

"AV mother, AV 7, acknowledge."

"Go ahead, AV 7."

"Prisoner and body now airborne, police have control of the van at the bottom of the drive. Area is secure, but we are still alert. Status on bomb squad please?"

"ETA 10, make sure they can get through; good job. Mother out."

"Jock, get down there and talk to our friends. We need to shift the van because we need to get the bomb guys in and get the gate open too. But the van may be rigged too, it must be checked first. Make sure the police stay clear until the bomb folks have looked."

Jock walked down the drive towards the National Grid van and the two armed police officers. He pulled his torch from his webbing and lit the way, just to make sure they had seen him fully. As he approached, he called out, "Friendly, Army, coming your way."

His hands were high, so were tensions, and it was too easy to squeeze off a round. As he got closer, he could see the police lowering their own weapons.

"You guys ok? Did you get them?"

"Yes, thanks, all good; two of them. We dropped one and the other one we managed to take alive, both have been lifted out. Both were women. Not nice for us, but not nice to imagine either.

"We have a bomb disposal team inbound, so we need the van moving, that can't be done until they have checked the van for any explosive devices. My advice is to park up in the warm down the road out of range. Let the bomb guys go to work, then if it is safe, we can move it. There is no way we can assume it is clean to move. If you block the road, they will need to stop and you can brief them. Thanks."

The Royal Logistic Corp bomb disposal squad could be heard long before they were seen, they must have driven all the way with their sirens going.

Just as expected, the police stopped and talked with the Bomb Disposal (BD) team. They wanted to be sure that there was no access at all to the B1090 from either direction. This was the case as it had been closed off by other police vehicles as soon as they were informed.

The BD vehicle asked the police to move back to the roundabout near the A1 and let them go to look at the van. They drove initially up behind the van and sat for a good 10 minutes just looking and talking. Was this van rigged?

Clearly, the terrorists had no concern for their own safety, so they would have no regard for anyone else. The chances were that it would be rigged.

"But how? How would we do it if we were rigging the van."

A discussion had started between the four-man team in the vehicle. These guys were highly trained in the removal of explosive devices. One of the best ways of understanding how to remove it was to create it. So, a large part of the training they received actually worked in the opposite direction.

"They needed to get out and take out what was in the back, their own devices to pop the tanks. So once they had what they needed and were clear, it had to be armed. But what could initiate?"

The conversation was going around all four men, back and forth.

"That means we are looking for two things, an arming mechanism and the initiator. Arming could be as simple as a switch somewhere, in the cab maybe, or it could be a timer. Timer would have been too risky as if set by mistake, we would have a hole in the A1 somewhere. No, has to be a manual arming mechanism."

"Yeah, I agree, there is a switch or toggle or something somewhere. But where? They had to open the back doors to get access to their gear, so the doors were not armed. PIR device would be too prone to mistakes. Has to be another switch or pull wire, somewhere."

The commander of the unit was a captain; he liked the pull wire.

"Pull wire, yes, good idea. Take your shit out the back, close the door almost, attach the wire. When we open the door, pull the pin out of a grenade. Bang. Then no arming switch and it is too simple to disarm. If there is a pull wire, my guess, it triggers an electrical delay. Get you inside the van and boom."

"So I am looking for two things. One, a switch of some kind in the cab that looks out of place. Two, a possible pull wire on the back doors. If the switch exists, we cannot just turn it off, it could be programmed to blow if this is switched over once armed. We need the pull wire."

"What about mercury devices, as they are used in IEDs? Move the van and bang?"

"Again, too much risk. It's windy, so if the van rocked as they walked away, they would have gone with it. Nah, got to be a pull cord."

The captain decided the plan of attack to check and defuse the van if it was booby-trapped.

"Brian, take Number 5 and go up to the side of the van, use the shotgun and punch a hole through, fire from down up, so the blast goes upwards to the roof, less chance of us initiating anything hiding in there. Stick the camera through and let's take a look. If the pull cable is there, we cut it."

Their truck pulled back and for the next 30 minutes, there was a careful preparation for what they would be doing. Lights had been set up, so it was easy to work without torchlight. The back of the truck was opened and a ramp pulled out; within minutes, No. 5 was being backed down the ramp.

No. 5 was their affectionate name for the remote-controlled bomb disposal robot. An electrically powered six-wheeled vehicle similar to a Mars explorer you see digging up the surface of the red planet.

One main arm had a variety of attachments, some permanent, some changeable. The arm could extend to 10 feet in front of the buggy and was narrow enough to be able to fit through smaller holes. At the tip of the arm was a camera.

Behind the arm was the main control camera, watching the arm, capable of normal, IR, and thermal views.

No. 5 had a wheeled buggy; the newer versions had tracks allowing them to even go upstairs. But for tonight's mission, No. 5 was ideal.

Also mounted on the arm of the robot was an L128A1 combat shotgun semi-automatic weapon. This was what would blow a hole in the side of the van.

45 minutes later, they were good to go and everything was in place.

"AV 7, be advised we are about to commence, we will fire one round. If it goes, it could be big, take cover until we release you. Confirm?"

"Cambs police, this is BD. Please pull back to 1/4-mile safe distance, we are about to commence. There will be one round fired and hopefully no bang. Confirm?"

Both confirmed and the police vehicle moved away quite fast.

No. 5 was controlled from within the truck. The truck itself was armoured to provide same safety for the BD operators. When everyone was back inside and safe, the captain took command.

"Ok, commence. Let's get to the side of the van and take a look. Before we do anything, check out the underside, make sure nothing bad is hidden there."

Off went No. 5 being controlled from a screen inside the truck slowly and surely heading towards the van. The van had been parked facing into the driveway facing north. The red and white barriers were still there but had blown over. No. 5 pushed them aside.

It was clear on the screen in the truck that the van's driver's door was still open, confirming their fears that the van had been booby-trapped and thoughts that some sort of switch had been used to arm the device.

"We have a live one, people, I think this is live and armed. Check the underside first."

The robot moved slowly up to the rear of the vehicle and lowered the arm almost to road level, then advanced on the van, the arm moving under the bottom of the vehicle. The camera on the end of the arm was moving back and forth as the operator and others looked for signs of a device, or wires, or anything that could be dangerous. Nothing.

"Looks clear, Captain, we are going to the driver's door now."

No. 5 backed away, the arm raised, and it moved down the offside of the van. As it got up to level with the driver's door, it turned to allow the camera to see inside the cab. Nothing was immediately obvious, no red lights or flashing or anything. But this was not a movie, this was real, and they were looking for something out of place.

"Use the arm camera, look under the dash."

No. 5 backed away a little and the arm deployed to the front laying almost flat to get low enough to see under the dash. It moved forward slowly and the arm moved inside the cab at a level with the edge of the seat and stopped. The light on the end of the arm made everything clear. As the camera panned from left to right across the dash, there it was.

"There, go back, a switch, cable-tied to the steering column just below the ignition cowling. Stop, right there, three pole switch, meaning these bastards have been sneaky."

"Where is the gas tank on one of these vans, any ideas? The filler cap is on the near side in the door jam; my guess is behind the passenger seats at the front."

Everyone agreed.

"Ok, blow the hole so that any shot goes up but also keep the fuel tank in the corner furthest from the shot. My guess is that any explosives will be against the fuel tank."

"Back out, blow the hole in the side and let's see what we have to play with."

No. 5 backed away and turned towards the south, it was at an angle of about 20° against the side of the van, facing southwest, the arm extended and lowered, then partly hinged upwards halfway down its length. The distance from the end of the arm to the side of the van was about 10 feet.

"Ready, OK to fire?"

"Fire."

The shotgun fired one round from 10 feet away and blew a hole about 18 inches across through the side of the van. Many smaller holes appeared in the roof as the shot continued through and out. Some could be heard pinging about inside but soon stopped.

"No bang, all good so far. Get the camera in and let's take a look."

No. 5 moved up and the arm re-orientated to allow itself access through the new window and into the back. The insides were full of smoke but the camera could see through using IR of heat. With the wind and the new forced ventilation system, it soon cleared leaving a clear view of the inside.

Attached to the rear door was a plastic-covered metal cable, stretching from the door to the corner of the back behind the front passenger seat, next to the fuel tank. They had used logic to figure out what they would do, given the same task.

"Bingo, cut the cable and get the rear doors open. Pete, suit up, go take a look."

No. 5 extended a pair of wire cutters, and with ease, cut the pull cable and withdrew. It should be safe to open the door but No. 5 would do the opening. If they opened ok, then Pete was going to take a look.

They moved No. 5 back and around to the rear of the van, then turned it to face north. Extending the arm once again, it rose slowly and took hold of the handle on the rear door, then started twisting it slowly a few degrees at a time. After what seemed like an hour, the door was free and No. 5 withdrew a metre back to allow the door to start to open just as slowly.

It did not get a chance; both doors were kicked open and in their place, stood a black figure with an AK47, and he fired. A hurl of automatic fire hit No. 5 and the front of the truck. He was crazy, spraying fire in all directions, not looking, just hoping.

"Shoot!" The captain screamed. "Drop him."

No. 5's controller hit the red fire button on the side of the console and No. 5 let loose another shotgun round which cut the shooter almost in half; it also hit the explosives at the back of the van and it exploded in a ball of fire.

The blast was small, and the number of explosives used was small. This was an anti-personnel trap. Kill some more only, there was no point in a massive hole in the ground here. There was enough to kill anyone looking at the van, nothing more. It was now a burning wreck blocking the entrance to where they needed to be.

"BD, AV 7, sit rep?"

"AV 7, van was rigged but also had a live trigger, which was the second shot; the robot got him but the shot initiated the explosives. Stand down."

The police cut in on the comms.

"We took the precaution of bringing the fire service within a mile, they are coming through now, assume no threat, confirm."

"Confirmed no threat, send them down."

Chapter 19

M6 Southbound, Birmingham
12 November, 2300

Following the deaths of the police officers on the motorways and the result of terrorist attacks, every police officer was now very reluctant to engage with vehicles that were breaking the law or just behaving badly.

The way that the motorway police had been targeted in such a horrendous way had destroyed just about everyone's will to get on with their job. Considering these officers were some of the most highly trained and motivated in any force, seeing them so torn between the need to do their job and their own personal safety was a difficult sight.

The job needed to be done and the officers needed protection, just how this could be achieved was going to be very difficult. Many hours had now been used looking at how to protect officers and how to deal with the deliberate 'baiting' of the police.

They were deliberately being drawn into a situation when they would normally stop a vehicle or try to stop a vehicle. Just to slaughter them. When this happened, the police had no choice but to react. If the driver had a bomb or something and failed to engage the police, it was entirely possible that they could have a secondary target—school, nightclub, shopping centre. Who really knows?

So, if they tried, the police would react, but now, they would react without question and without any real risk to themselves.

A plan of action and a plan of protection had been agreed jointly between the police command and the army. It was intended to use the army to help the police. Law and order could not break down.

Operating procedures had been changed and every officer who wanted to be armed and had been trained was now armed but with just a sidearm.

Marked police car crews were reduced from a crew of two to one in every case, with no exceptions. It was better to lose one officer than two was the thinking; hard, very hard, but sadly realistic.

All TPAC and similar manoeuvres were stopped, no close contact from now on, and everything was to be done at a distance. This included the use of a stinger.

On the brighter side, this also had the added benefit of doubling the number of vehicles on the road.

Each crew now had been assigned a member of the armed services onboard highly trained snipers. Plans were drawn up to ensure that no action was taken anywhere near the vehicle being stopped. Everything would be done from a distance. They had been issued with two weapons. A 50-cal. weapon with armoured piercing rounds. A big rifle that was accurate and fired one of the biggest rounds available from a handheld weapon. The armoured piercing rounds were marked with a red band as too was the magazine of 5 rounds.

He also had a L115A3 sniper rifle. Standard issue, 7.62 rounds. Highly accurate over a very long distance. This could drop a target up to a mile away. The new plans were not looking at having a mile in between them. They wanted to be safe but close.

Both weapons were too big and heavy to deploy from the car, but that was not the plan. The risk related to trying to fire from a moving vehicle in civilian areas was massive, even with fully trained military personnel. A stray 50-cal. round does not care where it ends up.

What was being planned was cunning and hopefully very safe for everyone involved. But it was just that a plan.

Many more unmarked cars were being deployed, making it more difficult for the terrorists to identify and bait their targets. They wanted the police to chase them to do this, they had to do something near a marked police car. So be it. The unmarked cars were to be the cavalry and would be used to strike back and stop these attacks. The aim was to identify any hostile vehicles quickly. This was to be done by simple assumptions.

- The vehicle will be one up, only the driver. They will not waste two suicide bombers on one strike in a car. One can do it just as effectively.
- The car will bait the police by some means. Speed, erratic driving, use of the phone, whatever it is, it will be a deliberate act. This will be the trigger for the police operation to start.

Once a police vehicle had taken the bait, it would remain at a safe distance, but then a huge operation would commence around the area to stop and destroy the bait car.

This type of proactive and aggressive attack on a vehicle, on the roads of the UK, has never been seen. There was a possibility that it may go wrong and someone totally innocent could get killed. Considering they would have needed to do something bad enough to get the police's attention to start with and then fail to stop, it was agreed the blame would rest with the driver. A benefit to the local gene pool.

The use of stingers to puncture the tyres of a bait car would work but would involve police personnel being way too close to the risk of the bomb. The drivers would be looking for the stinger, which meant at least two officers would be nearby. Game over, detonate there. The risk was unacceptable.

It could be argued that the whole operation was too risky and if the bait cars were left alone, then they would just go home.

Or they might go and park in the middle of a shopping centre and take that with them instead. Hard calls, hard facts; if the police were baited, then the new operation would swing into place and the bait car would be taken down using maximum force.

Approval had come down from the government to deploy the army alongside the police and provide the specialist firepower they would need. These were grim times and hard decisions were being taken by the government. They wanted this over and to stop the carnage on UK soil. The UK has some of the best military available and the best police force. Together, the bad guys were going to have a serious problem.

Exactly how they would be used was left to the joint task force that was now sitting in Lloyd House in Snowhill Queensway, Birmingham. Six people, three police, three army were set up in a large conference room, waiting. A mass of IT surrounding them, displays, keyboards, military comms, links to CCTV, and other road monitoring services such as the RAC and AA.

Every shift in each station that provided motorway patrols had been briefed by the six people sitting in this room. Shift by shift, linking up by secure video conference. Over the last 6 hours, everyone had been told the plans. They already had their new military partners.

Now they waited to see if any more attacks were planned. No one said they wanted to see any more attacks or any more risk to both the police and military.

But everyone deep down wanted revenge; they wanted to hit back, to make good of the deaths of the police officers that had been killed. They wanted to restore the pride that had taken such a beating.

Outwardly, they appeared passive; inwardly, it was now, 'Bring it on, motherfuckers, we have a plan', and so it began.

On 12 November at 2300, the motorway night shift went to work. For every marked vehicle that left, two unmarked cars also left. The patrol envelope for each marked vehicle had been limited, with more cars on the road, it was possible.

The unmarked vehicles were assigned to the same limits. One each side of the carriageway.

There were strict rules of engagement and the command had to approve any need to fire. But comms were good, and a separate frequency had been established and encrypted. There was no way anyone could listen in.

So it was that the army and the police went to war together to keep their colleagues and people safe. To stop the use of indiscriminate killing that was designed to break the will of our country.

By 0130 in the morning, nothing had happened. But it was the first night and everyone was so full of adrenaline, that it may have been the best thing that could have happened. But no, this was about to change.

An ANPR camera had pinged a BMW 330 saloon on the M5 heading north through Sandwell in Birmingham. The car had been reported stolen only 20 minutes previous from the car park at Sandwell General Hospital. Some A&E consultant was very pissed that her car was missing.

1 mile further along the M5, a speed camera recorded 110 mph and the motorway CCTV controllers had passed this to the police for their attention.

With the CCTV centre connected directly to the police frequency, they were tracking the BMW visually and updating the controllers accordingly. The was no link to the new army-police response teams. The FB crew's comms were now encrypted. The controllers would be relaying information as they thought it was relevant to the operation.

The joint vehicles had been assigned call signs FB for Fight Back. This made everyone feel good about what they were going to do. It was still a huge risk but a planned response that everyone saw the logic of had restored their will. There were a lot of seriously fucked off police out to get revenge and their first target was inbound.

Their comms came to life as their controllers started to pass the data.

"FB control, be aware we have a possible target north on M5, a stolen vehicle at high speed. Could go north on M6 or south, standby, standby."

The marked BMW X5 was approaching J7 of the M6 southbound. Pete, the police driver, had 15 years behind him; he was a highly skilled pursuit driver and the big V8 X5 was a very fast vehicle. He was hoping the car would come this way.

"I'm coming off at 7 and we will lay up on the slip road. If he comes south, then he will have to come under us. Unless they come up here too, and we will be buggered."

Pete was talking to Jack, a Royal Marine sniper, 28 years old, and had been flown up to join the operation from Portsmouth. He was hilarious and could not stop taking the piss out of Pete's Brummy accent.

"Mate, can you talk English, what did you say?"

"Just sort your fucking cannon out, sunshine, leave the roady bit to me. Make sure the fucking safety is on, yeah. By the way, where did you get that weapon? Is that off a tank?"

"Just drive, Granddad, let's go kill one of these motherfuckers."

Comms came to life again.

"BMW is southbound M6 from J8, be advised speed is still excess 100."

The X5 sat there out of sight halfway down the slip road, in gear, waiting. 15 seconds later, their first target T1 came passed under the junction.

"FB4, we have eyes on and are following as of now."

Pete hit the blues and on came the siren as he accelerated down the slip road and out into the M6, directly out into the carriageway and on after T1.

The first unmarked car was way ahead of both T1 and Pete, just approaching spaghetti junction (J6). The second unmarked car on the opposite side of the road was in between J6 and J7 where Pete had waited. They hit the gas and were now heading to flip-flop at J7 and get back after Pete to help.

In the distance, T1 had clearly clocked the police presence, he hit his brakes quickly, the natural reaction when the police are behind you. Pete was closing his speed was 120 mph, but he was looking for a sign of what was to happen. It did; T1 took off and floored the car.

"FB4, T1 is baiting us to chase. Acknowledge please, confirm go-ahead."

"FB, you have the go-ahead to follow, pick up the commentary."

This meant that they wanted Pete to give a commentary on what was happening. This was second nature to police drivers, all part of the advanced training for many different reasons.

The X5 was sitting at just over 150 mph and T1 was pulling away slightly. Whoever was driving that car was either very good or just mad. Or maybe had nothing to lose.

"You OK in the back, sunshine?" Pete shouted over his shoulder.

"Shut the fuck up and look where you're going, will you?"

Comms were now set to talk through; this meant the channel was open and anyone could talk as needed. Pete's commentary was continual, giving speed conditions, location, and T1 reactions.

"FB, CCTV have confirmed vehicle is one up only, single driver only."

One part of the rules of engagement had been met.

The speed of T1 dropped, rapidly, there was no junction anywhere soon, the next was J5, but he was slowing. Pete slowed to maintain a distance, large enough to avoid damage if he went bang. But T1 hit the brakes, a cloud of smoke came from the tyres, and he slid sideways, turning a full 180° to face Pete, then completed the doughnut and hit the gas south down the M6.

"Well, he seems very clear he wants us to follow." Part two of the rules of engagement.

"FB, T1 slowed and did a complete 360 on the road and is now accelerating away south. We have confirmed the bait."

"FB4, continue at a distance, we are instigating the response. We need an overhead."

Further down the motorway, other units were now setting up to intercept and stop T1. 2 miles ahead, an unmarked Vauxhall Vector was in the middle lane doing 70 mph. They need to confirm that only the driver was in the car, no one else. CCTV was not always very clear and open to misinterpretation. The easiest way was to assume the appearance of a stupid motorist hogging the middle lane and just drive.

Sure enough, T1 shot past the Vauxhall followed 15 seconds later by Pete.

"FB, FB7, driver only confirmed."

"FB, F4, be advised stop intended at junction 4, repeat junction 4. Drop back on approach, we will initiate before the junction."

Whilst Pete was following T1, other FB units were converging, and it had been decided to use J4 as the junction provided a bridge over the main motorway.

The junction had been closed across the motorway and was closed on all approaches. Two unmarked cars were stationary on the flyover. Below to the north, both lanes of the M6 were clearly visible, normally six lanes of solid traffic.

Traffic had been stopped as far back as J7 where this started for Pete and as far back as J1 to the south. The only vehicles on the road were T1 and the response teams.

On the floor lying prone were the two snipers. One had a Barrett M82 50-cal. rifle, the other had an L115A3 sniper rifle. Side by side lined up on the outside lane, listening to the commentary from Pete, now 3 miles out.

"FB, sniper 1, clear to engage confirm."

"Sniper 1, clear to engage, repeat clear to engage."

"Roger that, FB, sniper 1 will engage."

They had discussed the approach speed and targeting the vehicle at high speed may be difficult. It was agreed that if they were baiting and the police slowed down, then logically the target should slow. Massive assumption, but time will tell.

Pete heard the conversation with the snipers already set up and in position. So, he eased the speed down slowly. T1 had not moved out of the outside lane and did not look like it was going to. He moved his vehicle over into the inside lane. T1 may think they were giving up and slowing down.

Exactly what T1 did. Both vehicles slowed down and Pete eased back some more, his speed was down to 70 as they approached the junction. This had the extra benefit of moving Pete out of the firing line. If the round missed or ricocheted off the target car, he did not want to be in the way.

The 50-cal. sniper had his sights on the BMW sign right at the front of the car. He had been tracking the car as it approached, his position head-on for about half a mile. Relaxing, he moved his finger onto the trigger and pulled gently taking up the slack, waited, then took a deep breath, let it out very slowly, and as he exhaled, he fired.

The driver of the target car must have seen the smoke from the weapon, a little puff of grey smoke. But before he had time to register what it was, or may have been, or even was not, his life suddenly changed.

The round hit the car right through the BMW emblem on the front and smashed through into the engine block. A hot knife and butter. The armoured piercing round pierced through the metalwork at the front of the car and destroyed the engine block in a nano second.

Punching through at the point where the cylinder head meets the block. Aluminium is not any form of armour at all. The engine came apart. Ironically just a few miles away from the BMW, engine plant that had built it in Coleshill.

The tangled mess of rotating metal under the bonnet jammed, locking the transmission and the back wheels instantly. Clouds of smoke erupted from the rear and a cloud of steam from the front. The driver lost the back end as it swung violently towards the central reservation, but he still had the sense of mind to correct the skid, bringing the car parallel to the crossing. A sitting duck for the second sniper.

"Fire."

The second shot from the smaller calibre rifle still took out most of the other side of the driver's head. He was dead before the rest of his body knew it. His foot was still pushing on the brake pedal, muscle memory until it too realised, he was dead.

The locking up of the transmission, together with a lot of panic braking, dropped the speed greatly. The momentum of the car took it back across the road towards the inside lane, then across the hard shoulder and into a gravel area. The gravel took away the rest of the force. It sat silent, directly under the junction bridge, where the snipers above were now getting up very fast.

"Run, run for fuck's sake, go! Leave your shit and run!"

Four people took off running as fast as they could for the other side and away from where the car was now stationary underneath. As they cleared the bridge onto a grass area to the north, they dropped.

"Down. Take cover."

They hit the ground trying to be as flat as possible. Trying not to be there, waiting for the bang. Hands-on their heads, holding their breath, listening to their hearts banging away at breakneck speed.

5 seconds, 10 seconds, 15, 20, nothing; no bang came. 2 minutes passed before they did anything.

"It fucking worked, it bloody worked. Stop the car and shoot the driver."

"Yes, great, wonderful. We are still laying on the floor not far away from some dead cunt and a bomb."

"We need to get gone out of the way, let's get the kit and cars and remove ourselves."

Anonymity was guaranteed. The public, the police or the military would never know the names of anyone who had been involved in these operations. The only ones who would know were the men themselves and the terrorists whose warriors seemed to disappear.

Pete was half a mile down the road and he saw what happened. The car had stopped, and there was no bang. Was it good or was it bad? Had they just shot a joy rider? They had done their job and so had the army lads.

The rest of the operation was for others to complete and not the FB units. This response was now coming up behind them. Bomb disposal team to check the car and make safe anything they did not like. They would confirm and make safe any IED explosive, a vest or a bomb in the car.

The car had been stolen minutes before it was pinged by ANPR. There was no time to rig the car for explosives or a trap of any sort. It would be a vest or nothing. Even a vest would present many obstacles for the bomb lads. It would take time.

"Please don't let it be nothing!"

Pete was thinking, or so he thought, but he had said it out aloud.

"Don't worry, mate, we did our job. He did everything he could to bait us. Even if he is not a bad guy, I don't want that sort of twat on the road in front of me at any time. We did the world a favour."

The comms came back to life.

"FB, all involved units return to base for debriefing, we need to compare notes and learn from this incident. Hopefully, this was a good job. Well done."

The two unmarked on the bridge and the drive-by car together with Pete's unit went back to the same base. They parked up and made for the main briefing room. There was already coffee on the go and hot sandwiches for them, courtesy of the night shift. They had heard the news.

Within minutes, two uniformed officers came in. One a deputy chief constable, the other an army major.

"Gentlemen, please sit, relax, eat and drink; this is informal. We need to know your thoughts on what happened, the events along the way and the outcome. Where did we fail? Where did we get it right? This is not a witch hunt; it is fact-finding. Speak freely."

Over the next 2 hours, they all talked through their own parts in the operation, what happened, and how they responded. Bit by bit, they took it apart. They all had blood and a kill on their hands, this needed to be justified. Even within the strange circumstances they found themselves in now, following the attacks in the UK, they had to stick to the rules. Everything had to be documented and full statements taken. It would be examined to make sure the correct procedures had been followed.

"Gentlemen, thank you for your time and patience; you can now clock off for the night or go back out for the remainder of your shifts. Your choice."

A knock at the door surprised everyone, they had given orders to be left alone.

"Come in."

"Sir, sorry to intrude, we have just had word from the motorway that the bomb disposal team found a live suicide vest on the driver. It was a good kill, Sir." The tension in the room disappeared and from outside in the main offices of the police station, a small cheer went up.

The deputy chief constable stood up and went to each man in turn and shook their hands.

"That is good news for the teams. Good news for the planning and most importantly, good news for the policemen and women out there. Well done, good job, we have hit back, and we have clearly saved the lives of police officers tonight. Yes, it is good news, but we have a long way to go before we can all relax. My guess is that you lot want to get back out on patrol and catch another. Great, go, get out of here."

The body count had now started to rise. One kill on the motorway, two dead, and one in custody just over 100 miles away in Cambridgeshire.

History has always shown that to take a poke at the UK is a bad idea. Whoever this is, whoever has planned and carried out the attacks in the UK has the whole nation as one coming after them.

The British enjoy a good way of life and are a truly multicultural, multi-race society. Do not mess with our way of life. We may argue and moan about each other, but we will stand together as one people and fight back.

Chapter 20

RAF Waddington, Lincoln
12 November, 2330

The surviving prisoner from the aviation fuel storage site was transferred back to RAF Waddington with her dead friend. Although unconscious when she got into the helicopter, she had come around within about 5 minutes of being airborne.

The SAS team had redressed the cut to her head, but that was all it was, a minor cut just above her hairline to the front. Everyone knows that your head bled a lot, and a little bit of blood goes a long way. Although her face was still covered in blood, the field dressing and pressure had stopped it bleeding further.

She had been plasticuffed and was laying on her side, arms behind her back and these fixed to her ankles, which had also been cuffed in the same way. She was not going anywhere that was for sure. When she started to move, two boots were pushed onto her back holding her down. No chances were being taken, she had to stay alive.

The helicopter came in over the airfield and put down in a remote corner, very close to the buildings where the air ambulance operated from alongside the A15 road. The air ambulance was not there and had been operating in and around London over the last few days.

At the end of the runway, not more than 400 metres away, a C130 was lined up ready to go; all engines were running but the rear ramp was down. It was waiting.

The prisoner was lifted out of the helicopter by the four-man SAS team. Her ankle binds were cut, releasing her to walk. Two of the lads held her upright, whilst the other two, one in front and one behind, covered their arcs as they marched her away from the helicopter towards the C130. But stopped after no more than 100 metres. They waited.

Still, no chances were being taken, the two guards dropped and recovered their arcs. From the back of the C130, four men appeared and jogged over in a formation of four, two by two. They approached the group holding the prisoner and stopped. They were dressed in full camo, belt kits, and side arms. All wore a helmet and all had a mask. There were no military insignia on their uniforms.

"Nice job, lads, this one is ours now, thank you."

Two moved forward and took the prisoner by each arm from the SAS team, turned and marched off back towards the waiting C130. Nothing more was said. The SAS were stood down and a Land Rover was being sent to pick them and their gear up.

No sooner had the prisoner disappeared inside the huge aircraft, than the tailgate started to go back up and the aircraft started to move. As it taxied down the runway, the tailgate could be seen to shut fully. Turning around, the C130 roared back towards them but went airborne very quickly, tactical take-off, and climbed, disappearing into the night.

It went quiet. The lads grabbed their gear, jumped into the Landy, and headed off not saying a word. But they all wondered what the fuck had just happened. Even though they knew they had never seen it.

Location Restricted
C130 Airborne
12 November, 2355

The inside of the C130 was massive. No one normally gets to see the inside of a plane with no seats, nothing. All stripped out, almost a bare airframe. Designed to carry large cargo and men into and out of battle.

The forward cargo area had a row of red seats on either side of the body. Not seats as you would expect. Minimal steel frames and webbing to sit on. Nothing else. The rest of the space was designed to take vehicles or cargo.

There were five people strapped into the red seats on one side of the plane—the four soldiers that had taken over the prisoner and what appeared to be a civilian. The terrorist that had been captured near Sawtry was on the opposite side, strapped in and restrained. The inside of the plane was lit only by a red light. It was hard to see properly.

The prisoner had been blindfolded when they took her from the helicopter team and was now shackled to the seat with handcuffs. Apart from the normal straps on the seat, no other restraints.

The C130 went airborne and climbed at full rate, 2100 ft per minute. For 10 minutes levelling out at 20,000 ft. The flight crew were a special ops crew used to dealing with the demands and restricted nature of what they were sometimes asked to do.

Turning to the east, the flight crossed overhead Skegness, and out into the North Sea, then turned again onto a heading due north.

The flight crew had been told this was a training flight for the SAS, testing new deployment methods. They had no idea of what was being tested, nor were they going to ask. They were there to drive the airframe and nothing else. Even when they were asked to perform the tactical take-off and climb, they did not question anything.

On the climb after take-off, the prisoner would have had no idea of what was happening. Blindfolded and with no headset, the noise and disorientation must have been terrible. A 10-minute rollercoaster ride upwards, with your stomach in your throat, a huge amount of noise and vibration.

As the aircraft levelled out and the engines throttled back to normal flight conditions, it was as though someone had unplugged the noise. Everything seemed quiet.

The prisoner had vomited and covered her trousers and one side of her top in puke. She was still blindfolded and shackled.

The others released their own seatbelts and stood. Nothing was said; they deliberately did not want any talking or discussions. Two of the four soldiers left and went to the rear of the aircraft. The others brought out some boxes, placed them on the floor and opened them up.

Moving forward, the civilian approached the prisoner.

"I am going to release your handcuffs and you can then remove your blindfold. You are in an aircraft now, high above the North Sea. You have nothing to fear. Do you understand me?"

"Yes, I do. What are you going to do with me? Where am I going?"

"Nothing. As I have said, you have nothing to fear. I am going to move forward and release you. Please remain seated, do not get up."

He moved slowly towards the girl and at the same time, the remaining two soldiers moved one each side of the girl. If she did kick off, then they would restrain her.

"Right hand first, I will undo your handcuff."

This he did slowly and deliberately.

"Good, now the left hand too."

The handcuff was unlocked from her wrist. Both sets of cuffs were left attached to the chair.

"Great, your hands are free. Please remove your blindfold, then sit; do not stand and wait whilst your eyes get accustomed to the surroundings."

She did. Slowly pulling off her mask, then put her hands in her lap and sat very calmly and submissive.

From the box, a small bottle of water was taken and handed to the prisoner.

"I can't drink this; I am not stupid, you may have put something in it."

The civilian broke the seal and drank from the bottle, then handed it to the girl.

"Do not worry, we are not going to drug you or hurt you. We do need to talk to you and it would be very good for you if you are honest. Can you do that, can you be honest?"

The response was quick and with venom.

"I will not tell you a thing. I should be dead now anyway; I do not care what you do to me."

"Please, relax, drink your water. Then you can go and clean yourself up. Get some fresh clothes. We have brought something for you to wear."

Out of the box came a bundle of clothes and everything she would need to clean herself up. Not an orange suit but jeans, t-shirt, sweater, pants socks, soap, and deodorant. The civilian handed her the bundle.

"Please don't do anything silly. You are on an aircraft, there is nowhere to go or hide. The toilet is over in the corner, go and clean yourself, change and then, we will give you some food."

Rising carefully, she winced at the pain in her head. The dressing was still there. She touched it.

"When you get back, one of the lads will redress your head. It is not that bad but it did bleed a lot. You do not have to worry about it. Please go and make yourself comfortable."

She did. In the toilet compartment, there was a sink and a loo. She stripped off, washed herself, cleaned the puke from her skin and put the new clothes on, which were big for her. *Better big*, she thought. There was even a toothbrush and toothpaste. This put her at ease. They would not go to this trouble if they were going to hurt her.

She took her time, no rush they said, so be it. Eventually, she was done, having bundled the old clothes into a pile, she left them. She unlocked the door to the toilet compartment and walked back to her seat, head down, no eye contact.

The remaining three clocked that she would not make eye contact. They knew this meant that she had been given some training in how to deal with questions.

When she sat down, they handed her an egg sandwich and a hot cup of tea. Plenty of sugar. She took both and ate and drank greedily, not stopping until it was all gone. Another sign of training. Eat when you can and all you can.

"What's your name? I am John Hawthorn. I am a policeman; I am not a soldier."

This was true to a point as he worked for the Met anti-terrorist branch. He was seconded to the SAS and worked hand in hand with them stopping terrorist activity as they could. He now had a laptop open on his lap and was typing as he talked.

"So, what do we call you? Please be aware, that I can check everything you tell me very quickly. Please don't lie to us. We know you have been involved in the attacks over the past few days in London and elsewhere. We know that you should have died today blowing up some fuel dumps. Many people have died including many Muslim and non-British casualties. Your attacks have been indiscriminate. Targeting just anyone."

"I can't give you my name, it is forbidden."

"We have already sent your blood to be DNA traced. The dressing from your wound was taken. This is being worked on right now. I expect to be able to tell you who you are and where you live very soon. I will then also know every member of your family. We will know who you are, so why not tell us?"

"I am cold."

This was deliberate. It was cold in the aircraft. They all had thick coats and they were warm. She had a jumper but they knew she would be cold.

"We can give you a coat but you need to give us something too. We must work together now. The more you cooperate, the more you will help yourself and your family."

"What's my family got to do with this? They have not done anything."

"Really, that is what you are telling us after killing so many people. We do not know and we certainly do not trust you. Once we have your name and address, they will all be arrested and taken away. For their own safety and for us to make sure that none of them are involved. People are angry and want revenge for London. They would be at risk if we do not act."

"It's nothing to do with them, they don't know anything. That is not fair or necessary."

"Fair and necessary did not seem to apply to what you have done, did it? But without a doubt, they need protection if what you say is true."

"Don't talk to me about fair and necessary after what you did in Iraq and don't talk about indiscriminate, that's a word which does not apply to the West, does it? My name is Ellen Ammar, you will find this anyway from my DNA; there is no reason not to tell you. But this is all I will say."

A good start, John thought, *that was easy.* He typed the name into his computer which completed a search through both UK and Interpol databases. If she was known or being watched, then she would ping up. She did. 30 seconds after she revealed her name.

His mind was spinning over her comments about Iraq. What was that all about? She wasn't even born.

Ellen Ammar
52 Waverly Terrace Bradford
BD7 3HZ
Known to UK anti-terror
Not known to Interpol
Under surveillance possible threat.
No trace of family member
Mother Ishlam Ammar
Father Mohammad Ammar
Brother Mahar Ammar

"Ok, Ellen. Do you mind if I call you Ellen? You can call me John, that's fine."

"Yes, call me Ellen."

"You live with mum and dad at 52 Waverly Terrace in Bradford, you have one brother, Mahar. Is that correct?"

"You tell me, you have the information."

"Please, Ellen, is that correct?"

"Yes, yes, it is correct. So the fuck what?"

Ellen was getting either angry or scared. Why? This had to be as she feared for her family. She did not want them dragged into this. Or she did not want to have to watch whilst they were dragged into it. She was supposed to be dead and not seeing anything. *Weird*, John thought.

"There is no information that links your family to any acts or suspected involvement with terrorism. But we will still have to protect them and they will be arrested for now, for their own protection. You must also realise that they will be deported, sent back to the country of origin. The UK will get rid of them, to put it bluntly. We do not want families to remain in the UK that have had any links to attacks on people that live here. Whatever faith or belief, peaceful people deserve the protection of the UK."

"Don't make me laugh. Peaceful people, attacks on your people, you fucking hypocrite. Did you not study the history of the UK? All through history, you have slaughtered in the name of your God, or for wealth or conquest. Look in the heart of your own country before you judge. It continues today, in the Middle East, Iraq, and Afghanistan. What gives you the right to impose your beliefs or your ways of living on these people?"

There it is again, John thought. *Iraq, some sort of link back to Iraq, indiscriminate act. She had been told something. Something had happened and this was her justification to act and attack the country where she had lived.*

"Do you believe that it was right to just allow Iraq to invade Kuwait and take what they wanted, Ellen?"

"NO! But it was not your fight, it was nothing to do with the West. The Arab nations would have stopped it from happening. Always the West wades in with their bombs and missiles. Always the West kills indiscriminately because someone was in the wrong place at the wrong time. But oh dear! Look what happens when we do it to you."

The passion, the bile, the hatred from a young woman who was willing to lay down and die for that belief. Again, the word indiscriminate was used. Someone was in the wrong place at the wrong time. Someone had been killed clearly by UK forces that were in the wrong place at the wrong time. This was the basis for the hatred and for the attacks. It had to be. But it was so massive, so violent, so deadly.

"Tell me about the person that was killed in Iraq, Ellen."

"What do you mean? I did not say about anyone being killed. What do you mean?"

She was flapping and had realised from what she had said; a few pieces of a jigsaw had come together, to coordinate the attacks against the UK that had happened involved inside information.

John sent a message asking for any knowledge of anyone within the security services with family links back to Iraq and at a time during the Gulf War. It was marked urgent.

"Ellen, it is clear from what you have said that someone very important was killed. Wrong place, wrong time. Tell me about it. Who was it?"

She was mad. Mad with herself and mad at everyone. The temper was rising; she was going to let go and have her say. And she did.

"Fuck you, one person! Why just one person? Is that the only mistakes you think you made? The only person the UK killed or blew away, accidentally. Oops sorry! Really. Just how many innocent people did you kill? Does anyone care? You all fucking care now it has come back to haunt you."

So there it was, someone got killed and this was revenge! Now she was mad, John used it against her.

"Everyone you have killed was innocent. Over six thousand people, children, sick, everyone. Don't preach at me, you have no fucking right."

"Hurts, hurts, doesn't it? It's not over yet, it will never be over. Even your own are betraying you. Right now, right now as we speak. Not low-life people like me. You arrogant arsehole. People high up, people that are 'protecting the UK' as you put it."

She realised and stopped; her temper had always made her mouth run away.

"Can I have some more water?"

John handed her a bottle. No hesitation, she opened and drank.

"So, there is someone high up in government or the security services that has an axe to grind and this is the result. Who is it, Ellen?"

"I will never tell you; I will die first. I have said far too much already. No way I will ever say anything more about this."

"Will your family die for your beliefs and to protect this person, Ellen? Are you willing to watch them die for you, Ellen? Because they will die, Ellen. We will make sure you see too. You will spend the rest of your life replaying the video in your head, all alone in a cell."

"You would not dare, you would not be able to. Everything leaves a trace, people know I am here. You cannot do shit without it becoming public knowledge at some time."

"Really. No one knows you are here. No one will ever know. As far as anyone is concerned, we do not know you or have you, or even suspect you of being involved. No trace, you're in an aircraft over the sea. You will hit the sea as though it was concrete. You don't have your clothes on. Everything you are wearing is sterile. Don't fucking kid yourself, Ellen. You and the people you work with started this against the UK and you thought we would play fair. Wrong."

"Fine, kill me. You won't know then, will you? I can't talk when I am dead. Go ahead, shoot me, or throw me out of the plane, see if I care."

"All I need is a name. We will then put you into protective custody. You will stand trial as you should, but you will be given leniency for helping us."

"Fuck you, fuck your kind, fuck what your country did."

John thought for a moment.

He moved away from his prisoner and picked up an intercom phone to talk to the crew. The aircraft turned and started to descend. For about 5 minutes, they were going down, then it levelled out again.

"Gents, if you please."

The two soldiers took hold of the girl, one on each side, one on each arm. At the same time, a whirring noise started up and the tail opened and began to lower. The air rush was deafening. The soldiers put a hand on her back and pushed her hard forward to the rear of the plane.

John moved forward and put a set of headphones on her ears, then himself.

"Last chance, Ellen, last chance to help us. Last chance you have to stay alive. What do you want to do, Ellen? You want to live?"

"Fuck off!"

John stepped back and put on a red harness over his coat, stepping into it like trousers. To the back of the harness was a rope, this was under slight tension so that as he moved, the rope remained taut.

"Move her!" He yelled above the noise.

They pushed her backwards and stopped as she was on the break between the aircraft body and the ramp, which was now fully extended.

"Sure, Ellen? You ready to die? Are you ready to let this madness continue?"

"Again!" He shouted at the two soldiers.

Once again, they pushed her and she staggered backwards towards the open tailgate.

The two soldiers left her there and moved back into the main fuselage. John moved towards her. She was shaking with cold and looking forward into the aircraft.

"Ellen, I just need a name or something that can help me. If you don't know his name, what does he do? Give me something I can work with. Then this will stop."

"I do not know his name. I was never told who it was. I cannot and will not tell you more."

John pushed her hard. She fell back onto her bum sitting down. Reaching down, he pulled her up again, wrenching her arm hard.

"Ellen, your time is running out, tell me something, anything that will save you."

Her shoulder sank and John thought she was going to say something.

"I cannot tell you and betray my friends and soldiers. You do not expect me to tell you. You just want to kill me out of the way."

"Yes, you're right, I do."

He stepped forward right next to her, looking her in the eye, and put a hand on each shoulder, then pushed. Ellen fell back over the edge and disappeared.

5 seconds before John had pushed her, two figures in black, who were standing in the far corners of the aircraft, moved out and jumped. As they fell, they looked up and saw Ellen fall. The two flashing beacons now fixed to her back, put there by the other two soldiers as they first pushed her, could be seen easily.

The seasoned free-fall veterans manoeuvred themselves into position to intercept. They had around 60 seconds from her jumping to her hitting the ground.

They were on her in 5 seconds. They took hold and controlled her fall together. Then pushed a headphone on one of her ears holding it in place.

"I need a name or a position, or we let go."

They both pulled at the same time, with Ellen safe between them.

"Tell us, Ellen, or you will die right now. Who?"

She was cold, terrified, and about to die.

"All I know is that they are at the top of SIS in London. I don't have a name. As I told you in the aircraft. They would never risk telling us any names. It's one of the bosses. Go. Go and stop this madness and let me die."

She kicked out at the crotch closest to her. It hurt, he let go and she fell.

The aircraft was over the coast at Bridlington. There was little wind and the drop would have been straight down. They floated down the last 3000 ft after she had dropped, landing safely on the beach. 200 yards away were two flashing lights and what was Ellen lying face down in the sand.

"SF1, drop successful, request evac from beach Bridlington. One dead. Out."

The chopper came in from offshore, dropped down to where they were flaring, and four more guys jumped out. Less aware this time, they took some time to put Ellen into a body bag and loaded it up.

The jumpers collected everything and stowed it, checking the area for anything that had been missed. Then filled in most of the hole Ellen had left. Within 10 minutes, they were gone like it had never happened.

RAF Waddington
13 November, 0145

The same five men sat in a conference room. They were alone. All had coffee and sandwiches.

"Sir, I believe that she really had no name. She gave us the person, or a small group of people to work with. I also believe that she did this to stop what may still be coming. I must believe this is genuine."

"Ok, so we have a person or persons at the top or near the top of SIS in London. We need to act, so let us move this along and see what happens."

John picked up the phone, made a call and said just a few words.

Within 5 minutes, the main TV screen in the room came to life and three people appeared. One was a politician, the second was an army general, and the third was Sir Robert, the Met Police Commissioner.

It was the army officer who spoke first.

"Gentlemen, report please, tell us what happened this evening. Just the facts please, we do not need the how."

"Sir, the information we have is that someone or multiple persons close to the top at SIS are involved. This somehow relates to an incident during one of the Gulf Wars when someone got killed for being in the wrong place at the wrong time. The prisoner had no names, only the positions that these people held. It is claimed to be part of high levels within the SIS. I have already requested that checks should be done to look at if there are any links with present staff and Iraqi origins."

The commissioner then took over.

"John, good job by the way. Yes, I saw the request for your checks and I have stopped it. There were some strange things that happened recently which have been noticed. As a result, we are already working with one person under surveillance. I will say no more. But from what you are saying, there could be at least one more, perhaps several. This person at present is unaware of any action against them. It must remain this way. We will now expand our enquiries to look for other possible persons of interest.

"Everything that has happened and all the information that you have now in your hands is now classed as top secret, eyes-only. It is paramount that none of you discuss this with anyone. If this is who we suspect, or close to the top, then they would be one of the first to know that something is happening and your enquiry would alert them. Everything we do is being done outside of any involvement of the SIS. Am I clear?"

There was a brief silence.

"Then, gentlemen, all that remains is to thank you, and good night."

Chapter 21

Oswald Building, Queenstown Rd
London SW11
13 November, 0420

Si'ad lived in a second-floor apartment in the Oswald Building, Queenstown Rd. A modern, recently built complex of seven buildings adjacent to Chelsea Bridge.

He could walk very easily from here to the office, but his security level would not allow this to happen.

For him to be exposed for such a time along a route that provides many opportunities for someone to hit him, was not a good idea. Long shot, or hidden attack, it was too much of a risk without close protection.

The apartment was not a cheap place to rent. It was close to the river and had a view over the Thames, close to all the local amenities and Central London. If it was for sale, it could be valued at way over £1.5 million. £1.5 million for a flat. When you say it fast, it does not sound as mad.

He could afford it, easily, and he was paid very well. But the apartment was a sort of Grace and Favour arrangement tied to his job. It was chosen by the government, required to be secure and was swept very regularly. He was 'at risk'. Therefore, some of the costs were paid by HMG.

It was also close to where he worked.

Battersea Park was the opposite; this provided a host of recreational opportunities. Open space to walk or run, a boating lake, tennis, and even a Go Ape facility. Plus, the children's zoo and athletics track. More than enough for the residents to exercise and amuse themselves.

Si'ad would make use of the park for recreation, although this too could be considered dangerous. He did not normally risk meeting anyone in the park that was involved in his plans to cripple the UK.

Most of this communication was done through other means. Face-to-face at this stage was too much of a risk.

He was not asleep; it was just after 4.15 in the morning and Si'ad was awake. Sitting in the lounge with the TV on and his PlayStation was running. He was just sitting staring at the screen. The game had been paused and he was messaging people on the game's message app. A secure, difficult-to-find method of communication.

All messages were end-to-end encrypted and difficult to trace or intercept. A popular message platform for communication when it was necessary to remain hidden. It also kept the comms away from any phone that was provided internally, or his mobile.

There were eight areas of direct action in his plan. He knew them all by heart and had spent time planning each one to the smallest point. So far everything has been completed as planned with the expected results.

1. The gas supply: Shock and awe
2. London itself: Shock and awe
3. The Avgas supply: Shock and awe
4. The police: Demoralisation
5. Second gas attack: Demoralisation
6. Financial: Interference
7. Water: Demoralisation
8. Sterling Lines: Payback

Yes, there were always going to be casualties within his own people. They were to be expected. Each of them knew that their missions were a one-way journey. If they did survive, they would be hunted for the rest of their lives. But they still agreed to go, to take the fight to the enemy.

Oddly, it was not really their own enemy, it was a personal Jihad, simply revenge. Si'ad wanted revenge and they were happy to give their own lives, and willingly.

He had been very lucky in finding out about the report being compiled by the RAF on how to attack and cripple the UK. This was a stroke of sheer luck whilst he was digging through other secret information and classified documents. The document itself was a work of pure genius.

His level of security clearance gave him access to just about every document that was available. All are controlled by the login details from his laptop and the biometric passwords.

He took a copy of the RAF planning exercise document. He read this many times, taking note of parts that he felt could be used, and parts that may be useful. There rest was ignored from points of view concerning delivery of the strike, people needed, and of course, the ordinance.

He needed people though. It was impossible to complete what he was planning by himself.

But because of his job, he was ideally placed to be able to find and coerce anyone to help him. People who were already radical, people who would follow once he had shown them the evil of the Great British people. If he made them believe that they were doing Allah's work, ridding the world of the big Satan, they would follow him as they had ISIS in the past.

Many young people had gone to the Middle East to fight. If not for their own country, or where their roots lay, they went to fight the great Jihad, alongside ISIS. Worryingly for the UK Government, they were not all Muslim or Islamic.

The British Government had made it illegal to leave the UK and go to fight with ISIS or any other terrorist group. Many still went, but the risk of not being allowed back into the UK did not stop them.

In the eyes of the UK SIS, this could be a good thing. With luck, they would die fighting, removing possible future threats from the UK. Even removing them from the gene pool, protecting the future.

Why stop them going? Once they were gone, they were not allowed to return to the UK. Assuming that is, they survived.

It was true, many did go, in secret, moving through Europe and then through Turkey into the Middle East. No one knew about them leaving, only their families, and they could say nothing. But they left a trail, which was picked up again as they started to return home later.

SIS were tracking them all and Si'ad had all the resources he needed to locate them once they were back and then later, visit the ones he wanted.

The ones that did return mainly got home and quickly fitted back into their old lives, old jobs, and getting on with their lives. But the hatred was still there. By now, it was deep-rooted and Si'ad could make very good use of this.

These were the people that Si'ad wanted. He wanted that hate and that willingness to fight, the willingness and eagerness to die. They believed they were fighting a just war, they believed it was right. So, he slowly began to contact them and recruit them into his own personal cause. His own Jihad.

He would give them a renewed purpose and provide the fight that they so craved.

Over a period of almost 2 years, he met every one of them, spending some time talking with them and getting to know them. Nothing was mentioned of his plans until he was sure they were truly what he needed.

He chose carefully, making sure that those who he did want could fit in and live in normal society. A loudmouth radical, shouting every week outside his mosque or at a protest would attract too much attention. He needed soldiers who could hide in full view. One couple he recruited were even married.

It took time and careful vetting of everyone he was involved. They all knew the consequences of talking out of place or accidentally mentioning what they were doing. Si'ad was careful; they were all only told details of the part of the whole attack that they would be directly involved with. There was only one person who knew it all.

***

Unknown to Si'ad, the two teams organised by the Met Police Commissioner continued to follow him. They could not engage, they were tasked to observe and report back only. The communication lines were set in stone and no one was allowed to pass any information until they met, in person, in secret at 1830 in the evening.

But they were learning about him. What he ate, what he drank, how he amused himself. Any habits or interests he had; they saw and watched.

Si'ad was very much a loner; his job was the main cause. He could not meet anyone normally with the hours he worked and the need to drop everything when called. If he ever did have a date, then it would only last a few weeks before something got in the way. He could not make a show or was suddenly unable to meet her as planned. He would let her down.

He was wealthy to a point, and it was not long before the lads watching him found something that was not expected but welcome. Si'ad had a thing for call girls. Escorts, or street hookers. He did not care. To them, he was just another rich prick who wanted sex. He paid, they delivered. No strings attached sex.

He knew it was wrong and broke just about every rule in the spy book. He put himself at risk. But he was not stupid. He had divided his flat into two areas. His flat had two bedrooms. As you came in the front door, the bedroom directly opposite the door was smaller, but very useable. The small en-suite shower room provided facilities as required.

Any girl coming in was shown into this room and did not go anywhere else in the flat. In fact, the rest of the rooms were locked off.

The girls only went into his special room when he needed some life. It was totally clean, with nothing in there of any consequence. Nothing worth stealing, nothing that could identify him. Laid out like a studio, there was a small sofa, a TV on the wall, a nice view, a drinks cabinet, and of course, a bed. One door led off to the loo.

SIS understood that this was a guest suite and that the precautions taken were for good reasons. It did not.

Having gone for a short walk, he would return arm in arm with his chosen girl for the night and show them through into his guest room only. Everywhere else was out of bounds. The girls never questioned. They were there to provide a service. The room was warm and comfortable.

There was no weird business, straight sex, sleep, more sex, and they left. Anything kinky or otherwise would mean the girls may remember him. But it filled his need.

***

When Si'ad had walked away from the devastation that was his home, he was a boy of 15 years old. Suddenly, he was alone in the world. In the space of one night, his whole family and his whole life in Iraq were taken from him.

He had not seen what remained of his mother and sisters, but he had seen the body of his father. He was slaughtered by some unknown foreign soldier, just to steal his beaten-up old car. His father's life was worth no more than a rusty old truck.

That picture was burnt into his mind's eye. He saw it every time he closed his eyes. He saw his home smashed and burning. He looked forward to the day when Allah would call and he too would be taken; he could sit once again with his family in peace.

He was not going to stay in a place full of so much hurt and pain. Just to rebuild the devastation to be knocked down again when the president had another meltdown and attacked another neighbour. He had made his mind up to go. To go and seek a life where he was safe, could thrive and plan.

Crossing the border was not hard. The bombs had cratered the road and blown away the border fence. The fence was more of a symbol showing the borderline between Iraq and Kuwait. For generations, the people on both sides were friends and they lived and worked together as one. Yes, they were on different sides of a wire fence but they paid no attention to that, they lived as one.

With a small wrap of water and food, Si'ad set off to get away from the hell hole that was once his home and his family. Within 15 minutes, he was a mile into Kuwait. He had been taught how to use the stars to find his way. He was very used to desert life and used to living with very little.

His aim was to go south, almost due south towards the big cities of Kuwait. With the North Star behind him, he walked and walked. He was sleeping during the day and walking at night, eating what he could find or catch. He was worried that he could be mistaken for a spy, rather ironically.

He had about 140 miles to cover on foot, which was a huge task. He was determined to do this and get away. He had nowhere else to go or nowhere to be. He had no one waiting for him or looking for him. There was no rush and no real plan in his head. He wanted away from Iraq. He wanted a new life, and now most of all, he wanted revenge.

Revenge drove him on. Some days he would only walk a few miles and others, he would walk more. The terrain slowed him down or gave him speed. He was crossing land where goats were normally grazed, so at times was forced to hide away to avoid being seen.

Being caught was frightening. How would they treat him? Would they think he was a threat? Although this did concern him, he was far more likely to bump into a shepherd or another Kuwaiti farmer. These were ordinary Arab people. They did not want the war or the killing it brought with it. His hope was it would be one of these people that he met if he did.

The deeper into Kuwait he walked, the more confident he became. Walking more during daylight hours. He was less worried. There had been no sign of any military vehicles or soldiers and now he moved much deeper into the country. He started to relax a little and blend into his new surroundings. He was dressed as an Arab and looked like everyone else. He spoke their language.

6 days into his journey, he fell.

It was a windy day, warm, but the wind was blowing hard and it was noisy. Walking along the bottom of a deep wadi, he had his head down trying to avoid the sand that was blowing in his face. He did not hear the goats at the top of the wadi. When he did, he looked up in panic, there were the goats and two herders looking at him.

In his panic, he tried to run, lost his footing, and fell. His hands went out to protect the fall but his head hit a rock on the way down. Things just went dark.

Unknown to Si'ad when he woke up, he had been unconscious for 10 hours. It was dark when he came around. He had no idea where he was or what had happened. His head hurt like hell and it was covered with some form of dressing.

Where am I? Have I been captured? Have they sent me back to Iraq? Who took me from the wadi? Questions, questions, all going through his mind at 1000 miles per hour as he lay still on the bed.

I'm on a bed? How come?

He continued to lay still for some time and listened. He could hear talking not far away; men, several men, but also a woman's voice and children. He must be in someone's home. This thought gave him some comfort, but he was still very much aware and on guard.

The next time he opened his eyes, it was light. He had slept again. The bang to the head was still hurting and he still felt very weak.

"Ahh, you wake up, this is good. How is your head?"

His eyes were blurred, his head really hurt, and he could not really move that well. But he turned and tried to sit up. It didn't work, he went very dizzy, dry wretched and fell back onto the bed.

"Slowly, my son, slowly. There is plenty of time for you to recover. You are safe, you are in my house, do not worry yourself."

A strong hand lifted his head and shoulders and offered a cup of water to his lips. He drank, drank a lot, no concerns.

Over the next 2 days, Si'ad recovered and came to know the people who had taken him from the wadi to their house to help him. They explained he fell when he was scared and that he had a nasty cut to the side of his head in the hairline.

For the next week, Si'ad stayed with these people. He explained what had happened and they all knew he had come from Iraq to escape the war and the death. They took him in, fed him, and cared for him as one of their own.

This was the Arab way, peaceful people going about their simple lives.

But he knew he could not stay there forever and he talked to them about his wish to go to the big city and find a new life, but kept the secret that he wanted to quietly build his strength and plot his revenge.

The man of the house was a large man called Amal. He was huge, something not normally seen in Arab people. He may have been huge but he was clever and very kind. He spoke with Si'ad and probed the trouble that he could see in Si'ad's eyes.

"You are very troubled, my son. What is it that haunts you like this? Is it your family, what is it?"

Si'ad told him, told him of the promise he had made to himself to revenge the deaths of his family and to bring this hurt and heartache to those that had killed so indiscriminately in his hometown.

Amal listened; he said nothing until Si'ad had finished. Then he paused before replying.

"I can see that your mind is set on your plan for revenge, and I can see that nothing I say will change this in your head. So, you must now continue, go, seek this thing you want for your family. Tomorrow, I will help you to find your way to Kuwait City, from there, may Allah look after you."

The following day, true to his word, Amal put Si'ad on the right road to take him to Kuwait. They gave him food and water and set him on his way.

"Stay on the road, someone will stop and let you ride with them. You will be in the city today with Allah's help."

Amal had also told Si'ad that there was a square in Al Jahra near Kuwait City where people wanting work would gather. Employers would come and take the workers for the day, for the week, or sometimes permanent work.

The square was very near to the Al-Fath Mosque, meaning Si'ad could find it easily. This is where he would go. If he worked hard, he could earn money. The money would pay for education. He wanted to learn, to get clever, to understand the world, understand the West and learn why they were so barbaric.

It took 2 days to make the journey. He did get a lift but the driver headed to a different city and dropped Si'ad at a junction to try to get another ride. He did eventually get one but had to sleep overnight in the open, waking early to catch the busy times on the road.

Just as Amal had said, there were many people in the square when he arrived. It was early morning, and they all waited, hoping for work. Trucks and buses would come as the day began, men would select the people they wanted, load them into trucks and go. Later in the evening, they would return.

Si'ad was there for 3 days but he had no offers of work. He tried, would shout, and ask. They would tell him he is too young and not strong enough.

"Go home, boy, we need men."

And so, this continued for a week. Si'ad grew hungry, down hearted. He had water from a nearby well but there was no food without money now. He was not going to give up. He looked filthy after his journey. His clothes were dirty, he was dirty.

This cannot help me look so shit, he thought.

Overnight, in the cover of the darkness, he stripped off and cleaned himself using the water from the well and cleaned his robes. Washing them as best he could in just cold water. It made him feel better, feel cleaner. More self-respect. The following morning, he was there with everyone else waiting to be taken to work. It still did not happen.

He sat on a wall, opposite the mosque, thinking about what to do next. He had not given up; he was just rethinking. A short distance from him on his left was the Waha Medical Centre. He thought back to how he had cut his head. He could have had his head checked.

A car suddenly sped up to the medical centre and stopped with a skid and a screech. This startled Si'ad back to reality. The car was new, modern, and very shiny. Unlike his father's rusty truck. The door opened and an elderly man jumped out from the driver's door. He shouted at the medical centre aimlessly, it was too far to be heard he thought.

Opening the back door, he tried to pull out what seemed to be a boy, maybe the same age as Si'ad. The boy was floppy, not responding, and the old man could not manage to get him from the car.

Without thinking, Si'ad ran to the car and called for the man to let him help. He got into the backseat, put his arms under the boys arms and wrapped them around his chest, then pulled him from the car. He was unconscious, something was very wrong.

"He is choking, he is choking," the man kept saying. "Help me, help me take him to the doctor."

The boy was heavy, well-fed clearly, and dressed nicely. Pulling him up and out of the car was difficult, and Si'ad had to jerk him up a few times to get enough grip to hold him and move him.

As he pulled hard and up on the boy's chest, he clearly heard the air come out of him and a stone from the middle of a peach shot out of his mouth onto the floor. He started to breathe. Totally unknown to Si'ad, what he had done in lifting the boy mimicked the Heimlich manoeuvre.

His coughing and crying caught the old man's attention.

"What did you do? It is a miracle! What have you done, he is breathing?"

"I have no idea but let's get him to the doctor quickly. He is not well, go and tell them he is coming, I will carry him."

Si'ad carried and pulled the boy across the road and into the medical centre; the old man had alerted the staff, and they took the boy from Si'ad. He thought nothing of it, left the centre, and went back to his seat on the nearby wall.

It must have been about half an hour later when Si'ad noticed one of the doctors walking towards him. He was worried, maybe it was not his place to help the old man. Had he done something wrong?

He panicked and stood, grabbed his bag, and went to run.

"Wait, please wait. Nothing is wrong, come with me please, come to the medical centre."

The doctor stood, beckoning Si'ad to follow.

He is a doctor; doctors are good people. I can trust him; he is a doctor.

Si'ad followed but was on his guard. The doctor led him back into the medical centre and then along a small corridor. It was cool inside, with no midday heat. It was very strange; he had never felt the cool of air-conditioning. On the right of the corridor was an open door and the old man was standing in the doorway.

"Come, come, see what you have done for my family. Allah sent you today to be there for my son."

On the bed lay the boy from the back of the car. He was sitting up, supported by some pillows. Wires came from him to strange machines that made noise. He looked pale but he was awake and talking to the doctor.

Si'ad was puzzled; he looked from the old man to the doctor and back. He had no idea what was going on. He was unaware that in lifting the boy as he had done, caused the stone in the boy's throat to dislodge. He had saved the boy's life.

The doctor came over to Si'ad and held out his hand, when Si'ad responded, he shook his hand many times.

"You have saved this boy's life. What you did was amazing, very quick thinking. Who taught you how to do this? How did you know?"

Si'ad was no one's fool. He now realised what had happened when he lifted the boy. He had forced the air out of his lungs and moved the stone.

"I just did what anyone would have done to help the boy. He was choking, the man said he was choking. Is he ok? Did I hurt him?"

"You have saved his life. If you had not been there to help, he would now be dead. He owes you, his life." The old man came over and put his arms around Si'ad and hugged him tight.

"Thank you, thank you from the bottom of my heart, I owe you a debt that no one can ever repay."

Si'ad was taken back, shaken. One side of his head was saying he was a hero, the other side was saying he needed to go now. *Do not get caught, run the fuck away.*

"I must go, I am happy your son is well. I must sit and wait outside."

Si'ad turned to walk away and the old man stopped him, holding his arm. He lifted the side of Si'ad's headdress and saw the bloody wound dressing. The effort of lifting the boy had caused his own wound to bleed once again.

"Look, Doctor, he is bleeding. He has a wound on his head."

The next 30 minutes were just weird for Si'ad. He had never been to a doctor in his life, he had never been to a hospital. The lady in the village would help with fever. He too now lay on a bed and the doctor had sewn up the wound he had on his head. He did not feel it when the doctor had sewn his skin.

The doctors left and the three of them, two patients and an old man, talked about what had happened and why Si'ad was there in the first place. Si'ad told them the truth of what had happened in Iraq and why he had come to seek work. He was now alone in the world and wanted to make his way.

"The answer is very simple," the old man said. "You will now come and live with us, my son, Mohammad, and I. There will be no argument, you are now part of my family. Allah sent you today to help us, we will now honour Allah by helping you. You will now be as my son."

And so it was that Si'ad was adopted into the Sheikh's family and treated as if he was a son. Because of this chain of events, Si'ad met Sheikh Nazim.

A very wealthy land and property owner. He had one son, Mohammad; his wife had passed during childbirth 15 years ago. There had been no more children born to the Sheikh. Si'ad was accepted into the family as if he too was a true son of the Sheikh.

For the next 3 years, Si'ad lived a good life. He was made to study, to catch up on the missed time when he should have been in school. He was smart and learning was easy for him. The extra time needed for study meant that he was almost 19 when he graduated from high school together with Mohammad. They were both very clever and both wanted to continue their studies at university.

"You have both made me very proud, you have both done so well. None of this would be possible without Si'ad having come to our family when he did. So now it is time for you to fly and continue your studies at university. But where, where do you want to go? You must decide, I will make sure you can go where you wish."

Si'ad already knew he had been thinking of this for some time. If he graduated with the best grades, he could get into any university and the Sheikh would fund it for him. His mind was set. London.

Somehow, he now had to convince Mohammad that he too wanted to go to London.

London it was.

Chapter 22

Scotland Yard, London
13 November, 1830

The conference room was locked down as usual and the same people were there.

The police commissioner, Will, the SAS, and police units.

The room was buzzing with hushed conversation. Clearly what had been discovered was causing some light-hearted banter, but also a lot of questions.

"Gentlemen, if we may, thank you."

Bringing the room to some sort of order, he continued.

"So Marachi has a thing about the ladies, really? Well, that's something I was definitely not expecting. How can we use this to our advantage?"

The commissioner looked very surprised at what they had just been told but had already started to wonder just how this could be of use to them all.

"So how is he contacting them? I do not believe he is using the secure lines or his mobile. There must be another mobile, he has another phone. We need to find it and find it quickly."

One of the SAS stood and addressed the room.

"Sir, if I may…"

"Sit down, man, at ease, we are not in court. Relax, speak your mind. None of this regimental ballock for now please."

He sat, loosened his top button, and as with all the others, relaxed into what was to be an open discussion between some very time-trained professionals.

"I don't think he is using a phone, or anything else to meet a girl. It's all too risky and leaves a trail if he uses any device. I don't care how careful he is. We have seen him. Just like going for a walk and coming back with someone within 30 minutes. He clearly knows where there is a local place the hookers hang around. So simply goes and gets one when he feels the urge."

"Ok, so what intelligence do we have on any local hook-up points around his area? Must be within a 10-15-minute walk. Unless he jumps a cab. So, I need a list of all known places where these ladies ply their trade within 2 miles of his flat."

This time, it was one of the Met guys who stood and started to walk out.

"Let me go and ask around, perhaps Vice can give us the data…"

He stopped talking and it was obvious that his head was considering what he had just said.

"No, we cannot involve anyone outside of this room. We cannot risk letting him know we suspect him."

The commissioner was there already.

"Exactly, we must do it, or rather you lot have to do it. I still always want the normal Obs team on Si'ad. Nothing changes there. The rest of you get out there tonight and walk the area, I want a list of all places he could get to in 15 minutes to pick up some tart."

The commissioner fell silent, whilst the others mumbled again between themselves. They had just realised 12 hours on and 12 hours off had just changed to sleep when you can.

"So, does he have a type?"

"A type, Sir?"

"Yes, yes, what type of lady is our Si'ad partial to? Blonde, dark, small, big, fat arse or what. Does he go for a certain type of person all the time? If he does, maybe we could plant someone that he may pick up on."

"Do we have anyone that is willing to shag for their country, Sir?"

This made the commissioner laugh, along with everyone else. It was good and it broke the mood a little.

"Good point, but it may not come to that and besides, there is no medal I know of for that type of bravery. This man is the head of the SIS, he is highly trained and will plan everything to minimise any risk and to keep himself secure. So, my guess is that he will have one room in the house that is clean and he will use this for his lady friends when they arrive.

"But! Likewise, such a room would allow him to perhaps contact other people from a clean environment. He has no idea if his flat is bugged or not, so he will assume it is. Yes, they sweep it every week but we would not point out one of our own listening devices. Even if he found it, he can't move it. It's a perfect cover from the outside. Anyone, like we have, who notices his appetite for fanny would expect a clean room.

"Taking this theory one stage further, are these people hookers. For cover reasons, 95% will be genuine. It's the other 5% he wants. He can meet with someone in this room, posing as just another lady. But the room is secure from SIS or any other interested party that wants to listen. We need to be able to hear in this room. And quickly."

Will had been listening intently to what the commissioner was saying. It made a lot of sense to him and he could see the logic in Si'ad doing this and the commissioner's evaluation.

"The only way we can get a device into this room is for an agent to pose as a hooker. Then get Si'ad to pick her up one evening. That itself is difficult to achieve on many levels. Once we get her in the house, we cannot keep her safe, she is alone. That's a huge risk to her life."

"Will, you put your life at risk every time you got in your aircraft and flew. You even got shot at from a fucking pub you were about to bomb! Everyone with us here, knows the risks involved as would any female agent we choose to ask to complete this job. So? How many good-looking females do we have either SAS or SCO19? We cannot ask around but you lot have met them all, operated side by side under pressure. Time to spill the beans. Which ones are worth taking to bed as far as looks go? How many have the balls to do this? Excuse my pun."

There was a lot of joking and laughing and banter as you would expect from a bunch of men given the opportunity to say out loud which of their female colleagues they wouldn't mind going to bed with.

Two teams of guys, police on one side, SAS on the other, you would expect two answers, but this was not the case. The SOC19 guys spoke first.

"What was the name of the SAS Rupert that worked with us to take down that lunatic eco-activist that was going to blow up the nightclub last year? She was very good, on the ball, knew her stuff, and was not afraid. She walked right into the club dressed to the nines, looking like a million dollars. She knew there was a bomb in there somewhere and she was going to get it out. No question. Man, she should be your recruitment poster. All of us were all over her when we had a chance."

"You mean Grace Roberts. She is now a captain after that night out. You're right though, she is a looker. Not at work, she hides it all down. By the book. But seeing her dressed up, I agree."

The commissioner had come back to life and was on it straight away. He needed this woman.

"How do we contact her and how quickly can we get her here? More to the point, is she safe, can we trust her?"

"All SAS Regiments are now on active duty in the UK, either defensive or proactive in hunting these idiots down. Grace is with 22 and 22 is in London, so she will not be far away. I can try to get her now."

Again, the commissioner paused. He was about to break his own rule by allowing contact outside of his group.

"Find out where she is. Do you have your SAS comms with you and are they secure? Can SIS intercept?"

"SAS comms are encrypted, and the encryption cycles every minute. No one can hack them and if they do, it only lasts seconds. I can contact her. But then what, Sir?"

"Just get her location, prepare her to be picked up immediately, no questions, no refusals, this is a direct order from the top. She is to tell no one, say nothing, get in the car when it comes and shut the fuck up."

"If she is within range, she will respond, otherwise it will need to be relayed via Sterling. Are you OK with that? It will just be an order to EVAC?"

He was struggling with the risk of exposing his team and letting Si'ad know they were on to him. The commissioner knew that sooner or later it would get out; getting out now would just accelerate matters a little.

"Just do it, we need her."

From a large bergen wedged into the corner of the room, out of the way, the senior NCO retrieved his tactical radio TACCOM. Within seconds of turning it on, it went live and was working. He had to put the earpiece in place and hold the throat mike to his neck.

There was a lot of chatter but nowhere near what could have been expected considering the last few days. His commands were short and to the point.

"Captain Roberts, location…Captain Grace Roberts, location…"

She clearly answered but was unheard by the rest of the room.

"Sir, just off Park Rd NW8, Danubius Hotel. How long for pick up?"

The commissioner picked up his desk phone and dialled.

"I want a pickup from the Danubius Hotel, Park Rd back to Scotland Yard. Armed protection, two vehicles. How long?"

There was a pause for what seemed like 6 hours. He sat motionless waiting.

"Very good, do it and I want full security on this, you are collecting a high-value SAS Officer."

He then turned back to the room.

"15 minutes, get her ready to go."

"Captain Roberts, EVAC 15 police 2 pack, bring your gear. From the top. Don't ask, don't speak, over.

"All done, Sir, she will be there and ready."

***

As always when a shout comes in, you are having your rest break. The two crews of the armed response units were sat together. Two of them were halfway through huge plates of pie and mash, which was a known benefit of working out of Collingdale Nick. The other two were just returning to the table with trays of their own.

Collingdale had developed a reputation of having one of the best kitchens in the area, providing a combination of foods that was the envy of many Nicks in the Met. Sure, there was the fill-you-up stodge available, but they specialised in having a special plate every day. From pie and mash to jerk chicken, the daily special was talked about everywhere.

Almost everyone eating had been on shift for 12 hours or longer. Some had finished their food and were asleep on the arms in front of them. No one wanted to go home as everyone wanted to be working to help deal with and overcome what had happened.

They all knew their loved ones were safe, they wanted to work. Public service like this was a calling. The same as the NHS. Sadly, generations of politicians have taken advantage of this. But now, when the chips were well and truly down, everyone was in awe of the emergency services. Everyone would double their pay overnight.

All four of their comms units squawked into life. A beep beep noise meant an emergency response was required. With no hesitation, they left their food and ran back to the cars. En-route, they were told to collect a high-priority package as soon as possible from the Danubius Hotel and move them quickly to Scotland Yard, a fully armed security vehicle response.

The route would take them out of Collingdale Nick and south to the outskirts of Regents Park, across the road from the North London Mosque. Their package was waiting at the Danubius Hotel.

With the situation in London, many officers had now been issued with firearms, but the highly trained SOC19 officers were still deployed for response where it was possible that shots could be fired.

Each had their full body armour and tactical vest, sidearm, taser and sprays. The driver's HK MP5 weapon was alongside his left leg. Safe, but loaded and no round in the chamber. The front seat had a fully loaded MP5, safety on but ready to use.

From Collingdale Nick, they left joining the A41 Watford way. Lights blazing and full sirens, they had 5½ miles to cover as quickly as possible. Most of London was still shut down to allow easy access for emergency vehicles. The rescue and recovery operations were continuing. London was told to stay home.

Blasting through Hendon Central and down over the Brent Cross flyover, the route was almost straight through. Right turn in Finchley and in towards Regents Park.

They arrived at the hotel entrance 7 minutes after they left Collingdale Nick. For London, that was a very fast journey.

Captain Grace Roberts stood just inside the hotel lobby, close enough to the front to get a view, far enough back to make any shot very difficult. Not that she expected to be shot at really, but who the hell knows she thought.

She had battle fatigues on, her bergen was on her back. Sidearm, fully loaded vest, and her own MP5 across her chest. In terms of appearance, she looked as threatening as the four lads about to meet her.

The cars drew to a stop outside the hotel, all four got out. Three took up positions of defence whilst the fourth made his way to collect the captain. As she was the only soldier standing there, he assumed, rightly, it was her.

"Captain Roberts, come with us please, Sir."

"Ma'am…underneath this lot, I am female."

"Sorry, my mistake, follow me."

They left the lobby and headed for the two cars. The other three had not moved other than to cover their arcs of fire. They had no idea what may shoot at them but they would not take a chance. High-value package means someone could want them dead.

"In the back, Ma'am, please throw the bergen in first."

The others followed and doors banged as they made ready for the final part of the journey. The same two drivers took their positions, each one checking their weapon twice before getting back into the car. As soon as all were good to go, they were off.

"Ma'am, sorry, we need to check your weapons."

The captain did not respond. She took her MP5 and within seconds, broke it down into component parts. Then reassembled it. Pulling her sidearm out, she repeated the action with the handgun.

"Sorry, no one touches my weapons. They are safe."

"Did you just say ma'am?"

Grace didn't wait for the answer from the driver, she answered for him.

"Yes, I am a female SAS Captain, one of only two ever. I completed the same training exactly as the men and have fought alongside them in many places around the world. Now I am sorry, my orders are to ask nothing and to stay quiet."

"Woooh, no offence, Ma'am, just admiration. I wish we could get more female recruits into SOC19."

As the captain had said, the rest of the journey to Scotland Yard was quiet, uneventful, and very fast.

She got out of the car and the police repeated the defensive positions, one of them escorted her into the lobby and to security.

"Good luck, Ma'am. When this shit is all over, come back and visit us."

"Thanks, I will do that, and I mean it. But you have to promise to teach me to drive like that madman out there."

***

Security had been warned to expect the captain to arrive with the police escort. She was to be shown through immediately and the commissioner himself would collect her from the lobby.

Grace did not sit; she now had her bergen on again and was holding her MP5. Sitting was not very easy.

"Captain Roberts? Thank you for coming, not that you had much alternative I guess, but thank you anyway."

The commissioner greeted Grace and led them back towards the lifts. She had no chance to say anything, and could not get a word in backwards.

"This must all seem a little odd but bear with me. Once we get upstairs, we will fully brief you and get you up to speed. As you can imagine and clearly will know, the last days have been manic. With the devastation in Central London and the death toll still rising daily, we are stretched to the limits."

He led Grace from lifts along the corridor towards his own office. Every night, there was no one on this floor, except for the commissioner, his team, and the armed guards blocking all access to the commissioner's office.

As she was led into the meeting room, Grace's eyes widened. She recognised the four SAS lads who had just risen from their seats, along with everyone else. But she made no acknowledgement of their presence. She stood and waited.

"Please sit, Captain. You can put your gear over there where everyone else keeps their packs and weapons. I assume they are safe. Sorry."

Again, Grace did not react to the 'Safe' comment but she took off her pack and vest, leaving this ready to go quickly, alongside her MP5. Her side arm stayed put but she had noticed everyone else had a side arm too.

"Ok, we all owe you an explanation as to why you are here. Before we can discuss anything with you, I must inform you that what you will be told is classified at the highest level. Every one of the men in the room has signed a secondary addendum to the Official Secrets Act. You have already signed the OSA but I need you to read and carefully consider the document I will give you.

"This does not change anything or add anything to the original document you signed. It serves only to remind you of the obligations you have agreed to. Nothing more. If you sign, we will all continue. If you choose not to sign, then there are no consequences whatsoever. No one is aware you are here except us. We will return you to where we collected you and that will be the end of it."

Now Grace was interested, sign again meant really hi-classification security.

The commissioner handed the document to Grace, and she looked at it.

"Sir, would be OK if I grabbed some water?"

"Of course. Apologies, I should have said to make yourself at home."

Returning to her seat with the water, she removed the top and drank, then looked at the document carefully and began to read.

Two sides of an A4 page did not take a long time to read. 10 minutes later, she took the pen offered and signed the paper at the bottom as indicated. The commissioner signed next to her.

"Thank you, Captain. Now. I take it you know the four lads from your side of the fence. The other four are SCO19, some of the best we have. I will leave you to get to know everyone's names. In the far corner is Will. Will is RAF and he is helping in many ways, which we will go over as we lead you through what is happening and why.

"Firstly, outside of this room, no one knows of the existence of this team. We do not communicate at all. We meet here every day at 1830. Only then, do we discuss the business that we are all now involved with. Our presence is secret and we are guarded the whole time whilst we are together. No one within HMG knows what we are doing. No one within our own secret service knows what we are doing. We must not discuss anything with anyone who is outside of this room or outside of this team.

"Why the total secrecy of this team? That is simple but shocking. We suspect that the head of the British SIS Si'ad Marachi is in some way responsible for the attacks on London and other UK critical assets. We are investigating this possibility as we speak. Everything we do has to be completed by us without involving anybody, or service, civil or military. Nothing, or anyone, can be asked to provide info, intel, assistance, or something that could alert this man that we are on to him. As you can imagine, this is somewhat limiting."

Grace just sat and looked at the commissioner straight in the eyes. Didn't move a muscle, just one word came out of her mouth.

"F…U…C…K!"

"Exactly, I could not have put it better myself. Welcome aboard. Within this room, we are informal to produce an easier atmosphere. You can speak freely, totally freely. Consider the unit is on active duty. We are fighting a war inside our own country to stop this madman before he does anything else to Will's shopping list. What we are doing is highly dangerous, we are putting ourselves in the firing line. Plus, we may be totally wrong and all get shot for treason. But right now, we know we are right. We know this man is behind the horrible things that have happened."

The commissioner paused for breath and Grace was there.

"Will's shopping list, Sir?"

"Yes, sadly, it's like a shopping list of doom. I will explain. Group Captain Will Rivers is the Commanding Officer at JARIC, an operation you will be familiar with. A recent brief required the group captain, sorry Will, to produce a document that detailed just how JARIC would attack the UK and cripple it. This was a personal project that only Will worked on. It was so secret that only Will and two of his superiors were aware it was being done. The level of security required to access the document was such that only a few people in the UK could actually get to see the report. I was not one of these people, even had I known it existed.

"Shortly after the main attacks, I received a call from Will. Cutting a long story short, he told me about the existence of the report and that what had happened was part of the strategy he had devised himself to cripple the UK. His aim was to head off future attacks if they continued to follow his plan. This has been done successfully by preventing the second attack on the gas pipeline."

"Was that you? The first time our armed forces have been authorised to attack a UK target. You took out those bastards trying to blow the pipeline again?"

"Well, yes, it was coordinated from here by Will. Moving on, this was the first thing which flagged up that a high-level person in the UK with high-level security clearance could be leading the attacks. The same day before I had even met Will, I went to ground zero with the prime minister and Marachi himself to see the devastation that had been caused. Something strange happened.

"Marachi insisted we wear anti-gas suits and respirators. We stood looking at the scene as if we were on the moon. The whole site had been evacuated. Only much later did our people establish that there had been a leak of ammonia gas. Just how did Marachi know that the gas was present and take precautions? Not for us, for himself. He had prior knowledge. It was with this coincidence in mind that I assembled this team.

"Then, of course, I have the call from JARIC. One of the only people able to access and read the report from JARIC is Marachi."

Over the next 3 hours, the team brought Grace almost totally up to speed. She was engrossed on the whole concept of the head of SIS attacking the UK. She was also angry because of the last few days, she saw scenes on the streets of London reserved for a battlefield.

"As I said earlier. Fuck! So why am I here? What can I do?"

This time, the SAS lads described what they had been doing following and watching Marachi. Every movement he made was being watched. His liking of hookers and the fact that this has pointed them to believe he has a clean room in his flat.

The clean room was a means for him not just communicating, but also meeting his terrorist team members. They needed to get some form of a listening device into the room.

Then, the penny dropped.

"Oh! Now I understand. I'm here because I have a pair of tits!"

The commissioner was clearly flustered and tried to calm things a little.

"You're here because you were recommended for the job we have. Your past success in dealing with a situation where, shall I say, a nice-looking young lady was required preceded you. Add to this the fact you are SAS and close by."

"Please, don't get me wrong. I am not offended or anything. I was stating the obvious. You need a woman to try to get close to this Marachi. I'm in. I'll bite his cock off if I get a chance."

And so, the room fell into laughter and relief.

"One thing that no one has considered, is clearly, that he may be gay. Have you considered the people he takes back are men?"

The commissioner's eyes went very wide.

"FUCK!"

Chapter 23

Scotland Yard, London
13 November, 2030

The room fell back into discussion on just how Grace could get the attention of Si'ad. This could take time but they were all out of time. Somehow it needed to be done very fast.

"We still have no idea where he goes to pick up the girls. I know I know things are moving fast and we have not looked yet. We know how far he walks. It takes him roughly 30 minutes to get there and back, this includes time to chat with the lady I guess, agree terms, etc."

The commissioner was again considering breaking the silence and asking for help from the people on Vice. He had to reduce the time it would take to find where Si'ad was going and pick up the hookers.

"Who do we know in Vice, lads? Who do we know that is good, knows his job, and can help us and will not ask questions?"

The SOC19 lads had been out in support of raids related to Vice, taking down traffickers or dealing with nasty pimps and protectors. They had experience of the command structure in Vice.

"Mike, the DCI, he is one hard bastard. No room for any compassion with him. He knows his territory and works it to remove the filth that prey on the girls. He would know and I think we could rely on him."

"Call him, get him here asap. Tell him to say nothing and speak to no one again. Come directly to Scotland Yard, then wait in reception."

The call was made and Mike was told to report to Scotland Yard quickly. He was only 15 minutes away but he too would be blue-lighting it to meet the commissioner.

Mike was a big guy, Scottish, born and brought up in Glasgow and as hard as nails. Ex-army, joined the Met 15 years ago, and was doing well. He was known for being unstoppable and unflappable.

The commissioner showed him into the conference room. Mike did not bat an eyelid at the sight of the gathering.

"Please take a seat. We need your assistance. I can tell you absolutely nothing about what is happening here, sorry, that's just how it is. Need-to-know and all that ballocks. But we still need the benefit of your experience and know-how.

"If I lived in Queenstown Rd, near Battersea Park, where would I go, on foot, to pick up a hooker? It must be within a 15-minute walk, 30 minutes there and back. Our target is making use of the ladies frequently. We need to know just where he is going to find them. Any ideas?"

Mike thought for a short while.

"Is he picking up men or women?"

This amused the team but puzzled the commissioner. Grace looked very happy.

"Simple question, if he is straight or is he gay. If he wants fanny, then he will head for one place, or gay, he will head for another. Around here, there are not many places. On Strasburg Rd, there is a substation building. The girls tend to stand there. Easy for mobile pickups and out of the way of us lot.

"Further down Queenstown Rd, there is a car rental place, Sixt I think. The lads stand here. If he was not using these, then he would need to go further afield and use transport."

"Then this is where we will concentrate our efforts."

"Sir, your man, what race is he? It makes a difference. If he is any sort of Muslim, then he will not go looking for men. Gay Muslims are still very much in the closet."

The commissioner looked a little relieved.

"That has helped us a great deal; it means we are able to concentrate on one place and try to arrange the switch."

The DCI looked concerned.

"Sir, you are going to need some help if you intend to try to lure this man to pick up a plant. These girls can smell us a mile away, you will need them to work with you. Otherwise, your man will notice something is not right."

"Work with us, just how exactly can we manage that?"

"Sorry, I know this is some sort of undercover does not exist room, but you cannot just wade in with no experience with sex workers. Firstly, they will eat you alive because you are threatening their income for the night. Secondly, it will go around very fast that some new police operation is happening and they will all go to the ground. It could be that one will even tip off your man if he is a regular.

"I hate to suggest it but you need some help on this. More so if it is that urgent, I must come in from a job I was already on. Many of the working girls know me. We look after them, stop them getting beat on, or hurt. In the nicest way, they owe me and my teams. Maybe it's time to collect a little."

"Just how can we do that? We cannot tell them anything, give a reason for what we need."

"Exactly, Sir, they need to want to help. They owe us, so let them help us willingly. We could just say the operation is trying to draw out a really bad guy. We are using one of our own as a decoy and need their help to get her in place. If they see this as our way of protecting them more, they will help us. Sorry, Sir, I must ride along on this one."

The commissioner was deep in thought, then turned to Grace.

"Grace, it's your arse on the line, excuse the pun again. I'm getting good at this. What do you feel about what the DCI has just said?"

"It makes sense to me, Sir. As you say, it's my arse and if the girls help me out a little, we can do this. I want Mike to help us. We don't have time to mess about. This goes down tonight if our man decides he needs to get laid this evening."

Mike had no idea that one of the soldiers was a woman. He was turning to speak with a confused look on his face but Grace beat him to it.

"Oh, don't worry, Mike, I have tits I promise."

Which caused quite a stir, serving to calm the growing adrenaline within the team.

Mike continued. "I suggest we do the following. I will go in alone to start with and talk to the girls. We need to be sure that if your man comes along, there is little option but for him to approach Grace. If four girls are working, then four of you lads will roll up in cars, do a deal and take the girls away…for a coffee. This is a hands-off exercise. But you will pay them for their time and pay them what they ask.

"If there are three or two the same applies. We need to time the last one getting in the car as your man comes into view. He will just see Grace standing there. We need you lot looking normal-ish, with no guns anywhere in sight, and aftershave tonight. Time is 2115. Let us meet up at 2200 outside the front on the road.

"So, the lads in the cars, washed and ready to go. A tail team on your man, so we know when he is going to approach. Grace done up looking as hot as possible. Not stunning, a little slutty, show some flesh but not a lot. Finally, we need a few of the lads hidden away near to the target's place to go in and get Grace if she is in trouble. She must have comms somewhere, somehow."

The commissioner had never met Mike but he liked him already. His commanding presence, clear thinking, and the way he just sorted it.

"Agreed, gentlemen. Look after Grace, no one gets hurt tonight."

Grace pushed in as the commissioner stopped talking. "Urm, I am sorry but I have nothing in the way of clothes at all for a dressing to kill session. I need to find stuff to wear."

Mike was there again. "Oh, that's easy, I can arrange that. As I said, they all owe us big time. I need your dress size, shoe size, and bra size. The clothes can be here within 15 minutes together with makeup and hair stuff. Anything else you need?"

Grace shared some personal information and Mike made a call. Whoever was told to bring the gear exactly as asked.

"Grace, use my shower room through the door of my office. I will get the clothes to you as they arrive. We do not have much time, let's go and get this done. Good luck."

Grace took herself off to the shower and locked the door behind her. She had been on duty for 48 hours; this was a treat she had not expected. Before she was fully dry, a knock on the door startled her a bit.

"Grace, it's Mike, your clothes are here. There is a lady officer to help you if you need it."

The door opened and the officer disappeared onto a cloud of steam, then it closed.

At 2155, there were four cars with four drivers looking just normal. The fifth car was Mike's. He was sitting on his phone, waiting for Grace to arrive.

And arrive she did, dressed to the nines and looking very much the part. She had a long thick coat but it was flowing and not done up. It was 13 November, but not too cold. She got into Mike's car at the back.

"Ok, move to RV1." This was a point they had selected further away from where Si'ad would come from. There was no chance of passing him. When they were all there, Mike and Grace would then move to meet any of the normal ladies working that night.

There were only three girls dressed in a way like Grace. Mike had contacted one of his informants, a hooker herself. It was she who found the clothes so quickly.

He drove the small distance to where the girls were standing and parked a little away. Then walked over to the group of girls.

They stood and listened to what he was saying, and whatever it was, they were looking a little scared. Hands-to-mouth gestures and they all became obviously nervous. Less than 5 minutes later, Mike waved Grace over.

Grace sort of marched over with determination. The girls stopped her as she arrived. They were in awe.

"You really a copper, Miss? You need to come and work with us; you could retire in a year. Anyway, let us take a look at how you're dressed. Make sure we can see the tops of your hold-ups, and shorten the straps on your bra, stick 'em out more. The punters like that."

They fumbled with Grace for a few minutes, then looked at Mike, nodding.

"Ok, we are good to go. Ladies, thank you, when we get behind this man, the lads will pick you up one at a time for a short coffee break. Our treat and we will pay you as discussed. No funny business. We need these guys ready to work, not sleep. This will leave Grace here as the only option for our guy. Don't worry, there are a lot of very large men waiting to protect her."

Mike walked back to the car and drove away. Grace was alone, her first night strutting her stuff on the street. Totally unexpected and unplanned for, a car pulled up and asked Grace if she was working.

"You ain't got enough money, darling, sorry not tonight." Problem sorted.

Mike was on the comms briefing the teams.

"We have three workers, so only three of you to pick up. The fourth standby for the unexpected. We could get another girl to rock up. Follow team, are you in place?"

Back came a 'Roger that'.

"Protection, you in place?"

Another 'Roger that'.

"Protection, you only go in if Grace uses the help word. Do not shoot the twat, put him down."

Another 'Roger that'.

Just as he went to confirm with Grace, the follow team cut in.

"On the move heading your way, just left, ETA 10."

"All stations, we have a moving target, wait to confirm the route, standby."

"Target is moving in your direction, confirmed."

"Pickups 1 and 2 go, move the first two out. Follow team, let us know when you have eyes on Grace and the last girl."

It then went silent, deadly silent. Two of the cars stopped and called over a girl each. They got in and each car drove away in turn. Two left, Grace and the last working girl.

"Follow team, we have eyes on it."

"Car 3, go. Slowly, he needs to see."

The third car moved away, down the road and stopped, called over the girl, and she got in; as planned, in full view of Si'ad. He did a 3-point and drove away in the direction he came from, adding some normality to the scene.

Grace was standing alone and had moved towards the wall of the building. There was a slight breeze blowing up. Her hair was not very long but it managed to blow it a little. With her dress and the way she looked, the effect was stunning. She could see Si'ad still walking towards her, closer and closer.

His direction did not really show he was heading to talk to her. In fact, as he got closer, he was not really paying much attention to Grace. Either he was going elsewhere, or not interested.

"Follow team, he is not taking the bait, seems to be walking past… Hang on."

"You interested in some fun tonight? I'm all alone now, my mates have pulled."

As she said it, she opened her coat revealing her very short skirt, stocking tops and cleavage. Si'ad noticed too, just as she had hoped. He walked up and looked her up and down.

"You are very lovely. What shall I call you?"

"I'm Grace. Tonight is my first time doing this. I am very nervous, you look like a nice man. You interested?"

"Follow team, Grace sorted it, and told you she was good. She looks good too."

Si'ad looked up and down. Why? There could be many reasons. Looking for a tail, follow up, where the others had gone, who knows. But the sight of what was on offer allowed his other brain to take over.

"I only live around the corner. Shall we go back to mine? We can have some fun in the warm together."

"Ok, but I have been told to get payment before I leave here. Don't want to go before the deal is done. What do you want, you know the options, I guess?"

"Actually no, Grace, I'm not sure, and you're new. It would be fun for you to tell me."

Bastard, she thought, but had no choice. "Well, let me see. Hand job, £50; Blow job, £75; full sex with condom, £125; no condom, £175. Or £200 for an hour of anything goes."

Si'ad stood back and looked at her again. Inside, she was already fuming and wanted to punch him. He took his wallet from his rear right pocket and peeled out four £50 notes.

"£200 it is then, shall we?"

He held out his arm for Grace to hold and then walked off towards his apartment, his new lady on his arm.

"Follow team, Grace moving towards the apartment, we are with them. ETA 10-15, she is struggling with those killer heels."

Mike was back on the net within seconds.

"Car 4, back up, the protection team at the flat. No guns unless required as a last resort. Protection team, target is inbound, stay down out of the way. Grace, if you can hear us tap twice."

They waited and were rewarded with a tap tap. Her comms had been set so everyone could hear what was going on around her. But obviously, right now she could not speak.

The walk to the flat in the heels was making life difficult, so Grace walked slowly and carefully. Si'ad had sensed she was unsteady on her feet and had now moved his arm down and was holding her around the waist. Well, more over the top of her bum. Grace was good with that; reeling him in.

"Follow team, front door, they are going in."

Another set of 'Roger thats' came back.

Grace was now on her own and she knew it. She was not scared, a little apprehensive of what she was getting into, or what this man may expect before she could get out. She had the device concealed in her underwear, plus the tiny radio. Clearly, he was not getting anywhere near her knickers. So, his options were to be cut short.

The issue was that Si'ad also was a trained agent or spy. He may begin to suspect that Grace was not who she claimed. This was why she chose to use her own name.

On the way up the stairs, she wobbled a bit more, forcing Si'ad to hold her tighter, this time under her arms. His apartment was on the second floor, he never took the lift, so he walked with Grace up the stairs.

He held the door open for her, a true gentleman, then showed her through to the safe room.

'Tap Tap' was the sign that she was in and in the room.

"I won't be long; it seems you may benefit from a glass of water."

Si'ad left and Grace stood surveying the room quickly. She was deliberately walking a little as though she was drunk. I good hiding place was needed for the listening device where she could put it with little effort.

"Here, I put some ice in the water and some lemon. Sit down please, let me take your coat."

Grace moved towards the sofa and at the same time, started to take off her coat. With a few wobbles again, she sat down, putting the coat across her lap.

"Come on, don't be shy. I know you said it was your first time doing this. But I'm not going to hurt you, just make you feel good."

Leaning over, he kissed Grace lightly on the lips. He was a good-looking man and he was gentle.

Ok, that won't hurt, but you better be careful, Mr, Grace thought.

Grace's hand was in her coat pocket and in her hand was the listening device. She waited for Si'ad to lean in for another kiss; she did not resist and kissed him back. At the same time, pushing the coat off her lap.

Pulling away, she reached down, picked up the coat, and slid the device under the sofa towards the back, then sat back up with her coat in hand. Si'ad reached gently, took her coat, and put it over a table nearby, then went back in for another kiss.

He kissed her harder this time and his hand found her breast. She was expecting this, obviously; he thought she was there for sex and was going to try. She left it a short while then pretended to retch.

Pulling away, Si'ad looked at her with concern.

"I'm sorry, I was so nervous about doing this tonight that I had a couple of drinks. Where is the loo please?"

Si'ad pointed to the door in the corner. Grace rose and rushed into the loo, shutting the door, almost closed but not quite. Leaning over the toilet bowl, she stuck her fingers down her throat, reached once and threw up.

The noise was horrible and obvious when someone threw up. Si'ad realised his evening of sex with the beauty he brought home was over. But he was still a gentleman.

"Come, drink some more water. It seems perhaps we need to postpone our night of passion to another day. Don't worry, you do seem very nervous, but you should be very confident with a body like yours."

Handing her the water, he helped her to her feet and led her to sit down again on the sofa. This time, not interested in kissing anymore.

"Come, I will walk you home. I want to be sure you are ok."

"No, no, please, I have made such a fool of myself. Here is your money, take it back please."

"Keep it, I am in credit for when you are better. Maybe tomorrow night. I'll give you the number on my mobile. You can call me when you are working again. It would be good to complete our little arrangement together."

Si'ad reached into the drawer on his table and took out a business card. On it was a name address and mobile number.

Grace's mind was in overdrive. *Phone! How and where did he get that without anyone at SIS noticing?* She took the card and put it in her pocket, then reached a little and rushed back to the toilet. This time, it was for real, a result of the forced vomiting earlier.

"Please, I need to go. I do not feel well, I can see myself home, it is not far. Hopefully, I will feel better tomorrow and I will look for you tomorrow night. Same time. You seem a nice man. I owe you now. Maybe some extras for waiting."

Si'ad saw her out of the door and watched as she walked back the way they had come earlier.

"Follow team, Grace is on the move, something must have happened. We are on her."

"Roger that, make sure he does not follow, keep an eye on the flat."

"Grace, job done, package planted. I threw up, seemed to spoil his sex drive. I will walk back to the girl's place and wait for a pickup. One of you."

"Protection team, stay in place, take over the Obs for now. We need new orders from the boss."

20 minutes later, they were all back in the commissioner's meeting room. Hot tea and coffee and some sandwiches from somewhere appeared. The commissioner sat whilst the others talked about what had happened.

"Will, do we have contact with the device? Is it bloody working?"

"Yes, Sir, it's online. No chatter, he is in the other room I think."

"Right, Mike, great job. Impressive. When this shit is all over, we need to talk. Thank you, but sadly, I am unable to involve you any further."

Mike did look a little pissed he was being stood down but he knew the rules.

"Sir, no problem, you know where I am if you need me."

Grace walked into the room, still dressed for her night out. The lads couldn't help but tease her.

"Wow, just look at you, Miss Stunning, and to think I was stuck in a bunker all night with you once. But, great job, Grace. Amazing idea to puke, no one wants to kiss a bird that has just puked up."

Mike was leaving the room and stopped to shake Grace's hand.

"You're one brave lady, Grace. If ever you want to join the police, give me a call."

"Yes, well done, Grace, great job. No one got hurt, now we have work to do."

The commissioner called them to order and they all sat. In the background was a hiss of radio static that was coming from the receiver linked to the device Grace had pushed under the sofa. This could be found anytime if the sofa was moved but that was unlikely for a while.

"What have we got that is new?"

"He does have another phone. He gave me a card and the number is on it."

Grace put the card on the table. It showed Si'ad's real name, his real address, and his mobile number.

"So, the bastard does have an unknown means of communication. We need to trace this number, where is it registered, and where was it bought. It will be clean with no details but we need to check. Get on to the provider. I want every single call that phone has made or received and every single message, picture, or whatever else it can do. We need it very quickly too."

This was said to no one in particular, but as Will was a little out of things at this time, he offered to arrange the checks through his own routes.

Grace stood and looked at herself.

"Sir, if you don't mind, I would like to change back to my camos."

"Well, Grace, for us it will be a shame, but of course, please go ahead. You know where things are now."

Within 5 minutes, Grace was back, dressed as before in her camo suit, complete with a sidearm. She walked past the coffee and grabbed a sandwich, then past Will, who was sitting with his headphones on one ear, the other listening to the conversation in the room.

As she walked by, his arm shot up and he shouted, "SHHHHHH!"

The room went quiet. Will flipped a switch and what was in his ear now came from a speaker.

"He is on the phone, I heard it ringing."

Will leaned over and hit a red button on his laptop, the sound was now being recorded.

"Yes."

"We are not all ready."

"Why?"

"Almost, there is a problem."

"What?"

"No, I will come."

The phone went dead clearly. Si'ad could be heard slumping down onto the sofa.

"Fuck, Fuck! This is turning into a good night. First, I pick up the puking hooker, and now this."

More noises of movement, then the door could be heard to open and close. Si'ad had gone out of the room.

"He is clearly confident that the room is not bugged and is using it for any calls he needs to keep private. Someone is coming to see him; it sounds like there is a problem. Keep listening, Will. I think maybe it is time to let him know we are on to him, a small thing that he will pick up and then realise we know. Time to flush him out but we need to know what the problem is that he has. It does sound like some plans have gone wrong. Plans mean something is going to happen."

"Sir, the lads watching the flat say someone new has just gone in the door. Could be anyone, but could be our visitor."

The tension in the room was rising. There was an atmosphere you could cut with a knife. Everyone sat in total silence, waiting.

Over the speaker came the sounds of doors but no speech. Then the door to the safe room clearly opened.

"Assalamu alaikum. ladayna mushkilat mae 'ahad alrijal."

"Oh great, they are going to speak Arabic."

Grace was on it.

"Shhh. He said there was a problem with one of the men, listen!"

"Laqad fatih alsuma wahu alan maridi. sawf yamutu."

Grace responded, "He opened the toxin and is ill; he will die."

Si'ad exploded, he was clearly very angry. His shouts were now back in English from Arabic.

"What! Why? Why did he disobey me? Why would he risk everything? Let him die in agony, he can be the first. He can be at the bottom of the pile of the dead pigs. Where is he?"

"He is in his position, waiting as are the others."

"Where, where is this position? There are three."

"He is in the trees near the south bottom corner. He called to say he had dropped the vial and it had cracked. So, he put it into a bag and then sealed it. But then he got ill."

"Well, he will die, we cannot stop that. The British pigs will find him and deal with the toxin. This is no longer my problem. The plan will go ahead. Make sure no one else fucks with my plans. No more mistakes. Nothing will change. We stay to the plan, just one less bottle of toxin, will not matter. Nothing more will go wrong. We will poison their water; we will throw a dead sheep in their well.

"This is our final act, the biggest water treatment plant. Birmingham will watch whilst I kill two million people as they drink the water I will poison. Just like the British pig soldiers killed my father only to have his truck and just like they bombed my house and killed my family. I will have my revenge on this country. They will learn the wrath of the Koran, and feel the sword of revenge.

"I have waited many years to avenge my family's death and I will stand and watch whilst they weep. Now go. I will kill anyone that fails me and I will kill their families too."

The room was in total silence; everyone was stunned. No one had any words, except Will.

"This is one seriously fucked up, motherfucker. Is he for real?"

Chapter 24

Scotland Yard, London
14 November, 0010

"Ok, ok, calm down. One thing at a time. Obs, this is control. I want you to make sure that the same guy who just went in sees you two very clearly as he leaves. It is time to let our Mr fucking Marachi know that we know. Confirm."

"Roger that."

"Do not make contact, just spook him, get a picture."

The commissioner had moved into offensive mode; it seemed he was now worried.

"Will, find the two biggest water treatment plants that supply Birmingham. Get your fly guys in the air and I want thermal imaging sweeps of both plants constantly. We need to see who is on the ground, not in the plant itself right now but around it. Monitor any heat traces you get. Don't worry about the noise, it will make them realise we know.

"Contact the plants, ask them if they can just shut down for 24 hours or something. Then get their people out of there and away from danger, got it?"

"Yes, Sir, I'm on it."

He then moved to his desk and picked up one of two phones. This one was grey, the other was all black.

"Get me the prime minister. I am well aware of the time, just get me the prime minister."

There was a pause of about 5 minutes, then, "Commissioner, what can I do for you?"

"How long would it take to get COBRA sitting? If not COBRA, then we need you and some of the COBRA members at least."

"Most are nearby because of what has happened and what is going on. Why?"

"That, Prime Minister, we can discuss when I arrive. Shall we say, I will be there in 15."

"Very well, Commissioner."

Then he stood and looked at the team.

"Let's go and get this Marachi before he can do any more damage. Right, two of you on me to get me to number 10. Get your kit together and gun up. The rest of you, be ready to support the Obs team. Marachi is going to run, I think.

"Get three fast movers with fully trained drivers, I want the best. Cars out the front ready to go. If he runs, you lot are going after him. Will, warn Waddington to get the SAS Helo on standby and get them ready to go with no delays. We call for them, I want them in the air in seconds. I intend to brief the PM and get approval to move on Marachi. With permission from the top, we will have a green light for what is required, including the pre-emptive use of lethal force.

"Do not hang around waiting for my orders. Kill this bastard before he can kill millions. Clear? Right, let's go to number 10."

The commissioner's words were sent out across the comms system so everyone heard from the whole team.

"Obs team, we spooked the visitor and he disappeared. Then, we followed for a short while. He clearly sent a text message, so I think your man knows now. We need someone rolling to our position. If he does run, we will lose time going for the car."

"Roger that."

Two of the others grabbed their gear and jogged down to the lift, then through reception outside.

Three fully marked BMW X5 4X4s were stood waiting. All three were two up driver and front seat, all fully tooled up. They were outside of the vehicles scanning the area, weapons raised and ready. As the two lads from the commissioner's team came out, they did not stop, just shouted, "We off?"

"Yeah, one of you is, and quick, we need to get moving. You guys ready for a fight?"

They loaded into the first BMW bergens in the back, longs between their legs.

"Go, go, we will explain on the way. Head towards Queensferry Rd, near Battersea Park. Fast but no flashing lights and stuff."

As they moved, the lads gave their two new best friends a limited version of what was going on, why they were running about like madmen, and where they were going.

"If what you say is true and he runs, he will go north towards Birmingham. We would be better to wait up over Chelsea Bridge."

"Whatever you think is best, let's go and go quickly."

They shot down the embankment, past the Palace of Westminster and into Milbank, crossing over into Grosvenor Rd, then left in Chelsea Bridge Rd, finally turning left into Turks Rd. After a 180, they pulled up on the left and waited.

The lads from the Obs team had split up, no choice, they needed to get their car able to go quickly. One stayed eyes on the target building whilst the other went back down the street to get their own BMW saloon. This was not a police car, it was an SAS car. Unmarked, but still had blues and twos if needed.

***

The commissioner was shown into the cabinet room, and the two lads guarding him stood in the reception foyer of the building.

"Commissioner, please sit. Would you care to explain?"

"Prime Minister, think back to your visit to ground zero when both you and I were shown the centre of the attack by Marachi, the head of the SIS. He came prepared and provided us with HAZMAT suits and breathing gear. Did you not wonder why?"

"I assumed it was a precaution or standard operating procedure. Why do you think it was?"

"Sir, at that point in time we had no idea that there was a toxic gas involved in the attack. How did Marachi know that he needed to wear protection?"

"I see, so you think he knew in advance?"

"Yes, I puzzled over this for a few hours and was nervous about what I was thinking. Shortly after this, I received a call from the commanding officer of JARIC in Cambridgeshire. Long story short, he wrote a report on how to shut down the UK. This was highly secret and only three people knew about it."

"Well, I have not been briefed on this one."

"Exactly, nor had I. In fact, only a very few people in the country even had security clearance to read the document. Marachi was one. The RAF Office contacted me directly as he saw that the attack was following his report. This confirmed my suspicions about Marachi. Since that day, I have had a covert operation in place monitoring Marachi. No one apart from the team I used knows of its existence. Sorry, Sir, but even you were not told. It was too easy for information to get back to SIS.

"Last night, we also confirmed that he is the leader of some operation designed to cripple the UK. We have a recorded conversation, obtained by the insertion of a listening device, which talks about his plans to poison the water supply to Birmingham with a toxin. I have a lot of resources now at my disposal, it was me that killed the attempt to blow the gas pipes again in Cambridgeshire with the help of the RAF and SAS.

"I need your blessing to go after Marachi now before he can infect the water supply and stop this once and for all. He needs to be dead and dead very soon. I have already sanctioned an operation which is now preparing to take down Marachi and any more of his followers we can hit."

"How have you done this without being discovered or questioned? Why did you not come to us before?"

"There was no way of knowing who would hear, who would alert SIS or even Marachi. We had to tie this down 100%. Only myself and my team were involved. We used no communication, only eye-to-eye contact every day."

"What if you're wrong, Commissioner, what then? We just killed our own man."

"I am not wrong, Sir, not after what I have heard. If I am, award him a medal for dying in action and I will step down. But I am not wrong, Sir, and with respect, I need all the minutes I am using standing here asking for permission. Time is against us."

"Commissioner, step outside and give us a moment."

He left the room, the lads joined him on either side.

"Well?"

"Honestly, I have no idea. I told them the facts straight. I told them I was wasting time standing here talking, in the nicest possible way. I offered to quit if we were wrong. We are not wrong, we need to go."

The cabinet door opened and the prime minister walked out. He looked very white.

"Go, go and do what needs to be done. Stop this madness in our country. But, Commissioner, do not be wrong, please do not be wrong."

They turned and left, walking as fast as the commissioner could manage across the road and back towards Scotland Yard.

Once back in his office, he sat at the table, reached for the coffee, put his head in his hands, and said to everyone left in the room, plus live on the comms.

"Are we right or are we wrong?"

Unanimously, they all replied right.

"Then go to work. Is everyone ready? The four of you lads, load up downstairs now and be ready to roll. I still believe it's going to happen sooner rather than later. Grace, I have ordered another car, you're with me; no way am I going to miss this. Sorry, Will, we need your steady hand on the helm."

"Lady and gentlemen, the operation is live. Let's get to it."

The four remaining lads grabbed their gear and weapons and disappeared down to the front of the building. They loaded their gear in the boot, spare mags into their vests, and stood by talking to the police drivers. They all had the weapons ready if needed.

"We are going to war, lads, on our own fucking soil. We can't tell you until we go mobile and then we will brief you along the way. It may not happen right now but it is going to happen. Believe me."

Less than 5 minutes later, Grace appeared fully loaded with the commissioner in a set of blue fatigues and a side arm.

"You licenced to carry that, Sir?"

"I made the rules, I can break them Grace, just stay behind me if it comes out."

Grace and the commissioner got into the car. Both got in the back. The unmarked BMW 5 series had the similar two officers, a driver and a front seat. Both armed.

At the flat, there was movement obvious from the windows. Curtains were drawn but shadows were moving and quickly across them.

"Obs team, I have movement in the flat. He seems to be rushing about across the windows. Blinds are down but the shadows are moving really fast. I think our friend is panicking. I have eyes on the front door."

"Will here, where is his car and what is it?"

"Not sure about the car, we have not seen it. Would be in the garage I guess under the building. Access is possible through the elevator. Obs, can you see the garage exit?"

"Roger that, standby standby."

You could hear it before you saw it, a fast-moving Mercedes was coming from the south towards the Obs team.

"We may have trouble, standby."

The car sped up to the front of the building, yards from where one of the Obs team was watching the front door.

"It's going down, he is coming out. I have a fast mover inbound and Marachi is coming out, standby. Rog, get our fucking car moving."

It took less than 10 seconds, the car sped up and stopped, and Marachi came out around the car and into the passenger seat. It was gone, north, over Chelsea Bridge.

"He's running, north over Chelsea Bridge. Merc AMG, go faster. Light blue, Reg SW14BYX. Rog, where are my fucking wheels, buddy?"

The Merc went over the bridge and then north on Chelsea Bridge Road. Within seconds, he went past the front of the police X5 in Turk' Row.

Outside the flat, a second growling car could be heard, and another car rushed up and stopped.

"Come on then, you tosser, get the fuck in."

Around the car and into the front, they were gone, north after the Merc.

"All call signs CO2, we are northbound heading for the A41. Lead car is marked X5 with an unmarked SAS behind. He has a choice if this is going all the way to Birmingham, M1 or M40, standby."

The Merc was moving fast. London was at home, and the only traffic was still emergency services. No real obstacles with traffic or traffic lights, they were blasting through. Hot on the heels were the police X5 and the SAS.

"CO2, peel off in a blaze of blue and let the SAS unmarked take the lead. Grace, get your car in behind too. This must go all the way to Birmingham. Stopping Marachi will not stop the others intent on completing this tonight.

"Marked units, if they go M1, you go M40, and if they go M40, you go M1. We need everyone there in one piece."

Grace and the commissioner were now speeding through London chasing the lead SAS car. The Merc and the SAS were past Swiss Cottage and into Finchley Road going north. Grace was less than a minute behind.

"Fuck me, and you lot reckon we are mad. Who taught him to drive? Rog, we are on your six, settle in for the ride."

Within minutes, they were through Hendon and onto the M1.

"Will here, its northbound M1. I am going to route the rest up the M40 and get the locals to clear the way for everyone. Shut it down, we can have this crashing."

Will grabbed the phone and called the control room in Llyod House, Birmingham. This was where the 'Fight Back' police and army road crews were controlled.

"Scotland Yard here, we have an incident developing heading north from London. Inbound to one of the two largest water treatment works. We need you crews ready to respond, ETA 75 minutes. No details at this time, we will advise as we get more data."

Will then called the control room at RAF Waddington.

"Incident is live, we need the SAS Helo in the air now, head to Birmingham International, refuel and await instructions. We expect serious resistance this time, get your lads ready to fight in full chemical weapon gear. Plus, I need nine more sets of chemical gear on the helo. No one mentioned gas, Sir."

"Tell me about it. Just pass it on and scramble a medevac helo too, with gas gear. Same routine, get it to Birmingham International. One final thing, do you lot still use flame throwers?"

Will had arranged for the airspace over Birmingham to be shut down. There was very little air traffic, but now this air belonged to him. AWACS from RAF Waddington had been airborne on a continuous cycle over the UK giving military control of airspace in conjunction with the normal civilian services.

Will would now need to use them to keep control of the air assets he was calling in.

"AWACS, sit rep please."

"London, we have four Tornados running circuits over the two possible targets. We have no possible hostiles at one but keep getting blips of two possible three concealed at the other. Two helos inbound to BHI and will hold."

What was missing was the support they were going to need on the ground both for a good result and a bad one. The local civil defence planning needed to be woken up.

The police in Birmingham had already been made aware something was going on. Will had the Fight Back guys on standby and he was going to need these crews. What he also needed was the backup for everyone involved. Anything could go wrong.

Will called the same number he had less than 15 minutes ago.

"Scotland Yard again, incident is still heading your way to Minworth Water Treatment Works. We have both police and military assets involved. For now, please keep your lads away. I need the joint road crews ready to roll. Move them to forward holding points as follows:

- Two crews overhead junction 4 M6
- Two crews on slip road from M6 to M6 Toll northbound
- Two more overhead junction 9 M42

"Bring BUH to full alert for contamination response. Limited numbers plan for twelve."

Birmingham University Hospital was a known centre for infectious diseases and toxins. They had the facilities and staff to deal with anyone that happened to get contaminated.

"I need fire and ambulance resources waiting, park them up in Midpoint Park. Keep them out of the way until we call, if we do; better to have them and not need them. Finally, I need four dogs with armed protection."

Will had decided that they were heading for Minworth Water Treatment Works. This was the only one out of the two that had given thermal imaging results. That had to be the others Marachi was going to meet.

***

It was approximately 120 miles from where Marachi was picked up to the water treatment plant. According to the two SAS cars, they were now averaging 130 mph+ Allowing for the slower time out of London, this gives a travel time to the site of around 1 hour. So far, 30 minutes had passed.

Marachi would know there were two cars on his tail, and he would also know they were unmarked, meaning more than possibly SAS. The lads were hanging back giving the AMG Merc the road it wanted, and it was eating it up very fast.

"Grace, location please?"

"We are just passing Northampton, still 130 plus northbound."

"CO2, location please?"

"5 miles south of Leamington; looks like we are ahead of them."

"All units, this is heading to Minworth, repeat Minworth. I am vectoring other support into the area. I have chemical suits inbound for the lads. Marachi must be going to try to use the toxin on the freshwater storage tanks. There is no doubt about this. These are all underground with limited access. He cannot be allowed to get within 20 feet of any tank access.

"The issue we have is that we cannot stop him on the road now. We have no idea how many other people have the toxin and are waiting to meet him. They will know he is coming and have been told if we stop him to go ahead. We must let him meet his own people and attempt to complete his attack. They will all need to be taken down simultaneously. Which we will do. We will be ready and waiting for him."

With the operation now in full swing and out in the open, there was no need for further secrecy and Will had the full resources of the Met to use if he needed. He picked up the phone and called the main control room.

"This is Group Captain Rivers, working upstairs with the commissioner. Can you please mobilise the nearest bomb squad and get them to Midpoint Park, an industrial estate near Minworth? They can liaise there with local emergency services also on standby. We will contact them when required. Use channel 17 on military comms."

That was the last part of the chess set Will was assembling not just to take Marachi and his fanatics down, but to provide the highest protection for the lads going in. He then started the game moving.

"AWACS, move the SAS Helo to the target site, drop the men, let me know when they go live on the grid."

"Will do, over."

The engines on the helicopter were already running, the men were loaded, fully armed to the teeth. As the helicopter spooled up, they came on the grid.

"SAS Helo, we are airborne, 5 minutes out."

"Get the lads on the ground and get suited up asap. I need a sit rep of what it is like and where these bloody water tanks are. We have about 20 before they are likely to arrive."

"Roger that."

"SO2, use the A446 to get access to site, friendlies on junction 4 of M6. Gates are open, site is totally dark, all lights are off. Friendlies will show IR."

Any of the SAS or police active on-site would have an infrared beacon on their kit. This could be seen with the night goggles being used. The site being dark was going to delay Marachi.

"Grace, location…"

"Junction 2, speed 135 now."

"SO2, location?"

"Just crossed M6 junction 4, killing the blues, 5 minutes out."

Turning left at the roundabout on the A446, they shot through Curdworth and then left into the compound, through the gates. There were security people at the gate.

"Where are the main freshwater storage tanks?"

"Go left, under the pump house 100 mtrs on the left."

"Ok, now go, far away; get out of here."

The three X5s stopped in a line and they all got out. The lads grabbed their gear and started fanning out around the vehicles. The police went to get their own gear from the back.

"Thanks, guys, for the ride, we got this from here."

"Like fuck you have, we're coming, get used to it."

There were now six from the SAS Helo, twelve mixed police and SAS, three more and the commissioner behind Marachi.

"We are in the far north right corner of the site. We have the water tanks, which are under the pump house. Only access is the sample tube from the ground unless they get inside of the pump house. That is not going to happen."

"Stay put, we will meet you there."

Within minutes, they were all together. Nine chemical suits were dropped on the ground.

"Sorry, we only got nine."

"Not too late to go, no one will blame you."

"Fuck off, we stay."

They sorted themselves out, then stood looking at the scene.

"There are two sample access points, stick an IR beacon on each. We have the building; we need the high ground. We really need snipers; we cannot trust these to hit them right. We do not have snipers."

The comms were through to everyone. Whatever they said was being heard.

"Will here. Yes, we do. I deployed the joint police and army fightback crews. Those were the friendlies at junction 4. There are three more crews on standby not far away."

"Good call indeed. We need them here, now, time is running out."

Will issued the instructions and sent four of the crews from the holding points to the main gate and in to meet the rest.

The police drivers were relieved and sent to the ERV in the business park. The eight army guys sorted their kit.

"What have you got with you?"

"L11s and 50-cal."

"Fuck, that should stop them."

"We have some C4 with us and I suggest we wire the pump motors to blow if they manage to drop the toxin into the water. We asked but do not know if they shut down the supply. IF we fail, I am going to blow the drive motors."

Will cut in again.

"Better to have it and not need it, I agree. Heads up, it is almost certain that these people will have explosive vests on. If you hit them centre mass, they will go bang and disperse whatever it is they have. We cannot risk it going airborne. It must be a headshot, kill shot, immediate total failure. Once they are down, stay away. Once they are down, your job is done, move out and protect the permitter."

"Roger that. You lads get in there and get on the roof, work in your pairs, both shooters line up; if one misses, the other kills. No mistakes. We are going to fan out in pairs across the site, within 200 metres. We will not be within the kill zone. You shoot on command. What we don't know is if they will send everyone in or hold back a crazy in case they do get compromised."

"Just one question. We are on the roof, you really gonna blow those motors?"

"Yes, but we'll tell you first."

***

Si'ad had changed in the car, he was now all in black and he had put on one of the suicide vests. His driver had arrived already wearing one. He had seen that he had two tails but was not bothered. They couldn't catch him in this car.

He planned to rendezvous with the two of the men that were left. To the rear and east of the plant was some scrubland, which at one time could have been an old RAF station, now just a field. In the centre of the field was a group of old buildings. The two remaining terrorists had now met up in the buildings waiting for their leader. The third that had contaminated himself was either dead or near dead, somewhere nearby.

The AMG had left the M6 and was now on the M6 Toll, around 1 mile south of the M42 spur and exit road. The driver was now slowing down as though to come off allowing him to use junction 9 as well.

The two cars behind were hanging back waiting for anything to happen.

With no warning at all, as the big Merc joined the slip road, it baked hard, threw a hard left lock and did a complete 180. Both doors opened and the driver and Marachi jumped out. The driver lifted an automatic weapon. Marachi legged it around the back of the car, over the railing and down the bank away from the Merc.

Both of the cars behind did exactly the same, braked hard, straight line, all four front doors and one rear door came open, and five very angry people took up firing positions.

"Someone drop that cunt."

A single double tap rang out, hit the driver centre mass, and he exploded and the Merc with him.

"Down, fuck me."

Marachi was away and running. Less than 800 metres away were his two fellow terrorists. Grace and the other two SAS lads were gone in pursuit.

"Contact Contact, Marachi is away and running across the field to the plant. We are following up."

Will came up on the grid.

"Do not engage, let them come. Follow up only when we have them in sight. We do not know how many others could be there. Anyone checked the commissioner?"

"He's good, he has a gun don't forget. No worries, they are moving him now. He will take up control from the business estate."

Marachi soon found his men and moved out towards the far north right corner of the plant. As they ran, he encouraged them.

"They may have found out about me but they do not know what I have planned. They cannot know. Everything was done in total secrecy. They have chased me here but could not catch me, now their cars are blocked. We will continue."

Grace and the two lads found the derelict buildings and cleared them. As they did so, they were startled when a fast jet went over the top. It made them all hit the floor before they realised it had to be friendly.

Will was on the net within 2 minutes.

"All units, last pass showed three heat signatures moving roughly northwest towards the plant on what looks like an access road. There is a fourth splash to the west of this road in a thicket. But this is stationary. Suggest it is worth checking."

They were coming; Marachi was coming to complete his vow to avenge the deaths of his family, caused by the British armed forces. He wanted Britain to suffer and suffer again.

This time, he had made a mistake; he was arrogant enough to assume that no one really knew his target and that he had stopped them chasing him. He was wrong.

Chapter 25

Minworth Water Treatment Plant, Coleshill
14 November, 0400

The commissioner arrived on the industrial estate but was not happy he had been pushed behind the lines. He wanted to be in there. Command sometimes was not all it was cracked up to be. He must trust the highly trained people on the ground to do their job.

The lads had now spread out circling the buildings and the access to the sample pipes. They were all concealed and in the darkness, no one would easily see them. They would need to bump into each other.

From what was seen on the last flyby, there were three coming at them. Meaning, they did not need the fourth sniper team on the roof.

"One of you teams on the roof, get back down here. There are only three, we will put you in the building to protect the entrance."

"Oh, great. Let's get nearer the pump motors when they blow up."

"Ha ha, very funny, let's go, lads. Radio silence unless you see them."

So, they waited, and waited, for what must have been a very long few minutes.

Si'ad came along the part made up the road, almost to the top where it met with Kingsbury Rd. There was a gate preventing vehicle access but it did allow a way through to the footpath. On the roadside of the gate, someone had dumped a load of car and lorry tyres.

To the left of the road and Si'ad's left, there was a metal boundary fence, marking the perimeter of the plant, complete with sharp spiked tops.

Whilst the other three terrorists had been hiding up, waiting for Marachi to come, they had removed a few of the metal uprights. The pile of tyres against the fence provided a very helpful way of concealing the gap they had created. Within a few minutes, the tyres had been cleared away and they were through.

A small thicket of trees had been grown on the plant side of the fence, no more than 20 metres deep; once through the gap, they headed in a straight line through the trees and stopped at the tree line. Marachi was now running on pure adrenaline; it was so close.

"Heads up, I have movement, three tangos, black, with vests. Small packs on their backs."

There followed a load of clicks as they all acknowledged.

Si'ad looked around trying to look through the dark. The plant was dark but outside of the plant, all normal lighting was working. There was some ambient because of the streetlights on Kingsbury Rd.

"Wait, let our eyes get used to the dark."

"Why is it dark, Sir? Do they know we are here?"

"It is not possible that they know. Come, you know your stations; you go to the far sample point and I will go to the one nearest to us."

They moved out this time in single file, with Si'ad at the rear, up the plant boundary road and then left turn towards the pump buildings. The main building was quite large, maybe 60 metres. Distance from the corner to the far sample point was 100 metres.

"I have them, moving single file towards the pump building."

"Steady, lads. Let them come."

"Grace here, we are through the gap in the fence, following them, we are flaring."

"Stay back, Grace, you have no suit. If this fucker goes bang, you could be in trouble."

This put Grace and the other two lads directly behind Si'ad. As they got level with the first sample point, Si'ad stopped and waited. The other two continued walking another 30 metres and they stopped. To their right-hand sides were two stainless steel pipes rising from the ground, 150 mm in diameter with a clip cover which sealed it off.

"Can you hear me, Father? Can you hear me, Mother and Sister? I am finally here to avenge your deaths. I am here after many years to make good the wrong that this country did to my family and my country. I will show them the pain of such indiscriminate acts. I have already killed and killed many people, and now the final act. This is for you."

"Do not move, Marachi," the shout came from somewhere in the darkness.

"If anyone moves, you will all die."

"Sit rep, you on them?"

Three yeps came back.

"Do not take your sights off them. Headshots."

Marachi was really shocked; he wobbled on his feet and scanned left and right. This had thrown him; he still had the arrogance to believe that no one knew.

"Stand down, Marachi, stand down or we will shoot."

"There is no way you could have known I was to come here, only my closest officers knew of this plan; they are all here now. One of you has betrayed me."

"You betrayed yourself, you arsehole. You betrayed yourself with your lust for young women, young hookers; even had a special room, you fucking pervert."

Grace walked up from behind Si'ad, closer to him. Even though there was little light, there was enough. She unclipped her helmet, pulled out her hair, and let him see her.

"You arrogant piece of shit, it was me, you picked me up tonight. I'm the puking hooker. You actually made me sick."

"You! No, it cannot be so! How? Why?"

Marachi went mental. They had no guns; they did not believe they would need them. But they had their vests and he reached into his pocket.

"Vest, SHOOT!" Grace screamed the command and hit the floor.

Marachi just stood there, time had stopped, bolt upright. The rest of his body had not yet figured out that his head was missing. The 50-cal. round had decapitated him, along with his two friends.

"Targets are down, three dead."

The commander was on this time.

"Stand down, back away and RV at the front of the security house. We have decontamination units here waiting and you lot are going to use them. I am taking no chances."

"Rog," was all that came over the grid.

Grace was just getting up and was on one knee. From the hole in the fence and running along the road, the third thermal image came screaming. He had no weapon but he had a vest and held high something in a plastic bag. This guy was fucked up badly, something was very wrong with him.

He was about 75 metres away. Grace pulled out her sidearm, two hands, raised, aimed, and squeezed two shots. He went down like a sack of potatoes, with two rounds into his forehead.

"Fucking night of the living dead."

"We have another down, this one does not look well."

"Half of us are pulling out now, the rest will wait 15 to be sure no follow-up."

As they jogged around the corner to the security office, there was a decontamination unit the size of a 40 ft container. It was being guarded by both police and army.

At the front, there was a door, it said 'IN' and at the back, there was a door, it said 'OUT'. Next to the 'In' door was a sergeant major type.

"Come on, you know the drill, kit in box, one at a time, all except your camos. Fill the box, seal it up, write your name. Into the door, strip off clothes in the shoot. Walk through each stage, spend the correct time in the cubical, do not move on until the lights change. Ma'am, if you would not mind leading them in."

Grace had never done this for real but it was something that they practiced time and time again. It was impossible for a female member of the SAS to avoid having to get naked with her team there, or near, or even with her. Something she just shrugged off. In her mind, it was just as embarrassing for the lads as it was for her, so she just did it.

She went up the stairs into the strip area, took everything off, totally bare naked, then pushed all her clothes into the dirty shoot; these were collected for incineration. Once done, she stepped into the first shower cubical.

Hot water came out and a blast of soap solution. She knew what to do, no part of her could be missed. Washed all over, she stood in the warm whilst the flow washed the soap away. The lights changed, and she moved to the second shower, simply by walking through hanging strips of thick clear plastic.

As she moved on, Rog came into the first shower.

"Grace."

"Rog." All in a day's work. This continued through several different stages until Grace reached the end. At the end were white plastic boots, white coveralls, similar to forensic uniforms you see all over the crime TV shows, and thick coats. All done, down the stairs, they went, where the commissioner was waiting.

"In the minibus, Grace, we are taking the precaution of having you all checked over and you will stay over one night at BUH. Just to be sure."

"Can we get some water?"

"Not until the medics are done with you."

The bomb squad dealt with the vests, once it had been confirmed that the three containers of supposed toxin were intact and unopened. They were removed and made safe. The vests were disarmed and removed by the bomb squad.

Because of the issues with the toxin threat, they were all cremated nearby before the sun came up.

The third man, shot by Grace, was more of a problem. He had to be dealt with by a specialist contamination unit and the plastic bag was removed to be made safe. His bottle had broken and he had clearly been infected. Once the toxin was gone, a debate took place as to the best ways of destroying any possibility of infection or transmission or whatever. This had to be done without risking anyone coming into contact with the body.

After careful reference to some very clever people at BUH and St Thomas' in London, the conclusion was fire. The body was cremated where it fell. Will had thought ahead, once more. They still had flamethrowers available.

Luckily, BUH had ignored Will's suggestion of twelve people possible. Their internal plans called for three wards in such a situation.

Twelve lads from the three BMW X5s, Grace and two more lads, plus the eight Fight Back lads, twenty-six people that were on the ground and engaged the threat during the final part of this mission, all went through the decontamination and were shipped to BUH for observations, 48 hours in total isolation.

Most of which, they all slept. After the past few days and the very little sleep they managed to get, no one complained.

At the plant, the clean-up was taken care of by local resources with the help of the military. New drivers were sent up to bring the Met vehicles back at a more normal speed. The commissioner returned to his office at Scotland Yard.

SIS Headquarters, London
17 November, 0900

The team was now back in London. The Fight Back lads had returned to operations in Birmingham. Even though everyone believed they had cut the head off the snake, no one believed it was over.

There had been a lot of people involved in the planning, logistics, and taking part in the attacks within the UK. The priority now was to either catch or eliminate anyone remotely involved in what had happened in the UK.

SIS was, for the time being, without a leader. It would take some time and a lot of red tape to get a successor in place for Marachi. The whole SIS organisation was hanging its head in shame. No one within their ranks had any suspicion that their own leader was, in fact, rogue.

The commissioner has spent almost 6 hours briefing the PM on what had happened, from start to finish. How they did everything, what they had found, plus what he wanted to do next.

"Sir, we cut off the head. The body remains and will grow a new head. Make no mistake, someone will take up the sword to replace Marachi. We must now act quickly whilst they are confused and in turmoil. Marachi survived and remained unnoticed by lying about the truth. For example, he set up the raids around Manchester that failed but he targeted the real people involved in the plots. That was the genius, all the intel pointed to these people.

"I believe we have the data we need to quickly round up possibly 80% of anyone who is out there. The rest may take longer, and we may need to go global to hunt them down. Removing 80% of a threat to me is a good deal right now."

"What are you asking for, Commissioner?"

"Simple, Sir, control."

The commissioner got his wish and so it was that at 0900, he was standing in the largest meeting room within the SIS building. Everyone from the lowest analyst to what was left at the top was there. The room had been arranged like a theatre and they all sat mumbling and talking quietly amongst themselves.

The raised stage at the front had ten empty chairs; the commissioner stood at a podium, arranging his notes.

Like everyone does, he tapped the microphone, which brought some attention from the audience. Then he spoke.

"Ladies and gentlemen, can I have your attention, please? As you are all aware, three days ago a team of people, put together in secret by me, shot and killed the head of the SIS. Si'ad Marachi was personally responsible for the deaths of thousands of people in and around London, the destruction of the National Grid Gas pipeline and other failed attempts to destroy the British way of life. But he failed to achieve what would have been a huge disaster of untold misery.

"It will be hard for you all to hear these words, but responsibility for what has happened lies at your door. On your shoulders. No one suspected anything, you all assumed that the head of the SIS was clean, good, and above suspicion. You were all wrong. He played you all, he played your loyalty, and he slaughtered your countrymen. No one has ever raised any concerns, logged an inaccuracy, or logged a point that doubts his leadership or orders. That concerns me."

From near to the back of the room, someone stood and was about to speak but he did not finish his sentence.

"I am not here to debate this, or discuss it, or take questions. There will be time for this once we all know the job is done and correctly.

"There are ten chairs behind me. There are two hundred and fifteen chairs in front of me. Let me introduce to you the ten people who, working together with me, solved, acted up, and stopped this mystery. If you would be so kind as to open the door."

One by one, they filed in. The commissioner stopped each person and introduced them to the audience. Where necessary, their rank was included. First in was Will. As they were introduced, they took their seat on the stage.

"Group Captain Will Rivers, RAF, Sgt Robert Moore, MET SOC19, SAS Soldier 1."

No identities were given for the SAS lads. That would not be possible, even within this room and clearance levels.

"It was these very ten people and me that did not believe the obvious and asked the questions leading us to Marachi. It was us that killed him. It was we who took down the attempt to damage the gas pipeline again. No mercy, we killed them. And here we are."

You could hear a fly fart in the room. No one even coughed. No one knew what was coming.

"It will take 3-6 months to go through the protocol to appoint and instate a new head of SIS. Until such time as he or she is in place, your new boss is me! I will take over the helm of SIS and together with the ten people that I trust more than the sun rising tomorrow. We will now be running all operations within SIS but concentrating on hunting down and finding any remaining people involved in what Marachi did.

"All other projects as of now have been halted, paused until we are done with what needs to happen. I will listen to representations concerning what you feel is an urgent operation and should continue. As of today, everyone's security clearance has been reduced by one level. Many clearances were sanctioned by Marachi. We need to go back and be careful. No one is a suspect. We do not believe that anyone has betrayed the SIS. Believe is not the same as knowing.

"The eleven of us will operate out of meeting room 14 on the third floor. Our door is open 24 hours a day. There is no hierarchy whilst I am in charge, do not be afraid to come to us with any tiny piece of intel. If your guts tell you that what you have is important, you come to see us and explain. No information will be stopped whilst moving up through the chain of command.

"The operation that was carried out in Manchester to try to bring down the terrorists failed. Marachi staged this to take SIS off the scent. BUT! He used his own people, the real bad guys. He just warned them it was coming. Did no one consider that they had been tipped off? No, because you all believed in Marachi and the system. Clearly, the system was fucked up.

"So, we return to GO. I want each name on the list of targets tracked down. Wherever they are, whatever you need to do to find them, do it. We will plan for their families to be taken into custody. For their own safety on the outside but to make sure their sons or daughters or nephews involved in what has happened find out. If they don't give them up, then maybe some will surrender to protect their own. Yes, maybe it sounds like our own Guantanamo Bay, but the difference is this will be a nice safe place for the families to be at HMG cost whilst we hunt down their loved ones.

"At 0900 every day, we will meet here for 30 minutes to update everyone as to progress. I want a daily update on the hunt for each of the people on the original list. I want a second list compiled and reported on for any newcomers we agree need adding. When we find them, my new best friends sitting behind me will be sent to bring them in or eliminate them. The function of the whole SIS organisation is to locate the people we need to talk to. Bring them back and question them, or kill them running. There will be no mercy.

"Anyone with any moral issues about what I am saying can join us on a visit to the refrigerated containers where thousands of body parts and piles of bodies, babies, kids, mothers, grandads, are awaiting DNA tracking.

"Both Interpol and the CIA are lined up to help us find and take out these people. That is all I have to say, we are a team, we are the best, you have to restore the confidence in the SIS and we are here to help you do it."

A few people stood and applauded, others just sat. Some even ran out and vomited. But they had the message.

And so it was that SIS went offensive, driven and guided by a team of eleven focussed, crazy bastards that were set on stopping this from ever happening again.

Over the next weeks, whole families were taken into custody. Surprisingly, many White British families too. Some names were given up, as expected by the family; others did come forward and hand themselves in. Then there were the ones that ran.

Chapter 26
Epilogue

Part of the background for the novel was based on my personal experience of my career in power engineering. I got to see places and plant systems that were amazing.

From working on site, replacing filter systems on gas turbines, or control systems of huge engines, to consulting to get engines working more efficiently and with less emissions.

The power plant in Spitalfields exists, and to my surprise, a friend, who proofread this manuscript, had actually been on site and recognised what I was describing.

The details of the gas grid, the compressor stations, and the impact of targeting certain places, are facts. When I used to visit the compressors to help with operational cleaning or new filters, security was very low. Now this has been increased to a level where my attacks would not be possible.

Time spent working with the RAF cleaning their engines with soapy water got me on to bases and I learnt of the AV gas pipeline. I even lived in Sawtry, across the road from the storage tanks.

I was involved with the RAF just before Desert Storm working with the folks at RAF Bruggen in Germany, looking at quicker ways to clean the engines.

So overall, I have drawn on a lot of personal knowledge.

Certainly, the attack on the power station in London would have caused a huge bang. It was this thought in my head after I had been there that sparked this novel. It was a bomb sitting there, waiting to go off. Just needed some help.